Missouri

ILLINOIS

Knapp Plantation

...kes' child ...ried here

The Blue Teal sinks

St. Louis

Missouri River

Hermann
The Riley Home

Beaver House
home of Pierre

Jefferson City

Knapp House

Missouri ...ssembly

Race between THE HAWK
and THE SILVER STAR

Mississippi River

STEAMBOAT MILES

St. Louis — Missouri River 30 mi.
St. Louis — Hermann 120 mi.
St. Louis — Westport Landing 450 mi.
St. Louis — St. Joseph 546 mi.

DONALD T. PITCHER

THE RIVER WITCH

THE
RIVER WITCH

MARJORIE McINTYRE

CROWN PUBLISHERS, INC. · NEW YORK

To MOTHER *and* FATHER

BOOK I

MISSOURI GIRL

PART ONE

1

TRAVELERS GOING WEST in the 1850's were serious people, acutely conscious of the importance of an extra ration, or of the tragedy that an ailing horse or a broken wheel could bring. Yet the life of the emigrant was not barren; he took along a sense of humor and a hoard of songs and tales.

On the California trail, a ballad or a sad tale was better than a rocking chair or a rosewood chest. You could sing the ballad around the campfire of an evening or tell the tale to each new person you met—adding a bit yourself if you had a mind to.

It was along the Missouri River, the hub of westward activity, where travelers would surely have heard the strange ballad of "The River Witch." Intrigued, they listened and wondered about her. Who was she?

> "Now Cap'm Riley's daughter is a River Witch,
> A River Witch,
> Callin' for her baby . . . Oh.
>
> "Listen early in the mornin',
> Listen late at night,
> River Witch is callin' high, and callin' low.
> Cap'm Riley's daughter,
> Lonesome Missouri woman, Oh . . ."

If a traveler asked, some of the river people would shake their fists and declare The River Witch was a sinner; others would solemnly insist she was a saint. The few who knew her best said sadly that she was a girl who loved everything she loved a little too much. Usually the traveler never heard all the story but went on his way, humming or fiddling the haunting tune and retelling the story to suit himself.

Actually, there was no way of knowing or understanding the story behind the ballad unless one went back to a fall afternoon in 1846 and knew the young girl named Cordelia Riley some four years before she became the lonely, tragic figure known as The River Witch.

That autumn afternoon sumac was flaming like a crimson mantle on the bluffs, and cattails were standing like burned-out candles in the marshes, when Michael Riley, Captain and owner of the steamboat *The Blue Teal*, landed his boat at Hermann, Missouri.

He went ashore as soon as the stage-plank was in place. Crossing docks overflowing with produce and refuse, he threaded his way between sleeping dogs and lounging Negroes and climbed the stone steps leading to the town proper. His cronies would be expecting him at Rommel's wine cellar, and his wife and daughter were awaiting his homecoming in one of the more imposing bluff-top houses. His inclination was toward the wine cellar but he continued homeward. He had a fine present swinging from his arm for his sixteen-year-old daughter, Cordelia.

A few minutes later Michael was climbing more stone steps leading from the town to the bluff top where the Riley house sat like a massive German trunk upon a shelf—two stories of soft orange brick, with deep arched windows trimmed with limestone carvings. For a moment he looked at his house, then turned, as he always did, to look down at the magnificent view.

Michael never returned from a river trip without a renewed gladness that he had chosen this spot for his home. Below him spread the Missouri River, glinting in the afternoon sun and tossing restlessly in its bed. Bluffs rose along the river side, blue-gray and aloof, their alluvial soil autumn-rich with almost every kind of tree and shrub. Little farms dotted the landscape where the forest had been cleared and far down the river he saw a witch plume of smoke where another steamboat slapped her paddles in the murky water of the Missouri.

He looked with pride at his boat, *The Blue Teal*. She was a sidewheeler, especially built for use on the Missouri River. She drew only three feet of water, but she carried 300 tons of freight and 200 passengers. It had been less than two days since he had taken her from the wharf in St. Louis and brought her upstream, leaving the

Mississippi River behind for the twisted, tortuous channel of the Missouri. Enroute to Hermann, he had stopped at innumerable small landings to pick up or deliver produce from merchants and farmers. Now the trip on up the Missouri to St. Joseph lay ahead.

If he were lucky some of the legislators from the Assembly might come aboard at Jefferson City and entertain him with political talk at dinner. At Glasgow he could always figure on a heavy cargo since it had the best levee on the river. Those Brunswick merchants would be itching to get rid of their tobacco. He made a mental note to buy some new hawsers from the hemp man at Waverly. If my running time is good, he thought, there isn't any reason why I can't stop off at Westport Landing and watch that girl dance in the Yellow Dog Saloon.

Then Michael shoved his cap on the back of his head and laughed at himself. Here I am, he thought, a tough old channel-cat forty years old who's made more trips up the Missouri and back than I can count, and I'm still as excited about it as I was when I was a cabin boy of twelve. Then he forgot all about his boat and the trip ahead, for a lithe figure burst from the house and came flying down the path to meet him.

She held up the skirt of her dark brown dress and ran down the path like a boy, her black curls flying out behind her like woodsmoke from a steamboat. "Father! Father!" she called breathlessly, flinging herself into his arms. "I wanted to come to the dock but Mother wouldn't let me. I've been watching and waiting for over an hour. Oh, I'm *so* glad you're home! Tell me all about St. Louis, and *did* you go to the theater? Tell me quick before Mother hears!"

"Cordelia girl!" Michael gave his daughter a bear hug. "Not so fast and just one question at a time. Now, about the theater and the wicked painted women . . ." He drew his mouth down into a mock stern line. They came laughingly up the path, their arms about each other, and both chattering like blackbirds.

"What do you have in the box?" she asked, taking a tentative poke at the parcel he carried.

"Oh, a present for a woman I know," he said. "One who gets prettier every time I see her. Too pretty for her own good."

"Oh, Father, you mean me—I hope!" She flashed mischievous gray-green eyes at him and wrinkled her tip-tilted nose. "Is it something to wear?"

"No! Hymn books," he said solemnly and winked.

[5]

Margaret Riley appeared in the doorway of the house. She was thirty-seven, tall and slender like her daughter. Her black hair was drawn smoothly back from her pale oval face.

"Welcome home, Michael." She smiled decorously and put up a smooth cheek for her husband to kiss. Then she turned to her daughter. "Cordelia, you *must* walk, not run like a rabbit. What will people think! Will you never learn to be a lady?"

"I forgot. Oh, Mother," Cordelia burst out, "Father's brought me a package from St. Louis!" She snatched the box from him. "May I open it now?" Then, without waiting for his nod, she tore open the package. Out tumbled a deep green velvet dress with a little bonnet to match.

"Velvet! Velvet! I've been praying for a velvet dress. Oh, I love it! I love *you!*" Cordelia hugged her father rapturously.

"Velvet is much too old and does not suit a young girl," said her mother in a positive tone.

"Gr—ee—n," rhapsodized Cordelia. "It matches my eyes."

"Admiration of one's face is never to be commended," Margaret said firmly. Then she turned to Michael. "She's spent the last two weeks in front of the mirror."

"That sounds normal," said Michael, laughing. "Put the dress on, child. The best dressmaker in St. Louis made it."

"Michael!" exclaimed Margaret. "It must have cost a fortune!"

"Two fortunes," said Michael, "but we have only one daughter." Then he turned to Cordelia. "Try it on, child, and stop flitting about like a dragonfly."

"It will only take me a minute," said Cordelia breathlessly. "Of course I should have a dozen petticoats, but maybe four . . ." She flew up the stairs, the dress piled in her arms and the bonnet clapped atop her head.

"Honestly, I don't know what to do with her," said Margaret.

"I figure Cordelia is pretty apt to do for herself," said Michael.

And there she was, walking slowly down the stairs, coming forward timidly until she stood uncertainly in the doorway, her eyes asking for her parents' approval. Michael gasped when he saw her, with the creamy lace foaming about her throat and the taut bodice bringing out the curved lines of her breasts. Her mouth was a soft red *O* and her eyebrows were like black shooting arrows over her dancing eyes.

"And the bonnet!" She reached up and touched the plumes reverently. "The plumes are like silver frost." Michael laughed because in her haste Cordelia had tied it on crookedly and it gave her an impudent, saucy look.

But Margaret did not laugh. Looking hard at the velvet bodice and the low-cut neckline, she said, "The material *is* lovely and very expensive, I know. But it belongs in the theater and not on a young girl. I'm sorry."

"Mother!" Cordelia wailed. "Oh, *no,* Mother!"

"I'm sorry you've spent so much money, Michael," Margaret said reproachfully, "but as you can see, the dress is entirely unsuitable for a girl of sixteen. Perhaps you can make an exchange."

"Exchange!" Tears were beginning to come into Cordelia's eyes. "But I don't want any dress but this. It's the most beautiful dress in the world!"

"I can't exchange it. I had it made especially for her," Michael protested. "I think you're being unnecessarily strict, Margaret. You could put a little more lace on the bodice, but I like it the way it is."

"I'm truly sorry." Margaret compressed her lips and regarded them both with somber, gray eyes. "She simply cannot wear the dress."

"Oh, come now, Margaret," said Michael, "let's not be ridiculous."

"She can't wear the dress and that's that!" said Margaret firmly.

"Mother!" Cordelia let out an anguished cry, then, whirling, she ran halfway up the stairs, turned and looked down with blazing eyes. "I don't care what you say. I will wear the dress, I *will,* I will!" She walked up the rest of the steps, her back as stiff as a poker.

"You see," said Margaret. "She's got so she actually defies me."

"She has a mind of her own," said Michael. "It's time you let her have her way some of the time."

"But not about a dress designed for a strumpet," said Margaret sternly, her cheeks blazing from the use of the unaccustomed word. There was a long silence. Michael rose, went to the window and looked out at the river. Finally Margaret asked, "What time do you wish your dinner?"

"About seven." His voice was harsh. "I'm going downtown. I'll make it a point to be back by then—if it suits you."

"So you prefer the wine cellar to your own hearth!" said Margaret coldly.

"At least it's warm there," he said angrily. Then he turned to

[7]

Margaret. "Margaret, must you always be so cold and unyielding about everything?"

Margaret looked at her strong hands, twisting her fingers a little. "I always try to keep a good home, Michael."

He took her by the arms. "Look at me, Margaret. It's not keeping a house I'm talking about. Don't you understand the kind of welcome a man needs and wants when he comes home? Don't you understand at all?"

"Yes, Michael," she said, raising great, troubled eyes to his. "I understand you perfectly. But I should think that after eighteen years you would not come roaring in like some Irish sailor from the St. Louis levee!"

"I'm going to Rommel's!" Michael snatched up his cap and slammed out of the house, leaving Margaret standing still, with her hands clasped in front of her.

When dinner-time came, Michael left the tavern in the company of his young pilot, Pierre de Vries. He had asked Pierre home to dinner as a protection against Margaret's wrath and also in the hope of brightening the evening for Cordelia.

Both hopes proved to be failures. Margaret served a fine dinner, topped off with her truly superb burned-sugar custard, but she was scarcely more than civil after she sniffed the heavy aroma of smoke and wine.

Pierre was as charmed with Cordelia as he had been on other occasions when he had been invited to dinner at the Rileys' and he made every effort to be engaging. But Cordelia scarcely spoke and kept her eyes on her plate.

Shortly after dinner Cordelia pleaded a headache and went to her room. Pierre, realizing something was amiss, quickly excused himself and went back to town. By eight-thirty Michael and Margaret were alone in their sitting-room.

To Michael, as he sat in his big chair smoking his pipe and watching Margaret do fancywork in the lamplight, the austere room seemed unbearably dull. The furniture was heavy and uncomfortable-looking. The only bit of brightness was a crystal chandelier which Michael had installed against Margaret's wishes.

Its prisms answered the flames from the fireplace, casting a thousand lights on walls and ceilings. Margaret would not put candles in it, but even she could not keep its translucent splendor from dancing in the sunlight or answering fire with fire. He wondered what she would say if she knew it had once graced a bawdy-house in St. Louis.

Junk it for sure, Michael thought, studying his wife's face bent over her fancywork. Margaret was much prettier than most of the women who traveled on his boats, if only she would not dress so plainly. Of course if she wanted to look like a wren . . . but she had no right to bottle up Cordelia like a butterfly and to dress her like a nun! He bit hard on his pipe.

"I know you're dead set against it," he began, in a careful, reasoning tone although he was quite angry, "but I think Cordelia should be allowed to wear the dress and bonnet I brought her."

"It is not suitable for a young girl and you know it." Margaret's lips were a straight line. "You are thinking of those painted tarts who travel on your boats!"

"Good God, Margaret! Cordelia's a *woman*. A pretty one at that, and what have you done? Shut her up where she sees no one. I say let her wear the dress! Let her be happy. Better for her to make a few false steps on her own than walk a hundred miles with you telling her how to do it!"

Margaret remained silent, which meant she would not give in. Michael sighed. There had been too many silences between them lately and it would be worse when he was home for the winter, with the river holding his boats captive in the ice. When he was younger he had had bitter arguments with Margaret. But though he could order her to let Cordelia wear the dress and she would obey him, he knew she would find some way to defeat him in his absence.

He glanced restlessly out the window. There was a moon tonight and he could go upstream without waiting for daylight. There were plenty of dangerous bends ahead, but if you wanted a safe life you should plant corn, not own a steamboat. The moon was bright as day, a night for lovers. He rubbed his hand wearily across his eyes.

"Cordelia's too vain and willful as it is," Margaret said, breaking the silence. "Her needlework needs improvement and she has more of a head for figures than poetry. She even talks more like a boy than a girl—and you're responsible. Only yesterday I heard her boasting that you promised to take her duck hunting!"

Michael laughed. "I notice you always dress and cook the ducks she shoots." He thought lovingly of his lonely child. This winter perhaps they would have more time together.

Margaret made a French knot and bit off the thread. Michael

knew the subject was closed. She blamed him for having taught Cordelia to swim and shoot when she was a child. Now that she was grown up and he brought her pretty dresses, that was wrong, too!

Michael was a blithesome man, full of waggish good humor, fond of taverns, singing and hunting. It was strange, he mused, that in his youth he loved no woman but this one of stern principles, who would always be cold and unyielding.

Margaret was more agreeable now, and began to talk of the neighbors' doings, but Michael listened with only half an ear. He was thinking how lovely his daughter had looked in the green velvet dress and he suddenly realized that Cordelia was a dangerous mixture. She had inherited his natural love of life and her mother's stubbornness, a combination that didn't make for easy living.

Upstairs in her bedroom, Cordelia stood listening to the river slap and gurgle against the wooden landing as if it had half a notion to gobble up landing, boat and all. Then, as if changing its mind, the river would make a peculiar sucking, chuckling sound, familiar to all who lived on the Missouri River bluffs, and go on its way like a greedy old man sucking his gums in the dark.

All the past year she had listened to the rhythm of the water and felt an inner excitement in the sound of its perpetual cadences. Tonight the river ran in time with her pulse. Her mother would have thought her mad if she were to make such a comparison, but then her mother had not the faintest idea of what went on in her mind. Father knows how I feel, she thought. He knew how much I would love the dress he brought. He knows how I feel about the river.

She had often seen him stand on the bank with his black hair curling from under his cap, shaking his great hairy fist at the river, cursing it for a vile hussy and swearing never to take a boat up its cussed, twisting, muddy, shallow-bottomed channel again.

Every winter he told Cordelia and her mother that when the ice broke he was going to take his boat down the Mississippi and on to New Orleans. At least the Mississippi *had* a channel. But come spring, her father would be the first man to leave the Mississippi and take his boat up the Missouri. He ruled his crew with flailing fists, belted his boat through the bends, cursed the snags and vicious, whipping pieces of driftwood called sawyers, and said quick prayers for the sunken boats that dotted the river from one end to the other. For all his libel of the river, Cordelia knew her father loved the Missouri as passionately as her mother hated it.

Cordelia leaned far out the window, sniffing the damp air and · the musky odor of rotting leaves and water-wet timbers. Oh, it was wonderful out there now with the leaves blazing along the banks, their color spreading like slow-creeping fire onto sandbars and little islands. The cattails were standing like tawny sentries, their spear-like foliage sheltering mallards who paddled lazily at summer's end, their prismatic necks bowed to catch unwary insects.

Lung-fever weather, her mother called it when she had come up earlier to see if Cordelia were wearing her warm nightgown. She might have fainted had she known that Cordelia sometimes stood unclothed before the open window, letting the soft night air steal around her body like a caress.

Lung-fever, poof! she thought, as she folded a rug against the door-sill so her mother would not see the light from her lamp. She held the lamp close, scrutinizing her face in the mirror. The fall air made your hair curlier and your skin softer and your insides all a-tingle. She recalled, with a delightful shiver, the way Pierre, her father's young pilot, had looked at her across the table.

Restless, she set the lamp down on the washstand and went back to the window. *The Blue Teal* was half-outlined in the dark by flames from the pineknots burning in their iron baskets. They called them jacks, but to her they were like mammoth candles, casting silver paths on the water.

She had shed so many tears alone that afternoon over the velvet dress. She had flung down her books and she *would not* do fancy-work; instead, she had fled to the edge of the bluffs where she watched the roustabouts loading the lower deck of *The Blue Teal*. Sometimes she could distinguish the stalwart form of Black Button, her father's chief roustabout. She could certainly hear his voice above the rest.

Now it was dark and the boat was nearly loaded. She could hear the sounds from the cattle and horses on the lower deck, and faintly, ever so faintly, the strains of a waltz. She knew that in an hour or so the boat would be pulling out. On a night like this her father would not wait.

Oh, how she wished *she* were there, dancing in that beautiful green dress! Who had a better right to be on the boat than the own-er's daughter?

[11]

She had often explored every nook and cranny of *The Blue Teal*, from the back galley to the boiler room. But with the exception of one visit to her Uncle Otto's in St. Louis, Cordelia had never made a real boat trip. For three years she had pleaded to take just one trip and had promised to stay as close to the ladies' cabin as the Bible chained to the marble table, but her mother would not give in.

"Why?" Cordelia had demanded. "Why are we the *only* captains' women who never make a trip with them?"

"I am a *Knapp*," her mother had said, proudly, "and so are you. We do not go trailing our men about in boats." Her mother's people, the Knapps of St. Louis, owned a steamboat line, and her mother's older brother Otto owned the largest line on the river. It was true! Their women never traveled on a boat. Instead they stayed at home in a gloomy old house, sewing. There was no dancing or card-playing on a Knapp boat. How dull it must be on Uncle Otto's boats, thought Cordelia to herself. *I'd* never take passage on one of them!

When one of her father's boats docked, you could hear the sound of fiddles half the night and when the wind was right, wagon-folks singing and blowing on a jug.

The light-paths on the water danced and called to her. For a year she had wanted to slip aboard one of her father's boats, but she hadn't quite summoned the courage. But now she was angry and a little frightened. This very evening she had overheard her mother say to her father that since Cordelia was so willful and set on a river trip, why shouldn't they send her to Uncle Otto's in St. Louis for the winter?

Uncle Otto had been desolate since the death of his oldest son Charlie. He had been trapped in a cabin when *The Merry Widow* burned on the Mississippi. But Hugo, the younger son, had miraculously escaped death in the same fire.

Hugo! Cordelia made a face. She had always known her mother intended for her to marry Hugo. He was a Knapp. But Cordelia remembered that when she was a little girl he had pinched her, and on his last visit he had lifted her skirts with his eyes, while he decorously shared her psalm book. She would never marry a man unless she loved him—and she was sure she would *never* love Hugo!

It terrified her to think of being shut up in the gloomy Knapp house to have babies—and never to have gone up the river on a boat, never to have floated past fine houses set high on the river banks nor to have watched cottonwood logs bobbing past on their way to the

[12]

seal She suddenly decided to slip aboard *The Blue Teal* that very night.

Shucking off her nightgown, she tossed it on the bed. She put on shoes, stockings, her best drawers, a camisole and one petticoat. Hastily she put on five more petticoats and took up the forbidden dress. Oh, how soft the velvet was! Soft as a furry kitten, she thought, as she drew it carefully over her head. So tight in the waist she could scarcely breathe, which made it perfect.

When she had finished she looked at her reflection with satisfaction. Who would guess her to be sixteen? All she had to do was walk up the stage-plank of the boat as if she were a passenger who had strolled off and was strolling back on. If someone stopped her or asked her about her ticket, she would say she was going aboard to tell her father goodbye.

Studying her face in the mirror, she observed with satisfaction that she had odd-shaped gray-green eyes, black-lashed. Her hair was the color of woodsmoke, her father said. But her mouth was entirely too wide to suit her. Worst of all, her nose was tip-tilted. She guessed that was the Irish strain. Her chin was too square—that must be the German. She glanced down at her feet and wished they were tinier. Like her mother, she was apt to put her foot down hard and not move it for anyone.

She started as she heard her father's voice booming up the stairway. "Goodbye, Cordelia girl!" His voice was kind. She was counting on that kindness to allow her to stay on the boat when he discovered her presence.

"Goodbye," she called sleepily.

Quickly she slipped on her quilted pardessus, blew out the flame and waited. Everything, everything depended on timing. Her mother always accompanied her father as far as the front gate. What if she failed to go tonight?

She heard her parents' voices, then the door opening and closing. Had her mother gone to the gate? She listened intently. No sound came from the parlor. If her plan were to succeed she must get on *The Blue Teal* before her father came aboard. Now! Now was the time for her to go!

Cordelia held up her skirts and scampered down the stairway and out the back door, her heart thumping like a woodpecker on a hollow log. She did not follow the regular path but cut across the bluffs to a dirt slide used by the children of the town. Awkwardly she pulled up her pardessus, her skirt and six petticoats, sat down and gave herself a shove.

It was a short-cut to the docks, but she had a feeling her best drawers would be ruined.

2

CROUCHING BEHIND Cheatin' Charlie's woodpile, Cordelia saw it was just like folks said. Cheatin' Charlie could stack steamboat wood so you could toss a hat through it. Steamboat owners bought wood as it measured off and Charlie got paid for holes and all. Cordelia peeped through one of the holes at *The Blue Teal*.

How lovely it was—all white and gilt—with the pilot-house perched on top like a bubble. She heard music coming from the main saloon and saw dancers flash by the windows.

Roustabouts were rolling barrels of sorghum and fat on the lower deck, and there was a mingled smell of horses, cattle, muddy water, sweating men and decaying wood. On the passenger deck above, the carpets were thick and the ladies wore sweet-smelling scents. But how was she to get up there?

In daylight it was a simple matter to walk aboard, mount the great stairway and mingle casually with the crowd on the passenger deck. But at night all the ladies were inside and a girl alone would be quite conspicuous.

A steward she had never seen before was standing by the stage-plank. Wherever she looked she saw men, most of them tipsy. The dock was swarming with Negroes who always came down to watch whenever a boat landed or cast off. Anxiously, she glanced at the steps leading to the town. Her father would be along any minute and he must not see her there.

She threw back her head and stepped with more confidence than she felt from behind the woodpile. She was so intent on getting aboard quickly that she did not see the two men staggering in front of her. She walked almost into their arms.

[14]

"Well, well!" they hailed her. The men were well-dressed but drunk. "Chipmunks come beautiful these days," one said, each taking one of her arms. "Do you live in the woodpile all the time?"

"Please let me alone. Let me go!" She jerked her arms free and glanced up at the steps. She was not frightened by the men. Her only fear was that her father might discover her before the boat sailed.

One of the men laughed. "Don't be coy. Gimme a kiss, girlie." His sour-sweet breath was on her face and suddenly he was drawing her to him.

"Stop it!" she half-screamed, slapping him hard across the cheek. Now his voice changed. "Oh, a wharf kitty with claws! Well, I like kittens with spunk. Come here and let me tame you." The man pulled her roughly against him and her heart thumped with fright and anger as she began to struggle with him in earnest.

Suddenly, to her intense relief, she was released. It was as if the man had been plucked up by a giant and set down several feet away.

"Are you having trouble, miss?" she heard a deep voice ask. Cordelia looked up, shaken and trembling, to see that a tall, broad-shouldered man had thrust the two drunken men aside.

"Yes," she said, almost crying. "I don't know what I would have done if you . . . I had just . . ." Her voice broke.

The men who had annoyed her suddenly began to babble foolishly. "We didn't mean any harm," said the younger of the two. "A thousand pardons, Mr. Callahan, all in fun, you know . . ." said the one who had tried to kiss her. They both backed off and stumbled up the stage-plank.

"Well," said her rescuer, "there's nothing like a bad reputation to scare a coward . . ."

"I hope those two ruffians fall off the boat and drown!" said Cordelia, smoothing her rumpled dress.

"I doubt if you really mean that, miss," he said. "You don't look like one who would wish death to *any* man." Then he removed his hat and Cordelia saw his face for the first time.

He was a tall, rawboned young man with dark hair and high cheekbones. He had a long jaw and a stubborn chin. A small white scar showed faintly across his left cheek. The flickering fire from the pine-knots cast strange shadows on his features. Even in the dim light

Cordelia could see that his eyes were a brilliant blue. She sensed a great strength in them.

"Now tell me," he asked, "what is a young lady like yourself doing alone on these docks at night?" His voice became reproving. "Don't you know it is dangerous for any but an armed man?"

"I'm Captain Riley's daughter," she said. "I have an urgent message from my mother to my father. I'd be grateful if you would escort me aboard." She smiled tremulously, hoping he would believe her outrageous lie.

The man called Callahan glanced at her low-cut dress and plumed bonnet and a smile flickered across his face. "I don't believe your story, miss." His eyes bored into hers and she could not look away. "If you were two years younger, I'd spank you and send you home." Then he shrugged ruefully. "But I suppose you'll tell me it's none of my business. Besides, you are very pretty, and who am I to deny a pretty young lady her wish? Take my arm and I'll escort you to your . . . your father," he laughed.

Cordelia felt Callahan's arm, hard as iron, through the sleeve of his broadcloth coat as he shouldered his way through the crowd. He did not speak again but remained aloof, nodding only to the steward as they came aboard.

Safely on the lower deck, Cordelia disengaged her arm and thanked her rescuer as charmingly as she knew how.

"Oh, but I'll escort you to your father," he said, again taking her hand and holding it fast.

"That isn't necessary." Cordelia tried to withdraw her hand. How strong his fingers were! "I know my way."

"Look, miss," he said earnestly, and she saw that his eyes were concerned. "Whoever you are, I reckon you know what you're doing. But you look like a nice girl to me. I'm no angel myself—but before you go up those stairs, consider whether or not the man is worth it."

She jerked her hand free as if she had been burned. "You're like all the rest! You think nothing is of importance to a woman but a man!"

"Well, *is* he?" His eyes were no longer smiling.

Fascinated by his voice, confused because she did not know how to answer him, she ran. She ran willy-nilly between mounds of yellow pumpkins, bales of hemp and tobacco and barrels of fat and salt, bumping into astonished members of the crew. Finding the stairway at last, she scampered up toward the passenger deck. On reaching the top she paused and looked back. She hadn't intended to, but she couldn't help herself.

The young man who had aided her was staring up at her like one who has caught an exotic moth, released it and then wished he hadn't. He cupped his hands and called up to her. "Miss, oh, miss! If your plans don't work out, the steward can find me. My name's Josiah. . . Josiah Callahan!"

"Josiah," said Cordelia breathlessly to herself. "Josiah . . ." as she brushed past two women and fled up to the pilot-house, praying it was empty. Thank heaven it was.

Glancing quickly around, she saw a red curtain on a pole. The pilot hung his extra clothing there. She heard approaching footsteps. There was no time to look for another place of concealment —it was stay behind the red curtain or be caught. Flattening herself behind it, she took cover under some old jackets reeking of whiskey and tobacco.

She heard her father's voice only a few feet from where she lay in hiding. "River's quiet as the Brown Shanty Saloon in the morning," he said. "Moon's bright too, so we'll be all right if there's no fog in the bend."

"Moon or no moon, I still say we should wait until morning," she heard Pierre saying earnestly.

Another voice spoke, one Cordelia had never heard before. "I can shoot any bend and grasshopper any sandbar in this hussy river. This is a man's river," rumbled the voice, thick with liquor. "I say, them that's scared, let them go down on the Mississippi with the boys."

"You will not talk so big if we all get our feet wet!" said Pierre hotly. There was more argument, and Mr. Rumble-Voice won. Finally she heard footsteps going away and suddenly she felt a quiver and showers of wood sparks flew past the window. The boat shuddered hard and she heard the engines throbbing.

Myriad noises from below contributed to the general symphony of sound. Then the whole swelled to a strident crescendo. Cordelia shivered with excitement. *The Blue Teal* was ready to cast off!

Here in the pilot-house she could hear everything. From far below she heard Button singing. "Heave now, ho! Ho! I drags de line, I totes de hemp, till my back is bent. Libely, now, libely, ho! Drag, you nigger! Swing, you nigger, to make dis boat go."

There was the sound of giant hawsers being dragged across a wooden deck. Then loud and clear from somewhere came a man's

[17]

voice. A wagon-man, she guessed. "I tell you what I need now is a woman who will cook me up some hoppin' john." This was followed by guffaws and the scrape of a fiddle. Someone began to sing, "Oh, there was an old hen, she had a wooden leg . . ."

Closer, much closer she heard a worried voice. "Ma's pretty sick. Maybe we had ought to've got off here. Blue Mass don't do no good nor Bitter Apple either, seems like. Not even fever pills." Cordelia wrinkled her nose at the thought of medicine and listened to the voices again. Someone was speaking German, another French, and there was a drawling, unmistakably Kentucky-bred voice. Again she heard Button shouting, "Lift dat hemp! Roll dat barrel . . ." Button could lift more wood, heave more hemp, pull more rope and wield a knife better than any other man on the river!

Slap and slap-slap-slap went the paddle wheels. *The Blue Teal* was on her way upstream. Cordelia leaned against the wooden, oil-soaked walls and felt a great exhilaration. The pilot-house was the top of the world.

If only she could stretch a bit or steady herself against a support. Suddenly she remembered how strong Josiah Callahan's arm had been. Now there was a man who could hold you up, no matter what. Her cheeks flamed at what he had said.

It seemed an eternity before Cordelia dared peep out at the pilot. She hoped it would be Pierre, but instead she saw a tall man in a silk hat.

Cordelia's eyes widened. The pilot wore striped trousers, fine leather boots, a vest embroidered with gold flowers and a swallow-tail coat. A huge diamond glittered on his starched front, his hands were encased in saffron-yellow gloves, and two pearl-handled pistols bulged his hip pockets. He had a hatchet face, bushy eyebrows and graying red hair.

This must be—it *was*—Fancy Foot Morgan. Fancy Foot was the vainest, most temperamental, and best-paid pilot on the Missouri River. They had run him off the Mississippi because of his terrible rages and his unpredictable behavior. They said he hated women. There was no telling *what* he would do if he found her. Cordelia slid wearily to a sitting position.

By the time the orchestra had stopped playing she was very tired. Perhaps if she just curled up quietly on the floor . . . well, whatever folks said about Fancy Foot, he was a good pilot. The motion of the boat was like a swing. Swinging always made her sleepy. . . .

Cordelia was awakened by a sudden lurch which threw her against the side of the boat. Clang-clang-clang went the pilot's bell. She heard excited voices and running feet. Her father and Pierre burst into the pilot-house.

"I told you it was folly running this bend at night!" She peeped out and saw Pierre's face pale with anger. He shook his fist at Fancy Foot. "You're drunk! You'll ground us!"

"Drunk or sober, I'm a better pilot than you any time!" Fancy Foot deliberately spat a stream of tobacco juice in Pierre's direction.

"Why, you . . ." Pierre advanced toward Fancy Foot.

Cordelia's father stepped between the two. "Get away from the wheel, Fancy Foot, and let Pierre have it!" he ordered.

"No!" bellowed Fancy Foot. "I'm piloting this boat and I know what I'm doing. I drove it into a bank to avoid a snag. You couldn't see it, Frenchman, but I can. I have the best eyes on the river—and you try to tell *me* what to do!" A string of oaths followed. Clang-clang-clang! went his bell again—enough to drive the engineer below crazy. "This damned monster of a river is snapping her teeth at me, but no river is going to get the best of Fancy Foot Morgan!" There were inquiries from below, and Fancy Foot hurled an empty rum bottle in that direction. Sweat rolled down his face and he stripped off his coat and gloves and sent them after the bottle.

Pierre again attempted to take the wheel, but Fancy Foot shoved him aside. The boat was backing now and slammed into the opposite bank. The whole cargo shifted; there was the sound of rolling barrels, thudding pumpkins, bawling cattle and shouts from the passengers who had fled their staterooms in their night-clothes and were screaming at the pilot-house.

"We're going to take that wheel away from you, Fancy Foot." Cordelia's father advanced on the frenzied pilot. "Give it up peaceably or I'll lay you low."

"I'm the pilot. I know my rights. You can't take this wheel!" roared Fancy Foot. "If you do, you'll never get another pilot. I'll fix you so nobody will take you up this river. Now clear out of here. I'm taking this boat to St. Joe or bust her wide open."

Thud! The boat scraped against the bank and then righted itself.

"Fancy Foot, I'm warning you," shouted Captain Riley.

Pierre cut in, "But if you break the river law you may never get another pilot!"

"Pilot be damned!" said Captain Riley, grabbing Fancy Foot by the back of the neck and flinging him away from the wheel.

Fancy Foot, enraged, tore off his trousers, hurled them at Captain Riley and stood cursing him wildly. In his red underwear he looked to the horrified Cordelia like a demon from the flames of hell. "Nobody can do that to Fancy Foot Morgan!" he shrieked, preparing to rip off his under-drawers, too. Cordelia screamed.

Cordelia's father released the hard-won wheel, letting it spin aimlessly as both he and Pierre leaped to pull open the curtain.

"Mother of God!" breathed Pierre incredulously.

"Cordelia! Cordelia girl!" Her father looked from Cordelia, cowering under the coats, to Fancy Foot, who was trying desperately to fasten his drawers. Then he threw back his head and burst into a roar of laughter that echoed through the pilot-house and all over the boat.

Below, bedlam had broken out on every deck. Women were screaming, babies were wailing, cattle bellowing. The rumor had spread that the boat was sinking. Wagon-men rushed to their wagons, the gamblers stopped their game, dozens knelt in prayer around a preacher—while others reached for a jug. The laughter brought a sudden calm.

3

MICHAEL RILEY turned the wheel over to Pierre. That situation was under control, he could see. The boat was free, the damage probably slight and the men would take care of it. He turned and took his daughter to his stateroom. Now he was angry. He called her a disobedient, ungrateful child, threatened to put her in a convent, and certainly to send her home at the next landing. He said everything he felt was expected of him as a parent. Then he ran out of words and stood glaring at her. "Cordelia girl," he asked helplessly, "why did you do it when you know how your mother feels?"

"That's just it," Cordelia said. "I know how Mother feels, but she doesn't know how I feel. *You* know," she said. "You know I've never been anywhere or seen anything! Every day of my life I look from my window and see hundreds of people going up and down the river. Some are bound for the end of the world—almost! I can't stop thinking about it. What good does it do me to have a water road at my door, if I do nothing but sit home and sew? And now Mother wants to send me off to St. Louis to marry Hugo. I hate Hugo! I won't shut myself up in that old house. I'd rather be dead!" she declared passionately.

"Cordelia girl!" Her father patted her arm. "Nobody's going to make you marry someone you don't like."

"Mother never lets me see other men and she prays I'll marry Hugo. I've heard her," she said grimly. "Please! Please!" she begged her father and began to sob against his shoulder. "If I were a boy, you'd have let me come with you long ago."

Her father's face was sad as he put his arms about her and smoothed her hair. "It's true, honey," he said. "I wanted a son, just as any man wants a son. But that doesn't mean I'm not happy to have a wonderful daughter that I love."

He patted her shoulder. "You're a stubborn, willful child. I'm afraid you're going to have a hard time in this world." He wound one of her silky curls between his fingers. "It would be a lot better if you thought more about fancy stitches and how to please a man. Folks would understand that, but nobody but your father will ever know what you see in a muddy river."

"It's not just the river," she protested. "It's the people, too. All of them going somewhere. I wonder about them. I wonder what happens to them when they are a long, long way from this river."

"Don't go thinking that way!" Her father's face looked worn. "Nobody but a fool goes along in his mind's eye with those wagons full of men and women and crying babies. Nights when you're lying in your stateroom you can see 'em shivering, or think of them out there in the burnin' sand with Indians coming at 'em.

"Or maybe you haul an old man and his wife up the river and they buy a little piece of land with their last money. Then the next spring you go up the river and see that the old man has never built a dock and you look up on the bluff at his house and see sand blowing in where the windows used to be—and you start wondering what happened."

"You *do* know! You do know how I feel." She loved him so much she could hardly stand it.

"Now you listen to me." He did not smile and his big red face was sober. "Nobody but a soft-headed Irishman could think like that! You can't be thinking of this river as a road, and wondering what happens to people after they go off yonder. No, sir, if you're smart, you'll see nothing but a big river. A big river folks want to get themselves and their stuff up and down. You haul 'em and forget 'em. Load the boat with as much as she'll hold and charge every cent you can get to haul them up and down this river that isn't navigable in the first place. Make yourself a lot of money and keep your womenfolks home in a fine big house."

"Like the Knapps!" she said contemptuously.

"Like the Knapps," he said, smiling a little. "They are very rich, you know."

"But I like your way best," she said. "I love it!" With that she threw herself into his arms. "You will let me stay. Please!"

"All right, you can stay," he said, "but your mother will most likely blast us both out of the water."

The next morning Cordelia stood in the pilot-house with her father and Pierre. While the two men were deep in river talk, Cordelia watched the river.

She still had to pinch herself to believe that her father had sent a rider back at the first landing to inform her mother that Cordelia was safe aboard *The Blue Teal* and would finish the trip with him.

She was wearing a rose-sprigged dress and shawl her father had been fortunate enough to buy from a dressmaker who was aboard. The wardrobe had been intended for a young bride who had died suddenly of cholera. Wearing the pretty clothes of a girl who had met such an untimely death made Cordelia feel sad, grown-up and tragically elegant.

Her little stateroom had lace curtains, a washbowl and a pitcher with pink flowers, and there was a velvet rug on the floor. She was safe, too, safe enough to please even her mother. Her father had ordered Button to sleep on the floor outside her door where his great black hulk presented such a formidable sight that even the steward was afraid to knock.

But most exciting of all was the river, which had proved to be even more than she had expected. There were boils and eddies where cottonwood logs hung in a mad, gyrating dance until some whimsical current of the river sent them bobbing toward the Mississippi.

There were few broad, flat stretches. The Missouri flung itself across the fertile land in a series of serpentine bends and the landscape unrolled itself like a scroll, revealing a series of scenes like exquisitely embroidered miniatures.

Trees grew close to the water's edge, some dipping their branches in the river. But now and then she saw a clearing that looked as if some majestic hand had swept aside the curtain of the forest to reveal a little stage on which were set barns and houses edged about by fields.

At night the little towns made a friendly cluster of lights, pin-pricking the darkness, but the lights from the houses of lone settlers were the ones Cordelia loved the best. They seemed like low-set stars that had lost their way. She wondered what it would be like to live in a lonely, remote spot.

She looked fondly at her father, laughing over a joke with Pierre, and decided he was the most understanding father in the world to have allowed her to take this wonderful trip.

Her father turned. "Wouldn't you like to go to the ladies' cabin, Cordie? You mustn't go wandering about the boat alone, you know."

"Let me stay up here a while longer with Pierre. I want to watch the river," she begged.

"I shall take good care of her," Pierre assured him. "The very best."

Pierre's eyes were such a warm, shining brown. Cordelia found him a delightful companion. He knew when to talk and when to be silent as they moved along the ever-changing river. She saw a number of pretty little islands covered with willows, cottonwoods and luxurious undergrowth. She saw birds flitting through them like quick-moving shadows.

"Someday," she told Pierre, "someday I shall build myself a home on one of those and take out only enough trees for a house. I could live like a queen in my own kingdom with water all around me."

Pierre laughed and gave her a sidelong glance. "Your island is probably a sunken steamboat and more likely to be covered with water than surrounded," he said. "Those pretty little islands are the sad wrecks of someone's hopes—here today and gone tomorrow."

"Oh." She gazed thoughtfully at a wooded crescent of land surrounded by bobbing, rotting logs. "It makes me sad to think of anything so beautiful being washed away."

"Dream castles have a way of being swept away in a flood," he said, his strong face serious. "You must build a real home someday."

"But who wants a gloomy old house where you can't see the river!"

"No house is gloomy if the right person shares it," he said.

"Why, Pierre!" Cordelia exclaimed. "That sounds poetic."

Pierre's neck became very red. "Hardly that," he said hastily. "I was thinking aloud."

Cordelia did not know what to say. His eyes had said even more than his lips. Pierre seemed more gentle than most of the river pilots. He was young, quite tall, with brown, curly hair, a fair skin browned by the weather, and a quick smile. It made her feel important to talk with him, because all the ladies on the boat seemed to want to talk to Pierre. They were always crowding in the pilot-house, asking silly questions. But Pierre never looked at them the way he was looking at her.

"Those birds," he pointed skyward, trying to cover up the sudden awkwardness that had sprung up between them, "those birds are transients. But take the little blue-winged teal—he's the best navigator in the world. He's been going up and down this river long before steamboats and he'll be here long after they are gone."

"Gone!" Cordelia gasped. "You're joking. Steamboats will never be gone!"

Pierre did not have the heart to tell her that there was always something new to take the place of the old. Such a pretty, bright look she had! He had fallen in love with her the moment he first saw her, two years ago. But he had always known she was not for him. Her mother was a Knapp, who would not dream of allowing her daughter to marry a young river pilot.

"Come closer," he said, "and I will show you how to read the river."

He pointed to the high waves. "That is where the water is deep because the wind is upstream. If the wind were downstream we would know the water was the shallowest there."

"But how do you know where the channel is?" she asked. "The river looks so wide."

"You are really interested?" Pierre asked, amazed.

"Oh, yes, yes!" Cordelia leaned past him, her hair touching his shoulder as she peered down at the river.

Her hair is like black silk with smoke in it, thought Pierre. Her breasts are high and proud. What a woman she would be to love! But he *must* keep his mind on the river.

"The channel . . . who knows where the channel is?" he replied. "It is more a hope than a fact. Today it is here and tomorrow it is half-a-mile away. You learn to look for landmarks, rocks, hills and trees. Some people, like Fancy Foot, have the magic eye and ear. I've heard he can land a boat in a fog by the barking of a dog or the squealing of some farmer's hogs. I'm not that good a pilot. But that is not what I want out of life. . . ."

"What do you want out of life, Pierre?" Cordelia gazed up at him and he could see the green lights dancing in her eyes.

"I would like . . . I would like to own my own boat and a pretty house ashore, to be married to a girl I loved, to have children and much laughter," he said.

"Would . . . would you let *your* wife go up the river with you sometimes?" Cordelia searched his face earnestly.

"If she were the right girl," Pierre looked intently into her eyes, "she could go anywhere with me."

The two stared at each other and Cordelia felt her face flaming. "I think, I mean, my father said I should go to the ladies' cabin. Excuse me." She turned and ran down the stairway.

There she found herself in the midst of the afternoon lull. The ladies' cabin was furnished with thick carpets, carved tables and velvet chairs. Crystal chandeliers swung from the ceiling. But it was too quiet. Like a church or a funeral.

Stout matrons, sitting in a semi-circle with their backs to the windows, were crocheting and talking in murmurs like bees. They glanced up and nodded when Cordelia came in. She stood hesitantly, watching them. She supposed she ought to settle down with her fancywork, too. But she didn't want to and, besides, her mother said her work looked like chicken-tracks.

She examined the big Bible and idly traced the words *The Blue Teal* embossed in gold on its red velvet cover. She looked around the room again. To her delight she saw that she had overlooked a pretty young woman with red hair sitting at a table alone.

Cordelia sauntered over, hoping that the girl might speak to her. As she approached, she realized the girl was slapping cards down on the table before her.

Cordelia had never seen a woman playing cards alone before. "May I watch you?" she inquired politely.

The girl glanced up and Cordelia saw that she had eyes like tawny cattails and that her eyelashes were long and sooty. The girl was breathtakingly lovely, but not so young as she had first thought.

"If you like." She pursed her full red lips and studied the cards. Presently she pushed them together, shuffled the deck and began dealing out the cards again.

"Do—do you play cards often?" Cordelia asked.

"When I'm not busy," said the girl, sharply. She raised her long lashes and shot a resentful glance at Cordelia.

"Oh . . ." Cordelia began, observing her cherry-colored velvet dress trimmed with pink satin. Pink petticoats peeped from beneath her skirt. You wouldn't think of wearing pink with red hair, but on this girl the effect was spectacular. "Are you, are you an actress or an entertainer?"

Cordelia heard a loud gasp and she turned to see that the matrons had dropped their needlework and were agog, like a ring of geese.

"Miss Riley, Miss Riley!" called one old lady with a yellow cat. "Do come and see how cunning my Tommy is with his toy mouse!"

Another voice called. "Would you like to see a crochet stitch, brand new? My sister brought it from England. Come over, dear, and let me show you." They were crooking their fingers at her, insisting she come and sit with them.

Bewilderedly, Cordelia looked from the gaping women to the beautiful red-haired girl. What was wrong? Why were the women beckoning to her? Why didn't they want her to talk to this girl?

The girl turned around, smiled a crooked little smile, and rose gracefully. "You asked me what I do," she said in a clear, ringing voice, glancing coolly at the pale-faced sewing circle. "I market a commodity which those fat hens over there never had!"

Then, with a whirl of red skirts, she went out without a backward glance. Just as she went through the door she laughed, a dull, throaty laugh that sounded like water falling. Cordelia felt as if velvet had been drawn across her bare arm. Nobody had to tell her now what the girl was. That was a laugh any man in the world would follow.

The women flocked around Cordelia. "Sit down, dear. The nerve of her—that Red Maude! Never mind what she says, dear. You must *never* believe anything you hear."

"What things? That girl has such beautiful hair I . . ."

"That's her stock in trade," one said. "That's why they call her Red Maude. She's a strumpet. Her and her fancy skirts and curly hair!"

"But she's so pretty!" Cordelia protested.

[26]

"Pretty on the outside and carnal on the inside," said the old lady with the cat. "You're wrong. You'll understand when you're older." All the women agreed, nodding their heads and looking down at the fancywork they had taken up again, but still watching her out of the corners of their eyes.

Almost as if in answer to a prayer, a maid brought her a message from her father. Quickly she arose and excused herself. "I should love to learn a new stitch," she said, "but my father says there is to be a wood-loading contest, and he thinks I might like to watch it."

"Run along, dear," they said. "It will be a tiresome thing, but you should please your father."

Cordelia made a half-curtsey and tried to restrain herself from bounding out of the room. She glanced back and saw the women's heads together, whispering, whispering. What *were* they whispering about? The outside air struck her face. Oh, how fresh the air was! And how free!

4

AS SOON AS Cordelia stepped from the ladies' cabin she saw that the passengers and crew were swarming on the decks of *The Blue Teal*, making bets and waggish remarks to each other. The boat slowed to one stroke and slid into the landing at Franklin.

A steward pushing his way ahead of her made her a path through the jostling throng to the railing. At the railing she saw her father in earnest conversation with a tall, dark man. As Cordelia approached them, her father shouted and waved. The other man turned, his dark, arresting face expressionless except for his brilliant blue eyes that caught and held hers like a lodestar. She felt color flooding her cheeks as she recognized Josiah Callahan.

She had scanned every face in the dining room at every meal and had taken numerous turns about the promenade deck in the hope of seeing him again. But now that she had finally encountered him, she was afraid. Suppose he mentioned having rescued her from the ruffians on the Hermann dock? That was a detail she had not related to her father.

However, when her father made the introduction, Josiah gave no sign of having met Cordelia before. He bowed slightly, took her hand and said, "I had heard the Captain's beautiful daughter was aboard. I hoped to catch a glimpse of her, but work has kept me in my stateroom. Now that I have seen her, I find the reality even more delightful than the glowing descriptions." His eyes sparkled and the corners of his firm mouth twitched. She felt the warm, strong pressure of his fingers on hers.

"Don't turn her head, Callahan," her father laughed fondly. "She's vain enough as it is!" Then he leaned over the railing to bellow an order to the lower deck.

Cordelia knew Josiah was teasing her with his pretty speech and it made her furious. "Thank you for the compliment," she said, then in a low voice, "Your speech is pretty, but your memory is short!" Then she blushed and hated herself for blushing.

She looked up at Josiah resentfully and their glances clashed briefly.

He smiled and said, "I've thought of nothing else since I first saw you, but there were reasons why I could not seek you out. You must take my word for it. I cannot tell you why."

He is hard, Cordelia thought, looking at the firm mouth and the white scar across his cheek. I could never bend him with pretty ways and speeches. No woman could. But in a storm, she looked at his broad shoulders, in a storm he would be like a sheltering wall. And if he should love you . . . His mouth was firm but it was tender, too, and his eyes were like blue lightning. Suddenly it seemed as if a humming-bird were imprisoned in her chest.

Her father ceased shouting to the deck hands and, putting his arm about Cordelia, drew her to him. "You'll have to mind what you say to Mr. Callahan here. He's a lawyer and a member of the Missouri Assembly. When he talks down at Jefferson City, folks listen. Even Fiery Benton, I'm told."

"It's the other way round," said Josiah. "I'm the one who listens. I've learned a lot in Jefferson City, though I'll admit I've lost considerable hide doing it." Then he looked over the railing as if he saw something a long way off. "However, I'm no longer in the Assembly, Captain. I have resigned to go to Santa Fe or wherever our regiment will go. I had intended going with Doniphan this spring," he hesitated, "but personal matters intervened."

"You mean you're going to *war?*" exclaimed Cordelia.

"That's what they're calling it." Josiah looked at her keenly.

"Well," said her father, "I'll wager you were once with the old St. Louis Grays. You must have known Charlie Knapp, Cordelia's cousin."

"Charlie Knapp! I knew Charlie well," he said. "We were all saddened by his death."

"He'd be going with you, no doubt," said Captain Riley.

"Of course," said Josiah. "Charlie was the kind of man you'd like to have riding with you. We're a cavalry regiment," he explained to Cordelia. "Volunteers, and we like to think we're the finest anywhere," he added with pride.

"Well spoken!" The Captain slapped Josiah across his broad shoulders. "This country needs men in hickory blue to discipline those Mexicans. Insulting our minister and killing our men! The country needs for that territory to be free and open to trade."

Josiah shook his head. "Hold up, Captain. You're giving me more credit than I deserve. Missouri is my adopted state and dear to my heart. Wherever her volunteers go, I'll go."

"Let's hope they'll bring it in free," said Captain Riley.

"Free!" said Josiah. "Then we would have lost the war before we started. A free territory would be the ruination of the country!"

Cordelia had remained silent, carried away by thoughts of brave men like Josiah galloping over far-away trails to rout the Mexicans and make the territories safe for all the wagon-folks she had seen going up the river.

"I think it's wonderful!" she said. "Our country is like a big family and when one of us gets into trouble the rest have to come to the rescue, like brothers or sisters."

"Hardly that!" Josiah smiled tolerantly at her. "War sounds noble and romantic when you are standing aboard *The Blue Teal* talking to a pretty girl. But war is never romantic and seldom noble," he added dryly. "As for us being one family—let's say we're made up of a lot of families, each wanting the best for itself. But, I'm boring you with such talk."

"Not at all!" Captain Riley took out his pipe and tapped it hard against the railing. "But you're talking to the wrong folks. I understand you were born in Louisiana and that makes you a Southerner.

We're St. Louis German and Irish and not attached to any certain corner of this country. We think it's all pretty wonderful and we are grateful to be where we are. As long as it's America we're satisfied."

"Surely, Captain, you don't question the sovereignty of the state?" Josiah asked quickly. Then he shrugged. "Perhaps we'd better watch the wood-loading contest and not discuss politics. Is that the boat we're competing with?" He pointed to a gray steamboat tied up next to *The Blue Teal*.

"That's it," said Captain Riley. "It's *The Hawk*. The Knapp line's best boat. They think they have a roustabout who can lift more wood than Button." He chuckled.

"*The Hawk!*" Cordelia leaned over the railing, realizing for the first time that it was one of Otto Knapp's boats docked beside them at the wharf. "A Knapp boat! Then Button has to win," she exclaimed. "Besides, it will make Hugo furious, which is all the better!" She stopped abruptly, annoyed with herself for having been so artless.

"By the way," her father turned to her, lifting his eyebrows, "you might be interested to know that your cousin Hugo is aboard *The Hawk*. We have a bet up on our niggers." He bit down hard on his pipe. "From what I hear his nigger is big, and Button may be hard put to outdo him."

"What's going on here!" demanded an old lady in a high, querulous voice. "Betting!" She turned on Captain Riley. "I'm surprised you would allow such a practice, Captain Riley. Especially with your young daughter aboard. I think it's dreadful!"

"In that case, madam," spoke up a tousle-headed young man named Bird whom her father had pointed out to Cordelia as a traveling Methodist preacher, "I would suggest you go to your stateroom and close the door so you will not be a witness to such sin. I myself propose to remain here and get material for a sermon." A general laugh went up as the old lady retreated.

The minister reddened and Cordelia realized he had spoken sincerely. She felt sorry for him. She had noticed his shabby suit when she had seen him in the dining room and wondered what he could accomplish by going from town to town, farm to farm, with no money, with no real church of his own.

Maybe he didn't know folks didn't want to be reminded of their sins but just needed someone to "marry them tight and bury them decent." She looked at plain little Mrs. Bird standing beside her husband and holding fearfully to his arm. Cordelia felt even more sympathy for her. Then her attention was diverted to the dock where the townspeople were flocking to watch the wood-loading contest between the famous Black Button and some "yaller nigger" from New Orleans.

A shout went up from *The Hawk* and Cordelia saw her cousin Hugo and a man who appeared to be a Creole walking down the stage-plank toward the woodpile. Behind them shuffled a giant mulatto.

A groan went up from the crew of *The Blue Teal*. "Man, that yaller nigger is as big as a steamboat. Lord, lookit them hans! We is cooked possums."

"Blast Hugo," said Cordelia's father, standing with arms akimbo, squinting at the men by the woodpile. "He's got himself a half-witted creature who won't know when to quit." Almost as if verifying his statement, the mulatto, who was nearly seven feet tall and had hands like hams hanging by his side, grinned foolishly, turned his head from side to side and shuffled his feet.

Josiah turned to Cordelia. "Is the big blond man, the one with the tremendous shoulders, your cousin?"

"Yes, that's Hugo," said Cordelia. She realized for the first time how handsome Hugo must look to other people. From this distance you couldn't see how cold and gray his eyes were.

"He doesn't look a thing like Charlie," said Josiah, puzzled.

"He isn't like Charlie in any way," said Cordelia emphatically. Then she bit her lip as she realized she was maligning her cousin for no other reason than that he looked at her boldly and wanted to marry her. "I don't know the man with him," she hastened to cover her slip of tongue, "but I expect it's that Frenchman who tried to save Charlie when he was trapped in his cabin on *The Merry Widow*. Hugo brought him back to St. Louis afterward and the two have been inseparable ever since. He even lives at Uncle Otto's, so we've heard."

Captain Riley was absorbed in studying the mulatto. Josiah bent down and spoke quickly to Cordelia. "It is very important to me that I talk to you again. Can we. . . ?"

Before Cordelia could think of a reply, a great roar went up from *The Blue Teal*. Deck hands beat themselves into a frenzy as Button sauntered down the stage-plank and took his place on the dock. "Button, Button, we're countin' on you, Button!"

[31]

Black Button was not nearly as tall as the mulatto, although he stood well over six feet. He was twenty-six years old, a tremendous man, bare from the waist up, with a great silver chain hung around his neck. He stood, head up, proud and relaxed. When he moved, hard muscles rippled under his ebony skin.

"What a stallion!" Cordelia heard Josiah say under his breath, and he bent forward, excitement in his eyes. *Men,* she thought, watching him from the corner of her eyes. They're all like that. Let a duck fly, two men fight or a contest of any kind come up, and a woman is just so much dust!

She was hoping he would speak to her again when Fancy Foot Morgan took a position on the dock, drew his two pistols with a flourish and fired them into the air. The two Negroes approached the woodpile carrying knotted ropes. It was not how fast they could carry wood, but how much they could lift and carry.

Each looped his rope around several sticks of hickory, then drew the load onto his back while two men added sticks at their nods. Finally, when each had twenty sticks, the ropes were drawn taut across their foreheads. The mulatto motioned for another stick of wood, another and another, until there were twenty-four sticks of wood on his back.

Button nodded and an equivalent mountain of wood was placed on his back. Bare yellow feet spatulating, tendons knotting; bare black feet white between the toes on wooden planks, muscles tensing, thighs knotting and bulging, animal grunts as the two Negroes crept, half-crouching, up the stage-planks and dumped their loads on the lower decks of their respective boats.

Now the crowd began to clamor for blood. For the second load always decided the contest. Bets increased, fists were shaken and curses shouted. Feet began to stomp. Broadcloth brushed against linsey-woolsey, fine leather boots clattered beside a wagon-man's rude shoes and over all came the spat-spat-spat of the Negro roust-abouts' bare feet. Again the two contestants loaded twenty-four sticks of wood on their backs.

Each motioned for another. Twenty-five, twenty-six, now twenty-seven. A general hullabaloo ensued as the Negroes' knees bent lower and they rocked back and forth as if in pain. Cordelia could see Button's eyes rolling, white with strain.

"Button! Button!" She clutched Josiah's arm convulsively. Button had to win, he had to! Ever since Cordelia could remember, Button had spent the winter with them doing chores around the house. It was Button who had made her first swing and who had saved her life when she fell into the river. Who but Button could convince a wide-eyed little girl that there were steamboats with griddles so big that darkies had to put bacon sides on their feet like skates to grease them? Button! She called and waved to him.

Button's eyes rolled up at her. As if in answer he made a motion and still another stick was placed on his back. He stumbled, sank to his knees, rose and moved on. He moved like some gigantic black ant to the chant of the roustabouts. "Button, Button, carry that wood, man! Tote that wood or there'll be no hoecake tonight. Up!" Grunt. "Up!" Grunt. "Button, Button, tote that wood, man!"

At last Button made the lower deck, where he threw down his wood, fell and lay prone, gasping for air. Now every eye was on the mulatto.

He was shaking his head like a frightened horse, refusing the last stick of wood, but Hugo himself strode to the woodpile, took an extra large stick, loaded it on the protesting Negro's back and ordered him up the plank. Cries of encouragement came from *The Hawk.* The mulatto bowed his back, inched a few steps and collapsed on the dock.

A triumphant shout went up from *The Blue Teal* and groans of disgust from *The Hawk.* Cordelia caught her breath and looked away as Hugo, apparently losing control of himself, strode up to the mulatto and kicked him in the ribs. But Hugo's companion showed a little pity. He moved the wood aside so that the struggling mulatto could regain his feet and stumble off in disgrace.

"Oh, I could hug Button!" said Cordelia, clapping her hands.

"I'm glad you won," said Josiah, "but I wouldn't go that far."

Captain Riley laughed. "Cordelia's mighty fond of our Button. I reckon we do give him lots of privileges for a nigger. He was a slave on a neighboring place and he saved the life of Miss Puss here when she fell in the river. I freed him. We don't keep slaves," Captain Riley added. "My wife's opposed to it." Then he called a steward. "Send Button up here. I want to see him."

"How do you keep the patrollers from running your Button in?" asked Josiah curiously.

Cordelia and her father looked at each other and burst out laughing. "Well, my wife would throw a fit if she knew it," said Captain Riley. "When Button is out late at night I give him a paper signed by me that says, 'Anybody who bothers this nigger will get the hell beat out of him by me. Signed, Captain Michael Riley.' I haven't had any takers yet!"

"Do you have slaves?" Cordelia inquired of Josiah.

"A number on my place outside St. Louis," he said. "But I'm more interested in hearing how you're enjoying your trip."

"Oh, I love it!" she said enthusiastically. "The water, the people . . . everything!"

Cordelia's father pulled one of her black curls affectionately and then he said something Josiah Callahan was to remember all his life. "Cordelia has always loved everything she loves a little too much. Sometimes it gets her in trouble."

Again Josiah trapped Cordelia with his eyes. "I think it is better to love too much, no matter what the cost, than to love too little. Don't you agree?"

Cordelia agreed wholeheartedly and she was trying to think of a way to tell him so when the steward returned with Button. He was grinning.

"Button, you did it, you did it!" said Cordelia. "I knew you could!"

"Ah was scairt for awhiles," he said. "That big yaller boy, he was plenty man. I couldn't a toted that last stick if it hadn't been *The Hawk* we was aimin' to lick."

"Good enough, Button!" Cordelia's father roared. "Your wages are double this trip. You made me three thousand dollars off Hugo!" He looked over the rail. "Here he comes, too, and very unhappy if you ask me. Paying a three-thousand-dollar wager will near kill a Knapp."

"That was quite a wager on a wood-loading contest!" said Josiah.

"There were things at stake that don't meet the eye," said Captain Riley.

"Three thousand dollars!" Cordelia exclaimed. That was a lot of money, more money than she could think of. For the first time she understood why her mother was always putting money away for a rainy day.

"Here's Hugo," said her father. "He's smiling, but I wager he'd like to kill that nigger of his."

Hugo Knapp was a big fair man who gave the impression of being more stocky than he was because of his massive head and shoulders. There was nothing cherubic about his face. His gray eyes were glittering with repressed anger.

"Well, you got me that time!" he exclaimed with a false heartiness. Then he saw Cordelia. "Cordelia!" His whole expression changed and his eyes lighted. He took both her hands in his. "You grow lovelier every day." Then he drew her to him and gave her a kiss that was a little too long to be cousinly. "I heard at the last landing that you had run off on *The Blue Teal.*

"Oh!" He turned to the slender dark man who had come aboard with him. "Cordelia, this is Jean Austin from New Orleans."

"I am glad to know you," said Cordelia. "We are all grateful for what you tried to do for Charlie."

"It was nothing," said Austin, bending over Cordelia's hand. Then he raised his head and she saw his eyes, dark brown and melting. "Your Button is a most remarkable man, mademoiselle."

Button had been squatting by the rail, but when he heard this he rose, looked haughtily at Hugo and Austin, turned and left.

"The nerve of that black beast!" said Hugo.

"He *is* arrogant," said Josiah, who had been standing aside, watching the family talk.

"Josiah," said Captain Riley, "I don't believe you know these gentlemen. This is Josiah Callahan of the Missouri Assembly."

"Was," corrected Josiah. He turned to Hugo. "I'm glad to meet you. I knew your brother. If he were alive I'm sure he'd be mustering with the Volunteers."

Hugo shrugged. "He probably would. Charlie was always off on some fool's errand. It would be like him to gallop off to Mexico."

Cordelia saw a muscle twitching in Josiah's face and the white scar showed whiter. "I hardly think it a fool's errand," he said. "I myself am going to Mexico. I have not forgotten that only five years ago my older brother Tom, traveling with the dragoons on the Texas-Santa Fe expedition was beaten, tortured and marched two thousand miles over desert and mountain ice by Mexicans. I cannot forget that he died in chains in the filthy dungeons of Perote Prison! I'm sorry," he said, "I did not intend to make an oration. We Callahans have many faults, but a short memory is not among them."

Hugo forced a thin-lipped smile. "I suppose an apology is in order." Then he shrugged. "Granted your brother was ill treated, but Texans had no business trying to break up the St. Louis trade. Any expedition we send now will be as ill-fated as theirs. Between Polk and those effete infants prancing about at West Point, they may very well ruin the country with their idea of taking in the whole universe!"

[35]

"Come, come," said Cordelia's father hastily. "Let's not argue. Let's have a drink to Button's victory. I shall take your three thousand, Hugo, but at least I shall buy you a drink! Won't you join us, gentlemen?"

"Thank you," said Josiah, "I should like to."

Jean Austin hesitated. "I have things to see about ashore. Monsieur Knapp is buying a plantation here in Franklin, you know. I am assisting him in the construction of his house."

"A Knapp on a plantation? Here?" asked Cordelia, amazed.

Hugo shrugged. "It's my father's idea. He wants me to run the Knapp line and buy an upriver plantation. When I marry," he looked boldly at Cordelia, "I shall live here, and my wife shall want for nothing, eh, Austin?"

Cordelia turned and saw that although the Frenchman's lips were smiling, his eyes were not. "You must first get the wife, monsieur." He bowed slightly. "It has been a pleasure meeting all of you. Now if you'll excuse me, I'll see to the unloading of the marble for the fireplaces." He walked away, his back straight and somehow defensive.

"Come, come," said the Captain. "We men are thirsty. Cordelia, you must go to your stateroom. We'll remain here at this landing for the night, so you both will join us for dinner this evening."

"A pleasure," said Hugo quickly, "especially since we will dine with our lovely Cordelia."

Josiah bowed slightly and Cordelia held her breath. "I can think of nothing I should like better, but I have so many affairs to wind up that I shall have dinner in my cabin. Please excuse me," he said.

"We should love to have you," said Cordelia, hoping that her invitation would sway him. For a moment he looked at her, then shook his head and turned to her father.

"In fact, if you'll forgive me, Captain, I think I shall also forego the drink and finish my work in my stateroom."

"Certainly, certainly," said Captain Riley quickly. "I understand. A busy lawyer has many things to do before going off to war."

"Then I'll say goodnight." Josiah bent over Cordelia's hand. Then he was moving away, walking with long strides, tall and gaunt in his dark gray suit.

"Conceited ass!" said Hugo as soon as Josiah was out of earshot. "If you ask me he's no Missourian. He's a snob from Louisiana and always will be."

"I don't think so," said the Captain. "True, his family was of the old patrician school but Josiah is cut of different cloth. He is a friend of Benton's, I'm told, and of young Frémont. Like them, he's up to his ears in Missouri state affairs."

"Other affairs, too," snorted Hugo. "That's why he wouldn't have dinner with us. Every time he appears it sets people to buzzing like bees."

"Buzzing? Buzzing about what?" Cordelia asked.

"He just fought a duel on Bloody Island," Hugo explained. "Didn't you see the scar on his face?"

"A duel!" exclaimed Cordelia. "I didn't think they were allowed. Was it over a woman?"

Hugo threw back his head and laughed. "Oh, Cordelia, how innocent you are!"

"Well," she asked, "*was* it?"

"Of course!" Hugo narrowed his eyes a bit, studying her. "Don't tell me you're smitten! Why is it, Michael," he turned to her father, "why is it that when a man shoots another man over a woman it makes him irresistible to all women?"

"Stop making fun of me, Hugo!" Cordelia said fiercely. "It annoys me. Who *was* she?"

"A Jefferson City woman," her father explained, eyeing her with concern. "I believe her name or honor was sullied by a man. So Callahan, being engaged to marry the girl, shot the fellow."

"Did . . . did he kill him?" Cordelia gasped.

"No," said Hugo, "but I understand he's going to be a long time recovering. Callahan was grazed on the cheek."

"Then . . . then he married the girl?" Cordelia could scarcely ask.

"Of course not!" said Hugo smugly. "The woman was guilty as sin and everybody knew it but Callahan. He knows it now."

"Oh, how terrible!" said Cordelia, overcome with compassion. "No wonder he is fierce and hurt!"

"Better not tell him that!" said Hugo. "Fighting Mexicans is a good job for a hot-headed adventurer with pistols."

"I think you're horrid and cruel!" said Cordelia. "I'm going to my stateroom."

"Cordelia girl!" her father called after her, but she kept on going.

Once inside her stateroom she threw herself on the bed and put her hands to her temples. Her head had begun to ache the minute

[37]

she learned Josiah Callahan had been engaged to a woman in Jefferson City.

She rolled over on her back and stared at the swinging lamp and at the design in the lace curtains. Josiah must have loved that woman very much to have fought a duel in her honor. Still, he hadn't married her. It was quite cheering to think of that woman being left behind. It would serve her right if she never saw Josiah again.

Then a terrible realization came over Cordelia. Josiah Callahan was going to war. *She* might never see him again either, and if that happened, she knew her world would never again be so bright and shining.

5

THAT NIGHT the dining room of *The Blue Teal* seemed enchanted to Cordelia. She heard the high ring of crystal touching crystal as the passengers drank toasts to their victory in the wood-loading contest, to a general good time, and, as somewhat of an afterthought, to success in the Mexican venture.

The gentlemen were elegant in fine broadcloth suits, the ladies were dazzling in gowns of taffeta, brocade and velvet that fell in soft folds from their tiny waists. Overhead, five crystal chandeliers trembled, shaking gently like clusters of dewdrops and catching up the soft glow of silver from the tables below.

Cordelia scuffed the toes of her new shoes in the thick red carpet, but she sat very straight in her chair at the head table between her father and Hugo. She was wearing the green velvet dress. From time to time she touched the lace at her wrists to make sure she was really in the dining room of *The Blue Teal* wearing her lovely dress.

Hugo inclined his head toward her and made every effort to be charming. Cordelia, glancing around the room, saw that several women were frankly envious of Hugo's attentions to her. One of them was Red Maude.

Cordelia was staring at Red Maude sitting alone at a table, idly turning the pages of the St. Louis *Republican,* when Maude looked up and returned Cordelia's stare with a glance smoldering with resentment. Cordelia could not help but admire the woman's beautiful copper-red hair cascading down her back and the soft white breasts swelling above the low-cut bodice. She was so beautiful that Cordelia ventured a half-smile of recognition. But Red Maude looked away.

Hugo drew Cordelia's attention from Red Maude to himself. "So you ran away, Cordie," he said teasingly. "We'll have to put our pretty swallow in a cage so she won't fly away from us, eh, Michael?" He winked at Cordelia's father.

"Oh, she's got plenty of time to settle down—perhaps after she's married." Her father laughed. "I mean I *hope* she will."

"That's what I mean," said Hugo, devouring Cordelia with his eyes so she could not possibly misunderstand his meaning.

"Oh, Hugo," Cordelia said uncomfortably, "don't start that."

Cordelia's father cleared his throat. "That's a long way off, anyhow. Now," he deliberately changed the subject, "what's all this about your starting a plantation here?"

"Father's got a notion I ought to stay off the river, since I'm all that's left of the Knapps," explained Hugo. "First he didn't want me on the Mississippi and now he wants me off the Missouri. Maybe he's got a good idea at that. You never can tell, land along the Missouri might be worth money someday."

This touched off a discussion of land and townsite values between her father and Hugo. Cordelia remained silent, listening.

"Are you going to live up there alone?" asked Cordelia's father. "Running a plantation is big business."

"I'll have lots of niggers, of course. Jean Austin will be general overseer of them and the plantation. I hope to have a wife, too. Someday I wish to talk to you about that," he said, doggedly pursuing his subject.

For a moment there was silence. Then Cordelia saw her father look sharply at Hugo from under his black eyebrows. His eyes were hard and searching. "The first quality I shall look for in my daughter's suitors is kindness. I can't say you exhibited any, Hugo, when you kicked your mulatto when he was down this afternoon."

"Oh, that one! He was just a no-count nigger," said Hugo contemptuously. "I lost my temper with the stupid beast."

"That's what I mean," said her father dryly, "your temper." Then, without waiting for Hugo to reply, he beckoned to a steward. "If everyone has finished, clear the floor and call in the orchestra."

The dining room came to life with the sound of the first waltz and Cordelia watched, wide-eyed, at the women's skirts blossoming out like full-blown flowers as they whirled. From the corner of her eye she saw Red Maude rising from her table. Now she swept past them without so much as a glance of recognition. She wore blue satin tonight, and frothy lace peeped from beneath her skirts.

"I don't dance too well," said Hugo, "but would you like to try a waltz with me, Cordelia?"

"Oh, yes, I would!" she said. Then she looked down at her hands. "Only I don't know how. Mother has never allowed me to learn."

"Then I'll teach you sometime," Hugo promised. "Perhaps your father will let you walk outside on the deck and look at the lights of the village. If the moon is bright enough I will point out the house I am building."

"I'd love to," said Cordelia, grateful to Hugo for offering to teach her to dance.

"You don't mind, do you, Michael?" Hugo turned to her father. "After all, Cordelia and I *are* cousins."

Her father gave Hugo a long look. "She may go. But see that you remember you *are* her cousin, and take her to her stateroom early. She has been up much too late since she came aboard."

"Goodnight, Father." Cordelia arose from the table and bent to kiss her father. "I'll see you in the morning."

The night was sharp with the promise of winter and fog lay like a low-flying banner on the marshes. But the moon was bright overhead and the lights of Franklin sparkled like a handful of stars flung against the bluff.

Cordelia took a deep breath. "Oh, I love it!" she said. "I love the night, the river, all of it. I'm glad we came outside." Then she turned to Hugo. "Hugo, do you know this is the very first time I've ever been alone with a man at night?"

"I'm flattered," said Hugo. "I've wanted to talk to you for a long time. I was afraid your father wouldn't let you come. He doesn't like me," he said, suddenly bitter. "Not many people do."

This sudden admission from her arrogant cousin startled Cordelia. "Why, Hugo, what makes you feel that way?"

"Because it's true," he said. And now in the darkness his voice sounded bleak and lonely. "Take Charlie. Everybody liked him and even now after he's dead, they still go on talking about him."

"Oh, Hugo, you're imagining things."

"No." Hugo's shoulders slumped. "Do you know why my father wants me to come up here to live? Because every time he looks at me he wonders why it wasn't I who died instead of Charlie. My own father can't stand the sight of me! You'd think he'd want *me* now! But he doesn't!"

"You mustn't say that!" Cordelia touched his arm sympathetically. "You *know* he doesn't feel that way!" The arrogant Hugo had suddenly become pathetic to her. "I don't feel that way and I'm sure other people don't."

He turned suddenly and in the moonlight she could see his face white and drawn. Why, he was actually suffering, she thought. Then he gripped her arm and stared at her.

"Cordelia, do you mean that? You're the first human being who ever understood me. I never dared tell anyone else how I felt. But you understand." He shook her a little. "Marry me, Cordelia, and we'll show them. You and I can live up the river here and shut the world out. There will never be anyone else. I swear it. Oh, God, you don't know how lonely I've been all my life. With you I can be somebody."

"Hugo!" She drew back as his fingers dug into her arms. "You're hurting me. You know I didn't mean *that*. I don't want to get married—yet. I have to be honest, even if it hurts you. I just don't love you, but if I can help in any way . . ."

"Help?" Now his intensity frightened her. "You've got to *marry* me," he said fiercely. "I need you. You're strong and full of fire, and that's what I need. I'd have fire, too, and more strength. I've wanted you since that day when we were children. Do you remember? I teased you and you hit me with a stick. I took the stick away from you and hit you with it, but you didn't cry. You stood there, not whimpering, but flailing me with your fists. It was give-and-take. I *must* have you—someone between me and . . ."

"But I *don't* love you!" Cordelia was beginning to be terrified.

"Don't you know what it's like to want something, someone, until it eats at you like a disease?" he demanded, his arms tightening around her like a vise.

"Let . . . me . . . go!"

"Not until you promise," he said, shaking her. "Promise!"

"No! You're mad. Absolutely mad!" She struggled free at last. Desperately, she raked his cheek hard with her nails.

This seemed to bring Hugo to his senses. "I'm sorry I lost my head," he said, breathing hard. His eyes still glinted and his mouth was a straight line. "But I swear I'll have you. You know that, don't you?"

"No, I don't," she said. "And I certainly *can* see now why people liked Charlie and didn't like you!" He stepped back as if she had struck him across the face with a whip and Cordelia was quick to take advantage of her release. "I'm going to my stateroom and you may escort me or not as you like; it makes no difference to me." Cordelia wheeled and set off at a fast pace, Hugo following grimly.

"At least say you'll forgive me," Hugo pleaded as they approached her door.

"I don't want to talk about it," Cordelia said furiously. As she reached her door there arose the huge figure of Button, who stood towering beside her. "Goodnight, Hugo," she said quickly. "I'm *not* angry with you; I'm only very, very sorry for you." She slipped into her stateroom without waiting for his reply.

When she was sure Hugo was gone, Cordelia stuck her head out the door and whispered, "Button, Button, don't let anyone disturb me tonight, not anybody."

"They won't, Miss Cordie, they sure won't." She saw only the whites of Button's eyes in the shadows.

"Do you think I'm a scaredy-cat, Button?" she asked.

"Well, I tells you, Miss Cordie. When there's a big ole hound bayin' at you, it's a lot better to be a scaredy-cat in a tree than a smarty-cat on the ground."

Cordelia did not sleep well. Long after the orchestra had ceased playing she was still awake thinking about the evening. Toward morning she began to dream. She dreamed that she was running down a long stairway. There were footsteps behind her. No matter how fast she ran, the footsteps came faster. She looked back and saw that it was Hugo. She fell and rolled over and over. At last she lay terror-stricken as the relentless Hugo bent over her. He was picking her up in his arms! There was no escape from him!

His arms were strong, so strong. How could she ever escape? Then suddenly she did not want to escape, she *wanted* to be in his arms. He bent his face to hers and she saw that his eyes were the deepest blue. It was not Hugo at all—but Josiah Callahan!

"Oh, Josiah!" she said. "I'm so glad it's you. . . ."

"Come look at the moon," Josiah said, carrying her to the window. "I shot a man so you could have the moon," he said softly. She looked at the moon as it shone so brightly and she was filled with happiness. Then suddenly she saw it wasn't the moon but an embroidery hoop, and that the man who was holding her was Hugo after all. She screamed. She couldn't stop screaming.

She was awakened by Button's pounding on the door. "Miss Cordie! Miss Cordie! What's the matter?"

She stumbled to the door and opened it to his frantic pounding. "Button," she said, crying, "Button, I had a terrible dream, I never had anything like it before. I can't wake up." Her teeth chattered.

"Oh, Lawd," said Button, relieved. "You go on back to bed afore you catch lung fever."

Lung fever. Suddenly, for the first time since she had run away, Cordelia wanted her mother. Maybe it was only homesickness, for she knew her mother would have scoffed at her dream. But her father would understand. She must tell him about the dream and how Hugo had frightened her.

Dressing quickly, she opened the door and called Button softly. "Button, I've got to talk to my father. I want you to take me to him."

"Lawdy, no!" Button exclaimed. "You wait till mornin'. This no time of night for a lady to go to her daddy's cabin."

"Don't be silly, Button. I'll be safe with you."

"You safe all right," he shook his head, "but I ain't gonna take you nowhere."

"Oh, yes, you are! I'm going to my father and you can't keep me from it."

Button groaned. "Last time you say somethin' like that, I had to fish for you in the river. Please! Miss Cordie, I *cain't* do it."

"Very well, then, I'll go by myself," she said. "Stand aside."

Button remained in the doorway without moving. "I *cain't* let you go!"

"Button! You hear me? Stand aside!" she ordered. With flashing eyes she stared him down. Reluctantly, he inched aside. "Now, follow me," she said, setting off in the direction of her father's stateroom, with Button pleading with her at every step.

When they reached her father's door, Button made one last effort. "Please, Miss Cordie, for *Gawd's* sake!"

"Don't be such a goose, Button!" Cordelia raised her hand to rap when she heard her father's voice speaking. Then she heard a laugh. It was a laugh no one could ever forget; it was *exactly* as if velvet were drawn across your bare arm. Red Maude was in her father's cabin.

6

STANDING STRICKEN outside her father's stateroom door, Cordelia heard Red Maude's sensuous laughter, joined by her father's hearty chuckle. The sound struck her across the face.

"Miss Cordie! Miss Cordie! Come away!" Dimly she heard Button's anguished voice. "For Gawd's sake don't look like that!"

She felt as if she were made of glass. Her mouth was glass, too. "You were right, Button." She heard her own voice floating by her, high and disembodied. "It was too late . . . too late . . . too late!" And then she wasn't glass at all, only a thousand hurts. "How could he?" she moaned. "Oh, how could he?" Suddenly she was terribly sick. She swayed and clapped her hand to her mouth.

Scooping her up, Button ran swiftly with her to her stateroom where she burst into tearing sobs and began to retch miserably.

Button summoned two Negro maids who came running, wide-eyed. They were to take care of Miss Cordie, Button told them, and if they so much as breathed a word of what they saw or heard, he would cut out their hearts with his canning knife.

"I want to go home, I want to go home," Cordelia sobbed over and over while the maids bathed her face with cold water and patted her wrists with cologne.

She was so ill that Button became frightened and wanted to call her father, but Cordelia became more hysterical than ever.

"No! No! I hate him! I hate him!" she cried. And Button dared not call Captain Riley.

When *The Blue Teal* started upstream again, shortly after sunrise, Cordelia stopped crying. Turning her face to the wall, she ordered the maids to leave.

If her father loved her—or her mother—he could not have done this thing to them. How could a man and woman marry, have children, live together, and still want someone else? For the first time she was forced to think of her parents as people, loving—hating maybe. How different it was to think of them not as father and mother, but as man and wife. She could never forgive her father . . . never.

"I hate him. I hate him," she said over and over to herself. But in her heart she knew it was not true.

Cordelia did not appear for breakfast, which was not unusual among women passengers, but when she was still absent at lunchtime her father came to see if she were ill.

"I have a headache," she said, turning her face away from him.

"Are you sure that's all, Cordie?" He bent over her anxiously. "There's a doctor aboard, you know."

"I don't want a doctor," she said shortly, barely looking at him. How handsome her father was with his ruddy face and crisp curling black hair, his great shoulders filling out the blue jacket. She had always thought of him as her father. Now she saw how he must look to women like . . . Red Maude.

"I'll have the steward bring you some chicken broth. Wouldn't you like that?" he asked.

"I don't want any broth!" She was near tears again. Couldn't he see she both hated and loved him, and that she couldn't stand it?

"What's the matter, honey?" he asked, taking her face in his hands and turning it toward him. "Cordie! You've been crying!"

For the first time in her life she stiffened and drew away from him. "I want to go home!" she said, bursting into tears.

"Home?" her father exclaimed. "Are you homesick?"

"Yes . . ." She buried her face in the pillows.

"Well, I'll be blasted!" He rubbed his chin and narrowed his eyes. "I'll wager some of those catty women have hurt your feelings. By God, tell me who it is—and man, woman or child, I'll put them off this boat at the next landing!"

"No! No! Please! Go . . . away . . . and . . . leave . . . me . . . alone."

"Now, Cordelia girl, you don't want me to leave you. Tell your dad what it is."

"No. No. No! If you don't go away and leave me alone . . . I'll . . . I'll die."

The more her father tried to comfort her, the more hysterical she became. Finally he said, "I'm going to get to the bottom of this. If you're not better by dinnertime, I'm going to have the doctor take a look at you."

Outside, she heard him questioning Button sharply. Then Button's reply. "No, sir, I swear to de Lawd, Cap'm, I got no idea what's wrong with Miss Cordie. Young girls, they gets that way sometimes."

"How about Hugo?"

"It wasn't him, Cap'm. I was right here when he bringed her back. It wasn't *him*. Efen I was you I'd just let her be a little while— leastwise for de day."

About the middle of the afternoon a maid brought Cordelia a note from Pierre. It read:

> Your father tells me you are not feeling well, but if at all possible I should like to see you on the promenade deck. It is a matter of utmost importance.
>
> Pierre

Looking in the mirror at her swollen face and reddened eyes, Cordelia felt she could not see anyone, especially Pierre, who had such a keen way of looking at her. She answered his note by scribbling,

> Couldn't this wait until tomorrow? I do not feel at all well.
>
> Cordelia

Immediately an answer came back.

> This matter cannot wait. I implore you, if at all possible, meet me within the hour.
>
> Pierre

Cordelia could not imagine what could be so urgent, but she knew Pierre was not the sort of person to pretend things were more important than they were, so she agreed to meet him.

After she dressed, she dusted rice powder on her nose, drew her hair back into a net and put on a bonnet with a veil, hoping the ravages of her tears would not be too apparent.

She found Pierre pacing impatiently up and down as if he had been waiting for hours. "I was hoping you would come." He took both her hands. His brown eyes flickered over her face, but if he noticed her pallor and tear-reddened eyes he gave no sign.

"Come, take my arm and let us walk," he said. "That will give the ladies something with which to supplement their gossip. As you can see, *The Blue Teal* is making for that little settlers' landing. Some of the men are going duck-hunting for a couple of hours. Your father told me he hoped to have roast duck for your supper, since you are so fond of it."

"Yes . . . I am." Cordelia walked with downcast eyes, puzzled at Pierre's talk of duck-hunting while something urgent waited.

"Not many fathers would be that thoughtful," he continued.

Cordelia remained silent.

"The truth of the matter is," said Pierre, "your father uses duck-hunting only as an excuse. He really drops anchor here so that No Legs Harry can fish for the monster fish."

"Pierre," she interrupted, "what *is* it you had to tell me? Who cares about a fish?"

"The fish is very important," he went on. "All who have traveled up and down this river talk of the monster catfish in the channel. It is said to weigh 300 pounds." The boat had slowed to one stroke and was sliding into the landing. "Think what it would mean if No Legs caught this fish! Every man on the river would look up to him. He would have done something that men with legs have failed to do!"

"Pierre!" she said angrily. "Did you make me get out of bed to hear about a fish?"

"Just think," Pierre said earnestly, "your father knows the passengers would not stand for a delay while the cook fished, but they will stop anytime to hunt duck—so while they hunt, No Legs fishes for the great fish. There is not a captain on the Missouri who is as kind as your father, Cordelia."

"Pierre," she could not look at him, "I'm going back to my stateroom."

"Oh, no!" He took her firmly by the arm. "You must see No Legs fish." Before Cordelia could protest he was half-dragging her down the stairway to the lower deck.

"Of course," Pierre took no notice of her reluctance or silence, "ladies usually go only to the port galley where the chef can display his skill, but the captain's daughter really ought to see the whole boat, even the starboard galley."

"Pierre, stop dragging me! If this is your idea of a joke, I don't think it's very funny!"

"Here we are," said Pierre, ignoring her protests. "It is not pretty but I do not think you will be sorry you came."

The starboard galley would have horrified those who dined upstairs at the snowy-clothed tables, and Cordelia was forced to put her handkerchief to her nose as she approached the chicken coops. Chickens, turkeys, pheasants and squabs were carried alive in small odoriferous coops. Great caldrons of boiling water sent up steam and a black rat came out of a sugar barrel and stared brazenly at them. Bloody feathers and peelings lay in a heap waiting to be thrown into the river.

No Legs' high stool sat between the coops and the caldron of boiling water. He boasted that a chicken would not stop jerking before he had it in the pot. But today his stool was empty.

No Legs was sitting on the deck, holding a fishing line that looked more like a rope than line. He was a terrible-looking creature with a broad, coarse face and a nose that seemed to spread over half of it. His head was huge and hairless. But there was more than enough long black hair on his chest and overdeveloped arms. He looked up at them from under beetling eyebrows and motioned for them to be quiet. Cordelia tried to keep the revulsion from her face.

"Trying for the big cat?" said Pierre softly.

No Legs nodded and looked at Cordelia.

"Good afternoon, Harry," she forced herself to say. "I hope you catch him." She looked angrily at Pierre and turned to walk away.

But Pierre took Cordelia's arm and held it fast. "I understand Captain Riley stops here just so you can fish," he said.

"Ah, yes." No Legs showed snagged yellow teeth in a grin. "The Captain is a fine man. For five years now he has let me fish for the monster. He say to me, 'Harry, if you catch that fish you will be the tallest man on the Missouri River!' So," No Legs shrugged, "who knows? But today I catch him." He ran a hairy hand over his bald head and grinned at Cordelia. "The fish is as ugly as I am. He has seven hooks in his mouth already, one as big as a hay hook."

Involuntarily Cordelia drew back. But Pierre held her fast. "What do you expect to do with the fish when you do catch it?" he asked.

"Bring him in, of course!" No Legs glared at Pierre. "Frenchman, do you think because I have no legs, I have no strength, that I am

[48]

not a man? See?" He took up a barrel stave and snapped it in two like a match-stick.

Cordelia shuddered.

"You told us to be quiet," said Pierre. But No Legs continued, "The Captain knows I am a man, too. He says 'No Legs, you have the strength of two roustabouts!'" He turned to Cordelia. "I am going to give this fish to your father!"

"Oh . . ." said Cordelia faintly.

"Come," said Pierre, "we must go. We might frighten the fish," and he led the shivering girl into the cool, clean air.

"Pierre! How could you!" she said as soon as they were away from No Legs. "I think . . ."

"Just think," Pierre ignored her anger, "Harry was born without legs. He crawled through the world and no one . . . no one was ever kind to him before your father . . ."

"I didn't want to see him!" said Cordelia. "He looked as if God just started to make him and forgot to finish him! How could you make me look at . . ."

"Your father does not see him like that. He sees him as a man, as a human being." They were standing at the foot of the great stairway and Pierre took her hands. "Look at me, Cordelia. Surely now you will admit your father is one of the kindest men in the world."

Reluctantly she raised her eyes to his. "Oh, Pierre, what are you trying to say . . . you . . ."

"I saw you last night," he said. "You must promise me never to walk the deck at night . . . even with Button."

"Oh, I'm so ashamed, so . . ." She hung her head.

"You are angry and hurt," Pierre went on. "I do not ask that you understand your father's actions . . . someday you may, but not now. But I hope you will find it in your heart to forgive him. If you think him unkind, remember No Legs Harry and the rest of the crew. To a man, we respect and love him."

"Oh, Pierre," she felt the tears beginning to come, "you aren't a woman. You don't know . . . I don't think I can forgive him . . . ever."

"Someday you will," he said. "But I want you to remember I am your friend. If ever you need me, I want you to promise that you'll let me know."

She bowed her head and nodded, too overcome to speak.

"And now," he said, "would you like to go back to your stateroom?"

Cordelia looked up at the passenger deck and saw the women looking down at her. She did not want to see them or hear their whispering. Besides, she was afraid she might meet Red Maude. "Could we walk outside on the little dock?" she asked. "I see two or three ladies and their escorts are strolling about. Surely no one will mind that."

"Your pretty shoes will be ruined," said Pierre. "It's only an abandoned settlers' dock. . . ."

"Let's walk out there anyway," she whispered. "I . . . I don't want to walk past all those women . . . please, they'll see I've been crying."

As Pierre had said, the landing was an old one and some of the planks had fallen into the river. A dense woods marched to the river's edge and giant elms stood out here and there like sentinels. Suddenly the silence was split by the sound of a gun. The hunters had found their game.

Pierre and Cordelia walked back and forth slowly without speaking. Cordelia's mind was in a whirl and Pierre, as if sensing this, let her think in peace. They were strolling along the edge of the woods when the assistant engineer bounded down the stage-plank and dashed up to them.

"Come quick, Pierre! That fool Luke's drunk in the engine room. We got four yaller niggers in the wheel-house making repairs, and Luke swears he's gonna turn the steam on them."

"*Mon Dieu!*" exclaimed Pierre. "They will be roasted alive! I'm sorry, Cordelia, we must go back."

"Please," she begged, "let me stay here, Pierre."

"Well," Pierre looked around hastily, "I see the traveling preacher Bird and his wife. You may stay here if you'll remain with them. Come along."

What rotten luck! Pierre thought as he ran for the boilers. The first time I have Cordelia to myself, just when she needs a shoulder to lean on, Luke decides to boil the crew!

As soon as he had restored order in the engine room Pierre returned to the dock. The minister and his wife, he saw, were still there, but Cordelia was not with them.

"I was gone longer than I expected," he said, hastening up to Reverend and Mrs. Bird. "Did Miss Riley tire and go back to her stateroom?"

"No," said Reverend Bird. "We were talking with her when suddenly she thought she saw a wild turkey in the undergrowth. Before we knew what she was about, she had gone over there." He pointed to the woods.

"Not in the woods!" exclaimed Pierre. "Not by herself?"

"Well," the minister glanced at his wife, "she was so pale and she looked rather ill. We thought . . . well, it is a long way back to the ladies' cabin and we thought perhaps . . ."

A terrible fright gripped Pierre. "You mean she's been gone all this time? Why, man, I wouldn't go in there myself without a gun!"

At the sound of Pierre's excited voice a couple strolling by stopped. "What seems to be the trouble?" asked the man.

Pierre turned and recognized Josiah Callahan, the man from the Assembly. The woman on his arm wore a blue-striped dress and a blue bonnet with plumes. She was Red Maude.

Pierre saw it all. Cordelia, confused, had come to the wharf to think things out. Then the poor child must have looked up and seen the woman who had caused all the trouble coming down the dock. No wonder she had run into the woods! Cordelia, brought up by such a cold, uncompromising mother, was totally unprepared for this new side of life. Now she had run away rather than encounter Red Maude face to face.

"Quite some time ago," Pierre explained to Josiah, "Cordelia . . . Miss Riley saw a wild turkey and stepped into the woods to have a look at it. She has not come back!"

"In the woods!" Josiah's eyes met Pierre's. "How long ago?"

The minister's wife began twisting her wedding ring. "A half-hour ago . . . perhaps we *should* have called someone. There might be snakes or Indians. . . ."

"Now, Martha," scolded the Reverend, "you know there aren't any Indians, and if there were, they are friendly now. They don't kill people any more."

"Not *kill*, perhaps . . ." Josiah said, exchanging a long look with Pierre.

"Well," Red Maude interrupted testily, "thank you for escorting me down for a breath of fresh air. I'll escort myself back while you two gallants look for Miss Innocence!" With that she flounced back up the stage-plank of *The Blue Teal*.

"But what would make Miss Riley do such a foolish thing?" Josiah asked.

"She had had a bad shock. I can't explain now," Pierre said. "There is no time to lose. We must find her. I am sure we will. I am used to hunting in these woods."

"And I in the bayous," Josiah said quickly. "We'll find her."

"Certainly," said Pierre. "I'll go to the right and you to the left. If we fail, we'll meet in fifteen minutes and blow the whistle of *The Blue Teal* three times. As you search, you'd better call her name. It's Cordelia."

"Yes, yes, I know," Josiah said, drawing his pistol and striking out into the woods.

Pierre set off in another direction. There were Indians in these woods. Pierre had once seen a white girl after two drunken Indians had finished with her. "Mother of God," he prayed, "be merciful."

September shadows lengthened and the air was sharp with chill. The whistle of *The Blue Teal* had long since been blown, but there was no sign of Cordelia. The woods were no longer silent, but noisy with the creeping, crawling things that belonged to marshes and woods. And then it was night. Black and moonless.

Michael Riley was like a man possessed as he ordered every man on the crew to join in the search. His face was ashen, and deep furrows appeared on each side of his mouth. "Something was wrong," he kept saying brokenly. "Something happened to make her run away. She loved *The Blue Teal* and she wasn't the kind of girl to do a foolish thing like that. I can't understand it. I can't understand it!"

All the male passengers lighted pineknots and made sorties into the woods. *The Hawk,* coming up the river, saw the lights of *The Blue Teal* at the out-of-the-way landing and put in beside her. Hugo and Jean Austin organized a party from *The Hawk* to join in the search.

Flares blazed in the darkened woods and there was the sound of beating on bushes, as the men trampled through the underbrush.

Stumbling ahead was Michael Riley, calling in a voice hoarse with despair. "Cordelia . . . Cordelia girl! In God's name, Cordelia girl, where are you?"

There was such anguish in the Captain's voice and such terror in his eyes that Button, who walked beside him, could not bear to watch it. He took a flare and went off searching on his own.

But no one found a footprint, or a broken twig. The only sound came from nocturnal animals scurrying from the lights, and querulous frogs challenging the intruders. It was as if Cordelia had vanished from the earth.

In the late afternoon sun, only a few hours earlier, Reverend and Mrs. Bird were earnestly telling Cordelia how much the settlers along the river needed the gospel, when suddenly she glanced up to see Josiah Callahan coming down the stage-plank. On his arm was Red Maude!

She stared in panic as they approached the dock. Red Maude was devastating in a blue dress and bonnet, and while Cordelia watched she turned her lovely face up to Josiah and laughed. The sound of that intoxicating laugh made Cordelia hate her with such an overwhelming passion that she felt a wave of nausea again. She *would* not, she *could* not watch Red Maude captivate Josiah Callahan, too!

"Oh, look!" Cordelia pointed to the underbrush. "There's a wild turkey! Perhaps it has a nest close by. I think I'll see!" Without waiting for the minister's reply, she turned and fled into the woods.

Within the woods another world began. The trees grew dense on the marshy ground, so that it was like stepping into a softly-carpeted room. A thorny black haw caught at her dress, and everywhere there was the odor of tamarack bark and decaying leaves. It was as still as the stone church at home and almost like one, with the tree branches forming bleak arches to filter the blue-hazed light. Cordelia looked back at the dock and saw Red Maude smiling up at Josiah, one hand tucked in his arm and swishing her taffeta skirts with the other. She would walk a little way into the woods and stay until that hateful woman was gone.

Overhead, a fat robin, too old and dusty to fly south, began to scold her with a clack-clack. Underfoot, the ground was soft and spongy, and moss laid fuzzy green fingers over tree limbs and half-rotten stumps. Toadstools made soft white clusters at the foot of an old lightning-split elm. It was such a springy place to walk. She thought it would be even more pleasant if she could feel it with bare feet. But it was too cold and damp for that.

There were little puddles of stagnant water everywhere. Yellowed watergrass, rotting at the roots, sent up hopeful shoots. Even the undergrowth smelled musty, as if it had never quite dried out.

She had walked only a short distance when she felt a sudden movement in the grass at her feet and a shiny black cottonmouth slithered over her shoe. Cordelia let out a small involuntary scream and decided to turn back in the direction of *The Blue Teal*.

It seemed to be taking her a long time to reach the boat. Perhaps she had walked farther than she thought. The haze of light was rapidly turning to dusk in the tree-tops, and the frogs were tuning up. She should be there by now. She looked up and stopped. She must have been walking in the wrong direction. The sun set in the west; she wanted to walk east.

She began to retrace her steps. By now she was sinking to her ankles in mud, and her skirts were bedraggled, but she hurried faster because the sun was almost gone. The woods at dusk no longer looked attractive. Suddenly she heard three short blasts from the whistle of *The Blue Teal*. Her heart gave a leap. Oh, how thankful she was for the sense of direction the sound gave her. There were three more short blasts from the boat, closer this time—much closer, thank heaven!

She came again upon a little green-scummed pool she had skirted earlier. Across it lay an old cottonwood log, covered with moss, that looked like a short-cut. She had taken only a few short steps across it when it gave a sighing, sucking sound and began to move. Cordelia tried frantically to regain her balance as the log rolled over like a lazy alligator. She threw out her arms, swayed, slipped, lurched. Then her feet went out from under her.

Instinctively she threw out her hands to grasp whatever she could hold onto. The pool might be deep. But it was scarcely water! It was mud and quicksand that she felt on the lower half of her submerged body. Her arms and breasts rested across the slippery log. She lay there a moment, then attempted to pull herself up over the log. It was then she realized that her foot was caught in a branch underneath.

She dared not let go with her hands to free her foot for fear of losing her only anchor. She must free it! Cautiously she released one hand, and, holding on with the other, tried desperately to work her foot loose. Her efforts were futile; she succeeded only in slipping further underneath the log.

She was trapped by the slimy log and by her own stupidity. She didn't dare try rolling it from her; she might go down altogether. From the sound of the mud and the sucking on her feet and legs she knew what kind of pool it was. They called them sink-holes, places where the river had once been, or wanted to come. They were filled with quicksand—and they were bottomless.

Surely they'll miss me soon, she thought, her teeth chattering with cold. Who would have thought her hands would be blue and stiff so soon? She must work them, one at a time. Open her fingers, close her fingers. Oh, if only her father would come bursting through the clearing! She had thought she never wanted to see him again, but now she wanted him to come—and come quickly. What if she never saw him again?

She must keep such thoughts away. But when the sun was gone, she could no longer push the black thoughts from her. What if they *never* found her? She must fight! Wiggle her toes . . . but she couldn't wiggle her toes. There was no feeling in her legs at all. Minute by minute her hands numbed, so that she slipped still lower. Just when she could hold on no longer she heard faintly her father's voice calling, calling.

But her own voice was so weak in answering she knew no one could hear her. They must! She must make them hear her. In desperation she grasped what felt like a small tree limb. If only it would hold! She could pull herself back up on the log with the other hand. But the tree limb came loose—and to her horror she could feel that it was not a tree limb at all, but a bone. A bone from something or *someone* who had wandered into this abysmal sink-hole and had never been found.

She tried to scream as she saw the red glow of a torch, but succeeded only in filling her mouth with mud. For the first time she realized that she could die. Only this morning she had thought she wanted to die, but now, faced with the reality of death, she knew how much she wanted to live. She tried to pray, but she was too frightened.

How did she know God would hear her? All her prayers had been said kneeling in a white nightgown at her bedside or in church. That was the only kind of God she knew about. One who stayed in churches and who damned you if you did something wrong when you were away from church. Maybe there wasn't any God near a sink-hole covered with green scum.

But in spite of her terror she felt an invisible presence. So she prayed. She wanted so very much to live—she had never really lived at all. She made a vow: if God would rescue her from this green Hell, she would try never to hate anyone again—not even Red Maude.

7

WALKING ALONE through the dense undergrowth, pausing now and then to swing his pine torch aloft, Josiah Callahan forced himself to overlook nothing, although he knew the desperate urgency of haste. Unless Cordelia were found soon, she would not be found alive.

Moldy leaves squashing under his boots and a ghostly split elm standing grotesque against the dark woods reminded him of his native Louisiana and recalled all too vividly his unhappy childhood. His mother had died when he was five and he had spent many early years wandering through the bayous with a beloved older brother. But one day Tom, only seventeen, had run away with other adventuresome young men, all of whom had left G T T (Gone to Texas) notes. After this his father, already embittered over the death of his wife, took almost no notice of Josiah, but shut himself up in his law library with his memories and an inexhaustible supply of brandy.

When he was older, Josiah rode alone through forests hung with moss and ground sodden under his horse's feet. His sole companions were slaves, polite and withdrawn from his white man's world. After his father's death he had packed up his law books and had come to Missouri. When he received word that Tom had died in Perote Prison in Mexico, he was relieved his father had been spared that shock.

Missouri was a state for action. Only twenty, he had plunged into politics and helped to stir the political brew bubbling in the state capital. He had wanted action and he had had it, he thought, trying to shake off the depression of the damp woods about him.

An owl hooted. Where could Cordelia have gone? Not far alone. What if she were not alone? What if . . . there was that damned owl again. What a place! As he stepped into the marshy ground it was as if his last eight years had vanished and he was again a forlorn child wandering through the Louisiana swamps. He was so overcome with nostalgia and a strange sense of foreboding that he half-expected to hear Cain, his superstitious old slave calling, "Massa Callahan, come out of there! Things in there. Things in there gwine to get you."

Something slithered under Josiah's foot. He started. A cottonmouth! "Cordelia!" he shouted, quickening his steps. "Cordelia!"

I *have* to find her, he thought, swinging his torch savagely in a wide arc, turning to peer closely at the lightest movement between the trees. If it had not been for the scandal hanging over him from that stupid affair with Denise, he could have approached Cordelia immediately. As it was, he knew the most innocent conversation with the young girl would set tongues a-wag.

In a way, he supposed it served him right. He had planned to marry Denise, the daughter of a well-known politician, without feeling any grand passion for her. He was lonely and the political powers had made it known he should be married in order to give the impression of being well established. Denise had been attractive and willing—in more than one direction, he now knew. Denise had practically thrown herself into the arms of her wounded lover.

"Cordelia!" he called hoarsely, cursing his own hot temper for having rushed into that duel.

It had all cost him the one woman he wanted. For not until he had seen fiery Cordelia Riley defying the drunken man on the Hermann dock had he found a woman of his own mettle. The moment he had looked into her flashing gray-green eyes, he knew he had met his own kind.

The ground grew still softer under his boots. There was that scummy pool he had skirted before. It looked a little like the mouth of the River Styx. The slaves back home had once found a man's bones in a place like that. "Cordelia!" he called again, swinging his light across the pool, letting it play on a cottonwood log lying awry. There was a querulous inquiry from frogs and a muffled splashing from some animal in the pool. He called again, but heard nothing but the splash of the animal. Wearily he walked on. There was the splash again. Some sixth sense made him turn, swing his light over the pool and the cottonwood log again. It was then he saw Cordelia, almost completely submerged, apparently too weak to speak, clinging to the log with one hand and splashing desperately with the other.

"Cordelia!" he shouted. "Thank God, I've found you!"

Cordelia's mouth moved but no sound came. Her great eyes stared at him in anguished relief.

His knees trembled violently and his hands shook. Only then did Josiah Callahan realize how deeply he had fallen in love with this girl whom he scarcely knew.

"Hold on," he shouted. "I'm coming. Only a minute longer."

He stuck his torch in the ground and ran toward the log. He saw quickly that he dared not step on it for fear of pushing Cordelia under entirely. "A moment . . . I'll have you out in no time." He kept up a stream of conversation to keep her from slipping into unconsciousness, as he pulled off his coat and shirt and threw them down by the torch. He must have some dry clothes for her when he got her out. He tossed his pistol on top of his coat and waded out into the pool.

Quicksand! It was impossible to swim or wade. Her eyes met his, terror-stricken, as he retreated. "Hold on," he yelled. "I'll have to paddle out on another log." He seized a smaller cottonwood log, pulled it to shore and, cursing the delay, cut a pole from a fallen elm. Quickly he straddled the log, stuck the knife in his belt and shoved off with all his strength.

Cordelia's eyes were closing. "Open your eyes," he commanded sharply. "Do you want to drown us both?"

The bog seemed bottomless but his pole touched a submerged tree and he managed to slide in beside Cordelia. It seemed as if it had taken hours to reach her whereas actually it had been only a few minutes.

He leaned forward and grasped her under her armpits. "Now listen!" he ordered. "I will take one of your arms and you must hold on to me with the other. That will leave my hand free to shove away the log that is holding you. Don't grab, or we'll both go down."

She tried to speak but she was too weak.

He took her arm firmly in his. "Let's go!" he shouted. She obeyed and he gave the log that held her pinned a tremendous shove. It sighed, inched, but did not roll.

Despair showed in her eyes.

"Now! I'll get it this time," he reassured her. Josiah shoved again with all his strength, and this time the cottonwood tree rolled from her.

Sweat streamed from him. "Quick," he said. "I'll lift you over my log."

"My foot," she mumbled through the mud that bubbled from her mouth. "Caught . . ."

"Deep?"

"No . . ." Cordelia's eyes were closing.

"Cordelia!" he shouted. Then he slapped her. Hard, cruelly, but he was rewarded by seeing her quick, angry stare. He took his knife from his belt, ran his hand down her thigh until he found her foot caught in a split tree.

"I'll cut off your shoe," he said. He worked as fast as he dared. Better cut her a little and get her out quickly. At last the leather parted. He managed to work his hand below her arch. "It will hurt!" he warned, "but I'm going to pull!" He grasped her foot and pulled upward. The leather gave. Her foot was free. One final jerk now. Cordelia's foot was out of the shoe but his own arm was caught in the tree. God! he thought, it's like a monster lying in wait. He gave a wrench that almost tore his arm from its socket. Then, with a gasp of pain, he, too, was free.

Somehow, he never quite knew how, he reached the safety of the bank and staggered ashore with Cordelia in his arms. Not until then did he realize that his left arm was badly hurt. Blood streamed from the torn flesh.

Exhausted from his efforts, he made his way to the torch and laid Cordelia alongside it. When the light fell across her eyes she opened them.

"I didn't think you would find me . . . I was afraid . . ." she whispered.

He stood there, cold, dripping with mud, blood streaming from his arm and looked down at the scarcely recognizable girl. "You should have known that I would find you," he said.

A question flew into her eyes. "Why?" she whispered.

"Because I want you to grow up so I can marry you," he said gruffly.

"Then . . . I'd better grow up fast. . . ." Her voice trailed off as she lost consciousness.

Josiah realized that the shock and exposure might kill her. Quickly he piled the dryest branches he could find into a heap and set the torch to them. He cursed his injured arm. He knew that because of it he could not carry her to the boat and even if he could, she might not live to get there.

He picked Cordelia up, sat down, laid her across his knees and struck her hard on the back. She coughed, and mud flew from her mouth. She breathed more easily. Then he laid her by the fire and began removing her clothing.

Petticoats! More petticoats. Absurd things, full of mud, weighing her down like iron. They had nearly cost her life. Her stillness made him frantic.

When he had removed all of her clothing he put his dry shirt and coat under her and began rubbing her body with his bare hands. It caused him excruciating pain in his left hand but he dared not stop. He rubbed her skin until the mud was dry and blistered her white body. Then he wrapped her closely in his own dry clothing, went to the pool, skimmed up some water in his hat and gently washed the mud away from her mouth and eyes.

He took her in his arms and blew his warm breath into her mouth. At last she stirred slightly. Only after he had taken these emergency measures did he think of summoning help. He took his pistol and fired it into the air.

If only he had more dry clothing for her. He took her drawers and dress, wrung them out and hung them on a stick to dry. Then he took her in his arms again and sat close to the fire, hoping to keep her alive by the warmth of his own body until help came.

In a few minutes he heard shouts, and voices moving toward them.

"Here!" he shouted. "Here she is! Here!"

Torches flashed, undergrowth was trampled underfoot and finally Hugo Knapp, followed by Jean Austin, burst into view.

"My God!" Hugo's face was a white blur under his hat. "You've found her!" Then seeing the lifeless girl, "She's dead? Cordelia!"

"Not dead, shock," explained Josiah quickly. "She'd fallen in that pool over there and her foot caught under a log. In a few more minutes she would have been gone."

"She's moving!" said Hugo. Josiah looked up and thought, I believe the big oaf's in love with her—and I would have thought him incapable of loving anything!

Then Hugo's voice changed abruptly. "Why are you holding her like that, Callahan?"

"It's obvious," said Jean Austin, speaking for the first time, although relief shone in his strange dark eyes. "He's trying to save her life by keeping her warm."

"Give me your coat," Josiah ordered Hugo. "I want to put it around her."

"Was she soaked?" asked Hugo, peeling off her coat. Then he noticed Cordelia's clothing by the fire and saw that she was nude except for Josiah's jacket and shirt.

"My God! You didn't have to remove all her clothing!" he exclaimed.

Josiah kept his temper with difficulty. "Have you any spirits on you?" he asked Jean Austin.

"Brandy," said Austin, producing a flask and lifting Cordelia's head so that Josiah could let a drop or two trickle down her throat.

"How long ago did you find her?" asked Austin, quietly kneeling by the fire.

"Half-hour or so," Josiah began, chafing Cordelia's hands.

Hugo had been standing sullenly by, but now he burst out, "A half-hour! You've had her here a half-hour in this condition? As her cousin, I demand you explain that!"

Josiah stood up then and Hugo recoiled from the cold blue glitter in his eyes. "I don't know what is in that nasty little mind of yours." Josiah's cold, even voice sent shivers down Jean Austin's back. "Perhaps you're thinking of what *you* would have done under the circumstances. What would you have had me do? Deliver your cousin to the boat dead from shock and exposure in wet clothes, or try to save her life? If you don't like my methods, I'll settle it on your terms."

"Pistols again, eh?" sneered Hugo. "I hear you have a penchant for them. Well, as it happens, so do I."

"Hugo!" Jean Austin said quickly, stepping between them, "don't be a fool. Can't you see Monsieur Callahan is badly hurt? Look at his arm! He could not have carried your cousin out."

Hugo's gaze went to Josiah's blood-caked arm. "My apologies," he said stiffly. "I didn't see your arm. She is my cousin, you know, and I feel responsible for her. I'll carry her back to the boat."

"Effen you will allow me, sir, ah'd like to do it." The three men whirled and saw Black Button standing at a distance, dark and immobile as the forest itself. A torch blazed in his hand.

"It won't tire me none, and I carried her when she was a little girl and used to fall in the river. If she wake up, she won't be scairt if she find me carryin' her."

"That sounds reasonable," said Josiah. "The thing to do is to get her out of here as quickly as possible. The rest of us can carry torches."

"I'm her cousin and I'll carry her," Hugo insisted.

[61]

"Be reasonable, man," said Josiah. "This big strong nigger can walk her out of here in half the time. We'll be hard put to keep up with him with the torches. I presume you have your cousin's welfare in mind."

"Of course!" Hugo said stiffly. Again he and Josiah exchanged cold glances.

"Come then, let's go," said Jean Austin. "I'll put out the fire and carry her clothes."

"Pore Miss Cordie," mumbled Button. "Pore scairt little girl."

"You mean scared of living or of dying?" Jean Austin asked, walking almost at his heels.

"I ain't sayin'," replied Button. Then he cast a brief scornful look over his shoulder at Jean Austin. "But I'd a heap rather die what I *is*, than be like some folk and live what I *ain't*." He stalked on and Jean Austin did not question him further.

Once Cordelia awoke. At first she thought she was on *The Blue Teal*. Then she realized she was being carried. She moved her hand and it came to rest against a chain. Then it was Button who was carrying her. His chain was dripping wet.

"Are you crying, Button?" she whispered.

"Hush!" he said.

"Don't cry, Button. I won't die. I have to grow . . . up . . . fast . . . !"

A great sob tore Button's chest and tears fell on her face like rain. "Then for Gawd's sake, Miss Cordie, will you please quit fallin' in de water?"

8

SHOUTS, GUNFIRE AND BLASTS from the whistle of *The Blue Teal* spread the word that Cordelia had been found. The search ended, men and women stood in little knots, talking, speculating, or craning their necks in the hope of catching a glimpse of Captain Riley, or of Cordelia's rescuer, Josiah Callahan.

[62]

Michael Riley remained in his daughter's cabin while the ship's doctor examined her. Josiah Callahan, in dry clothing, and with his left arm bandaged from armpit to wrist, joined three other men who stood outside Cordelia's door, awaiting the doctor's verdict. They were Pierre, who was pacing back and forth, Hugo Knapp, arms folded across his broad chest and leaning against the door like a surly mastiff, and, at a distance, Button.

When Josiah appeared, Pierre rushed to him, extended his hand and said, "I can never thank you enough for what you have done! It must have been the Virgin herself who led you to Cordelia."

"She had a narrow escape." Josiah took the hand the Frenchman proffered. A nice chap, thought Josiah. It was fate that led me to the sink-hole, and woods-experience that helped me save her, but if he wants to give the Virgin credit, let him. He glanced toward Cordelia's door. "How long has the doctor been in there?"

"Over an hour," Pierre said anxiously.

"Doctors!" exclaimed Hugo sourly. "Their cures kill the patients, and their explanations, the relatives. If he had any sense he could tell right off about her!"

Another hour passed. Pierre's pacing increased in tempo, and he ran his hands nervously through his hair. "Merciful God," he prayed silently. "Forgive my jealousy. I wanted to find her myself, and I hated Callahan for doing it. Just let Cordelia get well and I'll never ask for anything else!"

Hugo Knapp remained passive, occasionally shifting his position as time passed, until the door behind him opened and the little doctor came out of Cordelia's room. His coat was unbuttoned and sweat poured from his face. He looked wan and haggard. The waiting men caught a glimpse of Captain Riley sitting by Cordelia's bed with his head in his hands.

"I *think* the girl will live," the doctor said slowly. "But only because she is young—and because she *wants* to live. You gentlemen might as well get some rest. She will not be conscious for some time, and then she must have no visitors. Now, if you will excuse me, I'll go to the ladies' cabin and inform them of Miss Riley's condition."

"I will remain here," Pierre said after the doctor had left. "Captain Riley may need me."

"I think I'll stay, too," said Josiah.

Hugo looked at *The Hawk* lying nearby. "I am more relieved than you can imagine," he said gravely, his eyes studying the other two men. "But since there is nothing I can do, I must take my passengers up the river. Goodbye, gentlemen." He nodded to them and strode off.

The two men were silent after Hugo had left, but Black Button still moaned by the railing. Maids came and went from Cordelia's room, but not once did Captain Riley appear at the door. Just after dawn Josiah and Pierre looked up to see a tall figure in a silk hat striding toward them. A great diamond glittered in his shirt-front. Fancy Foot Morgan, his red mustaches bristling, and redolent of rum, was bearing down on them.

"What's the Cap'm aimin' to do?" he demanded of Pierre.

"I don't know," Pierre said wearily.

"Then ask him, damn it!" Fancy Foot splattered the deck with tobacco juice. "I'm tired of sitting on my bottom!"

"I can't bother him," Pierre retorted angrily. "His daughter is close to death—as you well know!"

"That girl!" Fancy Foot let loose a blast of profanity. "She'll be alive and kickin' when the rest of us are rottin'." Then, sensing that he had blundered, he peered blearily into Pierre's face. "Pretty sick, is she, eh?"

"Very!" said Pierre shortly. "And you can't disturb Captain Riley!"

"By God, why didn't yuh say so? I can fix that!" He chuckled. Fancy Foot fumbled through his waistcoat pockets, and before Pierre's and Josiah's startled eyes he produced several diamond pins and rings. "Paste. To fool them boarding-house thieves." He then took out a watch and a key. "Cheap," he chortled. "In case them buzzards in Puke Row swipe it offen me." He rummaged still further and came up with a small dirty leather bag, which he handed to Pierre. "That'll fix her. Just you slip it under her pillow and she'll be up in no time!"

"What is it?" asked Pierre suspiciously.

"Injun magic! Beaver ha'r, unborn mice and such. Smells, but it works," Fancy Foot declared seriously. "Cajun wench gave it to me oncet. Cured me up quick."

"Cured you—cured you of what?" Josiah regarded the filthy bag dubiously.

"Never you mind what!" Fancy Foot said fiercely. "Just you put that bag under that girl's pillow!" He started weaving away, his coat-tails flapping behind him.

Pierre balanced the bag in his hand. Then he shrugged. "I suppose it would do no harm."

"No harm," said Josiah, "and no good either! Besides, it's filthy."

"Yes. I think, however, I will put it under her pillow," Pierre said slowly. "I want to place a piece of sacred bone there anyhow." Pierre took a tiny silk-wrapped parcel from his pocket, opened Cordelia's door and tiptoed into her room.

Beaver hair and sacred bone! thought Josiah. What rubbish! He gripped the railing hard. Cordelia was going to live! She was. She had to! It never occurred to him that he, too, was praying in his own way.

Sometimes Cordelia recognized her father bending over her, coaxing her to swallow broth or medicine. But when her head was raised, pain would shoot through her temple and she would lapse back into oblivion.

As the days passed, she gradually grew better. She became aware of the presence of a woman who rubbed her head, brushed her hair, changed her nightclothes and made her bed fresh and comfortable.

On the sixth day Cordelia opened heavy eyes to find that the walls of her room were no longer spinning. She turned her head experimentally. The pain was gone. "Josiah?" she called in a weak voice. "Where is Josiah?"

"Hush, dear," a soft voice answered, "Josiah's away, but he'll be back." Gentle hands stroked her forehead.

Cordelia raised her eyes and saw a young girl her own age bending over her. The girl had light blue eyes, bright blond curls, and she wore a white wool dress sprigged with blue flowers. She looked more like a doll than a girl.

Cordelia was perplexed. "Who are you?" she asked wonderingly. "Have you . . . have you been here long? Are you a nurse?"

"Mercy, no," the girl laughed, "I'm your cousin, Virginia Knapp, from New Orleans. I wish Papa had heard you say I was a nurse. He thinks I can't do anything. I'm good at head rubbin' and hand holdin', but I'm afraid the servants do the rest. I was visitin' at Boonville," she went on to explain, "when I heard about your accident. Naturally, since we're kinfolks, I came to take care of you." She seated herself by the bed, took out a lace handkerchief and patted her cheek.

Cordelia frowned and tried to concentrate. "You're *really* my cousin?"

"Yes, truly," the girl smiled. "And you don't know how glad I am to hear you talking. But I knew yesterday, when your fever broke, that you would be much better today. Oh, how you've worried us, and how glad I am that you can talk! Now I can get to know you!"

Cordelia was still foggy. "You're a *Knapp?* And your name is Virginia?"

"Oh, I'll admit I don't look much like a Knapp," said Virginia. "Mamma was even blonder than Papa. When Mamma was carryin' me, she read *Paul and Virginia* and she wept *buckets* of tears. That's why she named me Virginia."

Cordelia attempted to assimilate this information. She knew she had distant cousins in New Orleans. If Virginia was one it was a delightful surprise. How wonderful to wake up and find your own cousin caring for you! "It was more than kind of you to come and take care of me," Cordelia said gratefully. "And I'm sure I'm not closer than a third cousin, either."

"Fourth," said Virginia. "That means we will be friends. If you're too closely related, you always fight."

Cordelia did not know what to say to this, and she was awed by her beautifully dressed cousin, so she looked around the room again. What a relief to have the curtains stand still, instead of crawling like snakes as they had during her delirium. Then she realized *The Blue Teal* was not moving. "Where are we?" she asked. "We aren't moving."

"Why, hon," Virginia laughed. "Your father brought you back to Boonville, right where you've been for a whole week."

"Boonville!" Cordelia exclaimed. "But our cargo? Our passengers?"

"Your father sold his cargo," Virginia told her, "and sent the passengers up the river on another boat. I declare I never saw a father carry on so. He wouldn't leave your bedside until your fever broke and then we had to make him lie down. Confidentially," she leaned closer, "I think he was waitin' for you to call for him, but you never did. Just for your mother and," her eyes sparkled, "Josiah Callahan! And who wouldn't!" She rolled her eyes. "Mr. Callahan is the most dashin' man I ever saw!"

Cordelia felt her cheeks grow warm. What had she said? "He did save my life," she said defensively.

"Ah, ah, you can't fool me," Virginia scolded playfully, shaking a finger at Cordelia. An emerald ring caught sun-sparkles. "It was so romantic. That handsome Pierre de Vries pacin' one way, and that dashin' Mr. Callahan the other. Your father was in here wringin' his hands and that Black Button was prayin' Catholic prayers and tellin' his beads—and then he prayed in German—Lutheran, I guess, and ended up in plain nigger-shoutin'. Lordy, I wish I'd fallen in a pond myself!"

"Don't wish that!" Cordelia felt the horror of the sink-hole sweep over her. "Don't ever wish a thing like that!"

Virginia rose immediately. "Oh, I got you excited and I talked too much. Let me call Yellow Anna and have her rub your back. No one can do it like Yellow Anna."

Before Cordelia could reply, Virginia went to the door and called, "Anna, come in here. At once!"

A young girl about fifteen entered. She had softly waving black hair, a generous red mouth, perfect features and light skin with a slight apricot overcast. "This is Anna," explained Virginia. "Isn't she pretty?" The girl remained expressionless. "Papa let me bring her with me from New Orleans," Virginia said casually, as if she were speaking of a trunk. "I take her everywhere. She's a quadroon, but I swear she looks octoroon or even less. Don't you think so? All the men were after her, one old fat one in particular. But I fixed him up, didn't I, Anna?" Virginia's eyes danced.

"Yes, ma'am!" Cordelia saw that Anna's eyes were warm and lustrous and that her mouth curved proudly.

Anna's hands were strong and supple and, under their dexterous massage, Cordelia felt herself growing sleepy. She glanced down and saw Anna's arm moving across her own body. There was only a shade's difference in their coloring; strange to think *that* was the difference between freedom and slavery. Yellow Anna was indeed a soothing sorceress. . . .

She was asleep several hours and when she awakened, Virginia and Yellow Anna were gone. Even before she opened her eyes completely, she knew intuitively that her father was there. She let her eyelids flutter down, feigning sleep, and peeped at her father through her lashes. She was startled by what she saw.

Could this be the father whose handsome jocularity had so impressed her only days before? Could this be the man she had loved for his gay laughter and teasing ways? Great black circles ringed his eyes, and grief had cut two furrows on each side of his mouth. She had done this to him, she thought, conscience-stricken.

[67]

She could feel his eyes on hers, probing through her feigned sleep and she knew she could pretend no longer. "Father," she said, looking up at him and feeling the weak tears well up in her eyes. "Oh, Father!"

He bent over and clasped her to him as the tears rolled down his cheeks and fell on her gown. "Thank God! Thank God! Oh, Cordie, if I'd lost you."

"Don't cry, Father," she mustered a faint smile, "I'm going to be all right. I'm sorry . . . I'm sorry I caused you so much trouble. Virginia told me you had to sell off the cargo. . . ."

"Hush, girl," her father kissed her cheek, "you're worth more than all the cargoes on the Missouri." Then he laid his hand on her forehead. "But, Puss, it wasn't like you to go off like that. You don't have to try and fool me. Something happened, and I think you'd better tell me now what it was."

"I can't," she cried. "Please, please, if you love me, don't ask me!"

"We'll wait until you feel better," he said placatingly.

"I can't tell you ever," she cried.

"Not now," he said, "but someday when you feel . . ."

"Never, never, never!" she cried hysterically.

"But, Cordie . . . was it Hugo?"

"No! I won't tell you . . . ever. . . ." She rolled over and lay silent with her back to him.

Her father was baffled. How like her mother she was, with that straight unyielding back. What could have upset her so? He sighed. He knew that unless Cordelia *chose* to tell him he would never know; that was a Knapp characteristic.

Finally Cordelia asked, "Does Mother know?"

"Of course, child!" said her father. "I sent word back by the first downstream boat and I've been sending daily messages. I couldn't have her find it out from someone else first." He hesitated. "Your mother is strict and harsh at times, but she loves you very much. It's just her way."

Cordelia did not reply. She could not turn and meet her father's questioning eyes. She remained silent and finally she heard him tapping his pipe on the sole of his boot.

"There is another matter I want to discuss with you," her father said. "It's that fellow Josiah Callahan."

Cordelia felt tense. "He's a brave man and he saved your life for which I shall be eternally grateful. But," her father went on,

[68]

"I don't want you to be letting romantic notions sweep you off your feet. You're too young to know what you want."

"But I *do*," she said in a muffled voice.

"How could you, Cordelia girl? Look at me!" he commanded. He took her face between his hands and turned it toward him. Reluctantly Cordelia met her father's eyes. "You've never known any men. You must know *many* before you choose. Then it must be one of your own kind."

"Josiah *is* my kind!" she burst out.

"In a way, yes," her father said. "But you must listen to me." His tone was earnest. "Being attracted to a man is not all there is to it. Your world and Josiah's are a long way apart."

"How are they different?" she demanded. "How?"

"Well, for one thing," her father spoke slowly, almost as if to himself, "he believes in slavery. We do not. He has the stamp of the old patrician on him. I have grubbed my way up from the St. Louis wharves, an orphan Irishman who got his education on Battle Row, and was lucky enough to rise above it, at least financially."

"But Mother married you," protested Cordelia, "and Grandfather Knapp was of the aristocracy."

"The *German* aristocracy," her father reminded her. "That is very different. True, in his youth, your Uncle Otto did spend much of his time in tavern bouts with young bluebloods and commoners, at the university at Bonn, but once away from the Fatherland, he was no longer an aristocrat. He forgot about it and became an American business man. Germans are practical; they put away the old life. But your Josiah is typical of a certain class, a way of life about which you know nothing . . . a rather unadaptable way of life. . . ."

"You're prejudiced because he fought a duel!" Cordelia said angrily.

"Perhaps." Her father bit down on his cold pipe, then he smiled ruefully. "Let's put it this way, Cordie. Your ancestors knew when to put up their broad-swords, and I'm afraid your Josiah will never put away his pistols."

"You're not being fair!" she blazed.

"Cordie." Again he took her face between his hands and turned it to his. "Look at me, girl! You're too young to know. You can't be in love with this man. You've scarcely met him!"

Her eyes met his head-on. "But I *am* in love with him," she said. "I know I am."

[69]

Her father sighed. He let his hand drop, arose and walked away to stand looking out the window. "Your Josiah Callahan has spoken to me. At least *he* has sense enough to know how young you are, and that no decision can be made until he returns from the war."

"War!" exclaimed Cordelia. "Oh, Father, when will I see Josiah again?"

"Josiah left to meet some of his outfit as soon as you passed the crisis," her father said. "I promised him he could see you again before he leaves; I couldn't deny a soldier and a man who saved your life that. He will be here in two days."

"Two days!"

"Furthermore," her father continued in his strange new tone of voice, "I don't want you mentioning Josiah Callahan to your mother. There will be time enough to talk about him when he comes back. I don't want her worried any more than she has been."

How strange! He was concerned about her mother's every feeling, yet only a few days ago Red Maude was in . . . the memory made her feel sick and she turned her face away.

"I don't want you to get too tired, Cordie." He touched her cheek lightly. "I can never thank God enough for sparing you." He hesitated a moment, then presently she heard him leave, walking slowly and thoughtfully away.

It had been so easy to promise God she would forgive her father and not hate Red Maude when she was drowning. But now that she was in her own bed, it was more difficult than she had thought to keep that promise. Things would never be the same between her and her father. They couldn't be.

Presently her thoughts went back to Josiah. Two days! An eternity!

9

JOSIAH WOULD COME in the afternoon, her father had said, but Cordelia was awake before the sun was up. She spent the morning trying different ribbons in her hair, and drove her cousin Virginia frantic by changing her dressing-sacque every few minutes. She was too excited to eat breakfast or lunch, so that she was feverish by mid-afternoon when Josiah appeared in the doorway with her father. She could only stare at him wide-eyed and whisper, "Josiah!"

"Cordelia!" Josiah's face broke into a smile. "You look quite different from the way you looked when I saw you last. Your cheeks are pink and there is a sparkle in your eyes. In fact," he added, "I'd say you were downright pretty without the mud!"

"Oh, Josiah! Don't tease me!" She was so overwrought she felt the tears welling up. "I didn't know you would be in uniform. You look so different!"

"Don't let these trappings deceive you." Josiah looked down at his shining boots and touched his gold sash. "Your father will tell you we ride off in style, but we'll be in buckskins before it's over."

"That's true, Puss," said her father, as Cordelia still gazed wonderingly at Josiah.

"But I'm the same as I was without the uniform," Josiah said meaningfully, coming closer. He stood looking down at her. "And I didn't come to talk about uniforms. I have come to tell you goodbye." He glanced beseechingly at Captain Riley.

Michael Riley looked at his daughter's face, then hard into the eyes of Josiah Callahan. He laid his hand warningly on Josiah's arm. "I promised you a talk, but, remember, she nearly died and she is still quite weak. I'm going to leave you alone, but I shall leave the door half-open and remain outside with Button." Then he relented and smiled a little. "But I shan't be able to hear a word you say."

As soon as her father was gone, Josiah sat down by Cordelia's bed and took her hands in his. "How thin your hands are! You've been very ill. Are you sure you feel well enough to talk to me?"

"Oh, yes!" It seemed to Cordelia that the whole balance of her life was caught and held in Josiah's eyes.

"I don't want to be inconsiderate," he said gently, "but I have so little time. . . ."

"So little time!" she exclaimed. A heaviness seemed centered in her chest. "I don't want time to pass."

He put her hands to his lips. "But it will. I must ride back within an hour." He touched one of her black curls and the yellow ribbon in her hair. "What a child you look! What a child you *are*. When I was away I thought of you as a woman. But now I know I should not speak to you yet. Certainly I cannot ask you to wait for me."

"Oh, yes! Yes!" She started upright. "I will. I *want* to wait for you—there will never be anyone else!"

"Cordelia!" He bent over her, his face serious and unsmiling. "Do you know what you're saying? Are you *sure* you're not confusing what you think is love with romantic ideals?"

She drew away. "I *knew*. I knew the minute you called to me on *The Blue Teal* and told me where I could find you if I needed you, that I wanted to be wherever you were. I thought you felt that way, too!"

"You funny, wonderful, *honest* girl," he said. She lifted her eyes to his. He leaned over and kissed her gently on the mouth.

"You won't hurt me," she whispered. "I'm not *that* sick." In answer his arms closed about her like bands of iron. He lifted her up and crushed her mouth to his. Cordelia thought all the jack-lights in the world were aflame.

"Now," he said, laying her back on the bed and leaning over her, breathing hard. "Have you been well kissed, or shall I kiss you again?"

"Yes! I mean no. Yes!" She tried to laugh but she felt flushed and dizzy.

"Then listen to me," he said seriously. "My time is almost gone. I want you for my wife, to love always. I want you as the mother of my children. I want us to live together in this wonderful state of Missouri." The scar showed livid.

"I want you because you are straight and sweet, and because you're the loveliest thing I've ever seen. It won't be moonlight and birds-in-a-tree being married to me. I have my faults, and I warn you I have. Some people call me hard, others, an adventurer. Perhaps I am. But I promise you, Cordelia Riley, that I shall love you as no woman was ever loved." He took her face between his hands. "Do you understand? When I come home I want you to marry me."

"And we'll live in a house by the river?" she said dreamily.

"A house by the river you shall have," he promised.

"And you *swear* there will never be another woman—ever?" she demanded.

Josiah drew back, startled. "What makes you ask such a thing—at a time like this?"

"You must swear," she said stubbornly, "that there will never be another woman."

Josiah looked searchingly at Cordelia. "I cannot swear," he said at last. "All I can tell you is that I love you. Surely that is enough. What put such ideas into your head?" he asked sharply.

Cordelia could not tell him about Red Maude. Instead she said, "There was a girl in Jefferson City. Was she pretty?"

"Very." Josiah looked a little relieved.

"Did you make love to her?" she asked.

"How can you be jealous of something that's gone and forgotten?" Then, seeing her stricken face, Josiah drew her to him. "What is it? What *are* you afraid of, darling?"

"Of losing you," she said, trembling against him.

"You'll never lose me," he said, winding her hair around his wrist. "Never as long as I live. Is that enough?"

Cordelia rubbed her cheek against Josiah's uniform. "I guess so. . . ."

"Here," he drew a ring from his pocket, "this was my mother's wedding ring." He held up a little circle of rubies and pearls. "I want you to keep it while I'm gone. When I come back, you'll wear it."

He put the ring in her palm, closed her fingers over it, then closed his strong hand over hers. "Keep it. But if for any reason you should change, I want you to have it anyhow."

"Josiah!" She threw both arms around him. "I'll *never* change . . . never . . . never."

Michael Riley glanced inside his daughter's room. He started, frowned, then closed the door. He wished his daughter had hitched her cart to a less-spirited horse. But then he himself had always followed his heart rather than his head, so he could not help but sympathize with Cordelia.

Maybe he was worrying about nothing. Josiah Callahan was going to war and while he was gone Cordelia would grow up. There were other fish in the river—fine men like Pierre de Vries. Still, he thought, looking at the closed door, she thinks she's in love; then let her be in love. Let everything be perfect for now. She'll have time enough to find the flaws in love when she's older.

Several hours after Josiah had gone, Virginia swept into the cabin wearing a blue velvet dress and a bonnet covered with pink roses. "Why, hon!" she exclaimed. "You look almost well. And I bet I know why." Yellow Anna, who had followed Virginia, seated herself in a corner on the floor.

Cordelia smiled. "It was your wonderful care—and Anna's."

[73]

"Nonsense!" Virginia seated herself and spread out her skirt. "Nursin' doesn't make you look like that! Kissin' does. One kiss is worth a dozen herb cures."

Cordelia started to protest. "Now don't tell me different!" Virginia teased. Then she said, "What I really stopped in for was to tell you goodbye. Your father tells me you're going downstream tonight."

"He's had a chance to take a downstream cargo," said Cordelia. "And I think he wants to get me home." She touched Virginia's hand shyly. "I shall miss you, Virginia. I never had a real friend before. I wish you were near, so we could visit."

"Why don't you come to St. Louis?" asked Virginia. "I'm planning to spend the winter there."

"You are?" Cordelia sat up in bed in excitement. "Why, I may be going there to visit my Uncle Otto!"

"You silly goose, he's my uncle, too, in a way. Why, we'll see each other all the time!" Virginia leaned over. "I'll tell you a secret. I hadn't planned to spend the winter in St. Louis at all. But last month I came up on *The Hawk* and I saw Hugo, and I decided it was St. Louis for me!"

"Cousin Hugo!" exclaimed Cordelia.

"Isn't Hugo the handsomest man you ever saw?" sighed Virginia. Then she giggled. "I wrote Papa I had found the most wonderful music teacher in St. Louis and that I *had* to study with him. Papa swallowed every bit of it. But then he lets me do anything I want anyway since Mamma died," she added wistfully.

Cordelia thought of Hugo's bearlike grip. He would crush the fragile Virginia like a butterfly. "I like Jean Austin better," she said. "He is more gallant."

"Poof!" Virginia shrugged. "New Orleans is full of Jean Austins. Give me a real man like Hugo. Besides," she added in a low voice, "I know something about Austin. . . ." She turned to Anna sitting on the floor. "Anna, wait outside for me."

"Yes, ma'am." The girl rose gracefully and went outside, her hips swaying slightly.

As soon as the door closed Virginia spoke in a secretive whisper. "That Austin! He's got his eye on Yellow Anna. I think he wants her for his mistress. But it will certainly cost him a pretty sum."

"Mistress?" Cordelia gasped. "But Austin is *white!*"

"You *are* a baby," Virginia laughed. "Anna's *for* a white man—a nigger wouldn't dare look at her. Papa would kill him if he did. Yellow Anna is worth a fortune."

"Oh!" Cordelia felt old-fashioned and provincial beside her New Orleans cousin with her fine clothes and her knowledge of the world.

"Now tell me, hon." Virginia's blue eyes were avid. "Are you going to marry that handsome Mr. Callahan?"

Cordelia felt the ring under her pillow. She had made up her mind to tell no one—not even her father—until Josiah came home. "He's gone to war," she hedged.

"That's more romantic than ever!" exclaimed Virginia. "You can write him letters. And if he should be wounded you can . . ."

"Please," begged Cordelia, "don't talk about *that!*"

"I'm thoughtless, hon." Virginia rustled to her feet. "I've tired you. Now you take care of yourself, so I can see you in St. Louis this winter."

"I only hope I can." Cordelia clasped her cousin's hand. "I don't want to lose you for a friend."

Virginia kissed Cordelia on the forehead. "You couldn't lose me now, pigeon. Besides, wild horses couldn't keep me from St. Louis."

Virginia stood in the door a moment, smiling, waved gaily to Cordelia, and then she was gone.

In that instant, while Virginia had stood in the open door, Cordelia had seen Yellow Anna, of the lustrous eyes and satin skin, laughing up at Black Button. Button had hung his silver chain around her neck.

"Anna!" Cordelia heard Virginia's voice, curt and imperious. "Come with me! At once!"

Shortly afterward Cordelia heard the hawsers being dragged across the deck. "One fourth less twain," she heard the lead heaver calling. The engines shuddered, the paddle wheel slapped—and *The Blue Teal* had started downstream. How smoothly she moved. That was because Fancy Foot and Pierre were the best pilots in the world.

Pierre. Suddenly Cordelia wondered what had become of him. He was the only one who had not come to see her since she was better. Could Pierre be angry with her? She must find out. Besides, there was something she must know and only he could tell her.

She rang for a steward and sent a note to Pierre asking him to come and see her.

When Pierre arrived he looked almost as tired as her father had.

[75]

"Pierre!" she exclaimed contritely, seeing his haggard face. "You have worried, too. I was such a foolish girl—I should explain . . ."

Pierre's brown eyes looked into hers. "Do not explain to me, Cordelia," he said. "I *know* why you ran away."

"Oh, Pierre, you are the best friend in the world!" she said gratefully. "You understand everything."

"Friend," he said ruefully. "That is a fine word. But I think it is the soldier you have lost your heart to."

"Is *that* why you would not come to see me?" she demanded. Pierre managed a smile. "Yes, that is why."

"I have hurt you," she said, "and now we can't be friends."

"Nonsense!" Pierre's voice cracked slightly. "If you should ever need me any time, Cordelia, I will come. We shall always be friends."

"Pierre . . ." Cordelia hesitated. "Where is Red Maude?"

"Why? Why must you ask me these things?" Pierre looked embarrassed.

"I want to know where she is," Cordelia said stubbornly.

"She left the boat as soon as you were found. Women are more sensitive than men. I think she knew why you ran away." He shrugged. "God knows where she went."

Cordelia looked away.

Pierre took her hands. "Don't try so *hard*, Mimi." He slipped into a pet name unconsciously. "You do everything too hard. You think, you play, you laugh . . . and yes, you love too hard."

"You can't *love* too hard," she said fiercely.

"No, Mimi," he said, looking at her sadly, "perhaps not—but it can make one *hurt* too much."

Suddenly Cordelia reached up and drew Pierre's face down to hers and kissed him gently. "I shall never forget what you've done for me, never. . . ."

Pierre leaped back as if he had been burned. He started to speak, then turned and rushed from the cabin.

10

MARGARET RILEY met *The Blue Teal* with blankets, heated
irons and an assortment of household remedies. Cordelia, walking
with trembling knees down the stage-plank on her father's arm, felt
a great gladness when she saw her mother standing straight and tall,
her shawl draped neatly about her shoulders.

"Well, at least you can walk," her mother said as Cordelia and
her father approached.

"Oh, Mother!" Cordelia released her father's arm, and, for the first
time in her adult life, she threw herself into her mother's arms. "Oh,
Mother . . . Mother . . ."

She felt her mother's arms around her, but her mother's back was
stiff and her voice cold. She did not offer the warm comfort for which
Cordelia longed. "Thank God you're safe," she said in a low voice.
"Thank God you're home."

Cordelia looked up at her mother's pale, composed face. "Oh,
Mother! I'm sorry I caused you and Father so much worry. Please
don't be angry with me. When I thought I would drown, I thought
how terrible it would be never to see you again, never to see your
beautiful face. . . ."

Margaret Riley flushed and drew back. "You're feverish!" she said.
She appeared uncertain for a moment and Cordelia thought her
mother might kiss and comfort her, but instead she drew away and
turned to Michael. "You see," she said sharply. "That's what happens
on a steamboat!"

"Margaret!" Cordelia heard her father using a tone she had never
heard him use before. "I forbid you to scold the child."

Margaret turned back to Cordelia. "You've learned a bitter lesson.
We'll not speak of it again. What has happened is never to be men-
tioned in this household. Now come along home. Your room is ready.
I'll heat some soup."

When Cordelia walked into her own room, scrubbed and smelling

[77]

of lavender, she burst into tears. Oh, how she longed for her mother to tell her she loved her and to cradle her in her arms, just once. But Margaret Riley seemed unyielding. Her silence was worse than a tirade.

Later, when Cordelia was put to bed, Michael exploded in a burst of anger.

"Blame *me*, if you must blame someone for what happened. Do not take it out on the child! I can see by your eyes that you think it is my fault that Cordelia was almost lost to us."

"Wasn't it?" Margaret's voice was low and bitter as she faced her husband across the kitchen table.

"Not altogether," said Michael angrily. "Perhaps I *have* indulged her too much. But you—you have been so strict with her the girl thinks you do not love her!"

"I? *Mein Gott!*" Margaret gave an anguished cry. "When I found her gone I was beside myself. . . . Then, when I received your message about the accident I prayed that if one of us must die, that I should go and she be spared. Day and night I spent on my knees in prayer. . . ."

"Margaret, Margaret," he said, seeing the pain in her eyes. "Then why did you treat her so badly? Couldn't you see she was dying for you to make a fuss over her, to *love* her a little."

"Love her?" Margaret protested, twisting her apron. "I would *die* for her. Michael Riley, your idea of love . . ."

"Then for God's sake," he broke in, "couldn't you show her a little more affection! *Couldn't* you?"

Margaret stood up quickly and broke three eggs into a bowl. She began beating them furiously. "I cannot show my emotions like a waterfront woman," she said. "She must have discipline for her own good. What an idea, saying I am beautiful! Where did she get such talk?"

Making a last desperate attempt, Michael crossed the room. "Stop beating those eggs," he ordered, taking the bowl from her. Then he took her face between his hands. "You *are* beautiful, Margaret. You have one of the most perfect faces I have ever seen—if you would only smile."

For a moment he thought she would relent, but then she drew away from him. "It is difficult to smile when one's daughter runs away like a river tart and her own father encourages her." Then she clenched her hands. "If anything had happened to her—I could not have borne it."

"Then why not tell her so?" Michael shook her a little.

"Don't be ridiculous!" Margaret reached for the bowl. "That would be condoning her actions."

Without speaking, Michael turned on his heel, put on his jacket, clapped on his cap, bit down on his cold pipe and flung open the back door.

"Michael, where are you going?" Margaret paused with the beater in her hand.

"To the wine cellar!" he shouted between clenched teeth. "And I *won't* be home for dinner!"

By the end of October, Cordelia was completely recovered. In the afternoon, after her studies were over, she would run down the path, pretending she was going to the grove to gather hickory nuts. But instead she sat on the bluff and watched the river and dreamed of the time when Josiah would come home. From time to time she would touch the little ring she wore pinned inside her camisole. She was lonelier than ever now.

If there were only someone she could tell. If only her mother . . . but the very idea of telling her mother about Josiah was unthinkable. And she could no longer confide in her father; their old comradeship was gone. She knew that when the river was frozen and he was home for the winter, he would feel the barrier between them keenly. Because of this, Cordelia made no objections when her mother went ahead with plans to send her to the Knapps in St. Louis for the winter.

Of course that silly Hugo would try to make love to her, but she would not listen. She had Josiah's ring. The Knapp house was dull and the food heavy, but who cared? She would live anywhere, eat anything until Josiah came riding home in his blue and gold uniform. Then, too, there would be the thrill of riding on *The Blue Teal* again and going down the river she loved. Down the way the spinning cottonwood logs and rafts went, down to where the fierce Missouri flung itself in a chocolate foam into the Mississippi, and at last to St. Louis to the wharf where steamboats were tethered like snorting white stallions. Perhaps . . . perhaps she could even smuggle the green velvet dress with the low neck into her trunk.

While Cordelia and her mother sewed lace flounces, made linen collars and pressed ribbons in preparation for their visit to St. Louis, Otto Knapp made preparations of another sort.

In St. Louis Otto Knapp heard the early November wind whipping the Mississippi River into a froth, romping down the streets, playfully tapping the toe of the boot-maker's sign and shaking the shutters of his mansion. In his study he stretched his feet toward the fire and settled down in the heavily carved chair that had been especially designed in Berlin to hold his 300-pound bulk. He glanced at a long walnut table piled high with papers. Winter would soon be here, he thought. And according to his calculations this year had been even better than the last—only two boats sunk.

He had docks and warehouses heaped high with produce, boats plying as far south as New Orleans and as far north as Omaha, and a waterfront office where clerks were bent fourteen hours a day over bills of lading, but here in this room was the heart of his empire. The best year yet, he thought, and I am tired. Strange that I have never felt quite so tired before. It is the work, the crushing work, and I have no one to take the load from my shoulders. A man needs sons and grandsons to carry on his business. If only Charlie were alive. . . .

A log in the fireplace fell and sparks flew upward. Otto's great head sank forward on his chest and his blue eyes retreated beneath overhanging layers of fat. Automatically his pudgy fingers reached for a plate of confections on a table at his side. Worse than seeing the Knapp family line spun out to a puny thread, yes, worse than losing Charlie was the dreadful suspicion that had begun to grow in his mind. During the day he could put it from him, but at night it came out like a black rat and fattened itself on his very soul.

He heard the door open in the hall below. He rose quickly for a man of his weight, crossed the room, threw open the study door and stood looking down over the balustrade.

"Hugo!" he said. "Come up. I wish to speak to you."

Hugo stood in the lower hall, looking up at his father. The hall was paneled in dark wood and the stairway rose to a huge landing, which, like those on steamboats, divided and rose again majestically to the second floor balcony. Intricate carving embellished the bannister that followed the stairway and encircled the balcony. Several bedrooms opened off the balcony, but directly opposite the front door was his father's study, like a great eye watching the comings and goings of the household. He saw his father standing in the study door, framed by dark paneling and spindly railings, looking for all the world like a fat white spider in a dark web.

Ah, yes, thought Hugo wearily, come upstairs and take a scolding about a bill of lading. At least take a scolding about *something*, Hugo.

"Where have you been?" his father demanded as soon as Hugo entered the study.

"Out with some friends," Hugo said, flinging himself into a chair.

"Friends! Bah!" his father snorted. "You have been with those Liberals. I can see you now, swilling their bad beer and shouting Salamander! *Donner!* What a pass you have come to! A Knapp spending his time with what floats over from the Fatherland."

"I like them," said Hugo. "Whether you like it or not, there will be a lot more Germans in St. Louis before things settle down in the Fatherland. Besides, how can you be so smug? The only reason we are not called 'those Dutch' along with the rest of them, is because we are rich and Mother is the daughter of an English merchant, also rich."

"Silence!" Otto struck the table and glared at his son. "I don't care if all the peasants in the Fatherland come to sit in the beer gardens— *you* will not sit with them! What did you do besides drink beer?" he demanded. "Discuss radical ideas, no doubt!"

"We were listening to music," said Hugo. "There was a fellow with a truly fine voice singing parts of a thing Wagner has done. . . . It's called 'The Flying Dutchman.' You would like the story. . . ."

"Wagner!" The mention of Wagner threw his father into such a temper that blue veins showed in his temples. "That experimenter with Beethoven! Wagner's nothing but a vile romanticist!"

Hugo had deliberately excited his father to anger over Wagner, knowing that there would be less anger left to vent on him. He chewed on a spun-sugar confection and waited for his father to subside.

Finally the older man regained his composure. "I trust you will have enough sense not to spend your time in beer gardens when your cousin Cordelia is our guest, especially when my sister Margaret is here also."

"Certainly not," Hugo smiled, sure of himself now. "I expect to show my cousin every attention. That's what you had in mind, wasn't it?"

[81]

"It certainly was," said Otto. "It's time you married and had a family. Your cousin Cordelia is entirely suitable, even if she does have that waterfront brawler Riley for a father. She can have that trained out of her. She is a Knapp and I cannot think of a better mistress for your plantation or a finer mother for your children."

"We agree on that," said Hugo. "However, I may run into some difficulty. I think she has romantic ideas about Callahan . . . he's the fellow who rescued her from the sink-hole, you know."

"Surely a man 1,500 miles away is no threat!" said Otto contemptuously. Then his eyes grew cold and fixed themselves on Hugo's. "I've heard rumors that you've been paying attention to that empty-headed distant cousin of yours from New Orleans, Virginia Knapp. I've seen the girl—too skinny—and her bones are no good. I don't want you dilly-dallying around with a girl like that."

"No good for breeding, eh?" Hugo said sarcastically.

"Precisely," said his father. "Now about this bill of lading for hemp," he took a paper from the walnut table, "your laxness has cost me . . ."

An hour later Hugo left his father's study seething with anger. As he walked down the hall a door opened a crack and his mother's two spinster sisters peered out at him, then hastily shut the door. Aunt Helen and Aunt Opal, he thought disgustedly, have probably been entertaining themselves by listening at the keyhole of the study. As he descended the stairway, he saw his mother coming from the kitchens at the rear of the house. Alice Knapp was a tall, thin English woman with reddish hair.

When she saw Hugo she stopped abruptly. "Hugo! Where have you been?" She jerked her head nervously as if someone were peering over her shoulder. "Your father is in a temper. He's all worked up over the Rileys' visit."

"I know," said Hugo. "I've just had an hour's instructions on how to behave when they are here—as if I didn't know!"

His mother sighed. "You must remember your father raised his sister from the time she was a small girl after your grandparents' death. You know he and Margaret have been estranged for years over her marriage to that Irishman. She has been in this house only once since her marriage. Now your father has decided to patch it up. That's why he is in such a state. He's afraid Cordelia will find things too dull here."

"Why shouldn't she? This place is like a morgue," Hugo said bitterly.

"You won't believe it," his mother said, "but your father is planning a musical and perhaps a dance!"

"A *dance* in this house?" Hugo could not believe his ears.

"Your father is determined to go to any lengths to make your cousin content to be one of us."

"Oh, I see." The old hatred swept over Hugo. "He thinks I can't win my cousin on my own, that no woman would want me for myself!"

"It's just that he wants to give you every advantage," his mother placated. "You're all we have now that . . ."

"Don't say it!" Hugo almost shouted. "I'm going down to the office!"

Later, riding down to the wharf, Hugo thought, I'll show the old goat. When I marry Cordelia I'll take over the business. Father is getting old; soon *I'll* sit in his study. Then we'll see who cracks the whip. But in the meantime, he decided, he would not go to the office after all. He would go back to the beer garden and sit with whomever he liked as long as he liked. There people looked up to him and asked his opinion.

PART TWO

11

It was a gray, wintry day in November when *The Blue Teal* docked at St. Louis. During the trip downstream, Cordelia and her mother had kept to their staterooms or had sat quietly netting purses in the ladies' cabin. But at the sight of the St. Louis levee, Cordelia's sedateness ended. Oh, the sights and the sounds!

Steamboats festive as wedding cakes were docked so close you could almost step from one deck to the other. Flags ornamented with every conceivable insigne from angels to crossed swords flew from their jackstaffs. Cordelia caught her breath when she saw the docks swarming with people and heard the chant of the roustabouts as they rolled barrels of sorghum and shifted bales of cotton. There was the sharp, pungent smell of rust and wet hemp, and of wood rotting in the river. Over all the shouts, singing and bellowing was the sound of cackling chickens and pat-racking guineas in hundreds of crates.

Cordelia's eyes widened as here and there she saw men lying drunk or asleep, like so much driftwood cast up on the levee. Suddenly a whip cracked. Cordelia jumped and, turning, saw Negroes in chains being herded from a steamboat docked next to *The Blue Teal*. Behind the procession of Negroes walked an overseer with a whip and behind him, a big man smoking a cigar.

"Look!" she called, pointing to the Negroes in chains. "Look, Father! Where are they going with them?"

"To the slave pen, unless they are lucky," said her father.

"Don't look at such heathen practices," her mother said sharply. "Don't shout. Keep your eyes averted and hold your skirts carefully—it's windy."

Cordelia did as she was bidden about her skirts, but nothing could make her avert her eyes, for just as she stepped onto the docks she heard a fearful clatter. Looking up, she saw an enormous dray wagon, drawn by eight gray horses, clattering toward them. The horses were sleek and shiny, their harnesses a bright yellow. Black plumes nodded in the bridles of the lead team.

"Oh, look at the beautiful horses! Eight of them!" exclaimed Cordelia. "How I should love to go flying over the cobblestones!"

"Cordelia!" Her mother took her arm firmly. "What an idea! You see, Michael." She turned to Captain Riley. He, too, had been watching the magnificent horses. "Now you see why I had to make the trip with her!"

"Margaret! Margaret!" a deep voice called, and they saw Otto Knapp pushing his ponderous way toward them through the jostling throng. "Welcome to St. Louis, Margaret," he said, taking his sister's hands. "Captain Riley," he nodded, with bare civility. "So this is our little Cordelia! A grown-up lady, eh?" he beamed, pinching her cheek lightly.

Cordelia had always thought her Uncle Otto looked like a fat bear with a white fringe on his head. Today he looked like Kris Kringle—until she saw his eyes. They were small and blue, and were regarding her intently from under the fat, drooping lids.

Cordelia started to smile but seeing that only her uncle's mouth and not his eyes responded, she gravely acknowledged his greeting. Then she turned to greet her Aunt Alice. She had forgotten how thin and rusty-looking she was—even her hair. "Welcome, child," her aunt said. Her voice was kind. "We're glad to have you." She looked over her shoulder nervously at Uncle Otto.

Then her aunt's two maiden sisters, Opal and Helen, came forward timidly. The two old spinsters were dressed alike in heavily-beaded black velvet coats. Over the coats they wore black shawls, and on their heads little bonnets with black plumes. "Welcome, dear," they said timidly. They glanced inquiringly at their brother-in-law. Then they repeated, "Welcome."

With their long, thin faces, nodding plumes and vaporous breaths, they resembled the lead team on the dray. Cordelia caught her father's eyes. He winked. She smiled back at him and knew that he, too, had caught the resemblance. She felt warmed inside, almost as if the old camaraderie between her and her father were there again— almost, but not quite.

Just then Hugo came striding up.

"You're late!" said his father accusingly.

"Business," replied Hugo. "Aunt Margaret!" He took Margaret's hand warmly. "Captain Riley, sir!" he said respectfully to Michael. "And Cordelia!" He kissed Cordelia lightly on the cheek. "You'll never know how glad I am to see you completely recovered from your bad experience."

"Come along, Hugo!" ordered Otto. "You and I will ride in the carriage with our guests. Alice," he turned to his wife, "you and your sisters may follow in Hugo's carriage."

The two carriages proceeded at a fast clip for a block or so, but when they reached Levee and Morgan Streets they found the way blocked by horses, carriages and a milling, shouting mob. Smoke was pouring from the window of a two-story brick building.

"A fire!" shouted Otto. "Quick!" he ordered the driver. "Turn the carriage around!" But before the driver could turn, a crowd of men carrying fire-fighting equipment rushed past, firing pistols into the air. Immediately a shower of bricks rained down from the burning building.

Frightened, Cordelia looked up and saw men on the blazing building loosening bricks and heaving them at the men below. Pigs wandering through the streets squealed and a group of soldiers from Jefferson Barracks began to fight. Cordelia could hear her Aunt Opal and Aunt Helen shrieking above the din.

"Turn! I told you, turn! Here, you fool!" Uncle Otto jerked the reins from the driver. But the horses reared and balked, a pig was pinned under the wheels and nearly upset the carriage.

"Oh, what *is* it?" asked Margaret. "Why are they fighting?"

"It's that cursed Liberty Fire Company heaving their bricks again," shouted Otto. "Every dirty Irisher from Morgan to Locust has taken possession of the building. They will demolish it before they put the fire out!"

"In a pig's eye!" snorted Michael Riley, his eyes blazing. "It looks to me as if the Franklin Company is doing its own dirty work. Pistols against bricks! Pistols in the hands of those First Ward Germans!"

"German, Irish! Who cares! Why don't they put the fire out?" demanded Cordelia.

"Because," Hugo laughed, "both companies have to prove to all of St. Louis that *they* have the best volunteer unit. When there is a fire, they both come dashing to put it out, but they end up fighting to see who is going to do it."

"But the fire!" exclaimed Cordelia. She and her mother cringed as more bricks showered down.

"It burns," said Hugo dryly.

"Turn!" shouted Otto. "Turn!" His whip cracked out over the horses. One lunged and almost fell, but the crowd prevented their turning. Again bricks rained down and struck a man who fell almost under the carriage wheels. Hugo leaned out to look and a man running by saw him.

"Hugo! Hugo Knapp!" he shouted. "Get out! Get out and help us blast those dirty Irish out of the building. Then we'll burn every coffeehouse on the row!"

Otto leaned out and cracked the whip into the crowd. A way was opened and the crowd parted, cursing and screaming. Then quickly he struck the horses again and again. The carriage swayed, bumped, and a wheel almost gave way, but they negotiated the turn, the second carriage close on their heels.

"*Donner!*" said Otto. "What a foolishness! It is seldom like this," he explained to Margaret, who was white. Cordelia caught flying glimpses of galleried houses, masses of locust trees, and wooden fences, and once she saw a girl in wooden sabots jumping a mud puddle with a flurry of red petticoats.

"Goodness, Otto!" said Margaret, glancing at Cordelia's excited face. "I hope St. Louis isn't always like this."

"This is most unusual and regrettable," said Otto.

Hugo laughed.

The Knapp mansion was a two-story house, impressively built, with pillars running across the front and fierce stone lions guarding the steps. But the front door was so small and dark that, to Cordelia, the house looked like a fat face with too small a mouth. She remembered her father had said once that the house was a combination of baronial splendor and Knapp stinginess. She glanced at her father, but he seemed preoccupied as they mounted the steps.

Once inside, the Rileys were escorted up the long stairway and shown to their rooms. Cordelia dismissed the maid who had been sent up to help her unpack. What a stuffy room, she thought, looking around at the dark mahogany furniture and marble-topped tables. Silken draperies and lace curtains completely covered the windows.

Still, she guessed she could stand it for the winter. She could stand anything now, because she was in love, and she was waiting for Josiah to come home!

She took out the little ring she had hidden away and looked at it. After her mother had gone home she would hang it on a chain around her neck. She kissed it now and tucked it away. Then she began to put her clothes away in the great dark wardrobes and in the bureau drawers. When she had finished, she put on a plain gray dress with a white collar and went downstairs to join the family for dinner.

Dinner in the Knapp house was an important affair. They were seated around an immense table in high-backed chairs. First Otto read a few verses from a huge Bible, then he offered up a long prayer. Finally, he signaled for the servants to begin serving.

Cordelia observed that her Aunt Alice, at the far end of the table, appeared somewhat distracted and that she spoke very little. She found herself looking at Uncle Otto, sitting in his great armchair, and back again at Aunt Alice. They acted like people who scarcely knew each other. Then she saw that her Aunt Opal and her Aunt Helen were watching her over the rims of their glasses and carrying on a whispered conversation. Her father was restrained, not his usual self at all.

Mother once sat at this very table, she thought. Did Aunt Alice rub her forehead worriedly then, and did Uncle Otto read the Bible before every meal? Did they always have *three* kinds of pie and cake?

She noted a certain defensiveness about the way her mother sat while Uncle Otto spoke authoritatively on shipping, the Whig Party and the evils of Matt Murphy's beer. She noticed her mother even frowned a little now and then.

Then Cordelia caught her father looking at her, and she smiled almost shyly. "Have some cake, girl," her Uncle Otto insisted in his booming voice. "It will put meat on your bones."

"Yes, have some cake," said Aunt Helen, almost like an echo.

"I don't care for cake," Cordelia said. "I never eat it."

"I don't blame you a bit!" said Aunt Opal suddenly. "I hate it!"

"Opal!" gasped Aunt Helen.

Otto ignored Aunt Opal. "I fear, Margaret," he turned to his sister, "that your daughter is just like you. You wouldn't eat cake either."

"No, I wouldn't," her mother said in a strained voice. "And I remember how you would sit in front of me, tempting me, so you thought, with confections. I fear you have put *too much* meat on your bones!"

"Not too much!" Uncle Otto patted his huge stomach and laughed. "Eating keeps me young! And what keeps *you* young, Captain Riley?" he asked her father, making an obvious attempt to be hospitable to the man they all knew he detested.

Cordelia saw the corners of her father's eyes crinkle a bit. "Taking boats up the Missouri," he said. "The Missouri will trim any man down to size."

"Bah! I whipped the Missouri a long time ago," said Otto Knapp smugly.

"To the tune of two or three steamboats a year," Hugo put in, goading his father deliberately.

"Oh, how can anyone say they have conquered that river?" Cordelia broke in excitedly. "She flows so *free*—that's what I love about her. I think she laughs out loud at people!"

"Really?" Otto's brows drew together. "What an idea! What an idea for a *woman* to have!" He turned to Cordelia's mother. "It's a strange chick you have hatched, Margaret."

"What's wrong with my idea?" Cordelia asked before her mother could reply. "I love the river! I don't care if she is fierce and rough. I love her. What if I *am* a woman? I can think, can't I?" she demanded.

There was a silence. Aunt Helen cowered in her chair. Aunt Alice sat transfixed, her fork in mid-air. The silence was broken by a funny, rusty laugh from Aunt Opal. Cordelia saw that her uncle seemed to be choking.

"Cordelia!" Her mother's face was flushed.

"Bravo!" Hugo threw back his head and laughed, but Cordelia knew it was not in her support, but to spite his father.

Then her father came to her rescue. "Perhaps our chick does seem strange to you," he said evenly, but his eyes were bright with anger. "If so, you must remember she is half-Riley."

Uncle Otto's face was purplish. He took a swallow of water from a huge tumbler and set it down with a shaking hand. "I am not likely to forget," he said hoarsely. He was obviously making an effort to control his temper but he glared at her father. The strongest of men looked away from Uncle Otto's stare, but her father's eyes remained cool, almost amused, and they did not drop.

Then he looked at Cordelia. She guessed he liked meekly bowed heads around his table. Well, *she* was half-Riley. She stiffened in her chair and met her uncle's gaze defiantly.

The day her parents left, Cordelia regretted that she had not resisted more strongly her mother's decision to leave her in St. Louis for the winter. As she stood on the dock with her Uncle Otto and Cousin Hugo, she felt the keenness of the wind and saw that the Mississippi was choppy. Soon it would be winter and the river might freeze over. She did not want to be away from home in the winter.

"Mother!" she said, touching her mother's arm. "I wish I were going back with you!"

Her mother's eyes clouded for a moment. "This visit is for the best. You will see."

"Mother . . ." she said wistfully. "It will be spring before I see you again. Won't you miss me a little?"

"Miss you? Of course!" Margaret looked hard at Cordelia. "What ails you, child? If there is something you need to tell me, speak up!"

How she longed to tell her mother about Josiah, but she was afraid to. "No, nothing," she said slowly. "It's that I've never been away from *both* of you before . . ."

The whistle of *The Blue Teal* sounded. "Oh, Father!" She turned tearfully to him as he bent and kissed her. "If I hear news from Santa Fe, I'll let you know," he whispered in her ear. "Goodbye, Puss," he said aloud.

"Oh, Father, you know . . ." Tears filled her eyes when she saw the answer of understanding in his. "I wish I . . ."

Otto broke in. "Here, here, we'll take good care of your daughter. Don't worry, Margaret!"

"I'm counting on that, Otto," her mother said. Then she looked levelly at her brother. "I also want her to be happy."

"Oh, Mother, Mother!" Cordelia gave her mother a sudden hug and kiss.

"Come on, Margaret," said her father. "Goodbye, Cordelia girl." And then her parents were leaving, going up the stage-plank, her father holding her mother's arm as if she were a queen.

Cordelia noticed that her mother carried herself proudly. Her well-cut dark skirt swayed gracefully in the breeze. Her wrap, edged in fine fur, was draped just so across her shoulders. There was no artifice about Margaret Riley. Her clothes were not fashionable and her hair was drawn back too severely from her face, yet there was *something* about her. Cordelia saw that every deck hand turned to look at her mother.

Almost as if reading her thoughts, her Uncle Otto said, "Margaret always did carry herself well—better than any girl in St. Louis. Shall we go back to the house?"

"Oh, no!" said Cordelia, "I want to watch *The Blue Teal* cast off."

Her uncle hesitated. "Very well," he said, at last, in the tone of one indulging a small child.

Cordelia watched with an aching sadness as *The Blue Teal* went churning up the Mississippi, headed for the Missouri. She watched until even the banner of woodsmoke was lost to sight. "Come, child," said her uncle, "being here with us is not the end of the world."

"I don't want to be an ungrateful guest," she said apologetically. "It's just that I've never been away from both my parents before."

"You will not be lonely," he said. "I have planned a number of amusements for you, and there's Hugo and a distant cousin of yours, Virginia Knapp . . ."

"Virginia!" said Cordelia. "Oh, I do so want to see her. Will she be here soon?"

"Day after tomorrow," said her uncle.

"Father's planned quite a party for you, Cordelia," Hugo said. "You should feel flattered."

"It is nothing," said Otto. "I want you to meet suitable young people of the city and we want you to be one of us. Shall we go home now?"

As the carriage proceeded, her uncle continued. "Hugo can show you that we Knapps are not all shillings and strudel," he said. "Eh, Hugo?"

"Cordelia and I can . . ." began Hugo.

"I have ordered a fine saddle of venison for the party," Otto went on, ignoring him. "Hugo is the finest carver in St. Louis," he added. He warmed to the subject of the party. "And music. I have something special, a new trio. An Irishman who plays the violin, a Spaniard the guitar, and a Frenchman the flute."

"What, not a *German* in the lot?" asked Hugo mockingly.

"They are *directed* by a German," his father said, giving him a hard look. "A man educated at Emmerich. What music they play! Mozart! Beethoven and Hummel!"

"No Wagner?" asked Hugo wickedly.

[92]

"No Wagner!" roared Uncle Otto, frightening Cordelia.

"No Wagner," he repeated, breathing hard. "And not another word from you!" he ordered.

Hugo laughed, and Cordelia shrank back in the corner of the carriage. Not another word was spoken as they rode in silence, the two men staring at each other like two fighting cocks trying to decide when to spur.

Once back in the Knapp mansion Cordelia hurried to the privacy of her room, flung herself down on her bed and wept with loneliness. Presently she fell asleep.

In the room next door, Opal and Helen sat crocheting. "Sh . . ." said Helen, opening the door and listening. "She's stopped crying."

"Not for long—not in this house," said Opal grimly, beginning to crochet a stitch of her own invention.

It was dark when Cordelia awakened and the room seemed close and stuffy. She drew aside the heavy draperies and opened the narrow window. The wind blew raw and cold against her flushed face and she heard it howling through the bare trees. A light rain had begun to fall and below she saw the slate roofs glistening. Lights gleamed wetly through the dusk, and in the street below she heard a bell. She leaned out as far as she could and saw an ancient bell-ringer, muffled to the ears and carrying a lantern.

As he shuffled along he rang his bell and called, "Lost child! Lost child! Lost child!"

Cordelia shivered, closed the window and drew the curtains tightly together.

12

PREPARATIONS FOR Cordelia's party began the morning after her parents' departure. To Cordelia's amazement her aunt had very little to do with readying the house. It was her Uncle Otto who personally superintended every detail, from the preparation of food to the dusting and polishing of furniture.

Aunt Alice pleaded one of her headaches and remained in her room. Aunt Opal and Aunt Helen did not appear at all, so Cordelia, not knowing what else to do, tagged about at her uncle's heels.

She watched the maids, standing on chairs and ladders, dusting the crystal chandelier in the dining room. The great prisms danced and clinked musically under the energetic polishing.

"I never saw such a lovely chandelier," she told her uncle. "We have one at home, but not nearly so grand as this. This must have a thousand prisms!"

"Three thousand," her uncle told her. "I brought it from Munich. In my old home in the Fatherland we had such lights in every room. You should have seen it when all the candles were blazing!"

Cordelia was entranced with the rosewood piano in the front parlor. When the cover was removed, she touched the keys experimentally. The piano had an exquisite tone and she struck a series of melodic chords, sending a shaft of sound through the gloomy old house like a flash of exotic plumage against dark undergrowth.

Upstairs, Aunt Alice, hearing the sound, sat up and smiled. Then the smile faded and she lay down again and turned her face to the wall. Helen and Opal dropped their embroidery work. "Music!" said Opal. "I hope she can play! Though I suppose Otto will insist she play all those dull, stupid *Prussian* pieces!"

"Opal!" Helen watched her sister anxiously. "I don't know what has come over you. Ever since that girl entered the house you've been acting strangely!"

In the kitchen the cook paused and listened. Then he absently took up an onion and began cutting it into minute pieces.

"Karl!" exclaimed the serving maid. "You know Herr Knapp will not allow onion in the dressing. He loathes it."

"He will not notice a very, very small one," said Karl.

"Then why risk putting it in, if it is so small?" she asked.

A smile crossed Karl's heavy face. "But *I* shall know it is there," he said.

"Music!" said the maid. "I haven't heard that piano since I've been here."

"That is because you are new." Karl began mixing the onion in a huge bowl of stuffing. "A long time ago Frau Knapp played—and very well, too. Those tinkling little English tunes. Not much meat in them, but they made you think of grass and meadows. But Herr Knapp did not like them."

"So," said the maid, making a face, "he made her play German tunes."

"You have been here longer than I thought," smiled Karl, "but not long enough to know Frau Knapp. It is true she stopped playing the light English music—but she didn't play what he wanted either. That is why the piano is always covered."

In the front parlor, Cordelia dropped her hands from the keys. "What a lovely tone!" she said.

"It is always kept well tuned. You may take lessons this winter, if you wish," said her uncle. "I know a musician, educated in Emmerich, who is very good."

"Oh, thank you," said Cordelia gratefully. "I should love that!"

Later, Cordelia watched wide-eyed as servants brought tremendous silver platters and tall candlesticks from their hiding-places in the cellar.

"All this will be Hugo's someday," explained her uncle. "I only hope he will choose a wife who will appreciate them."

"Appreciate them!" exclaimed Cordelia. "Anyone in the world would love them." She looked up and saw her uncle smiling at her so kindly that she decided he was only a benign old bear after all. Was he not inviting young people to meet her? And, wonder of wonders, was he not having a small *tanz* in her honor? Dancing had never before been permitted in this house, and yet he was giving a supper-party for her.

The following evening, Cordelia felt wildly excited as she dressed for the party. She was downstairs a full hour before the guests were expected, looking at the blazing lights overhead and pointing an experimental toe across the gleaming walnut floors. She peeped into the front parlor. Yes, the musicians were already there. The dining room was dazzling. In the center of the long table was a platter of spun-sugar confections. She was admiring a pink sugar rose with glistening leaves when she heard her uncle's voice.

"Cordelia, you're down early," he said.

Cordelia turned to see her Uncle Otto, resplendent in a velvet coat, fawn-colored trousers and a vest of crimson brocade. An enormous diamond glittered on his shirt-front. "Oh, Uncle Otto! You look like a baron or a count—absolutely magnificent!"

"Thank you!" He smiled in a pleased manner. "Perhaps it is because I *am* a count." Then he studied her for a moment. "You look very lovely, my dear. However, you must change your dress—it is cut much too low."

"But my father bought it for me!" Cordelia protested, touching the lace at the throat of her beloved green velvet dress. She had smuggled it ever so carefully into her trunk inside a drab brown dress.

"So I thought!" Her uncle's face was bland, but his eyes were unrelenting.

"Uncle Otto," she said determinedly, "I know you don't like my father. But if you really knew him . . ."

"I know your father very well," her uncle said coldly. "Far, far better than you can possibly imagine."

Suddenly she knew. Her uncle knew all about Red Maude! "But I like the dress." She faltered now, uncertain.

"I am sure you have something more suitable. I expect you to wear it," he said firmly, turning and walking away.

Cordelia was angry, but since he was giving the party in her honor she had no choice but to wear whatever her uncle wished her to. She changed to a demure gray taffeta with lace collars and cuffs. She disliked her dress even more when she saw her cousin Virginia, who was the first to arrive.

"Cordelia!" Virginia came in with a flurry of rustling silks, trailed by Yellow Anna. "Cordelia!" She hugged her. "You'll never know how glad I am to see you! I was so afraid you wouldn't really come to St. Louis."

"I'm here," said Cordelia, "and I'm ever so glad to see you. How lovely you look!"

"Do you like it?" Virginia pirouetted about, then tossed her wrap to Yellow Anna. "My dress is new," she said gaily. Virginia wore a mauve satin dress, cut much lower than Cordelia's green velvet. A delicate lace scarf was thrown carelessly over her shoulders. Her blond curls were caught in a net sprinkled with stars. Delicate amethyst earrings swung from her ears. And Cordelia was sure her lips were rouged.

"You are *very* lovely," a man's voice called from the balcony. Both girls looked up and laughed when they saw Hugo. But when Hugo descended the stairs, the color drained from Virginia's face and her

[96]

eyes fastened on his. Like a bird with a cat, thought Cordelia, watching.

Hugo kissed Virginia lightly. "We're not kissing cousins, but perhaps one can bring the relationship closer?" he teased her.

"Why not?" Now Virginia's face was stained with deep color. "Why not, Hugo?" she asked coquettishly.

Cordelia knew Virginia would have stood gazing at Hugo all evening, so she said, "Come upstairs, Virginia. We'll talk until the other guests come. I'm dying to hear about your music lessons and what you've been doing."

Once the two girls were in Cordelia's room, Virginia collapsed on the bed. "Music lessons, silly! Who cares about music?" She threw her hands over her face. "Oh, I'm mad about Hugo! Absolutely mad. When he looks at me, I shiver all over. Have you ever felt like that?"

"No." Cordelia frowned. "I didn't feel exactly *that* way."

"How did you feel?" Virginia asked, her blue eyes inquiring. "How did you feel when Josiah Callahan kissed you?"

Cordelia did not want to say, but Virginia was insistent.

"All warm, that was the way I felt," Cordelia finally said, "a little shivery, but safe, too, as if I'd been caught in a storm and suddenly found a house and had run inside."

"How dull!" said Virginia. "I can't breathe and I feel very *unsafe* and I *want* to be!" Then she jumped up and put her arms about Cordelia. "I'm a selfish little beast. I haven't asked you if you've heard from your dashing Mr. Callahan."

Cordelia shook her head. "This is war, Virginia. They say it takes a letter nearly two or three months. It may be a long time before I hear."

"But how can you wait?" asked Virginia.

"I can wait," said Cordelia, gently touching the ring inside her dress. "I can wait forever."

"Oh, fiddle-faddle!" Virginia patted her hair and smoothed her dress over her tiny waist. "Nobody waits forever!"

There was a knock on the door. "Girls! Cordelia, your guests are arriving. You must come down and receive them." Cordelia opened the door and found her Aunt Alice waiting outside.

Her aunt was regal in dark red velvet, a paisley shawl and a pearl collar. "Oh, Aunt Alice, you look wonderful! I'm glad your headache has gone. I hope it will stay away!"

"That depends," said Aunt Alice cryptically. Then she smiled.

[97]

"You look very nice, dear, although I imagine you'd rather wear a dress like your cousin Virginia's."

"Well, I had a green velvet dress . . ." Cordelia said hesitantly.

"Yes, I know." Her aunt shrugged. "I prefer a low-cut dress myself. High collars nearly choke me to death. But you and I, my dear, must be covered and content while the men—your uncle and your cousin included—gaze at other women's low-cut bodices!"

"Oh, Aunt Alice!" said Cordelia. She was not only astounded by what she had said, but by the odd aroma about her. It was like lavender—but also a little like rum!

"Come along, my dears," said her aunt. "I hear your guests in the hall below."

Cordelia soon forgot her plain dress, for it was such a wonderful party. The young men were resplendent in light trousers, colored velvet coats, with diamond and pearl stick-pins glittering from every shirt-front. Their partners were all beautifully gowned in satin and lace. As they moved, their skirts billowed out like colored mushrooms.

Although Cordelia declared that she did not know how to dance, it proved to be an advantage, for every young blade fought for the privilege of showing her how to waltz. Naturally graceful and light on her feet, she was soon being whirled from one young man to another.

Around and around she danced beneath the twinkling chandelier. Was there ever so much fun in all the world before? Truly St. Louis was a wonderful place. And then in no time at all it was midnight.

At midnight all the young people trooped into the dining room and gathered around the long table. A saddle of venison was placed at one end. Suddenly the cry went up, "Hugo! Hugo! Let Hugo carve."

Hugo smiled, turned back the cuffs of his blue coat and stepped to the table. Confidently, he took up the great shining carving knife. She watched, fascinated, as meat, dark and succulent, fell in paper-thin slices under the precision of Hugo's razor-sharp knife. A murmur of admiration went up.

Cordelia looked around for her uncle and saw that he was not present. This was strange, since he had been mingling jovially with the crowd all evening and overseeing every detail of the party. On the dance floor he had maintained a benign but watchful eye, so that no man dared hold any girl closer than two feet. But now both he and Aunt Alice were gone.

A young man offered to fetch Cordelia an ice and she accepted. But suddenly the room seemed stuffy and too full of rich food odors. She saw that Virginia was talking gaily to Hugo and playfully toying with the carving knife.

Perhaps she had better let well enough alone. Her young swain was having to wait his turn at the confections so Cordelia decided to slip into the hall for a breath of fresh air.

Virginia was making the most of her opportunity with Hugo. "I never saw anyone so skillful," she said. "But then I guess you're good at everything."

"Not everything." He looked at her, interest lighting his eyes. The little flirt, he thought, like a delicate kitten.

"Oh, come," she pouted. "You're very good at dancin' and ridin' and runnin' boats and carvin'. What else is there?" Her eyes looked deeply into his.

"I suppose you mean love," he said, loosening his collar a trifle.

"Maybe . . ." She hesitated, giving him a sidelong glance. Then she laughed and deliberately turned her back on him. She had beautiful shoulders.

"I shall be at home tomorrow evening," she said lightly over her shoulder. Then she sauntered away swinging her fan. What a tiny waist the minx had—a man could easily span it with two hands!

As soon as Virginia was out of sight, Hugo looked around for Cordelia. Who would have thought she would be so popular? He had scarcely had a chance to speak to her all evening. He looked about at the guests all happily eating and laughing, but Cordelia was nowhere to be seen. Surely she would not leave the party! His father would be furious.

Then he realized with a start that his father was absent, also. Even his mother was missing. Curious, he worked his way through the crowd and out into the hallway. He stepped into the hall just in time to see Cordelia holding up her skirts and running up the stairway.

"Cordelia!" he called. But she did not answer. Hugo looked up to see light streaming from his father's study and to hear the sound of voices. Just then he saw Cordelia disappear into the study. Hugo rushed up the stairway after her, two steps at a time.

When Cordelia had stepped into the hall she had looked up toward the balcony and had seen the light coming from her uncle's study. Urgent business, she decided. She heard her uncle speaking in a loud, excited voice. She wondered what was disturbing him, but deciding that it was none of her affair, she started for the dining room. Then she heard another voice coming from the study. The sound spun her around.

"Pierre!" she called out involuntarily. "Pierre!" she called again, recognizing his voice. But how could Pierre be here when he had sailed on *The Blue Teal?*

"Pierre!" she called, running up the stairway. On the landing she stumbled over Yellow Anna, who was wide-eyed with terror. Cordelia rushed on and burst into her uncle's study.

She took one swift look and her steps faltered. Her uncle was bowed over his desk as if in pain. Then she saw Pierre. But he looked like a haggard, older man, not like the Pierre she knew. He wore rough clothes, and there was a stubble on his face. "Pierre!" She flung herself at him. "Pierre, what has happened?"

"Sit down, child. You must calm yourself!" Her uncle's voice was harsh and broken.

"Come, dear." Aunt Alice drew her to a chair.

Why were they staring at her? She jerked herself away from her aunt. "Pierre, what has happened to my . . . my . . ." Her voice trailed off. "Oh, no!" she screamed. "Not my father and mother. Oh, no, Pierre, they didn't . . ."

"Oh, Mimi, Mimi!" Pierre tried to comfort her. "*The Blue Teal* went down. We hit a sawyer . . ." There was a great roaring in her ears.

"Margaret is dead. Dead in the river!" said Otto Knapp grimly.

Pierre took Cordelia's hands. "Your father was thrown free, Cordelia, but your mother was trapped in her stateroom. He went back after her. Button found them, but it was too late."

A moan came from Cordelia's lips. "And I never told them. . . . Oh, Pierre! I never told my father or mother how much I really loved them. I wanted to tell my mother about Josiah . . . there was so much. . . ."

"Margaret carried herself so well," mumbled Otto Knapp. "I never saw a girl who carried herself so well . . ."

Then the real impact of what Pierre had told her began to hammer against Cordelia's brain. "Josiah! Oh, Pierre." She turned like a lost

[100]

child, swayed and collapsed. Pierre sprang forward to catch her as she fell, but it was Hugo Knapp, striding in the door at that moment, who caught her in his arms and carried her to her room.

13

WANDERING THROUGH the Knapp house like a lost waif, Cordelia felt not only an inconsolable loss at the death of her parents, but she was overcome with remorse because she had not entirely forgiven her father, not told her mother that she loved her. If only she could have told her about Josiah! Now her mother would never know.

She felt alone in her grief in this alien house. Numbly she donned the mourning dress her uncle had ordered for her, touching the dreary folds of material and thinking how her father would have hated to see her dressed in black. Tears welled in her eyes at the thought.

With the exception of Virginia, there was no one to whom she could turn for consolation. Virginia was the one bright spot, the one who offered her sympathy and understanding, but Uncle Otto made it plain that he considered Virginia giddy and not welcome in a house in mourning.

Aunt Alice had immediately shut herself up in her room, appearing unsteadily at dinnertime and, although Cordelia tried not to notice it, smelling rather like Rommel's wine cellar. Aunt Helen and Aunt Opal produced embroidery hoops and linens and attempted to show her fancy stitches. But try as she would, Cordelia could produce no more than the "chicken tracks" about which her mother had so often chided her.

Karl, the cook, tried to tempt her with rare delicacies, but she had no appetite for them. So, in desperation, she turned first to Hugo, since he was nearer her age and appeared sympathetic. However, his condolences were always accompanied by half-caresses so that she couldn't help feeling his solicitude was merely an excuse for familiarity. She had an impulse to talk to her uncle, even though he was hot-tempered and gruff. Once she had seen a look in his eyes that made her believe he was almost as lonely as she. But any understanding she might have reached with him was foredoomed by an angry scene that took place only two weeks after her parents' death.

Summoned to his study, she found him seated in his great chair holding a sheaf of papers. "Sit down, Cordelia," he said, motioning to a huge high-backed chair. "Do not look so forlorn and bewildered," he added. "This is your home now and I will take care of you."

She saw her uncle studying her from under his eyelids. "Thank you," she said, sinking into the chair.

"Now, of course you are a woman and know nothing of business." He tapped the sheaf of papers. "But you will at least understand what you are worth when I am finished. Now," he pursed his lips and scowled at some letters, "*The Blue Teal* was a complete loss. There are no damages, since shippers ship at their own risk. You of course still have *The Silver Star*. In addition, you will have about twenty-five thousand dollars when the Hermann property is sold. In fact, my girl, you are quite well off. Do you understand?"

"Yes, I understand," she said, "but I don't care about money right now."

"I know. . . ." Her uncle's eyes were almost kind. "But whatever happens, money *is* a handy device. I shall run *The Silver Star* with the Knapp line, if you wish. As you know, I never have an unprofitable enterprise."

Cordelia felt small and defenseless. "I should like for you to do that," she said. "However, I must be sure that Pierre de Vries is the pilot, that Button is the chief roustabout and that a legless cook called 'No Legs Harry' is kept on."

Her uncle studied her a minute, shifted his bulk and reached for a confection. "I approve, though I'd say you're being unnecessarily sentimental. I hope your interest in Pierre de Vries is purely business. I've seen that handsome young Frenchman, and you're inclined to be romantic. He's a good river pilot, but impossible as a match for a girl of your standing. I'm sure you understand that."

"I can assure you that Pierre is only a friend," said Cordelia, "because . . ." She took a deep breath, drew out the gold chain she wore around her neck and held up the ring Josiah had given her. "I'm engaged to marry Josiah Callahan and intend to do so as soon as he returns from the war."

[102]

Her uncle almost choked on the spun sugar. "What? Are you demented, girl? I heard you murmuring idiotic things the night Margaret was lost, but I thought it was delirium! It *is* delirium!"

Cordelia felt her knees trembling beneath her skirts as her uncle glowered at her. "I assure you I was not delirious. I have every intention of marrying him."

"That's impossible! I won't have it!" Her uncle's hand made a fat spat as it hit the table. "That fellow is a no-good adventurer, a hothead, and he's got a plantation full of niggers. Furthermore, there are other things . . ."

"If you mean his duel, I know about that," she said. "And he did save my life," she reminded him.

"You can't marry Callahan and that's final!" Her uncle's lower lip came out menacingly. He lowered his head and thrust it forward until he looked like a sullen old bull. "You must think of the family, now, girl—carrying on the family!"

Cordelia rose from her chair and faced him. Although she was quivering, she managed to keep her voice low and even. "I do not like to cross you or anger you, Uncle Otto, but nothing on earth shall keep me from marrying Josiah!"

"You! You slip of a girl, how dare you defy me?" Her uncle's voice was thunderous. "Just twenty years ago your mother stood right here in this study where you're standing now and said those same foolish words. And you see what it got her! A lifetime of sorrow with a drinking, philandering Irishman and a grave in the river!"

Suddenly Cordelia's whole world turned topsy-turvy. Her mother, her own mother, had defied Uncle Otto to marry Michael Riley! What courage it must have taken to leave this house, after having spent her whole life here. Cordelia tried to maintain her dignity, but the tears began to run down her face. The hurt was widening —that she had never understood her mother. And now it was too late.

"I think . . . I *know*," she said in a low, sobbing voice, "I *know* my mother would rather be dead in the river than to have been married to any man than my father. And that's the way I feel about Josiah!" she burst out. "And neither you nor anyone else can ever make me feel any other way!" She turned and fled from the study, and, reaching her room, flung herself trembling on her bed.

After this her uncle was no longer jolly, but watched her with a cold reserve, and, gradually, Cordelia came to feel as if the very walls of the house disapproved of her. Christmas in the Knapp house would be a dreary affair at its best, but with the house in mourning it was suffocation. The rooms remained shuttered, with the curtains drawn. As Christmas Day approached, Cordelia felt increasingly desolate. Sadly she recalled past Christmases with goose roasting in the kitchen, mantels festooned with spruce and red berries. Her father always gave her an exciting present, bought on his last trip down the river, and her mother always gave her something beautifully made by hand.

On Christmas Eve they always went to church together—one of the few times her father attended services—and they would sing "Good Christian Men, Rejoice." Her mother would be straight and beautiful in a new shawl, and her father's black unruly hair would be brushed down. There would be a whiff—a little whiff—of wine about him.

On Christmas morning she and her father would skate on the river. Her mother would scold them when they returned half-frozen, then serve them a dinner fit for kings.

Christmas Eve in St. Louis was quite different. Cordelia saw the surrounding houses aglow with bright lights, and watched parties of people stamping along in the snow, calling greetings to each other and swinging lanterns as they walked. Only the Knapp house remained dark and gloomy. Even Hugo deserted her and went off somewhere, resplendent in a new waistcoat and a fine beaver hat.

On Christmas Day she looked from her window and saw that the outside world was white and silver. She heard the church bells chiming, clear and sharp on the frosty air. The Knapps remained inside and her Uncle Otto read for an hour from the Bible in German.

The day after Christmas, Cordelia felt she could stand the stifling house no longer. "I was wondering," she ventured timidly at dinner, "I was wondering, Uncle Otto, if someday soon when you drive down to your office at the docks, I might not go with you. I should like to see the river frozen over and the boats covered with ice."

Aunt Alice continued cutting her meat, but her Aunt Helen emitted a squeak of protest. "To the river?"

"To the river?" Uncle Otto echoed, gazing at her in astonishment.

"Come, come, Cordelia!" Hugo shook his head, and made signs for her to change the subject. "I should think you'd never want to see the river again."

"Never see the river?" she asked, astounded. "But I *love* the river!"

"What they are trying to say," her aunt regarded her hazily, but kindly, "is that they think that since your parents' death you would never want to see the river again."

Cordelia looked at Aunt Opal, crumbling cake, and thought, they must think I am unfeeling. "I loved my parents more than anything in the world," she said slowly. "Surely you know that! But I love the river, too. My parents are gone, but I still have the river, don't you see?"

Uncle Otto didn't "see." "Alice," he bellowed, "call a doctor at once. The girl is feverish! Wants to see the river—the river that took Margaret! If it hadn't been for that cursed Irishman, Margaret would still be. . . ."

"Otto!" said Alice Knapp sharply, speaking up for the first time in years. "Do not speak ill of the dead! I forbid it! Forbid it, do you hear?"

There was a choked gasp from Aunt Helen. Dinner was concluded in painful silence.

Later that evening Virginia called, but Uncle Otto remarked that her bonnet was far too giddy and that she was an undutiful daughter not to have gone home to New Orleans for Christmas. Cordelia was eager for a comforting talk with her cousin, but her uncle did not allow them a moment alone. Virginia left early and Cordelia went to bed.

The following day when both Otto and Hugo went to the docks Cordelia was not asked to accompany them. But in the afternoon, almost as if in answer to a prayer, she received an invitation from Madam de Vries, Pierre's mother, asking if Cordelia would spend New Year's Eve and New Year's Day with them. The note added that since Cordelia was in mourning, the evening would be spent as quietly as possible, with only the family for dinner.

Cordelia was delighted. Pierre's vivacious little mother had been a guest several times at the Riley house when she had accompanied her son on trips up the river. Cordelia remembered her as an apple-cheeked woman with black hair and dancing eyes. She immediately dispatched a servant with her acceptance. She was anxious to see the de Vries', but more anxious to get out of the Knapp house.

At first her uncle forbade her to go, but when he found she had already accepted and was determined to go he ordered Hugo to drive her there. Perhaps throwing the two together on a sleigh ride might do no harm after all.

About three that day Hugo brought around a trim little cutter drawn by two prancing black horses, and Cordelia stepped outside and took what seemed to her the first breath of fresh air since the death of her parents.

Otto Knapp, watching Cordelia clap her hands at the sight of the cutter and horses, withdrew from the study window, satisfied. If only that Hugo had half a head on him he would have the girl eating out of his hand in no time.

The snow had been heavy and it had melted enough during the forenoon to turn the city into a fairyland. Locust trees stood like white sentinels, drifts made scallops along the fences and ice hung crystal lace from every gatepost. Men in mufflers were shoveling snow from stoops and breaking icicles from the drip-line on roofs. Cordelia saw that wreaths still ornamented some doors, and that brightly colored strings hung from trees holding tidbits for the birds.

"Oh, Hugo! It's a fairyland!" Cordelia forgot her sadness for a moment. They passed an apothecary shop with its windows filled with shining bottles. Down the street was a boot shop, its peaked roof dripping long icicles. Even the little boot hanging over the doorway was encased in ice. "Look at the little boot!" she exclaimed. "It looks as if it were made for an ice prince!"

"What a ridiculous girl you are!" Hugo teased her. "But I'm glad to see some color in your face. Cordelia, I wanted to take you out before this, but you know how every one would have talked."

"You *have* been kind to me these past few weeks," she said. "I don't know what I'd have done without you."

He patted her hand and tucked the fur robe around her. Then he halted the horses, sprang from the carriage and with a flourish attached a string of silver bells to the harness. "I thought you'd like them," he explained.

"Why, Hugo, how thoughtful!" she said gratefully. "I love bells."

"Cordelia," he said suddenly, taking both her hands in his. "Now you are looking at me the way I want you to. I know it's too soon, but promise me you'll marry me in the spring. We'll live on the plantation—away from this place and its reminders. . . ."

Suddenly Cordelia realized that the bells were not a kind, impulsive gesture, but a carefully planned setting for his scene. She drew her hands away. "Oh, Hugo, why won't you *listen* when I tell you I'm going to marry Josiah Callahan?"

"You're a fool!" said Hugo angrily. "He'll never come back to you. He'll amuse himself with a dozen Spanish wenches before . . ."

"Hugo!" She was trembling. "I swear I'd like to slap you!"

"You won't!" His eyes bored into hers. "And I swear I will not let that fellow have you. Never!" He sent the whip curling over the backs of the horses and the cutter leaped forward. The rest of the ride they sat in cold silence. Cordelia turned her face away from him and studied the houses.

She saw that the streets were different here. Houses were surrounded by high walls and fences, and all kinds of small buildings clustered around the main dwellings. She realized these must be the early French houses because of their small-paned windows, long narrow galleries and great stone chimneys, dwarfing the walls.

The de Vries' lived in such a house, not a mansion, but certainly not a cottage. It had an earthy look, as if the old stones had sprung up from the earth itself.

Hugo, who was still in a sullen mood, escorted Cordelia up a narrow, winding brick walk to the front door. The door was of wood, inlaid in herringbone fashion, and emblazoned on it was an enormous brass beaver head.

"Oh, look at the beaver head! And the little mullioned windows!" she exclaimed.

"That's because it is a very old house," explained Hugo boredly. "Pierre's father had a reputation as a beaver trapper and this is his way of showing it, I suppose."

"Oh, Hugo, don't be so dour," said Cordelia, tracing the beaver's nose with her finger.

"Then stop mooning over your cavalier in blue and . . ."

Just then the door opened and Pierre greeted them.

"Cordelia!" he exclaimed, his brown eyes dancing with delight. "We thought you'd never get here—Mother has been in a frenzy. And Monsieur Knapp! Come in, come in, both of you," he invited.

"No, thank you," said Hugo stiffly, remaining on the stoop. "I have to meet a business acquaintance shortly." He turned to Cordelia. "I'll call for you tomorrow at three o'clock sharp. Think over what I said." Then taking advantage of the situation, he kissed Cordelia on the cheek, strode to the cutter, leaped in and drove off at a fast clip.

14

As soon as Cordelia entered the house, the de Vries' swarmed around her. Pierre clasped her hands warmly, Madam de Vries took her in her arms and kissed her on both cheeks. "Mimi! You poor little bird! How glad I am to see you, and how sad for your poor papa and mamma!" She began a stream of condolences in French so fast that Cordelia could not follow her. "Janette! Cecily!" Madam de Vries called.

Immediately Pierre's two young sisters came running and took Cordelia's wraps. They were merry girls, with brown hair and sparkling eyes, and they revolved around Cordelia like curious, friendly chipmunks. "Oh, she *is* pretty, Pierre!" they exclaimed. "And her hair really *has* blue in it," they chorused.

A general laugh went up as Pierre turned a brick red. Embarrassed, but pleased, too, Cordelia looked about her and saw a great fire roaring in a stone fireplace, light, comfortable furniture and tables and chairs nudging each other in friendly profusion. A ball of yarn had fallen from a basket and a gray cat was lazily batting it with its cushioned paws.

"Do sit down, child," said Madam de Vries, drawing her toward a chair by the fire.

"Oh, no, Mamma!" the de Vries girls protested. "She must come directly to the kitchen and watch the cook making *croquignoles*." Without waiting for Cordelia's assent, Janette and Cecily took her by the hands and propelled her toward the kitchen, chattering like magpies. Although the girls were near her own age, Cordelia felt almost grown-up in her mourning dress.

In the center of the kitchen Cordelia saw a long table covered with a dazzling white cloth. It was heaped high with golden brown *croquignoles*. Cordelia watched, fascinated, as the cook cut out the curious shapes and dropped them into great kettles of boiling fat. "Emil is the best cook in the whole world," said Janette.

Emil looked ready to burst with pride as he turned two fat pheasants suspended before the fire and pretended to test the venison popping and sputtering on a spit. Suspended overhead were shining pots and pans. The whole kitchen was full of brightness, laughter and tantalizing smells.

Pierre came into the kitchen, took up a *croquignole* and handed it to Cordelia. "Eat this!" he ordered. "Emil will think you do not trust his cooking. Besides, Mimi," he added in a low voice, "it makes me unhappy to see you so thin and sad."

"Oh, Pierre, I cannot help my sadness." But she obediently ate the *croquignole,* and wished she could soak up some of the gaiety of this kitchen and take it back to the Knapp house with her.

Suddenly above the chatter and noise in the kitchen they heard a stout knocking at the door. "Oh, it's the Abbé," the girls shouted. The de Vries' rushed in a body toward the front door. Cordelia, curious, followed and saw the family enthusiastically greeting a chubby little priest with white hair and red cheeks.

Pierre drew Cordelia forward. "Father, this is our dear friend, Cordelia Riley. Cordelia, this is our esteemed Abbé Choate. He is our Father Confessor. He comes to us in sickness and stress—and always when I have good gooseberry wine."

"Shh." The priest's eyes twinkled. "You will shock your pretty guest!" They all laughed good-naturedly and sat down to discuss the news of the day. The war with Mexico—a topic which Cordelia drank in—and tidbits of news about neighbors which excited Madam de Vries to vivacious chatter.

Presently Pierre arose and went to the kitchen. He returned with an old glass decanter filled with wine. Janette brought some glasses from the sideboard and Pierre poured a little wine into each. When the glasses were raised for a toast, the family looked at the priest. "To Beaver House," said the priest, "and to the New Year."

"And now, Father," said Pierre, "to Cordelia!"

Cordelia had been too long exposed to the dreary Knapp house. So much warmth and happiness at once released her emotions like fast-melting snow. Tears began to run down her face.

Immediately Madam de Vries rushed to her, enfolding Cordelia in her plump arms. "You poor little pigeon. We have been thoughtless. She has sustained a terrible loss, Father, only a few weeks ago," she explained to the priest. "Her mother and father, Captain and Mrs. Riley, were lost in the Missouri, aboard *The Blue Teal.*"

"I heard of it," said the priest. "A terrible loss, my poor child," he said sympathetically. "God have mercy on their souls. You, of course, are of the Faith?"

"No, Father," said Pierre quickly. "Cordelia is of the Knapp family here. Protestant."

"Yes, yes, I know of them," said the priest. "Long prayers, these Protestants, and no laughter or wine." Then he smiled kindly. "But well-meaning people. If I can ever be of help to you, child, do not hesitate to come to me."

Cordelia raised her head and met the priest's sharp old eyes. "Thank you, Father, I shall remember." She began to dry her tears.

"That is right, dry your tears and do not forget to smile," he said. "I'm sure your parents would wish it that way. And now," the priest raised his glass to Pierre and the girls, "to my dear friend and your father who is gone—Jacques de Vries!"

"To Papa!" said the de Vries' with shining faces. "To the greatest beaver trapper in all the world!"

The priest saw the questions in Cordelia's eyes. "Ah, my child," he said, "you should have been here in the old days when Jacques de Vries and his men came home down the Missouri. Late in the fall you could hear the shouting and the singing of the *voyageurs*, long before the mackinaw boats and canoes came in sight. They were truly a fine sight, and no man was as handsome as Jacques de Vries. He always came in the first boat, riding like a king on his beaver pelts. As I recall, there was a certain young lady who almost fell from her window waving to him."

"Oh, Mamma, did you really almost fall?" The de Vries girls laughed.

"Never you mind." Madam de Vries tossed her head. "You young people know nothing about real gaiety. Such dancing we had!" She looked at the walnut floors. "Tonight, the *Jour de L'An*, was always the gayest night of all."

"Tell Cordelia about the bean cake," said Pierre.

"It was the custom," she told Cordelia, "and still is, to bake a cake with beans in it. I remember I was but sixteen when I received my first piece of cake with a bean in it. Ah, such a *Jour de L'An* that was! *Mon Dieu,* but I was excited, for that made me a queen! Queens could choose a king for the ball, so . . ."

"So you picked Papa," laughed Cecily.

"That Jacques!" said Madam de Vries. "He was very naughty. The next night he could choose another queen and the queen another king. That way we could keep our balls going to Shrove Tuesday! But that Jacques chose me again, which was almost a scandal, as no one can be a queen twice. So to get even, I chose him to be a king again!"

"That's when he asked you to marry him," Janette said.

"Well . . . I will not say. But I did marry him before he went away again. Up the Missouri with those savages."

"But he always came back to you and to Beaver House," said Pierre gently.

"*Oui*," she smiled and nodded. "He always came home to Beaver House—and to me."

The fire snapped and leaped up the chimney. This is the way death should be, thought Cordelia, a tender remembrance, not remorse. For the first time since her parents' death she felt somewhat at peace.

"But you, Pierre," the priest turned to Pierre, "you belong to the younger generation. You have none of your father's understanding of virgin forest, teepees and campfires. All you young fellows know is the blast of whistles, and barrels rolling on a dock."

"That's what I like," Pierre laughed. "The more whistles and barrels, the better."

"And what do you like, daughter?" The priest suddenly turned his wise old eyes on Cordelia.

"The people!" said Cordelia without hesitation. "I used to watch them going up the river. I could see each family in its new home with lights in the windows and cattle in their barns." There was a silence and the priest looked at her keenly. "Ah, my child, yours is a rare gift," he said. "To see man—not as what he is or was, but what he is to become—is a gift from the Virgin herself. Although I must warn you there will be few who understand it. And now," he rose from his chair, "I must go home and prepare for the morrow."

"Stay for dinner," the de Vries' begged.

The priest shook his head. "No, I need rest. Tomorrow is the New Year, which means it will be full of confessions for the sins of the old one."

After dinner that evening Cordelia was aware of much whispering in the kitchen. Presently Janette and Cecily came out giggling and tied a handkerchief about Cordelia's eyes. After much whirling and turning, they untied the handkerchief so she could see the "surprise" they had for her.

[111]

She found herself in the kitchen facing a huge Negro. "Button!" she cried. "Button! Is it *really* you? How . . ."

"I got no place to go winters now," Button explained, tears in his eyes. "So Mistah Pierre he let me stay in the house out back and help with the fires."

"Oh, Button!" she said, remembering. "They told me you were the one who found Mother and Father . . ."

"I found dem," he told her gently. "Your daddy was holdin' to a log with one han' and holdin' your ma with the other. I seen your ma was gone, but your daddy, he don't seem to know it. I gets dem both to shore, and then your daddy, he see your ma ain't breathin'. So it look like he just quit breathin' too. So . . ." he looked down at the floor, "I lays dem side by side, like dey was asleep and I set down and wait for the white folks to come and take 'em away."

"Thank you, Button," she said humbly. "I'll never be able to thank you enough!"

"Mighty little to do for folks you loves. . . ." Then he burst out, "Miss Cordie, it break my heart to see you so peaked."

"I'm all right, Button," she reassured him. "I think I'll be all right now." She talked to Button several minutes, reluctant to let go of the one link with her childhood. Presently she observed that the giant Negro was troubled.

"Aren't you happy here?" she asked.

"Yes, ma'am. No, ma'am," he said.

"Is there something you want? Something I can do?" She saw he was twisting his hands nervously.

"Nothin', Miss Cordie," he said. "Some things ain't right if you're a nigger—and I'm a nigger."

"What is it, Button?" she demanded. "You can tell *me*."

"Miss Cordie," he burst out, "what you think they do to a yaller girl if they catch her with a black nigger like me if she a high-priced yaller girl that ain't free?"

"Button!" She looked at him in alarm. "You don't mean Yellow Anna?"

He nodded miserably. "Do you reckon they kills us if they knowed we jumped the broom together?"

She took his arm and whispered fiercely, "You know very well slaves can't marry, or jump the broom, or anything, without their master's consent!"

"I knowed it, Miss Cordie." He looked down at his feet. "But we done jumped de broom by ourselves."

Cordelia was frightened for Button. "You must never tell. Never. Do you hear me?" Then a thought hit her. "Oh, Button, what if . . ."

"Anna, she know conjure things," he said, "so there won't be no black babies like me."

Cordelia flushed. "Be careful," she warned. "Oh, Button, do be careful!"

Later that evening the de Vries' were sitting about the fire, waiting for the New Year, when there came a tremendous thudding and shouting at the front door.

Pierre opened it a crack and was shoved aside as a motley crew of young men wearing odd clothing and grotesque masks burst in. A dragon demanded sugar, flour and all kinds of spices in a hoarse voice. A frisky blue turtle capered about, made a low bow to Madam de Vries and held open an empty sack.

Then to Cordelia's delight, all the young men began capering about and singing, "*Bon soir, le maître et la maitresse et tout le monde du logis. . . .*"

"Enough, enough!" said Madam de Vries, laughing as she and the girls hastened to the kitchen and brought forth provisions, placing them in the sacks.

Immediately the blue turtle, who seemed to be the leader, kissed Madam de Vries on both cheeks, and the young men began to dance a gay dance which Cordelia had never seen.

"It's 'La Guenille,'" Pierre explained. "They call it the rag dance."

"Ah, ha!" The blue turtle snatched up what was left of the gooseberry wine. "Thank you for the wine, Pierre!" Then he impishly kissed Cordelia, bowed low and said, "*Mam'selle, je vous souhaite une année belle et heureuse, et un gros mari à Paques!*" With more shouts, they departed. Cordelia could hear them singing as they went down the street.

"They knew you!" she said to Pierre. "Are they your friends?"

"My very best," laughed Pierre. "They will cut a lot of capers before the night is over."

"Why aren't you with them?" she asked.

"Because," Pierre gave her a steady, tender look, "I would rather sit by the fire with you than do anything else in the world."

"Oh. . . ." Cordelia dropped her eyes and changed the subject. "What did the man dressed as a turtle say to me?"

[113]

"Oh, didn't you know?" asked Janette. "He wished you a happy New Year and a big husband at Easter!"

There was a silence and they all gazed at the fire intently.

Suddenly the silence was broken by shouts and laughter, and church bells began to chime. "It is the New Year!" said Pierre.

For a moment it seemed that all of St. Louis was laughter and chimes. The New Year, thought Cordelia. Tomorrow I must leave Beaver House and go back to Uncle Otto's. It would not be easy.

15

THE SPRING OF 1847 came early, heralded by the sound of breaking ice, as the upstream thaw reached the Mississippi and St. Louis.

Cordelia, in the Knapp mansion, heard the popping and grinding of the river and sadly remembered other springs, standing on the banks of the Missouri with her father, watching to see the first dark seam appear in the frosty white coat of the river. She recalled listening for winter's reluctant groan, as its icy fingers were pried from the throat of the river. How she wished she could go down to the levee and see ice piled as high as a man's head. But Uncle Otto had expressly forbidden her to go near the river.

Then one windy March day when she knew the ice was gone and she heard steamboats whistling like hounds that had just found their voices, Cordelia felt she had to get out of the house. She must see the river, even if it meant walking alone on the levee—something no decent woman would dare do. She was leaning wistfully from her window watching housewives in their back-yards airing their good comforters, when she saw a carriage stopping in front of the house. She was overjoyed to see that it was her cousin Virginia. The two girls had become very close friends since Cordelia's parents' death. Virginia called often, in spite of Uncle Otto's outspoken disapproval.

Cordelia watched with delight as Virginia alighted from the carriage, followed by Yellow Anna. Virginia was wearing a dark blue dress, topped with a priceless India shawl, and her bonnet was pink, encircled with pink velvet flowers.

Cordelia observed that Yellow Anna no longer looked childish, but more like a full-blown yellow rose. She wondered about her relationship with Button. Just then Virginia looked up and saw Cordelia.

"I'm going for a drive. Do you think you could go?" she asked.

"Yes!" said Cordelia. "But don't ring the doorbell. Wait on the porch and I will let you in!" She raced to the stairway, then on sudden impulse, lifted her skirts, slid down the long railing, and leaped nimbly off when she reached the bottom. She ran to let Virginia in.

"Virginia!" she said, embracing her cousin. "You'll never know how glad I am to see you!"

At the sound of Cordelia's running feet, Aunt Helen and Aunt Opal opened their door. They thrust their heads out just in time to see Cordelia sliding down the railing in a flurry of petticoats. "Goodness!" they said in unison. Then they went back in their room and took up their needlework.

"I believe Cordelia is half-acrobat," said Opal admiringly. "Imagine having the nerve to slide down the railing in this house!" She smiled as she began working on a half-finished monogram on a large linen cloth.

"Opal!" Helen spoke reprovingly. "You sound as if you admired that girl's giddiness. What has come over you? You know Otto is worried about her skittishness. And look at poor Hugo! The girl treats him as if he were dust."

"I only hope she doesn't have to give in," Opal sighed. "But I suppose Otto will win in the end—he always does." She jabbed her needle savagely into the linen.

"I wish this Callahan she talks about would come home from the war. A lot of them are coming back since their enlistment is up," she went on. "I'm afraid the girl will have been married to Hugo and had her first child by the time Callahan gets here."

"Oh, the war will not last that long," said Helen.

"Long enough!" said Opal bitterly. "These Knapps are fast and determined on breeding. Did you ever notice how Hugo looks at Cordelia? It makes me feel strange."

"Opal!" Helen said sharply. "What kind of thoughts do you have in your head?" She regarded her sister over her glasses.

"I feel sorry for Hugo," Helen went on reprovingly. "He will be going up to the plantation in a few days and then he won't have a chance."

"I hope he stays there!" Opal flung down her scissors.

"Nonsense!" Helen exclaimed. "You get the wildest ideas about people! Sh . . ." She cocked her head and listened. "I hear voices. The girls are in Cordelia's room."

She opened the door a crack and listened some more.

"Sh . . ." said Helen. "Opal, those girls are planning on going down to the river! Imagine! After all Otto has said. He will be furious. I must tell him!"

Suddenly Opal jumped to her feet, and caught her sister's arm. "Oh, no, you won't. I won't let you."

Helen drew back as if she had been struck. "I think you must have lost your mind!"

"Let them go!" Opal said agitatedly. "It's time somebody got out of this dreadful place. It's spring! Look at us! Look at us, sitting here with linens in our hands, the way we do every spring."

"Opal!" Helen was frightened out of her wits. "Be careful what you say! You know we're dependent on Otto for every bite of food, every bit of clothing. It's only because we're Alice's sisters . . ."

"And look at Alice—she's been sick for days with a headache. She always has a headache—if you want to call it that—and you know why? Otto Knapp!" Hysterically Opal snatched the scissors. "Knapp!" she shouted. "I hate all the Knapps." She plunged the scissors deep into the tablecloth and whacked the monogrammed "K" into shreds.

"Sister! What will we do? What will they say?" Helen shrank back against a bureau and wrung her hands.

"I don't care what they say!" Opal snatched up the remains of the cloth and threw it into the fireplace.

Opal watched fiercely while the cloth burned, but the minute it was reduced to ashes, her defiance was gone and she burst into tears.

Immediately Helen rushed to her. "My poor, poor sister!" She led Opal to the wide feather bed and made her lie down.

Opal lay with closed eyes as Helen bathed her forehead with cool water. "I won't tell about the cloth," she reassured her. "Or about the girls going for a ride either," she added magnanimously.

In a little while, Cordelia, Virginia and Yellow Anna were driving along the waterfront. On the levee they saw horses pulling lumbering dray wagons and barrels being rolled by sweating Negroes. Strolling hands and dock workers shouted at them, but the girls paid no attention.

The March breeze carried the pungent odor of hemp and wood, mixed with the indefinable odor of spring on the river. Steamboats kept up a continual blast.

Virginia ordered the driver to halt, and tactfully remained silent while Cordelia watched the river. *The Blue Teal* had such a lovely whistle, thought Cordelia. But she will never whistle again. She is at the bottom of the Missouri.

At this remembrance she closed her eyes, and then she thought of the little islands Pierre had pointed out to her. "Sunken steamboats," he had said. Little by little, currents would send black soil over *The Blue Teal's* hulk. Someday it, too, would be a little island, harboring old logs and growing trees where birds might build their nests.

Somehow it comforted her to think that *The Blue Teal* would never be entirely gone, that it would become a new part of the earth —a small jeweled island in the river. But there were so many things she needed to know, and now there was no one to ask.

Finally Virginia asked, "Would you like to drive on or do you wish to stay a while longer?"

Cordelia roused herself. "Oh, Virginia, I have been selfish, using up the whole time for myself. Drive on, by all means."

Virginia took Cordelia's hands. "Oh, Cordelia! I wish you were happier. If only I could help you a little! Have you had no word at all from Josiah?"

Cordelia shook her head. "But there have been battles fought," she said. "I read about it in the *Republican*. Oh, Virginia, I'm afraid!" And then, in a sudden burst of confidence, "I'm afraid because they are trying to make me marry Hugo. I can't and I won't!"

Virginia turned pale. "Cordelia, you wouldn't! You don't love him!" Then suddenly she burst into tears. "Oh, why is life like this? I would give my soul to marry him . . . and you . . ." She turned fiercely to Cordelia. "Do you swear you do not love him?"

"I swear!" said Cordelia, gazing wide-eyed at the distraught Virginia. "I wish you didn't feel that way. . . . I'm afraid for you, too."

Virginia laughed off-key. "I know what you're thinking. That he's a brute, and I'm soft as butter. But let me tell you something—my butter is all on the surface. I want Hugo and I'm going to get him!"

"How can you do that?" asked Cordelia.

Now Virginia was her old self. She dried her tears and patted the roses on her hat. "If you don't know, I shan't tell you." Excitement was already sparkling in her eyes. "I know a certain way to win!"

"Virginia!" exclaimed Cordelia. "You wouldn't!"

Virginia laughed. "Listen, hon, I'm a New Orleans lady—but when I see a man I want, I aim to get him—and then I can be a lady again. I may need your help," she added soberly. "Let's make a pact. Whichever one of us needs help, the other will come to the rescue."

"I'll be glad to help you, Virginia," Cordelia promised, "but I wish you didn't care so much for Hugo. He's so . . ."

"You're scared of brutes," Virginia laughed. "I'm *not*. I know how to tame them. You'll see, I'll have him eating out of my hand in no time."

Virginia was still laughing when the two girls returned to the Knapp house. Just as they entered the front door Otto Knapp appeared on the balcony.

"Cordelia!" he called down in a harsh voice. "Where have you been?"

"Oh, hello, Uncle Otto," Virginia called out gaily. "I took Cordelia for a drive. It is such a lovely day."

"Where did you go?" he asked.

"Oh, out to the park," Virginia hesitated, "and over to see some friends of mine from New Orleans who are visiting . . ."

"Why are you lying?" he asked. "I saw you girls down by the wharf, like two women of the streets. What have you to say to that?"

"We were only driving, Uncle Otto," said Virginia.

"Come up here, Cordelia! I wish to have a talk with you! As for you," he scowled down at Virginia, "this is *St. Louis,* not New Orleans, and I should think you would have the decency to remember you are a *Knapp.* I can't understand why your father doesn't make you come home, why he lets you run helter-skelter spending large sums of money."

"My father is very liberal," said Virginia sweetly. "You see, Uncle Otto, my father has a new mistress this year, and he is glad to have me out of town.

"Goodbye," she whispered to Cordelia. "And if he gets too cross, stick your fingers in your ears. I always do."

Upstairs, Cordelia faced her angry uncle. "That girl! That girl! talking like that about her father. No respect!" he growled.

"She is only teasing," said Cordelia. "Virginia meant no disrespect."

[118]

"She is a giddy girl, and you're not to go out with her any more. Why," he demanded, "did you disregard my orders?"

"Uncle Otto," Cordelia began patiently, "I went to see the river. Surely there is no harm in that."

Her uncle drummed his fingers on the table. "I'm responsible for you, you know. Your actions reflect on me. You need a home and children. Hugo tells me he is very much in love with you. Why do you not marry him?"

"Because," Cordelia managed to keep her voice even, "I do not love Hugo. I love someone else. I have told you that before. . . ."

"Love—bah!" Otto Knapp made a contemptuous gesture. "That foolish word, invented by foolish people to circumvent the truth!"

"It is not!" she cried hotly. "How can you say such a thing? That there is no love." Then she lost her temper. "You, you of all people, to say that—when everyone *knows* you loved Charlie so much that you were sorry Hugo didn't die in his place. Everybody knows how you loved Charlie . . ."

Cordelia was not prepared for his reaction. Two red spots appeared on Otto Knapp's face, and he trembled all over. "Silence! How dare you? You . . . you! Saying such a thing to me! Go! Go!" He pointed with a trembling hand. "Get out! Get out!" He fell back into his chair and appeared to be choking with rage. His face and neck had turned purple.

Terrified by his sudden outburst, Cordelia fled from the study. But she had not reached her own doorway before she realized she had been deliberately cruel to mention her dead cousin to her uncle. She turned, and with quaking knees, walked back along the balcony. She stopped in the study door. "Uncle Otto," she said in a low voice, "I'm sorry. I shouldn't have. . . ."

For a moment she stood there, not knowing what to do. The great Otto Knapp, his head buried in his hands on the desk, his great shoulders shaking with uncontrollable sobs, was the most disconsolate sight she had ever seen. Long after she had tiptoed from the room, the sound of his weeping rang in her ears.

Later that same night Cordelia stood by her window, watching the moonlight shimmering on the roofs. The window was narrow, and the branch of a tree grew across like a great dark arm flung up to obscure the spring night.

She leaned out and saw that the streets were diffused in a silver mist. Directly under the window she saw a lantern glowing like a gigantic firefly. She heard a woman's laugh, warm and teasing, and a man's gruff, bantering reply. Then the lantern was gone and there was only stillness and the scratch-scratch of tree branches against the house.

She must escape this house! She must! But where could she go? As she stared at the moon, she felt the nightmare she had dreamed last fall was coming true, that Hugo had trapped her and that she could not escape from him. She was imprisoned in this dreadful house. It was closing in around her. The nightmare was real, her moon *had* become an embroidery hoop, soon she would be completely encircled by it. "Oh, Josiah!" she whispered, burying her face in the draperies. "Please let me hear from you soon! Please. . . ."

After she went to bed she slept badly and was awakened a short time later by what she thought was moonlight shining in her eyes. But as she started to turn her head, she realized that there was someone in her room.

She was too frightened to cry out. She tried to lie still, and then, feigning restlessness, took a terrified peek through her eyelashes. A man standing by her bed threw a dark shadow across her covers. A scream rose in her throat, but no sound would come out. A great heaviness came over her, as if the shadow itself were a suffocating weight, crushing the life from her. The man was Hugo.

Desperately she tried to keep her breathing even. There was such a terrible look on his face, a strange mixture of animal passion and bleak loneliness, that it seemed as if her very breathing would stop from fear. It seemed hours that he stood there before he turned and went softly out. She heard his key click in the lock.

Hugo had a key! A key to her room! She felt sick at her stomach. Had he used it before? She shuddered; she knew he would surely use it again.

Early the next morning, before the household was awake, Cordelia dispatched a note by the one servant she trusted, with strict instructions to tell no one where he went, and to bring back the reply to her alone. Within two hours she had the answer. Then she sent for Virginia Knapp.

Virginia was deeply puzzled by the note:

If you care anything at all for me and will keep your promise of yesterday to help me, come to the house at once. Say you are not well and that you wish me to go to the doctor's office with you. Say something, if they question you. I *must* get out of the house today.

Cordelia

Virginia dressed immediately and set out in a hired carriage for the Knapp house.

A maid admitted her into the hallway. What a musty old place, thought Virginia. Now if this were mine, I'd throw out those dreadful chairs. And that sideboard—ugh!

"Is Miss Cordelia in?" she asked in a low voice.

"Upstairs," said the maid, "and you don't need to whisper. Mr. Otto and Mr. Hugo have gone to their offices and the missus is lying down with one of her headaches."

"Thank you," Virginia said, lifting her skirts and running lightly up the stairway to the balcony. She tapped at Cordelia's door. A door down the hall opened and she got a glimpse of Aunt Opal, peering at her, then hastily closing the door.

"Cordelia!" Virginia called as she knocked. "I'm here—it's Virginia!"

Cordelia opened the door and Virginia popped inside.

"Virginia!" cried Cordelia, "I knew you would help me! I knew you would keep your promise."

Virginia saw that Cordelia was already dressed. She was busily stuffing everything she could fit into a large reticule.

"Cordelia!" demanded Virginia, "What *are* you doing? Where are you going? You aren't *leaving*?"

"Forever!" said Cordelia, drawing up the strings of the bag. "And don't ask me where I'm going. Then you won't know when they ask you."

"But when will I see you? And why are you doing this?" Virginia asked, astounded.

Cordelia hesitated. How could she tell Virginia about Hugo being in her room without making it sound ridiculous—or something worse? Virginia was in love with Hugo, and women in love did and thought strange things. "Someday I'll tell you, Virginia," she said at last. "But let's hurry!"

Cautiously the girls opened the door and looked up and down the balcony. "If Uncle Otto should come in you've got to lie as you've never lied before in your life," Cordelia warned Virginia.

The doors were all closed, but just as the girls reached the top of the stairway a door suddenly creaked open. Cordelia turned, startled,

[121]

to see Aunt Opal beckoning to her. She was dismayed, but she knew she would have to see what the old lady wanted.

When she approached Aunt Opal she asked, "Was there something you wanted me to get for you? We are just going for a short drive."

Opal's thin hand clutched Cordelia's arm. "You're running away, aren't you?"

Cordelia's eyes flew open wide. "Oh, please don't tell! Please!"

"I knew it!" The thin old mouth worked. "Here, girl, take this!" Hastily she put two worn bank notes into Cordelia's hand. "Now hurry," she whispered, "and don't ever come back. Ever!" Before the astonished girl could thank her, the old lady shut the door of her room.

"Hurry!" whispered Virginia. "Hurry! I'm good at lyin' but not to Uncle Otto!" The two girls sped down the stairway and out into the front hall, through the vestibule, past the stone lions, and down the steps to jump into the waiting carriage. "Your note sounded so desperate," Virginia said, panting, "that I didn't even bring Yellow Anna."

"I am desperate," said Cordelia. "Drive fast!" she ordered the driver. "I'll tell you where to turn. Please don't ask any questions," she begged Virginia, "it will be easier for you if you don't know."

Cordelia sat forward on the edge of her seat, clasping the reticule tightly in her hands.

How pale she looks, thought Virginia, almost as if she were carved from wax. Virginia was bursting with curiosity, but Cordelia's intense attitude forestalled questions.

"Turn right!" Cordelia spoke to the driver. Virginia saw they were approaching an older part of the city. The houses had mullioned windows, long, low galleries, and many of them were surrounded by high fences. Presently Cordelia ordered the driver to stop in front of a stone and timber house. It was a quaint place with a huge stone chimney. A winding brick path led to the door.

Almost as soon as the carriage came to a stop, it seemed to Virginia that people began popping from the house. First came a little Frenchwoman with apple cheeks. When she saw Cordelia she turned and called. "Janette! Cecily! She is here!" Out sprang two coltish girls with flying brown curls. They ran toward the carriage. "Mimi, Mimi, you poor little pigeon!" they chorused. "Come in at once!"

Cordelia turned to Virginia. "I can never thank you enough. You have proved today to be my dearest friend." She kissed Virginia lightly on the cheek.

"But, Cordelia, when will I see you again?"

"I'll let you know, Virginia. I know where you are, and you must forget where I am."

Cordelia squeezed Virginia's hand, then she alighted from the carriage and started up the walk, the girls and the woman chattering all at once.

Virginia was dumbfounded. Who were these people? Cordelia had not introduced them. They seemed quite friendly. Definitely bourgeois, though, she thought. Then to her further amazement, the door to the house opened again and a little old man in a priest's garb appeared on the doorstep.

"Well!" Virginia said aloud. "Now what do you think of that!"

"I don't know, miss," said the driver. "I'm only a driver—and I don't think about what people do. It's best not to. Where to now, miss?"

"Drive me home," Virginia said slowly. She was worried about Cordelia, but the worry was tempered by the thought that now she would have Hugo to herself. And if one were given opportunities, one should not question them too much. "Yes, home, driver," she said, "and be quick about it!"

As the carriage started up, Virginia looked back and saw the group entering the house. As the great wooden door swung to, Virginia saw it was emblazoned with an enormous beaver head.

The door of the Beaver House closed behind a thankful Cordelia Riley.

BOOK II

MISSOURI WOMAN

PART ONE

16

Upon discovering Cordelia's absence, Otto Knapp began shouting so that his wife locked herself in her room. Finally, Aunt Helen, trembling and self-righteous, crept to the study to tell him that Cordelia had run off with Virginia.

"Virginia!" exploded Otto. "That girl's a disgrace to the name of Knapp!"

"Oh, I don't think Cordelia's still with *her*." Helen smiled coyly, enjoying her brief moment in the center of the stage. "She's gone to the house of that French river pilot, I imagine."

"Pierre de Vries?" Otto rose so suddenly that his chair crashed to the floor. "If you knew this, why did you not send for me?"

Helen drew back, frightened. "I didn't think . . ." she murmured.

"Of course! No one thinks around here!" Otto went to the door of the study and bellowed to a servant scurrying past. "Bring my carriage around. At once!"

Just as Otto was ready to drive off, a young man came riding up on a bay mare. "Wait!" he called to Otto. "A word with you!"

"You here?" exclaimed Otto, recognizing the horseman as Pierre de Vries. "I was just on my way to Beaver House to settle with you."

Pierre dismounted and looked at Otto. "Beaver House has come to you, Monsieur Knapp," he said. "I think we should discuss this matter in private."

Otto looked at the resolute face of Pierre. A river pilot—another Michael Riley. Aloud he said, "Come in then, though what you have to say is of no consequence."

Otto seated himself in his study and left Pierre standing, hoping to wilt the Frenchman's feathers in a hurry. "First off," he said, "I am Cordelia's legal guardian, and if she is with you, you'd better return her here immediately."

"No," said Pierre. "She is miserable in this house. She's come to stay with my mother and sisters until her fiancé comes home."

"A likely story!" exclaimed Otto. "And if she *is* waiting for her fiancé, as you say, he'll never come back. The fool's out there with Doniphan in the desert. The whole lot of them will be carcasses before the month is out."

"But Cordelia doesn't know that," said Pierre. "And if she does receive bad news, we want to comfort her."

"You are a romantic fool!" sneered Otto. "I see through your game. Callahan won't come back. Then she'll turn to you for sympathy. Well, I can tell you right now that no niece of mine will . . ."

Pierre cut in. "You won't relent?"

"Of course not! You're being ridiculous." Otto smiled. This was no Michael Riley. This was only a soft-spoken Frenchman, fired with sentiment.

"You are leaving me no choice," said Pierre, seating himself.

"I do not recall asking you to sit down," said Otto.

"Monsieur Knapp." Pierre leaned forward. "You are forcing me to do something I do not want to do—the sort of thing I never thought I would do. I have tried everything, but you will not listen to me. Now I must break a vow . . . I beg of you, don't force me to do it. Forgive your niece, leave her in peace . . ."

"We have nothing further to discuss," said Otto. "My niece must come home at once!"

Pierre leaned back in his chair. "Very well. Then I must break my vow to prevent a worse thing." Then he went on slowly, measuring his words. "You once had a boat—*The Merry Widow*. It burned on the Mississippi."

"So it did." Otto's eyes had suddenly become still and watchful. His pudgy fingers were still, too.

"There was a steward who served aboard your boat," Pierre plunged doggedly on. "He also served on *The Blue Teal*. He was fond of rum—and talk. . . ." Pierre paused.

"Well, go on." Otto shifted irritably.

"Are you sure you want to hear the rest?" Pierre asked.

"I said go on!" Otto's eyes were like agates.

"You lost your son Charlie in that fire." Pierre paused as Otto

[128]

reached for a spun-sugar confection. Then Pierre continued in a reluctant voice. "This steward told me that your son Charlie's door . . ."

"Yes! Go on!" Otto let the sweet fall on the table.

"Your son's door was locked and barred when the boat burned," Pierre said slowly.

"People on steamboats usually lock doors." Otto's voice was husky.

"But," said Pierre, never taking his eyes from Otto, "Charlie's door was barred from the *outside*. I questioned the steward closely and he told me that Hugo and Charlie had been arguing all day, that there were shouts, threats and bitter words. Later when the boat was burning, he heard Charlie begging Hugo in the name of God to unbolt the door." Pierre hesitated. "The steward said he saw Hugo standing outside Charlie's door. He was laughing. The steward tried to open the door after Hugo left, but the flames were too high. I'm sorry, Monsieur Knapp," Pierre added in a low voice. "But I gave you every chance. You drove me to it."

Otto Knapp remained as motionless as some unfathomable Buddha in his walnut chair. His eyes grew blank and his soul appeared to retreat to some distant place, leaving his body behind like a discarded beetle husk.

When finally Otto did speak, it was in a flat monotone. "What is the price of your silence, Frenchman?"

"That you let Cordelia remain at Beaver House—and turn over all her property, including *The Silver Star*, to the Abbé Choate and myself, to be held in trust for her until she reaches the age of eighteen or marries."

There was another long, frigid silence. Then Otto Knapp bestirred himself, as if awakening from a deep sleep. Slowly he reached into a drawer, removed a sheaf of neatly bound papers and shoved them across the table to Pierre.

"These are the ownership papers for *The Silver Star* and the receipts from the sale of her home," he said.

"These are *all* the papers?" asked Pierre.

"All," Otto replied in the same flat voice. "You do not doubt my word?"

"No," said Pierre, "I do not doubt it."

"Then," Otto had reached the breaking point and his voice grew rough, "you may go. And you may tell Cordelia that I wish never to see her again. She is no longer a part of the Knapp family."

"Do not be vindictive," Pierre begged.

"Goodnight." Otto's voice broke at last. "You know the way out." Pierre left, without looking back.

Slipping quietly in the front door that same night, Hugo Knapp was startled to look up and find his father standing on the balcony, staring down at him.

"It is after three." His father's voice sounded strange.

"I went to a party," said Hugo defensively.

"Come up!" ordered his father in that same peculiar voice. "I wish to talk to you."

Suddenly the warm glow Hugo had felt from wine and a feminine conquest vanished. In its place crept a cold premonition.

Standing before his father in the study, he was acutely aware that his waistcoat was too gaudy. He glanced surreptitiously at his shoulder to see if traces of rice powder or blond hairs might give him away.

When Hugo started to sit down, his father said, "Don't. You haven't time. I have a boat leaving for upstream at seven this morning. You will be on it. It is March and time you were at the plantation."

"I don't want to go up there yet," Hugo protested. "Cordelia . . ."

"Cordelia," said his father harshly, "has gone to live with the de Vries'. She will not return."

"You're joking!" Hugo said, unbelievingly. "She can't do that!"

"She has already done it." His father looked at him coldly. "She says she will remain at Beaver House until that Callahan comes home."

"Then she'll have a long wait," sneered Hugo. "Everybody knows Doniphan's men are outnumbered five to one—and cut off in the desert. She'll be glad enough to be running back when that fool Callahan's dead—and eaten by the wolves."

"Callahan's a fool," said Otto, "but at least he will have *been* something, *died* for something!"

Hugo gaped at his father. "What's come over you? You've said a thousand times the Mexican war was a fool's errand. From the way you talk one would think you wished I were out there, too."

"I wish," Otto's voice was hard and bitter, "I wish you had died of pneumonia—or were buried of cholera at Carmugo. *Mein Gott!* A thousand times better that you were dead in the desert, your bones bleached white, than what you are!"

"Are you mad?" Hugo rose to his feet and stood staring at his father.

"Mad! Why . . ." Otto's voice broke. "Why did you bar Charlie's door when *The Merry Widow* burned? Why, why?"

"How did you know?" Hugo mumbled, caught off-guard.

"Why, why did you do that to Charlie?" Otto's voice was anguished.

"Charlie!" Hugo said venomously, recovering from his shock. "He's all you ever thought about! Well, how about me? *Me!*" He saw his father crumbling before his eyes. "I'm a Knapp, too, and I'll never let you drag our name in the mud. Besides, you can't prove anything."

"*Mein Gott!* Not even the decency to deny it!" Otto cried in a thick voice. "Get out! Get out!"

"I'll leave, gladly," said Hugo, speaking boldly now that his father was breaking, "but someday I'll be back—and then we'll see who sits in the driver's seat!"

In reply Otto hurled the heavy Rodalstalt plate, laden with sweets, at Hugo. It struck the doorsill and lay shattered on the floor. Hugo strode away without looking back.

"Swine!" Otto shouted after his son. Exhausted, he turned slowly to the fire to warm himself, but it had gone out. "Hugo," he muttered, weeping, "how *could* you have done it?"

17

IT WAS MAY NOW and Cordelia and Madam de Vries were walking in the garden. Cordelia was admiring the tiny fleur-de-lis that made a blue carpet of the moist earth. "Here are some seeds for you," Madam de Vries said. "Give them away and keep some yourself for good luck. The blue lily will bring people a bit of home wherever they are."

"I love lilies," said Cordelia. "I'm going to plant them around the house Josiah is going to build us, just as you have done here at Beaver House."

"I hope you will have your house soon," Madam de Vries said slowly.

Looking up, Cordelia caught a look of pity in the little Frenchwoman's eyes. "Oh, I will!" she said. "Josiah promised."

"My dear, there are other things in life besides a house by the river, and you must remember that men cannot always keep such promises." Madam de Vries touched Cordelia's shining hair.

Cordelia almost dropped her seeds. "I'm afraid," she said. "I can't understand why I haven't heard from him."

From the street came the sound of shouts and running feet. Going to the fence they saw a motley crowd rushing past singing, "Old Zach's at Monterey . . . Bring out your Santa Anner . . . Every time we raise a gun . . . down goes a Mexicanner."

Pierre, home from a river trip, came out to see what had happened, and, at the women's insistence, shouldered his way into the crowd to learn the cause of the celebration.

Presently he returned, bringing the Abbé Choate with him. "Such a business," said the Abbé, straightening his frock. "Victory may well be worse than the war."

"Victory?" Cordelia gasped.

"Yes, yes," said the priest, puffing and fanning himself. "Victory for our Missourians. Doniphan, with only 800 half-clad, half-starving Missourians has defeated the enemy—4,000 strong. A military victory, but a crime against a devout people."

"An incredible feat!" said Pierre.

The priest shook his head. "We have captured a nine-pound cannon, cast from church bells."

"A cannon from church bells!" Madam de Vries crossed herself.

"Never has this country fought so unpopular a war," the priest went on, "yet listen to them shrieking. They break into my church to ring the church bells."

"It is for the sons and sweethearts that they are grateful, Father," said Pierre gently. "One cannot forget that a handful of men have won a battle."

"Perhaps," said the priest wearily, "but one can well lose the world in such a war."

Pierre looked at Cordelia who still remained silent, her face rapt. "One can lose the world in many ways, Father," he said. "War is only one of them."

Words like "hungry," "ragged" and "diseased" flowed around Cordelia but made no impression on her. In her mind's eyes she saw Josiah dressed in his blue uniform, riding up the hill, firing his pistols. The Abbé said he was one of those who had charged ahead and drawn the enemy's fire. Josiah Callahan was a hero, and now that the battle was won, surely he would come home to her.

Less than a week later Cordelia was startled by the sudden appearance at Beaver House of Aunt Opal. The little old lady stood on the doorstep, looking like a small black bug in her somber dress and beaded shawl. Two red spots of excitement burned in her face as she thrust a dirty packet toward Cordelia. "I intercepted it," she said in a shrill voice. "I think it's from your soldier!"

"From Josiah! Oh, give it to me quickly!" She snatched the parcel from her aunt. "Come inside."

With trembling hands Cordelia unwrapped and tore open the soiled letter. "My beloved Cordelia," she read. "It *is* from him!" she shouted joyfully. "It *is!*"

Slowly, lovingly, so as not to miss a word, Cordelia read the letter through. She was beginning to read it for the third time when she saw Aunt Opal sitting on the edge of her chair like a tired sparrow waiting for a crumb.

"It was written the day after the battle at Sacramento," she told her aunt. "He wrote before, but . . . but the courier was found dead. This was his first chance to . . ."

"He's not hurt?" Aunt Opal leaned forward.

Cordelia bit her lip. "He was wounded at Brazito, but he says his life was saved by a gallant person."

"Is it true that there is nothing but flowers and dancing in the streets there?" her aunt asked, avid with curiosity.

"Josiah speaks of moonlight on the chaparral," Cordelia said shyly.

"And what of love?" Aunt Opal held her breath.

"He loves me very much and he will be home in a month or two!" Cordelia said in a delirious rush.

Aunt Opal burst into tears. "Oh, I could not have borne it if he were not still in love with you!"

"Why, Aunt Opal, don't cry!" Cordelia flew to comfort the old woman.

The minute her aunt left, Cordelia took a carriage and set out to see Virginia. She couldn't wait to share her wonderful news.

Her cousin was a long time answering the door and when she did appear Cordelia was surprised to find her disheveled and wearing a loose wrapper. Everywhere there were evidences of packing. Listlessly, Virginia bade her be seated.

"Virginia! Are you leaving? Why didn't you tell me?" Cordelia exclaimed.

Virginia folded a petticoat so that the ruffles were inside. "I've been meaning to tell you," she said, avoiding Cordelia's eyes. "I'm going up to the Knapp plantation tomorrow. Hugo and I are being married."

"Married!" Cordelia asked, astounded. She threw her arms about Virginia. "And you didn't tell me!" A sudden fear for Virginia swept over her.

"I didn't tell you because," Virginia said calmly, "Hugo himself doesn't know it yet."

"Oh, Virginia!" said Cordelia. "Look at me!"

Virginia raised her blue eyes to Cordelia. "I've just found out I'm going to have a baby in October."

"Oh, Virginia," she shook her cousin a little, "you can't go up there and beg Hugo to marry you! What if he won't? Oh, if only I had told you . . ." She stopped.

Virginia shook her off. "Please don't worry, Cordelia. Hugo will have to marry me. I told Uncle Otto, and he is going with me."

"It must have been terrible telling Uncle Otto!" Cordelia said.

"Yes. He shouted, of course," Virginia rammed some hat-pins into a velvet cushion, "but the family comes first. By the time I left, he told me that if the baby is a boy, he'll send him to school in Emmerich." Virginia gave a short laugh.

In her concern for Virginia, all thoughts of Josiah fled from Cordelia's mind. "Are you *sure* you love him, Virginia? Because if you don't, no matter what, you shouldn't marry him!"

Virginia drew away from Cordelia's comforting embrace and stood looking out the window. "I only know I can't live without him," she said. "It's like being thirsty and wanting water or . . ." Then, seeing the tears in Cordelia's eyes, she added, "Don't feel sorry for me, Cordelia. I can make him love me. I know I can. . . ."

Cordelia was so upset over Virginia's news and her cousin's white, drawn face that she did not tell her about Josiah's expected return.

But when she started home she took out his letter and pressed it to her cheek. It was covered with brown stains. She must ask him about that, and about the gallant person who had saved his life.

18

ALL THROUGH the sticky summer months, steamers from New Orleans brought home discharged soldiers. The city of St. Louis was beside itself. Orations were made from flag-draped balconies, bonfires burned in the streets and church bells clanged.

Early one July morning Janette burst into Cordelia's room shouting, "They're coming! Our own men are coming in on *The Harpy!* They say they have the cannon and the black flag with them!"

Cordelia leaped from bed and in less than a half-hour she, Madam de Vries and the two girls were ready to leave for the docks.

Just as they were entering the carriage they were joined by the Abbé, who came out of the parish house to wish them well.

"Come with us, Father," begged Madam. "Yesterday a bully tried to snatch Cordelia."

"Small wonder," the priest smiled, "the way she looks these days. Very well, I should like to go with you." Then he added, "Though I fear I'm so old only my cloth is protection from bullies."

On the way to the dock he spoke seriously to Cordelia. "This is a great day for you, child, but do not expect too much of your soldier. It has been a bad war," he shook his head, "a very bad war."

By the time they reached the docks, Cordelia saw, to her great excitement, that *The Harpy* was already putting in to shore. A cry went up from the crowded levee and it was answered by the gaunt, ragged men on the decks of the steamer.

"They can't be soldiers, can they? Where are their uniforms?" Cordelia asked bewilderedly.

"Rags in the desert," said the Abbé. "They were without pay the whole time they were gone, remember. Perhaps they did not bother to get uniforms in New Orleans."

"But they look so . . . so strange," faltered Cordelia, watching the emaciated men with flowing beards emerge from the lower deck.

"They are some of the worst and some of the best," said the priest, "but they have shared a terrible experience which will make a bond. Remember that, Cordelia."

But Cordelia did not listen. Men leading horses emerged from the boat and formed a line on the dock. "There he is!" She jumped up and screamed, "Josiah, Josiah!"

Madam de Vries pulled her down, but Cordelia was wild with excitement. "I would know him anywhere!" She caught her breath. "But he is so thin and he is limping! Look at that beard! I must go to him!"

"No, no." Madam held on to her. "You could not reach him in this crowd. He must come to you."

"But I can get through!" cried Cordelia. "I know I can!"

A brass band began to blare. The honorary fire companies formed a line to keep the friends and relatives back. A parade was planned and the politicians waited at Planter House to make speeches.

Wives and sweethearts cried as they were swept back. The St. Louis Grays rode about on prancing horses. The Jaegers and Dragoons formed an escort.

"I want to see Josiah," cried Cordelia brokenheartedly.

"Oh, look, look!" Cecily was pointing excitedly. "There are women on the boat, too!"

Cordelia tore her eyes from Josiah's face long enough to see a heterogeneous mixture of humanity straggling from the steamer. Women in bedraggled finery were followed by a theatrical troupe in harlequin clothes, carrying a banner that read, "The Lady and the Devil." As they came onto the docks the theatrical troupe beat on a drum and the women stepped ashore, tossing the feathers on their hats and lifting their skirts to show the tops of their boots. They were greeted by a roar from the sailors and deck hands.

"Mother, who are those women?" asked Cecily.

"Don't be such a goose," said Janette. "They're camp followers."

"Camp followers?" Cordelia looked questioningly at Madam de Vries. "You don't mean those strumpets went to war?"

"Hush, child," said the Abbé. "Such is the way of nature. In times of war it has always been thus."

Cordelia cast anxious eyes at Josiah's dark face and saw that he was mounted on a big chestnut horse, waiting for the parade to begin. A group of the camp women were picking their way over the docks past the soldiers. The men kept their eyes straight ahead, not daring to show an interest in front of their families. But one girl stopped. Cordelia drew in her breath sharply. The girl was speaking to Josiah!

They talked a few minutes and then the girl walked on, looking back at him over her shoulder.

"Madam de Vries!" cried Cordelia. "Did you see that woman talking to Josiah?"

"It is nothing, child," said the Frenchwoman. "Such women are always bold."

"But, did you see that woman's *hair?*" Cordelia's hand closed tightly about the older woman's wrist.

"It is very red," said Madam de Vries nervously.

"Beautiful hair," sighed Cecily. "Like red gold."

"Oh, silly!" said Janette. "She probably looks like a mud turtle close up."

White and stricken, Cordelia watched the woman who had spoken to Josiah. She could not be mistaken. The camp follower was Red Maude.

"Cordelia, are you ill, child?" asked the priest.

"No," said Cordelia faintly. "No, I don't think so."

The Liberty Fire Company band struck up "Yankee Doodle," and the Franklin Fire Company struck up "The Girl I Left Behind Me." The parade was on. Tall, gaunt Missourians, turned savage from dragging heavy artillery and wagons across mountains, bitter from lack of pay, with no medicine for wounds and nightly burial of friends, marched and rode proudly, a humorous twist to their lips at the irony of the gala reception.

As Josiah passed Cordelia's carriage, she called and waved frantically, but her cries were snuffed out in the din. "Follow them! Oh, please!" she begged.

"Very well," said the Abbé. "To Planter House. It's the first stop."

"Hurry!" urged Cordelia.

Madam de Vries, who was busily wrapping a handkerchief around her wrist where Cordelia's nails had dug in, caught the Abbé watching her and knew that he, too, had observed Cordelia's reaction to the camp follower.

Cordelia fared no better at Planter House. Although she jumped from the carriage and tried to fight her way toward Josiah, she lost her bonnet, tore her dress and was pushed back.

"Come, child," said the Abbé, "you are overwrought. He will find you by tomorrow at least."

[137]

"Tomorrow?" wailed Cordelia. "That's a hundred years from now!"

Back at Beaver House, Madam de Vries made Cordelia lie down and put a cloth on her feverish head. But Cordelia could not rest. That *was* Red Maude. She knew it. Red Maude had gone to war, had come home on the same boat with Josiah. He'd even laughed when she spoke to him. Cordelia got out of bed, dressed and stole from the house. Swearing the de Vries coachman to secrecy, she ordered him to drive her to Planter House.

She hesitated when she saw soldiers swarming at the entrance to the hotel. Indians squatted against the building, and slaves stood holding horses for their masters. Nowhere was there an unescorted woman. But Cordelia swept up the steps to Planter House, with her head held high. Men stared, but Cordelia tipped her parasol so that it nearly hid her face.

Inside, the high-ceilinged lobby was jammed with men. An Indian wrapped in a blanket stared at her unwinkingly and a planter in a big hat looked at her calculatingly. She went directly to the desk.

"Have you . . . have you a Mr. Josiah Callahan registered here?" Her voice sounded quavery even to herself.

"Captain Callahan?" The clerk chuckled. "Right over there in the corner."

Cordelia followed the clerk's gesture. It was Josiah! What would she say, now she was here? Would he think her a hussy for coming to the hotel? She walked toward them, but she could not get inside the ring of men.

"I tell you," said a wizened little Irishman, "we fit for nothin', if that territory comes in free."

"Wal," a lanky man spit tobacco in all directions, "dad blame it, us that fit fer the land aims to have plenty to say about that."

Desperately, Cordelia tried to catch Josiah's eye, but he had straddled a chair and was puffing on a cigar. He looked quite masculine and alien.

"This difference of opinion is going to split this country wide-open someday, mark my words," he said firmly.

"Do you figure Californy is a gone goslin'?" asked the tobacco chewer.

"Not if I can help it," said Josiah. "I may go out there myself and take a hand in politics."

"Josiah!" Cordelia cried out, forgetting everything. Her parasol hit the floor. "You *can't* go to California! You've just come home!"

The men parted as if struck by lightning, and Cordelia stood

[138]

trembling and flushing under Josiah's gaze. He had jumped up and was staring at her as if she were an apparition.

"Cordelia!" he exclaimed, his eyes an intense blue. "Cordelia!" Now he was walking toward her, and she toward him, like two lodestars. Her knees gave way and she would have fallen had he not caught her in his arms.

Three hours later in a shady place by the river, Cordelia's head stirred sleepily on Josiah's shoulder. They had had so much to tell each other. He had not known of her parents' death, and when he had called at her uncle's, he had been refused any information. But now for the past half-hour they had been silent, lost in loving contentment.

"I suppose I must get back," Cordelia said. "I slipped out of the house. The de Vries' will be worried."

Josiah traced her eyebrow with his finger. "I'll always be grateful to them for taking care of you. I'm surprised you haven't fallen in love with that handsome Pierre," he teased.

Cordelia hid her face happily. "He's away on my boat, *The Silver Star*. He will always be its pilot."

"You have a boat?" Josiah laughed.

"It was my father's boat," she said. "Josiah, you don't mind?"

"Of course not! When I describe my wife I shall say that she has hair like smoke, lips like velvet—and that she owns a steamboat!"

"Silly." Cordelia snuggled down against Josiah and traced the thin white scar on his face. "We're going to be happy in our house by the river, aren't we?"

"Hmm? Hmm? House, what house?" Josiah asked.

"Why, Josiah, you remember," she said. "The one you promised me when we were on *The Blue Teal*."

"Oh," he said. "Of course. We'll have a house someday but I have a lot of things to settle first."

"Let's build it as soon as we can." Cordelia settled down with a sigh. "Kiss me again, Josiah. I used to dream how it would be—but this is better."

The locust and elm leaves almost hid them; a robin flew close to investigate the intruders, then flew away. The summer afternoon was a slender thread on a bobbin and now it was almost spun away. Cordelia sat up and brushed her hair from her face. "Josiah," she asked, "who was that woman I saw you talking to on the docks? The one with red hair?"

Josiah was silent a moment. "Just a woman I know," he said.

"But she looked like a camp follower," persisted Cordelia.

"She was," Josiah said casually.

"But why did you talk to her?" Cordelia demanded. "Why would you be talking to a woman like that?"

"Because," he said reluctantly, "she was the person who saved my life. She came along in her wagon and saw me in the sand, left for dead. She kept me from bleeding to death and nursed me afterwards."

Josiah shrugged. "She might not have been so apt to stop had she not recognized me. She was aboard *The Blue Teal*. You may have seen her on your trip. They call her Red Maude. And now, we'd better go," he said, "or your friends will have the police looking for you."

"Josiah!" Cordelia flung herself against his chest. "Promise me! Promise me you will never speak to Red Maude again as long as you live!"

"Cordelia!" Josiah held her away from him. "I can't promise anything of the kind. The woman saved my life, don't you understand?"

Cordelia was shaking so hard her teeth chattered. "I don't care. You must promise. You must! If ever you should . . ." She began to cry.

"Here, here." Josiah took out his handkerchief and wiped her eyes. "You're overwrought and you are barely seventeen. I'm thoughtless, keeping you out here so long!" He smoothed Cordelia's hair and she began to relax. "You didn't want her to leave me to die, did you?" he teased her.

"I'm sorry. I'm such a silly goose," Cordelia said contritely, rubbing her nose on his shoulder. Never could she tell anyone, not even Josiah, why she hated Red Maude so, or why the very mention of that hateful name filled her with nausea.

Later, when she entered Beaver House, dreamy-eyed and disheveled, the de Vries' turned anxious faces toward her.

"Where have you been?" they demanded.

"With Josiah," she breathed. "We're to be married in September."

"Cordelia Riley! You have frightened us to death!" Madam de Vries began scolding her in pepper-pot French.

"Oh, Mamma," said Cecily, "don't forget you fell from a window waving to Papa."

The little Frenchwoman flushed, then smiled and held out her arms. Cordelia ran into them.

19

IN THE DAYS that followed Cordelia moved through the preparations for her wedding in a trance. Several times Josiah took her to dinner at the Planter House, but she was too excited to know what she was eating. Sometimes he invited other people to dine with them, but as they usually talked politics Cordelia found herself not listening but studying Josiah's face, his mouth and broad shoulders. Sometimes she was sure everyone could see her pulse beating eagerly. About the middle of August, Josiah decided to make a quick trip to Louisiana to attend to his father's estate. He would return only a few days before the wedding.

One hot steamy day Cordelia, who was too excited to know whether she was wearing silk or linsey-woolsey, was trying on her wedding dress. "If you do not stand still," said Madam de Vries, half-scolding, "we shall all go mad." Relentlessly she pulled on Cordelia's corset-strings. "Make the waist seventeen inches," she told the dressmaker.

Cordelia protested that her waist was really eighteen inches but held her breath obediently while the dressmaker measured. Cecily came running into the bedroom, her eyes wide. "There's someone in the parlor to see you, Cordelia. It's your cousin Hugo Knapp!"

"Hugo?" exclaimed Cordelia. "Why should he want to come to see me?" Then she thought that perhaps something had happened to Virginia, so she hurried into the parlor, where she found Hugo, dressed in a light suit, wiping the perspiration from his forehead. He did not look worried. In fact, she had never seen him look more pleasant.

"Cordelia!" he said, rising and taking both her hands. "It's been a long time."

"Yes, Hugo," she said stiffly, "it has been. I'm surprised to see you in the city in this hot weather. I should think you'd stay on the plantation."

"Aren't you a little glad to see me?" he asked. "After all, I'm not only your cousin, but Virginia's husband, you know."

Cordelia caught the old mocking light in his eyes. "Yes, I know," she said. Then, looking him squarely in the eye, she continued, "And you'd better make her happy."

"Don't be antagonistic, Cordelia. Let bygones be bygones. I made a special trip to the city entirely in your interest. Something that concerns you very much. I have something to show you."

"Show me?" she asked suspiciously.

"Cordelia," he said, smiling, "won't you believe any good of me at all? Here," he drew out some papers and handed them to her, "read these." His face was stern. "You'll see I have made this trip only because I'm interested in your welfare."

Cordelia glanced at the papers. "Well, as far as I can tell, Hugo, they are only bills of lading from one of your boats."

"I know," he said. "Read them."

Cordelia ran a practiced eye over them and read: "Marble for eight fireplaces; 300 feet of the finest walnut paneling."

Hugo unbuttoned his waistcoat. "I think you'll be interested in how they are made out. *I* was!"

Cordelia glanced again at the papers. Her eyes widened. "They're made out to . . . Josiah Callahan!" Then, recovering herself, she said, "What of it? Why shouldn't he buy marble and lumber?"

Hugo's eyes narrowed. "You're determined to go ahead and marry that adventurer you know nothing about, aren't you? Well, it's time you found out about him. Just where do you think that material is going, Cordelia?"

"Why . . ." Then a thought crossed her mind and she smiled. "He promised me a house by the river and I think he has already started it—to surprise me."

Hugo gave a short laugh. "He has surprised you all right. I can tell you where that material is going because I took the trouble to find out. He's building a house for another woman!"

"I don't believe you!" Cordelia cried. But a sudden fear stabbed her. "You're making it up. All your life you've spoiled everything that was beautiful. You're saying it just to spite me."

"Have it your way." Hugo shrugged. "But everybody in St. Louis knows he's building a place up near St. Joe for a common camp follower called Red Maude!"

Cordelia sagged against the chair. She felt as if all the breath had been squeezed from her body.

[142]

"Evidently," said Hugo, "he's more anxious to get a whorehouse started than his marriage. Naturally, I couldn't let you go and marry a fellow like that."

"Go away!" said Cordelia. "Please go away. If you don't, I think I might kill you."

"I see you still have your temper," said Hugo. He rose and caught her wrist. "If you don't believe me, just ask your cavalier about the 'lady' he brought back with him. Ask him!"

The following week Cordelia lost nearly ten pounds and there were shadows under her eyes. The de Vries' attributed it to excitement and loneliness for Josiah.

The morning Josiah was to return from Louisiana, she told no one where she was going, but slipped from the house and went to meet him in a carriage alone.

When she saw him coming toward her, all her doubts and fears crumbled, and when she felt his arms around her and his eyes looking into hers she knew Hugo had lied. But she had to be sure.

"Meeting me alone?" Josiah raised quizzical eyebrows. "Aren't you afraid of being gossiped about?"

Cordelia swallowed hard. "I met you alone because I want to talk to you," she said. "There's something important I have to ask you."

"Well, ask away and don't be so solemn." His eyes twinkled. "Did you miss me?"

"Oh, terribly!" She twisted her hands together.

"Then I'll drive us to a secluded spot so you can tell me how much," he said, putting his hand over hers.

Josiah stopped the carriage in a shady lane and drew Cordelia toward him. His mouth was hard and eager against hers. "I've been gone too long," he said. "Only four days more and you'll be my wife. There'll be no more kissing in a carriage, but *holding* you close the way I should." Then sensing her lack of response, he put her from him. "Cordelia!" he said. "Something has happened. What is it?"

"Josiah," she burst out, "that woman who saved your life when you were left for dead, are you sure she doesn't mean anything to you?"

"Oh, Cordelia!" Josiah looked relieved. "Of course she doesn't!"

"Then why," she burst out agitatedly, "why are you building her a house up by St. Joseph?"

Josiah's face sobered. He did not answer for a long time. At last he asked, "Who told you that?"

"My cousin Hugo," said Cordelia. "He saw the bills of lading. Oh, Josiah, tell me it isn't true. I know it isn't, but tell me."

A muscle twitched in Josiah's face. "So I have your cousin Hugo to thank," he said. "Yes, Cordelia, I am building Red Maude a house."

"But you can't! You couldn't do that to me!" she cried.

"I told you," he began patiently, as if describing something to a child, "that I had been left to die. In a short while I would have died had she not come along, recognized me, gotten out of her wagon and taken care of me. Even the army surgeon said it was a miracle that I recovered. I asked what I could give her in repayment—what she wanted most. She said she wanted security, a fine house of her own. I promised to build it the moment I got back."

"She'll use it for a whorehouse!" Cordelia lashed out. "Oh, Josiah, she took advantage of you!"

"Perhaps." His mouth was firm. "But you can't blame her. She's lived like an alley cat, taking scraps from life. Women like Red Maude have to take what they can get any way they can get it."

"You can't do it! You can't build that woman a house! Oh, Josiah!" Cordelia burst into tears.

Josiah put his arm around her. "Cordelia, I'm sorry you found it out like that. I wanted to tell you, but you have such a terrible aversion to strumpets, as you call them. It's nothing for you to bother your head about."

Cordelia burrowed her head in his shoulder. "Oh, Josiah," she said, "I knew you wouldn't build that awful woman a house when I asked you not to."

"I didn't say that," said Josiah patiently. "I said it was nothing to either of us. Only fulfilling a promise to . . ."

Cordelia jerked away from him as if he had slapped her. "You don't mean you're going ahead with it? I won't let you!"

"Cordelia!" said Josiah with annoyance. "You aren't very old, but surely you know by now that there are some things in life you have to do whether they are expedient or not. That when you make a promise like that—as a gentleman—"

"But not Red Maude!" she cried wildly. "You don't bargain with women like her. I hate her! Josiah Callahan, either you stop building that woman a house or I won't marry you—ever!"

"You're talking childishly, Cordelia, and you know you don't mean that. I've already started the house and that's all there is to it. Come, sweet," he took her hands, "here we are quarreling. The house will make no difference to us, one way or the other . . . don't you see?"

[144]

Cordelia withdrew her hands and sat with her back stiff and straight. "But it does make a difference," she said. "Either you stop building that woman a house or you'll never build a house for me."

"You're being ridiculous, Cordelia. You know I can't do any such thing," said Josiah angrily.

"Maybe she did more than save your life," Cordelia said. "Maybe she . . ."

"Cordelia . . ." he began wearily.

"Josiah, I told you," she said. "I told you when I promised to marry you, that the one thing I would not have was a husband who was interested in other women."

"Good God!" shouted Josiah. "I'm not interested in her, and you know it!"

"Then will you stop building her that house?" demanded Cordelia. Her chest was hurting terribly, but she must make him see.

"No." Josiah's face was pale beneath its tan. "I won't."

"Then," Cordelia caught her breath, "our engagement is broken. I won't marry you—ever."

"Cordelia!" He caught her to him and shook her. "You know you love me. From the very moment we saw each other we have belonged together, and you know it!"

Cordelia's eyes were enormous. "I didn't say I didn't love you." Her voice broke. "I may never stop. But unless you do what I ask, I'll never see you again."

When Cordelia returned to Beaver House, Madam de Vries, Janette, Cecily and Pierre got to their feet at the sight of her.

"Mimi!" cried Pierre. "What has happened?"

"The dressmaker is waiting for you to try on your wedding dress, child. Where have you been?" asked Madam de Vries.

"I won't need the dress," Cordelia said in a flat, tired voice.

"Mimi!" Pierre crossed to her. "Do you know what you're saying?"

"You can burn the dress," said Cordelia. "Because I will never marry Josiah Callahan as long as I live." She went into her room and closed the door.

"She has wedding nerves," said Madam de Vries. "I will go talk to her."

"No, Mother," said Pierre. "I think I'd better do it."

"Cordelia," Pierre opened the door gently, "I mean to get to the bottom of this. What has Josiah done to hurt you?"

Cordelia raised anguished eyes and looked at him. "The one thing you know I would never forgive."

"Now, Cordelia," reasoned Pierre. "It is true that Callahan is not a pipe-and-fireside man, but neither is he the kind of man to amuse himself with a pretty face. I would say he was as near a one-woman man as a man can be."

"You won't think that, when I tell you that he is building a house for a camp follower," she said.

"For the one who saved his life, yes," said Pierre. "I was hoping you wouldn't find out. But then that's too much to expect when all St. Louis is buzzing with the story."

Cordelia whirled on him. "You knew!" she blazed. "All the time you knew it was Red Maude, and you didn't tell me!"

"I know why you feel as you do about the woman," said Pierre. "I didn't want to hurt you. But in time you'll see you're being unreasonable. I thought you weren't going to hate her any more."

"But I do!" Cordelia cried. "And why are you staring at me like that?" she demanded.

"I was only thinking, Mimi," said Pierre slowly, "that your resemblance to your mother is startling."

20

DESPITE PIERRE'S continued reasoning, Cordelia remained adamant, moving pale and silent through Beaver House. Then one afternoon in September, long after the wedding date had passed, Cordelia dressed in her best silk dress, drew her curls severely back under a velvet bonnet and set out on a secret errand.

Her carriage moved through streets she had never seen before to a section of the city built on a grand scale by early merchants, and now deserted for more fashionable neighborhoods. She stopped in front of a big two-story house, conspicuous because of its twinkling glass door. She was trembling, but she marched up the steps and rang the doorbell. She heard it reverberating throughout the house.

She was peering through the outer glass door into a tiled vestibule and through an inner glass door into a large hall, when suddenly the door was jerked open by an enormous Negro who stared coldly at her from his great height. "You got the wrong house, girl," he said as he shut the door hastily.

Determinedly, Cordelia rang the bell again. This time, as soon as the Negro opened the door, she said, "I want to see Red Maude on a matter of the utmost importance."

"Red who?" asked the Negro. Then a grin broke over his face. "Oh, you mean Miss Maude Renfrew." He looked at Cordelia's severe dress and her pale oval face. "White girl, are you sure you want this job? Are you sure you got the right place?"

"I'm sure," said Cordelia, walking past him into the hall. "Call her, please." Evidently the Negro thought she was applying for a job as a . . . ! She sat down on a pink velvet chair because her knees wouldn't hold her up any longer.

While waiting, she looked about at the richly appointed room. Pale draperies and thick rugs made it look like anyone's well-furnished parlor.

She started at the sound of footsteps scurrying overhead. There was a low murmur of voices and a man's laugh rang out. Cordelia shrank back in her chair, clutching the arms tightly.

Someone was descending the stairway. She finally raised her eyes to find Red Maude staring at her. Red Maude wore a light blue dress with a low-cut bodice, and her fabulous hair was caught in a blue silk net. As Cordelia stared back she thought, she has wrinkles at the corners of her eyes, but she is beautiful . . . the most beautiful woman I have ever seen.

Red Maude's black lashes lowered slightly, but if she recognized Cordelia she gave no sign. "Did you wish to see me?" she asked in her husky voice. "Do be seated. Oh, but you are already seated, aren't you, dear?" she went on, making Cordelia feel more childish and awkward by the minute. Red Maude tipped her head slightly. "Have we met before?"

Cordelia's composure deserted her. "I'm Cordelia Riley, and you know very well we've met before!"

There was a long moment while Red Maude studied her. "Oh, yes," she said. "I believe you were the little girl on *The Blue Teal*, the one who had never seen a game of solitaire. As I recall, you wandered away in the woods and got lost. I have a feeling," she raised one rounded shoulder, "that you're lost again."

"Miss Renfrew," Cordelia said angrily, "I didn't come here to be made fun of. I came to ask a favor of you. I am—I was engaged to marry Josiah Callahan."

"Josiah?" The black lashes lifted and the tawny eyes grew amused. "Wonders never cease, do they? Isn't it a small world?"

"Miss Renfrew," Cordelia plunged on desperately, "I'm grateful to you and always will be for saving his life. But I beg you to release him from his offer to build you a house. He was sick when he promised you. Why wouldn't quite a lot of money do instead?"

Red Maude played with a fan dangling from her wrist. "I take it that you don't like the idea of your Josiah building me a house. Is that why you came to see me?"

"Yes! It's ridiculous!" said Cordelia sharply. "Besides, I know very well what you're going to do with it!"

"Do you now?" asked Red Maude insolently. "I wouldn't have thought you'd know. However, for your information I intend to have the best house on the Missouri River."

"You're being cruel and unreasonable, holding Josiah to such a promise!" cried Cordelia.

"He has not asked to be released," said Red Maude amusedly. Then she added softly, "And he never will."

"Of course not, he's a gentleman!" Cordelia was furious. "That's why I came to ask you to take money instead."

"How brave of you!" Red Maude's lip curled. "The noble little virgin. I wager he doesn't know you're here."

"What kind of woman are you?" demanded Cordelia. "Have you no heart at all? No decency?"

Red Maude stood up then and her hair tumbled from its net. "I'll tell you what kind of a woman I am," she said fiercely. "I'm a woman who's been kicked around. But nobody is going to kick me any more. Of course I won't give up that house! It's going to have all the mirrors the walls will hold, and plenty of fireplaces to warm all those who are not in bed. And I'll tell you why. It's so that when I'm old I can sit by the fire and laugh. They'll never look down Battle Row and say, 'There goes Red Maude, the poor worn-out bitch!'"

"Oh!" Cordelia jumped to her feet. "You're even worse than I thought!" Her bonnet fell off and she picked it up and clapped it on her head. She ran out the door with Red Maude's throaty, contemptuous laugh ringing in her ears.

Years later she still could remember how it sounded.

PART TWO

21

IN THE SPRING of 1849 St. Louis became a beehive of activity, teeming with people who had caught the gold-rush fever. It was from St. Louis that the wagon trains and dreams were launched. Every town and hamlet along the Missouri River resembled an up-turned ant-hill alive with human beings, scurrying about trying to find someone to haul their possessions. And the first to feel the pressure was the Missouri River steamboat trade.

In February, Pierre de Vries had broken the ice with *The Silver Star* to take westward-bound men, women and children up the Missouri to St. Joe and Leavenworth, where they camped, thousands strong, waiting for the grass to grow green on the prairies.

Now he was returning home. Home to Beaver House. As he stared out at the eddies and boils of the Missouri, watching with narrowed eyes a whipping sawyer, his heart lifted because he was homeward-bound. He thought of Cordelia, who had been his wife for more than a year now, and of their small daughter Marguerite, a baby of only three months. Was ever a man so fortunate?

His mind went back to the summer and the dark fall when Cordelia had moved silently, heartbroken and unyielding through the house, all the brilliance gone from her smile—and Josiah Callahan had gone to Jefferson City to establish his law practice.

Pierre knew he had asked her to marry him too soon after her broken engagement, but she was estranged from the remote family left to her and seemed so alone. Besides, he loved her so much he could no longer keep silent.

She had been very honest. Even now he could remember her grave eyes and serious voice when she had replied, "Of course I will marry you, Pierre, if you wish. But you know it is only a great tenderness and closeness I feel for you. . . ."

"You must have someone to look after you, Mimi," he said. "You will learn to love me. I shall teach you."

"It's not fair to you," she had said. "I'm not sure I can love anyone —now. But I will try."

Cordelia had held back nothing, he thought. She had tried. Sometimes too much to be natural, it seemed. But her young body was so sweet to him that he put aside whatever doubts entered his mind.

He was the one who was alarmed when she became pregnant so soon. But Cordelia was gay. "Oh, poof!" she had said. "I'm no longer a child with notions about babies." She had thrown herself wholeheartedly into preparing for the child, even to doing all kinds of fancywork which he knew she detested. She seemed so intent on keeping busy that again he wondered if she would ever be really happy.

They never discussed Josiah Callahan after their marriage, and only twice had the subject come up. Once, when Josiah had made a speech on the floor of the Missouri Legislature, Pierre saw Cordelia reading the account. The other time was too painful to remember, even now.

Cordelia's labor with the child had been hard and prolonged. Her slender body would not give up its burden. Pierre had been frantic, hovering outside her door, listening to the low moans coming from her room.

"If only she would cry out!" said his mother, coming out and wringing her hands. "I am afraid. She is out of her senses. She does not even know me."

Pierre could stand it no longer. He burst open the door, brushed the midwife aside and flung himself down by Cordelia's bed. Her face was swollen beyond recognition and she turned glazed, unseeing eyes on him. A spasm of agony passed over her and in terror he seized her hands and held them tight. "Cordelia!" he said. "Cordelia!"

She screamed once. "Josiah!"

"The baby is coming at last," said the midwife, drawing her hands from under the covers. "Go, go! Husbands are no good at a time like this."

Pierre stumbled from the room, and the Abbé who had been sitting outside the door came to him.

"You heard her cry?" asked Pierre numbly.

The Abbé's hand closed on his shoulder. "She will not remember, my son, and neither must you. When the child is here it will be different. You will see."

And it had been different, thought Pierre. Cordelia's gaiety was no longer forced, and in their marriage relationships she was not always trying so intensely to make her part a success.

Pierre's thoughts were interrupted by Fancy Foot Morgan, who had thrust his head in the door of the pilot-house. "What are you trying to do, Frenchman?" he bellowed, his mustaches bristling. "Send us to the bottom? Ever since you married that gel, you ain't had enough sense to keep a boat offen a sandbar." He withdrew, muttering to himself.

Pierre laughed. Fancy Foot was half-right at that, he decided.

Two days later he was striding up the walk to Beaver House. During the past year Cecily and Janette had both married and moved away, and Cordelia and his mother lived together in perfect harmony.

He flung open the door and saw his mother sitting by the fire. He scooped her up and swung her around and around.

"Put me down, you big bear," she said, kissing him on both cheeks. Then smiling, she added, "Cordelia's gone to put the baby to sleep, but I think she's still playing with her."

Pierre opened the door to their bedroom and saw Cordelia in a pale pink dressing gown bent over the baby's crib. She was laughing and dangling a locket before the baby. Marguerite's feet and tiny fists were kicking and beating together.

Then Cordelia looked up and saw Pierre. "You're home!" she exclaimed and ran to him, her dark hair falling over her shoulders. Finally she drew away. "You can admire your daughter while I dress. Emil has been cooking something special for you since morning."

"I've admired our daughter, and the food can wait, can't it?" He held her closer, cupping his hands under her breasts.

"Of course," Cordelia let her dressing gown slip from her shoulders, "if you wish."

It was at times like these that Pierre de Vries forgot that his wife had never said she loved him.

After dinner he suddenly remembered something. "Mimi," he said, "I have a letter for you. I almost forgot. It is from your cousin Virginia. I docked at their landing and she came down and gave me the letter herself. She wanted it delivered by me personally."

[151]

"Virginia!" said Cordelia. She had had few replies to her long letters to Virginia and only a polite note when Marguerite was born. "How did Virginia look?" she asked.

Pierre frowned. "Not too well. She was very thin and quite nervous."

Hurriedly Cordelia tore open the letter and read:

Dearest Cordelia:

I pray you will remember the pact we once made. I need your help desperately. Say nothing to anyone. Say I am ill, only come at once.

Love,
Virginia

Cordelia had no desire to see Hugo, but holding Virginia's letter in her hand and remembering how quickly Virginia had once come to her aid, she knew she could not refuse. "Virginia is ill and needs me," she said. "I should go." She bit her lip. "But I don't see how I can take the baby; she is so small."

Madam de Vries said, "If your cousin needs you urgently, then you must go. Taking the baby would be dangerous. Perhaps your cousin has something contagious. We will get a wet-nurse for the baby and I will see to her like the old mother hen that I am."

Cordelia looked inquiringly at Pierre. "You had better go, Mimi. If anything happened, you would always blame yourself. However, I am afraid," he frowned, "that you will have to take passage on some boat other than *The Silver Star*. She won't be ready to cast off for a few days."

"It would seem strange to be traveling on some other boat," said Cordelia, "and stranger still leaving my baby and you."

"I'll get you passage on *The Swan*," said Pierre. "Traveling nowadays is bad. Every man has a family, a wagon and a team, and is determined to get them upstream. I'll send Button with you," he decided. "Then I know you'll be safe."

At the mention of Button's name, Cordelia felt an errant surge of excitement, remembering how it was when she had run away on *The Blue Teal*. Once again she was going up the wide Missouri, once again she would hear it chuckling in the daytime and muttering to itself at night. Then she was heartily ashamed of herself. What was she thinking of? After all, she was a married woman now, with

[152]

a devoted husband, and an adorable baby. And she was almost nineteen years old.

22

TWO DAYS AFTER receiving Virginia's letter, Cordelia boarded *The Swan* for the upstream trip. At the last minute she had been panicky at the thought of leaving Marguerite, and only Madam de Vries' reassurances had kept her from getting off the boat and going back.

But when *The Swan* began to creak and groan in casting off, she came out of her stateroom and watched the scene on the lower decks. Momentarily she forgot her worry over the baby. She knew she would never fail to get a feeling of excitement as she heard the roustabouts singing, their backs bent under bales and boxes.

She felt ashamed of occupying the only good stateroom, which Pierre had managed to get for her, when she saw sun-bonneted women with babies in their arms crowding the decks. Seeing them, she wondered if she would have had the courage to take Marguerite on the long trek to California.

Later she went to the ladies' cabin and spent most of the afternoon staring out at the river. She saw matrons clucking their tongues and clicking their needles and it seemed as if they might have been the same women with the same knitting she had seen three-and-a-half years ago on *The Blue Teal*. There was also a young girl sitting alone in a dress cut too low. Cordelia sighed. She guessed there were always women like Red Maude.

Immediately she put the thought of Red Maude from her mind, but she grew restless and began pacing up and down the cabin. Then she sat down abruptly. She was behaving as badly as she had when she was a mere child. She wished now she had brought Marguerite. Less than a day had passed and already she missed her baby terribly.

Glancing out the window at the landscape she saw the ice was gone and the fingers of spring had reached to the river, turning the willows green. In the clearings, brown turned furrows promised corn in summer.

But in many fields Cordelia saw plows that were left to rust. At every landing emigrants waited, their pitiful belongings grouped about them, waiting to start for California, the land of gold. Late in the afternoon *The Swan* picked up such a group. There was a man and a woman with several small children clinging to her skirts. A small dog danced about and Cordelia noted the high color of excitement on the man's face and the pale composure of the woman.

After they had come aboard, the man joined the other men on the lower deck, but the woman stood by the rail, looking back as long as she could see, as if she were still setting to rights the house she had left forever. Cordelia saw that she carried a twig wrapped in a rag, perhaps a rose-cutting. On impulse she sent for Button and sent him to her with some of the fleur-de-lis seed she was taking Virginia.

At dinner that evening several men tried to get Cordelia's attention but she looked away. She had forgotten how conspicuous a woman alone could be. She supposed she should have remained in her stateroom, but she wanted to see the dining room and hear the music.

She had just finished ordering when she glanced up and saw a dowdy-looking little couple being shown to a table. She recognized them as Reverend Bird, the traveling preacher, and his wife. Signaling the steward, she had him ask the Birds if they would like to be seated at her table.

Mrs. Bird was pleased. "Imagine seeing you again, a grown-up woman! It seems only yesterday when you ran into the woods and that man found you . . ." She broke off at the Reverend Bird's frown.

Cordelia smiled. "I really am grown up," she said. "I am now married to Pierre de Vries. Perhaps you remember him as the young pilot on *The Blue Teal*. And we have a little baby daughter," she added proudly.

"A baby!" Mrs. Bird's face lighted up. "I do so love children. May I see her?"

"She's at home with my mother-in-law and a nurse," Cordelia explained. "My cousin is ill and I'm going up the river to see her. It was too dangerous to take the baby. My baby is named Marguerite. After my mother who died," she added.

Reverend Bird turned his deep-set eyes on her. "I read of the

[154]

tragedy of *The Blue Teal* and I said a prayer for your parents. I presume, my child, that you are saved?"

Cordelia looked down at her plate. "I took the Catholic faith when I married Pierre. He is a devout Catholic."

"Most unfortunate." Reverend Bird shook his head. "Catholics mean well, but they take the easy way out."

There was an awkward silence. Finally Cordelia asked, "How are you doing with your preaching, Reverend Bird?"

"Not too well," he said. "Iniquity abounds along the Missouri River."

"Now, Judd, you're doing all right," said Mrs. Bird defensively. "We've got a little church in the first village below St. Joseph. Just logs, but we built it ourselves," she added proudly.

"Judd gets discouraged, because of that awful woman who built that—that house on the bluff right across from the church. No matter how much Judd warns them, the men still go there."

"What woman are you talking about?" asked Cordelia clutching the edge of the table.

"Why, that terrible woman who has the place called The Petticoat," said Mrs. Bird. "Folks call her Red Maude."

"Oh, yes," said Cordelia faintly. "I've heard of her."

"Who hasn't?" asked the minister bitterly. "That Jezebel and her harlots are known from one end of the Missouri River to the other."

Suddenly Cordelia could hear Red Maude saying, "They'll never look down Battle Row and say, 'There goes . . . the poor worn-out bitch.'"

"Why are you traveling, Reverend Bird, if you have a church?" she asked, anxious to change the subject.

"In the spring and summer I travel around and preach to the Negroes. You're a young wife and mother and know nothing of this sinful world." He gave her a look that said she had no business gadding around in it alone. "Right now I'm headed for the Knapp plantation where I heard the behavior of the Negroes is nothing short of heathen."

"Knapp?" exclaimed Cordelia. "That's where I'm going—to see my cousin Virginia Knapp. Perhaps I shall see you there."

"Could we?" Martha Bird let eagerness and loneliness leak out in her voice. "We have a little room in the village. . . ."

"Come, Martha." Reverend Bird rose. "Duty comes before pleasure. If you'll excuse us, we must get our rest for the Lord's work."

[155]

Cordelia smiled to herself. She knew they were scurrying off so as not to witness a sinful waltz. Then, thinking of the little log church pitted against Red Maude, the smile faded from her lips.

Later that night Cordelia found she could not sleep. She thought of Pierre and the baby. Her breasts were hot and aching from unused milk, and she crossed her arms across them hard to ease them. The Birds had brought back a flood of long-buried memories. Finally she recalled what the minister had said about the Negroes. Thinking it over, she became curious.

Cautiously she opened her door and whispered, "Button, Button, are you there?"

Silently, his great black hulk arose from the floor.

"Somethin' wrong, Miss Cordie?" he asked.

"No. I just thought I'd step out a minute."

"You cain't stand out here, Miss Cordie. Mr. Pierre wouldn't like it," Button protested.

"I guess not," she assented. Then on impulse she asked, "Button, how often do you get to see Yellow Anna?"

There was a silence and Button's voice was a little distant when he said, "When we docks at the Knapp landing."

"That's not very often, Button," she said.

"No, Miss Cordie, it ain't," said Button. "But Yellow Anna, she's my woman and she knows I come when I kin. Wishin' won't make things different. We takes each other and things like they is."

"I wish I could do that," said Cordelia slowly. "Not many people can."

"That's 'cause I'se a nigger," said Button proudly. "You is white—and white folks butts they head on the wall."

He's right, Cordelia thought, I've done it all my life. Then she said, "Button, the preacher tells me you do wicked things in the grove. What do you do?"

"Nothin'," said Button.

"But what?" she persisted.

"Dancin'," he spoke reluctantly. "We kills a set-down hawg and roasts him."

"Good heavens, what is a set-down hawg?" asked Cordelia.

Button's voice was dignified. "Why, everybody knows it's a hawg that got hisself so fat he can't carry hisself around. He jist sets down all the time."

"Never mind!" Cordelia wanted to laugh. "I'll wager it's Mr. Hugo's sit-down hog and I don't care."

"Better go in now, Miss Cordie," said Button.

"I guess so," she sighed and looking down on the lower deck said, "Look at them down there. It makes me a little sad, thinking of all those people going way off to California. But then, folks have always been going somewhere. I wonder," she added wistfully, "if they ever think about people like us who help them get where they're going, but never get to go anywhere ourselves."

"Please, Miss Cordie, go inside," urged Button.

"Listen to them," she said, ignoring Button. Below, some men were fiddling and singing. "To hear them you'd never know they were going to cross mountains and deserts, would you? Some of them will never get there." There was a shout of laughter and now the little group of men stood up. Their good-natured chatter and loud good-nights carried up to where Cordelia stood. There was a dull glow of a lifted lantern swung high by a tall man. For a brief moment it threw his face into relief. Involuntarily, Cordelia let out a muffled cry.

"Yes, Miss Cordie, it's *him*," said Button sadly.

"Not Josiah Callahan! Not on this boat!" she cried wildly.

"I seen him come aboard," said Button. "He's takin' wagons to Californy. I pray to the Lawd you not see him."

Cordelia was shocked into silence.

"There won't be no call for you to see him, Miss Cordie," said Button gently.

Her throat was dry. "Of course not, Button!" she said sharply.

She went into her stateroom and fell across the bed. Josiah Callahan. On this boat and going to California!

In that brief moment when she saw Josiah's dark face in the fire-fly glow of the lantern, she realized she *dared* not see him again.

The next morning Cordelia had breakfast in her room, but sent back the food untouched. At noon she decided to risk going to the dining room. If she saw Josiah, she would nod briefly as if to a passing acquaintance. But he did not appear.

She would not speak at dinner, she decided. She would let her eyes drift on and over him. She was safe from such an embarrassing encounter, as he did not come to dinner either.

She saw him as she was leaving the boat. She was descending the great stairway, holding up her skirts, when she heard her name called.

[157]

"Cordelia!" She would have known his voice anywhere, but she hesitated and then turned slowly, to find Josiah looking up at her. She came down to the last step and leaned against the bannister for support. "Why, Josiah," she said in a cool, even voice. "I didn't know you were aboard this boat."

He was more tanned than she had ever seen him and the white scar on his face looked whiter. He wore a big slouch hat and boots. "Didn't you?" His eyes caught and held hers and she knew that he knew she was lying.

"I'm on my way to visit my cousin Virginia," she said breathlessly. "You know, the one who married my cousin Hugo." She ought to go on, instead of standing here staring at him.

"Yes, I know the one," he said. A smile lifted one corner of his mouth. "I know also you have a baby daughter now."

"You knew?" asked Cordelia, startled. "She's a beautiful baby," she rattled on. "We named her Marguerite, after my mother."

"Marguerite," said Josiah. "That was my mother's name too, you know."

"No, I didn't know," said Cordelia, in a high voice. "I suppose you are going to California, like all the rest of these people?"

"Why not?" shrugged Josiah. "There is nothing to keep me here, and I always like traveling around. Politics out there need a hand, too." He looked so at ease and Cordelia felt so completely upset that she wanted to hurt him, goad him.

"That makes me remember," she said. "My father once said you were an adventurer who would never put away his guns."

Josiah flushed and looked down at his perfectly matched silver-handled pistols. "Your father was right," he said easily. "I am not the sort of man to put away things easily. Neither my pistols," then, in a low voice, looking into her eyes, "nor my love."

Cordelia's face flamed. "I'm sorry," she said. "I didn't mean to be hateful—it's just that I . . . Josiah, California is a long way off—you *will* be careful. I've heard such terrible stories about wagon trains. . . ."

"Cordelia!" He laid his hand on her arm and it burned like fire.

"Goodbye and good luck, Josiah," she said in a high, gay voice, not meeting his eyes. "Come, Button. I see Virginia waving to me from the docks."

But after she had crossed the stage-plank she looked back. Just as, long ago, she had looked back at Josiah, she looked now. Pierre, the baby, time vanished and she was again sixteen, looking at Josiah and he at her. Only this time the gulf was far wider than the staircase of a steamboat.

23

WHEN CORDELIA stepped onto the landing Virginia ran forward with outstretched arms and threw them around her neck. Cordelia tried not to show her shock at the change in her cousin. Virginia's skin was transparent and she was thin to the point of emaciation. "Cordelia!" she exclaimed. "How I have longed to see you!" Then putting her mouth to Cordelia's ear she whispered, "I told Hugo the trip was your idea and that you came to see David."

"I've been lonely for you, too." Cordelia felt Virginia's thinness, like the bones of a fragile bird, through her dress.

Cordelia had been so upset over her encounter with Josiah and so shocked at Virginia's appearance that she failed to see Hugo's bulky form until he stepped forward and kissed her on the cheek. "Well, Cordelia," he said, smiling at her look of distaste, "Virginia told me you planned a visit. I expected you to bring your daughter. It *is* a daughter, isn't it?" He implied that since Marguerite was not a boy, she was of no consequence.

"She is too small to travel," said Cordelia.

"Then I'm surprised that you would leave her." Cordelia saw that Hugo's eyes were cold and watchful.

"I couldn't wait for her to grow up before I saw your son and Virginia."

"Well, I'm sure you'll agree that our son is a Knapp," said Hugo proudly. "There's no doubting his paternity!"

"Hugo!" Virginia's hand flew to her mouth in a nervous gesture but she forced a wan smile. "Come, let's go to the house."

It was beautiful—built of soft pink brick with white columns spaced majestically across the front. Lawns rolled gently away from the house and huge clumps of elms and walnuts grew in graceful grouping.

"It's one of the most beautiful houses I ever saw!" exclaimed Cordelia.

"It cost enough," said Hugo. "I presume you and Pierre still live at Beaver House."

"Of course," said Cordelia. "Why do you ask?"

"Oh, nothing," he said. "It was just that you used to spend all your time talking about a house by the river."

"I had forgotten all about that," she said. "All about it!" she said again, vehemently, still shaken from her encounter with Josiah. "I don't even want one now."

Hugo let the two women out at the front steps and drove on off to the stables. Virginia hurried Cordelia into the vast hall. Cordelia was exclaiming over the beauty of the curving stairway, when suddenly a door opened and a tall, slender man appeared.

Both women jumped. "Oh, Austin, it's you," said Virginia nervously. "You remember Jean Austin, don't you, Cordelia? He's Hugo's overseer."

"A pleasure," Jean Austin said and bowed. "I believe your name is now de Vries, is it not?" Then, turning to Virginia, he said, "If your husband has returned I should like to see him on business."

"He's at the stables," said Virginia nervously, tugging at Cordelia's hand and drawing her toward the stairway.

Upstairs Virginia looked in every direction, as if expecting to see someone. Then cautiously she opened a door into a large bedroom carpeted in a soft shade of rose. There were lace curtains at the windows.

"We can talk in here," she whispered. "You can go now, Nee." Virginia addressed an old Negress who was holding the baby.

"So this is David." Cordelia took the baby from the nurse, studying his gray eyes and small perfect features. "You're a lovely little boy," she said. "He is precious, Virginia." Then involuntarily she said, "He has red hair . . . like Aunt Alice's—and Charlie."

"Yes," said Virginia, "and how Hugo hates red hair!"

Studying the small, squirming boy Cordelia was fascinated by the child's resemblance to Charlie. Aloud she said, "I suppose Uncle Otto is beside himself since the baby is a boy."

"He hasn't seen him," said Virginia tensely, sitting on the edge of the bed, creasing and uncreasing the folds of her dress.

"Not seen him?" exclaimed Cordelia.

Virginia bit her lip. "It's Hugo's idea of getting even. I never liked Uncle Otto . . . but," her voice shook, "he begged me for a glimpse of David and Hugo wouldn't. . ."

Without warning, Virginia fell across the bed and burst out sobbing. "Oh, Cordelia, you've got to help me! I'm so frightened and I have no one to turn to."

Cordelia placed the baby in his crib and put her arms about Virginia's thin, shaking shoulders.

"What's wrong, Virginia? Are you ill?"

"I brought it on myself," sobbed Virginia. "Yes, I'm sick, sick inside. I thought I could make Hugo love me, but he hates me. He hates me because I trapped him with the baby."

"Not really hates you," said Cordelia. "No one could hate you."

"The nights are the worst." Virginia began pacing up and down. "It's as if he had some terrible hatred or resentment and must take it out on someone. Afterward . . . he falls asleep and dreams terrible dreams, because he cries out."

"What do you want me to do?" asked Cordelia, bewildered and shocked.

Virginia went to the window and looked out. "Buy Yellow Anna," she said desperately. "You've got to!"

"Buy Anna?" Cordelia exclaimed. "You want to get rid of Anna?"

"I love her," Virginia said, "if you can love a nigger. She's all that's kept me from going crazy. But don't you understand, Cordelia? Hugo wants her! I can see it when he looks at her."

"Virginia," said Cordelia, "surely you're . . ."

"He's building her a little house away from the rest . . ." said Virginia. "Then he can have her to himself. Anna is terrified of him . . . that's how I know. She told me."

Cordelia felt the color draining from her face. Thoughts of Button flashed into her mind. But she knew she dared not tell Virginia about Button because Virginia was a New Orleans girl who would be more shocked that Anna had chosen a black roustabout for a mate than if she were to become a white man's mistress.

"You've got to get her away from here," said Virginia hysterically, "or I think I'll kill myself." It took Cordelia several minutes to calm Virginia.

"I'll try to buy Anna tonight," Cordelia promised her worriedly,

[161]

smoothing Virginia's soft golden hair. "I'll do my best, but you know how Hugo is. He's clever at keeping people from having the things they want the most."

Hugo had never been more charming than he was at dinner that evening. He sat at the head of the table in a big gilt chair. He was smooth-shaven and his light hair was brushed until it shone.

"What do you think of my son?" he asked, playing the perfect father. "Isn't he a healthy youngster?"

"David?" Cordelia glanced at Virginia. "I think he's lovely!" She was deeply puzzled at the change in Virginia.

She was gay and her color was high. No one would guess that she had wept so piteously only a few hours before. Then Cordelia added, "But of course I think our daughter Marguerite is prettier."

Hugo laughed. "It amuses me to hear you talking like a young matron. I didn't think you would ever settle down and be a housewife. You were well rid of that Callahan. De Vries will do well as a river pilot."

"He's doing very well," Cordelia said. "For that reason," here was her opening, "I'm wondering if you would do me a favor and sell me Yellow Anna for Marguerite's nurse. A little girl needs a good nurse like Anna."

Slowly, carefully, Hugo put his knife down. He shot his wife a suspicious glance. "Since when," he asked, "did our branch of the Knapp family start buying slaves?"

"Oh, Hugo, I don't think of Anna as a slave," said Cordelia. "I simply need a good nurse."

Hugo laughed. "My dear," he turned to Virginia, "did you ever hear of anything so funny? Thinking you would part with Anna after all these years!"

An answering mirthless giggle escaped Virginia's lips as Hugo reached over and took her wrist. "You couldn't possibly part with Anna, could you?" he asked.

Virginia swallowed audibly. "I think that since Cordelia has a little girl, it would be nice if . . ."

"But think of the sentimental attachment . . ." Hugo's grasp tightened on Virginia's wrist. "After all, we shall have other children . . . several perhaps. Who is to say," he looked hard into Virginia's eyes, "that one of them will not be a girl?"

Cordelia caught a glimpse of the three of them in the gilt-framed mirror. It was like a horrible play with all the players wearing masks. She herself, sitting straight, rosy and bright-eyed, and Virginia like a doll, her head beginning to bob as she smiled weakly at Hugo.

"Oh, darling," Virginia said breathlessly, "I just thought that . . ." With moist lips and shining eyes she gave Hugo her other hand.

Hugo smiled triumphantly at Cordelia. "Do have some dessert, Cordelia," he said in the same tone his father used to use.

"I never eat it," she said between stiff lips, "as you very well know." The scene nauseated her. "If you'll excuse me . . ." She rose from the table. "I don't feel well. The trip was tiring and I think I shall go to my room."

"I'll go with you," said Virginia hastily.

"I couldn't help it," Virginia whispered later. "Maybe I imagined the way Hugo looks at Anna. She *should* have her cabin apart. She's almost white, you know."

"Yes, I know," said Cordelia wearily.

Virginia began to cry. "Oh, I know you think I'm weak and stupid, but you're married to Pierre and it isn't like this."

"No, it isn't," said Cordelia, "but I'm suddenly very tired and I'd like to go right to bed."

Virginia's head drooped. "I guess you must be angry with me, writing for you to come 'way up here, and then not letting you help me."

"No," said Cordelia, "I'm not angry. But since there isn't anything I can do to help you, you will understand that I must go back on the next boat. I left my baby in order to come, you know."

"I'm sorry," said Virginia.

24

CORDELIA'S CONCERN over Virginia, and the memory of her encounter with Josiah made sleep impossible. She tossed restlessly on the wide bed and finally arose and went to the window and looked out. A full moon silvered the trees and touched the Missouri with magic. A boat rode at the landing below. *The Swan* was still tied up. Somewhere on those decks Josiah slept with his wagon train, as remote as if he were a thousand miles away. What was the matter with her? She wished for Pierre, for Marguerite, the symbols of her newly found security.

But her restlessness increased and later she became aware of a sound, breaking the stillness of the night. Scarcely audible, it could not be defined as an actual noise. It increased, died away and increased again, inconstant, yet rhythmical, like the beating of a great heart in the earth.

For reasons she could not explain, Cordelia threw a cloak over her nightdress and stepped into the hall. A Negress materialized out of nowhere, the whites of her eyes luminous in the dark. "Best you not step out alone, Missy," she warned.

"I'm only going to the porch for a breath of air," said Cordelia. "It's safe there."

The Negress shook her head warningly as Cordelia slipped down the wide stairway and out onto the porch.

Looking across the moonlit meadows she saw trees marching like a dark army down the hillside where they camped to form a dense grove. Gradually she became aware that the beating sound was the same tempo as her own pulse.

Insidious as a whisper in the night, indistinguishable as the leaf patterns on the bricks, came the cadence of drums—until the earth quivered and the night tingled. The unexpected pulsation detached Cordelia from past and present and made her a subject of spring and moonlight.

She started as she heard footsteps, and, turning, she saw two dark-clad figures rounding a curve on the path near the house. They carried a lantern. Standing motionless, Cordelia watched the taller figure raise his head and she recognized Reverend Bird.

Relieved, she called softly, "Reverend Bird, it's Mrs. de Vries. Is something wrong?"

The minister and his wife started as Cordelia stepped from the porch and walked toward them.

"Mrs. de Vries! You up this time of night?" Then answering her question, "We heard there were heathen goings-on in the grove among the Negroes and we aim to see for ourselves if it is true."

"Reverend Bird," said Cordelia hastily, remembering Button's reticence in discussing it, "don't go to the grove. Darkies have their own way of having fun. I wouldn't bother them."

"How will I lead them to God if I don't know about their wicked ways?" he demanded sternly. "All that these slave- and land-owners want me to teach their niggers is to mind better, so they'll wear white aprons when they get to the Big Kitchen. But black or white, I say a body's got a soul and I aim to save it!" Taking up his lantern, he strode off, his wife clinging to him.

"Wait," called Cordelia, "if you're determined to go, I'm going with you." She knew Button would be there, and if there was trouble she might be able to help the Birds.

The minister strode down the rocky path like an avenging angel, carrying the lantern high so the two women could see to follow. The strange trio walked past walnut trees, past the locust ridge and down a path worn smooth by bare feet. All at once the path dipped sharply and Cordelia saw the flicker from a fire in the center of the grove. The sound of the drums was deafening now. The minister extinguished his lantern and they crept through the trees until they could see a band of Negroes gathered around the fire.

Cordelia's first wonder was where they had all come from. Some came from steamboats docked for the night, she knew. Others were workers on the Knapp plantation, but for the most part they might have sprung from the earth. Nearly a hundred Negroes were seated in a circle around the fire where "set-down hawg" was roasting on a stick. The air was pungent with the odor of roasting pork and frying cornmeal.

Cordelia located the drums. A young buck was beating on a primitive cowhide drum, another was rattling bones, long white polished ribs. As one, the Negroes swayed to their rhythm.

An old crone, bundled in rags and wearing a red bonnet, stood up and began to set a pitch. "Ahh-ah-ah," she intoned. "Ah-ah," she set a high tenor pitch. "Lawd, Lawd," the Negroes chanted. "Oh, Niggerdemous he clumb the sycamore tree. Oh-Oh-Oh Niggerdemous he clumb the sycamore tree . . . tree . . . tree . . ."

Their voices were warm and liquid as their chant rose into the night. Firelight flickered on black faces and on the shining whites of eyes and on work-gnarled hands, softly clapping.

Cordelia felt her heart beat faster. "Well, at least the poor souls are trying to sing religious songs," whispered Reverend Bird.

"Let's go back, Judd," pleaded Martha Bird. But now the drummer stopped and the Negroes remained motionless and waiting. Cordelia caught her breath as the drummer brought his hands down savagely, and more savagely still, until the rhythm became urgent and relentless. It was body-rocking. The Negroes stirred, grew excited. "Lawd, Lawd," the old crone screeched. The young girls squealed. It was then that Cordelia saw Yellow Anna.

She had not noticed her before because Anna looked so dark sitting there in the shadows. She did not look white at all but as if a sudden shadow had crossed her face. Her tawny eyes glowed like a cat's in the firelight. She swayed gracefully on her little rounded hips and she wore a crown of leaves in her hair.

The fire snapped and popped and the flame from the roasting hog soared. As if by a signal a young, almost-naked buck rose and began to dance. He danced effortlessly, bending low, stamping his feet, beating his thighs and throwing his head back to call out his urges in a kind of chant. It was no recognizable dance, no particular chant, merely the outpouring of his emotions concerning the night and the young girls sitting cross-legged by the fire.

He was joined by another buck, then another and another, until the camplights gleamed on more than a dozen glistening black bodies. By the fire an enormous old woman rose, her mountains of fat shimmering under red calico.

"Heathen! Just as I thought!" said Reverend Bird.

Cordelia was unable to reply. The pounding of bare feet and the cloppity-clop of the bones had started a pulse beating painfully in her throat.

Out of nowhere, Button emerged from the bushes, stepping high with a cup of cider on his head. The bucks drew back and joined the circle as he began to dance alone, putting his great feet down on the earth. His face remained expressionless, his cup immobile, but his rhythm increased. Great drops of sweat ran down his body. Faster and faster he danced, now whirling, now stomping, until the grove swelled with the drum and splat of his feet.

The drum rolled to a crescendo and crashed to a sudden stop. The drummer's hands remained suspended above the drum and left the night crying. Button had stopped in front of Yellow Anna and he stood there a moment, breathing hard, hands hanging by his sides. Then he tossed the cup of cider away, bent down, effortlessly lifted the slender girl in his arms, and, carrying her over his head, stalked off into the night. Anna laughed, and like some golden priestess performing a rite, took the crown of leaves from her head and put it on Button's. Other Negroes were drifting into the trees . . . even the fat woman in the calico dress.

"That's outright fornication!" said the Reverend Bird. "I'm going in there and teach them the error of their ways."

"Oh no, you're not, Judd!" Martha began to cry hysterically. "I beg of you, come away." She pulled on his arm.

"Martha, what ails you?" asked the minister.

"Please, Reverend Bird!" Cordelia pulled on his other arm. It seemed as if a slow, spreading fire had entered every nerve and fiber of her being.

"You sniveling women leave me no choice," said the minister disgustedly. "But I can see there is work to be done and I aim to do it. Come along," he said crossly. He lighted the lantern and stalked ahead, his back stiff and disapproving.

Back in her room, Cordelia threw herself across the bed. The years of cold restraints and inhibitions were broken, the hot blood of Michael Riley thundered in her veins, and she knew a thousand yearnings.

Going to the window she put her feverish head against the windowpane. Looking down, she saw that *The Swan* had taken advantage of the full moon and had cast off. Josiah was gone. A sharp pang of disappointment stabbed her.

She buried her face in her hands. She was no better than the Negroes in the grove. In her heart she knew she was not one whit better than Red Maude, for had Josiah appeared suddenly before her only a few moments ago, she knew she would have followed him willingly, joyously, wherever he might have led. She would have been his to command.

25

WHEN SHE RETURNED to Beaver House, Cordelia flew into such a fury of house-cleaning, sewing and caring for Marguerite that

Madam de Vries protested. "You will wear yourself to the bone, child."

"My linens are out of order." Cordelia jabbed fiercely at a tiny break in a tablecloth. How she hated mending linens!

"There is something troubling you, Mimi?" Madam de Vries asked.

"Of course not!" Cordelia put the tablecloth down and picked up Marguerite. How could she explain that this quiet room hemmed her in?

"Perhaps Pierre is too much occupied with *The Silver Star*," said her mother-in-law. "He was born to the river, you know."

"As I was," said Cordelia quickly.

"And you miss it—the boats, the excitement . . ." said Madam de Vries softly. "It is too bad you are a woman, a mother and cannot . . ."

"And why not?" asked Cordelia. "Why can't I go on the river with Pierre?"

"You could, I suppose, but Pierre wishes to protect you, to take care of you."

"Yes, yes, of course," said Cordelia. "If you will take care of the baby I think I'll walk in the garden." How could she explain to anyone the deep restlessness within her? The need to be a part of the world, to see, to feel and touch it. Here in quiet Beaver House she was missing something out there that drew her. But how could she explain that to Madam de Vries, or even to Pierre?

She had been home from the plantation about two weeks when a note arrived from her Aunt Opal saying there was sickness in the Otto Knapp household and that she was needed there.

Puzzled by the note, Cordelia decided Aunt Alice's drinking had brought her to a bad state. Remembering the kindnesses her aunt had done her, she decided to go to the Knapp house, regardless of the fact that her Uncle Otto had told her he never wanted to see her again.

It was with mixed feelings that she approached the gloomy old mansion. The lions no longer looked fierce, only rusty, and their claws were filled with leaves.

"Miss Opal is upstairs taking care of her sister," said the maid who admitted her. "The Madam has a terrific headache this time."

Cordelia raised her eyes and saw that her uncle's study door was half-open and she wondered if he were there. She went on upstairs and paused outside Aunt Alice's door. Her aunt was speaking unintelligibly and Aunt Opal was replying in a patient, persuasive tone.

Cordelia raised her hand to knock, then decided to wait until Aunt Opal came out. Again she glanced at her uncle's door. Three years had passed since she had run away. Surely he could not hold a grudge that long. After all, he was an old man now.

She tapped at the half-open door. There was no answer. Cautiously she pushed the door wide and spoke in a low voice, "It's Cordelia, Uncle Otto. I've come to see Aunt Alice. I hope you won't be too angry."

The curtains were drawn but she could see a bulky figure sitting in the great chair. "Uncle Otto," she said again in a low voice, "please don't be angry. It's been such a long time."

The figure moved, straightened, and she saw it was not her uncle at all, but Hugo. "Come in, Cordelia," he said. "Apparently you do not know that my mother has only had too much brandy, as usual. It is my father who is ill."

"Hugo?" Cordelia retreated a step.

"Come on in," he said. "Sit down." His eyes showed he was enjoying the situation. "Apparently you didn't know," he leaned back in the chair and put his highly polished boots on the table, "that my father had a stroke a few days ago."

"A stroke!" exclaimed Cordelia. "Then Uncle Otto is very ill."

"Very," said Hugo gravely. "I came at once, of course." He shifted in the big chair and stroked the smooth arms with his hands. "He is confined to his bed and cannot walk. I must take over the business, naturally."

"You're coming back to St. Louis to live?" asked Cordelia.

Hugo nodded. "I will spend part of the time here and part at the plantation. Virginia will remain at the plantation." A triumphant gleam came into his eyes.

Cordelia was revolted by Hugo's smug, self-satisfied air. "From the way you look I think you're glad to sit in that chair!"

Hugo's mouth thinned. "It fits very well, don't you think?"

"You can sit there from now to doomsday," Cordelia flared, "but you'll never be half the man your father is—much less the man Charlie was!"

Hugo's face turned ashen. "Be careful, Cordelia," he warned. "You're jealous because I have what I want at last and you never got what you wanted, did you? No, cousin, you never got your house

[169]

by the river. Your blue-coated soldier built it for a whore—and you can't quite forget it!"

In reply, Cordelia rose quickly and struck Hugo across the mouth. Then, appalled, she drew back, shaking.

Hugo grasped her by the wrist. "So you've still got fire, haven't you? I knew that you'd be burning—all the time you pretended to be a *hausfrau*. Your river-pilot couldn't quench that fire and I daresay he's no match for it either! But I am, I could bring you to me begging for . . ."

"Take your hands off me!" Cordelia said fiercely, trying to jerk away from him. "Or Pierre will kill you!"

"That Frenchman!" Hugo sneered, but he dropped her wrists long enough for Cordelia to put the desk between herself and Hugo. "My father was a soft old fool, but I warn you, Cordelia, I am not. If ever you cross me again I shall run you and your puny boat off the Missouri!"

Suddenly the door opened and Cordelia was relieved to see her Aunt Helen carrying a tea-tray. "Oh, Cordelia, you here?" Her nose quivered like a rabbit's as she set the tea in front of Hugo and stood awaiting his approval.

"There isn't any cream," Hugo said sternly.

"I'll get it. It will take only a moment!" Aunt Helen trotted out of the study.

Hugo laughed. "See that? Already this household knows which side its bread is buttered on!"

"I'm going to see your father," Cordelia said fiercely.

"Go ahead, for all the good it will do you!" said Hugo.

Cordelia was shocked at the sight of her uncle. Only his eyes seemed alive. "Margaret?" he whispered as she approached his bed.

"He doesn't know people half the time," said the nurse.

"It's Cordelia, Uncle Otto." She leaned over and looked into his eyes, shocked to see the once-active man lying so helpless.

When she saw slow recognition dawn in his eyes, she added, "I've come to tell you that I've seen your grandson!"

"The baby . . ?" Otto dragged the words out. His once-cold eyes now pleaded for more.

"Yes. He's a beautiful child, with red hair and blue eyes. Strong and healthy. He looks," she added slowly, "exactly like Charlie."

The mountain of flesh that was Otto quivered. "Won't let me see him. Send him to school . . . Emmerich. . . ."

"There, there." Cordelia laid her warm young hand on her uncle's cold one.

"Margaret!" Otto said. "Michael Riley will bring you no good. I forbid you to marry him. I don't hate you, Margaret, it's that I know best."

Pityingly, Cordelia looked down at her uncle. His eyes were closed now. Softly she went out of the room. Hugo was standing in the doorway of the study, arms folded, watching her.

She felt a great need and urgency to be out of this house. Aunt Alice's door was still closed, so she left without seeing Aunt Opal.

Back at Beaver House she found Pierre was home, and she heard the baby laughing as she came in the door. "Mimi!" he called, greeting her joyously. He looked in fine spirits, and she was glad because she did not know how he would react to the request she was going to make.

26

"BUT WHY SHOULD YOU want to bother your head about *The Silver Star*, Cordelia?" Pierre asked next morning. "And as to going up the river with me, you know how badly crowded conditions are now. Perhaps sometime next year . . ."

They were at breakfast, and Cordelia broke open a roll and regarded its steamy contents. "Then you have forgotten that you once said I could go with you anywhere?"

"No, no . . ." Pierre regarded her anxiously. "But are you not happy here at home? Sometimes my mother is inclined to interfere . . ."

"I love your mother, Pierre. It's only that I never see the river any more. I miss the boats and watching the people. I guess it's the river I miss most. I have spent my life watching it, you know."

"Aren't you satisfied with the way I am handling *The Silver Star*?" There was a little edge to his voice. "We are doing so well we will be able to buy another boat next year—if you like."

"Oh, Pierre, I didn't mean it like that! I'm cross, and you're so good I don't deserve you," she said contritely.

"Mimi!" said Pierre angrily. "Don't say that again—ever!" There was a silence. "You haven't been yourself since your visit to Virginia. You have been restless and preoccupied. And now you want to go upstream with me—take a small baby into that terrible crush—because you say you miss the boats and the river. What *is* wrong?"

Cordelia could not meet his eyes. How could she tell him without hurting him? "Of course I don't mean I would snatch up our child and leave with you this morning." I would, I would, though, she thought. "But I do want to go with you soon. Next time, maybe?"

"I will be late," Pierre said. "We are due to cast off at around ten, and these days passengers are in a frenzy. Goodbye, sweet." He put his hands under her chin. Then, seeing her eyes, he said, "I have failed you, Cordelia."

"Oh, no, no!" she said vehemently.

After he was gone, Cordelia remained in the garden. In addition to her overwhelming desire to see the river was another worry. In yesterday's paper had been an account of a wagon train, which must have left for California about the same time as Josiah's, which had been cut to pieces by Indians.

She took a little stick and poked at the earth and saw that tiger lilies were green at the roots and that the lilac was faintly tinged with purple. She dug on and on. The exercise and the warm sun on her head lessened her inner tension.

She must have been in the garden longer than she thought, because when she rose to go into the house her back and knees were stiff. She was rubbing her hands together to rid them of soil when she smelled smoke. Looking toward the house with alarm she saw that it was quiet. Then, looking at the sky, she saw it was hazed over. Toward the levee there were billows of smoke.

Frightened, she ran to the fence as some men came hurrying past.

"Where is the fire?" she asked.

"I don't know," said one of the men. "But we heard *The Algonquin* is on fire."

"*The Algonquin?*" echoed Cordelia, clutching the railing. "*The Algonquin* was docked next to *The Silver Star!*"

"They say the fire companies are already fighting," said the man. "It will be quite a show, and we don't want to miss it."

Looking with anxious eyes toward the levee, Cordelia saw high billows of smoke beginning to mushroom up against the spring sky. Now came the hollow hoot of a steamboat, followed by another, then another. She did not know where to turn.

Picking up her skirts she ran to the little parish church and burst into the Abbé's study. "Forgive me for bursting in, Father," she said, "but I'm so frightened. I've just learned *The Algonquin* is on fire, and *The Silver Star* is docked next to it. Pierre was to have cast off, but I don't know . . . . I'm afraid . . ."

The priest rose and took his hat. "I will go to the docks and find out," he said. "Try to be calm, stay inside and, if possible, keep Madam de Vries from finding out."

"Father . . ." Cordelia felt his eyes on her. "If anything should happen to Pierre . . . I mean, he has been so good to me, and I have given him so little . . ."

"Come, child," the priest said gently. "Go back into the house and stay with your mother-in-law and your child."

But there was no keeping the fire a secret from Madam de Vries, for shortly all of St. Louis was choking in smoke, and flames of fire licked against the sky.

Madam told her beads and Cordelia held Marguerite, who sensed her mother's tension and cried nervously.

It seemed hours before the Abbé came puffing up the winding brick walk, his face blackened with smoke.

"Pierre?" Cordelia asked fearfully.

The Abbé shook his head. "I could not get near," he said. "It is a sea of flames from Cherry Street to Duncan Island. The streets are impassable. Worst of all is the fighting."

"Fighting?" cried the women.

"The sailors and the firemen," explained the Abbé.

"Then you could see nothing, nothing of *The Silver Star?*" faltered Cordelia. "Oh, I pray to God it has already cast off!"

The priest did not meet Cordelia's eyes. "I must go back," he said. "Many will be wounded. Horses have broken loose and people are fleeing on foot."

"I'm going with you," said Cordelia. "I must know for myself that Pierre is safe."

"No, no," said the priest hastily. "You would be trampled to death —or worse. I will bring you word as soon as I can."

Cordelia pretended to agree, but as soon as the Abbé left she threw a shawl over her shoulders. "I must go," she told Madam de

Vries. "I *must* know what has happened to Pierre." Madam agreed tearfully, admonishing her to be careful.

Within a short distance Cordelia was forced to abandon her carriage. All of St. Louis seemed to be rushing toward the levee. Housewives on their way home from market were caught with baskets of food. Negro roustabouts, their eyes wide with terror, sailors, traders, women in carriages, men in broadcloth, and women in shawls were all milling about. Some were intent on getting away, but most were running toward the docks, to save a loved one, a boat, a few bales of hemp, a bolt of calico, crates of guineas, a warehouse—or just to look.

Running through the smoke, Cordelia coughed, stumbled and almost fell. Finally she met an immovable wall of humanity. No matter how she pushed, pulled and clawed, she could not get through. She lost her shawl, her hair came loose, and once she was knocked down. Burning debris showered the crowd and from somewhere a pistol shot rang out. More shots were heard, close now, and the crowd stampeded. Carried like a leaf on a swiftly moving stream, Cordelia was hauled, pushed and pulled into a coffee house.

Terrified, she flattened herself on the floor behind the bar while men dragged mugs and every available missile to doors and windows to bombard the advancing firemen. A brick sailed through the window, shattering the bar mirror and Cordelia threw up her arms to shield her face, feeling the hot prickle of flying glass against her shoulders.

"Come on out and fight, you dirty Irish!" bellowed a fireman, brandishing a shotgun through the hole in the window. He was answered by flying mugs.

The fight raged across the floor, over the bar and on upended tables. But at last the battling men swept out of the door and on down the street. Cordelia remained on the floor. Dizzily she raised herself to a sitting position and was struggling to her feet when a departing fireman, seeing only the top of her head, seized a chuck-a-luck cup and let it fly. It struck her on the temple and she fell without making a sound.

She awakened to find a face floating over her.

"Are you hurt bad, dearie?" a rough voice asked.

"I . . . don't think so . . ." Cordelia tried to focus her eyes on the face.

It took shape and she saw it belonged to a blowsy woman. "Would

[174]

you be tellin' me what the likes of you are doing lyin' on the floor of a Battle Row saloon?" she asked.

"My husband is the pilot of *The Silver Star*," Cordelia gasped. "I was trying to get to him." She swallowed hard.

"Oh, you poor darlin'," said the woman. "You got caught up with them villains."

They were interrupted by the sound of cannon. "Heaven strike them divils dead!" The woman shook her fist. "They have tore up Dennis Murphy's boardin' house and Terence O'Brady's coffee house and now they've got a howitzer. Little match it'll be for one good Irishman!"

"Oh, my head!" moaned Cordelia.

"It's a nasty lump you've got there, dearie," said the woman, applying a cold cloth to Cordelia's head. "And if I hadn't been safe under the kivers with me sweetie, I might have had the same bad luck as you."

Groggily Cordelia staggered to her feet. "I've got to find Pierre. He may need me."

"You can't get through," the woman said. "There's dead horses and people . . ."

Cordelia swayed and began to retch. "Oh," she said apologetically, "all over your dress!"

"Oh, I never mind a little puke," said the woman blithely. "I wouldn't be workin' here if I did."

Some way, Cordelia never quite knew how, the barmaid found a carriage and drove Cordelia back to Beaver House.

All night long Cordelia waited, her head throbbing painfully, but there was no word, either from Pierre or from the Abbé.

The following day smoke still hung over the city and the streets echoed to the sound of rioting. But along toward evening Cordelia heard a vehicle coming down their street. A cattle-drawn cart came with wooden wheels clacking, driven by a browned, gnarled farmer. He urged the cattle on with "chucks" and "sees" until they reached Beaver House, then he stopped.

The Abbé Choate, his habit torn and sooty and his face grim, rode beside the driver. Madam de Vries screamed, threw her apron over her head and sank to the ground. The Abbé had brought Pierre home in the back of the cart, wrapped in old coats and blankets. He was barely alive.

Cordelia, stricken with grief and remorse, scarcely heard the priest

[175]

tell of how he had found the unconscious Pierre lying under a pile of debris.

Cordelia threw herself beside Pierre. "You are so good, Pierre," she sobbed. "I have tried to love you the best I know—the very best— but it isn't good enough. Oh, Pierre, what have I done to you?" She clung to him.

"Come," the priest drew her away, "we must get him inside at once. There is a chance that he may live, though I have given him the last rites."

"He must live!" said Cordelia. "I didn't love him the way I should have. And he knew it! Just yesterday I saw it in his eyes!"

"You judge yourself too harshly, child," said the Abbé. "Who can measure love? You must take comfort—he still may live."

But Cordelia would not be comforted. All through the night and the next day she sat by her husband's bed. She felt she had failed Pierre and if it took her the rest of her life, she would make it up to him.

27

PIERRE HAD RECEIVED a terrible blow on the back of the skull and lay senseless to all that went on in the household. Even if he recovered his senses, which was doubtful, the doctor predicted his legs were so badly burned he might not walk again.

Ten days later Cordelia was summoned from Pierre's bedside by Emil, the cook. At the back door she found Button shuffling his feet.

"Oh, Button!" she exclaimed in relief, realizing that she had not shown proper concern for the crew of The Silver Star. "I was so glad when I heard you weren't hurt. You *are* all right, aren't you?"

"Yes, ah is, Miss Cordie," he said sadly. "But it break mah heart about Mistah Pierre—he so good to us. Everybody on de levee talk about how he save The Silver Star."

"Button, please!" Cordelia said. "I can't talk about it— Isn't there something I can do for you?"

"Miss Cordie," Button spread his hands out helplessly, "how us gonna live if you don't run no boat?"

"I don't know," she said slowly. "I've been trying to think . . . I'll pay your wages as long as I can. Some people think I ought to sell *The Silver Star* . . ."

"Sell your daddy's boat? Oh, Miss Cordie! Why, folks is trying to get out yonder to de gold, and no boats to haul 'em. Yestiday a wagon-man he take out his ole shotgun and he say, 'Nigger, that boat ain't burnt. How come its owner so high and mighty he let his boat set in water like a duck?' You better come and see, Miss Cordie," he begged.

"Today?" she asked.

Button looked at her reproachfully. "If Mistah Pierre could save de boat you ought leastwise come see it."

Cordelia saw that Button's clothes were ragged and burned. Then she realized that Emil had been listening to their conversation and was peering at her anxiously over his pots and pans.

Now, for the first time, she realized how far-reaching was the influence of *The Silver Star*, how many people depended upon it for their very existence. Besides herself there were Pierre, Marguerite, Madam de Vries—a whole world of people; cooks, stableboys, roustabouts, engineers—all of whom had for a generation depended upon the name of Riley for their livelihood. "Very well, Button," she said. "You may accompany me. I shall go see *The Silver Star* now."

The levee was a scene of desolation, with smoke-grimed men picking their way through rubble. Worst of all were the steamboats. They lay piled against Duncan's Island like skeletons on a burnedout funeral pyre.

Wagon trains waited miserably for transportation, and as Cordelia passed one wagon, a woman in a sunbonnet stared at her hopelessly. A pale little girl of about three peeped out with round, frightened eyes.

Just then a fiddle began to scrape and the child clapped her hands. Cordelia smiled at her, and, turning, she saw a tall lanky man fiddling away and singing in a rusty voice, "Oh, Californy, that is the land for me. I'm bound for Sacramento, with my washbowl on my knee."

Then as Cordelia watched, the man drew the bow across the fiddle, put his head down and spoke softly as if to an old friend, "Did you ever hear of the mountain boy named Joe, died of the plague when he was but four-and-twenty?"

The woman's eyes met Cordelia's. "You'll have to excuse my husband," she said. "All Pa does is make up fiddlin' songs about everybody he meets. Little it matters to him we're left in this place," she added bitterly.

"There will be boats going upstream in a few days," said Cordelia.

"Little good it'll do us," said the woman. "Pa lost our passage money to a slicker," she gestured toward the little girl, "and with a sickly one to boot."

"I hope everything works out for you," said Cordelia sympathetically. She patted the little girl's brown hair and picked her way toward *The Silver Star*.

The pilot-house was smashed and the chandeliers were shattered, but otherwise *The Silver Star* was undamaged.

Soberly, Cordelia surveyed her boat. It made her feel ill to see the beautiful white hull blackened and water streaked, and the lovely furnishings wrecked. Everyone wants me to sell it, she thought. But can I? And yet, she looked at Button waiting patiently for her, the crew must eat and there will be doctor bills for Pierre. I must do something and do it quickly.

Thoughtfully she crossed the stage-plank, troubled by the knowledge that if she sold *The Silver Star*, many of the crew who had been with her father for years would not be able to find other employment. They would be forced to become part of the human flotsam that ended up on the levee. She had seen them—old men, born to the river, lying drunken, hungry or sick among the barrels and lumber on the docks. The cargo was cared for but the only time anyone took care of a homeless old steamboat-man was when he died.

She was so deeply worried that she did not realize a crowd had gathered on the docks and was shouting at her.

"There she is, there's Pierre de Vries' wife!" a bronzed man shouted. "Lady," he bellowed, "are you going to let that boat set there and us and our wives and children suffer?"

Another man called to her, "We'll get caught in the winter going to Californy!"

Dismayed, Cordelia looked at the crowd. "Either I must sell this boat, or find a master and a pilot," she called back. "As you know, my husband is badly injured."

"But we can't wait," they shouted. There was some fist-shaking now. Then suddenly the crowd parted and Cordelia was almost relieved to see Hugo shouldering his way toward her.

"Cordelia!" he said, placing a protective arm about her. "You have no business on the docks!" Then turning to the crowd, he said, "I am Hugo Knapp of the Knapp lines. By tomorrow morning I shall have four boats to take all of you up the river. Sailing times will be posted."

The crowd murmured. "Now, along with you," Hugo waved them away, "and quit hounding this poor young woman."

A general cheer went up and the people began to disperse.

"Thank you, Hugo," Cordelia said. "They were in a nasty mood."

"I see *The Silver Star* is in fair condition," said Hugo, looking at it speculatively. "I'll take it off your hands and pay you well for it."

Cordelia looked at him suspiciously, "I need time to think, Hugo. I don't want to rush into things or to be taken advantage of just because Pierre is ill."

"I'm serious," said Hugo. "I'll pay you well. I can afford to. I will charge those fools triple fees to get them on their way."

"Hugo!" Cordelia exclaimed. "You don't mean you would charge those wagon trains three times the regular fare? They can't afford it. Besides, it isn't right."

Hugo burst into laughter. "Oh, Lord, Cordelia! You'd better sell me *The Silver Star* before you give it to someone."

"Not if it rots on the river!" she said fiercely. "Neither Pierre nor my father would have allowed *The Silver Star* to take advantage of people like that. They loved their boat, their river—and their passengers!"

Hugo's good humor vanished. "You know you have to have the money, and you can't get a pilot and a master on your own."

"I'll take that boat up the river myself before I'll let you have it!" Cordelia declared fiercely.

"You?" Hugo snorted. "A woman take a boat up the Missouri?"

"With a pilot, of course," said Cordelia hotly.

"And just how would you go about getting one?" Hugo sneered.

"Fancy Foot Morgan will go," she snapped. "He knows the Missouri River better than any man alive!"

"That drunkard? He's been drunk ever since the fire!" Then Hugo narrowed his eyes. "I believe you are serious."

"I am," Cordelia said, making up her mind. "I'll take that boat up the river. And I'll take them at regular prices."

[179]

Hugo's nostrils flared with anger. "If you try it, the Knapp line will run you off the river! Don't forget that."

An unreasoning anger swept over Cordelia. She stood breathless, looking into Hugo's cold eyes. Then she said in a low voice, "There is something *you* should not forget either, Hugo. I also am a Knapp." She turned. "Come along, Button. We're going to find Fancy Foot Morgan and sober him up!"

When Cordelia returned to Beaver House she was still trembling from the ordeal of watching Button drag Fancy Foot Morgan from his littered pigsty of a bed in a bad-smelling boarding house, shake him into sensibility and threaten him with a canning knife if he took another drink. But now, three hours later, she knew Fancy Foot would attend to getting *The Silver Star* in shape and would pilot it up the Missouri when it was ready.

"I'll see you tomorrow, Button," she said wearily.

"Miss Cordie, is you really goin' up that devil river yourself?"

"Yes, Button," she said, "I am, and I don't want any arguments from you. I'll have enough from Madam de Vries."

"But how about de li'l' baby?"

"I'll take her and a nurse," said Cordelia. "Madam de Vries has all she can do to care for Pierre."

"I doan know . . . steamboats and a li'l' baby . . ." Button wrinkled his forehead.

Cordelia lifted her head. "My baby's living will come from boats and rivers. Some women take them across the country—in wagons —clear to California. . . ."

"Maybe you right," said Button hesitantly. "If you'd married Mistah Josiah, you'd been takin' a li'l' baby to Californy."

Cordelia winced at the mention of Josiah's name. She started to remonstrate, but one look at Button's artless face and she said simply, "Yes, Button, I guess I would. So," she said briskly, "a trip up a river is nothing for a baby. Now off with you. I'm very tired."

Cordelia met with violent opposition from both the Abbé and Madam de Vries. A woman taking a boat up the Missouri! Impossible! Such a thing was unheard of. It was dangerous, and if Pierre knew of it he would never allow her to do such a thing.

In vain Cordelia tried to explain the economic situation to them, but it was a world apart from Madam de Vries and the Abbé. In spite of their protests, Cordelia took Marguerite and boarded the patched-up *Silver Star* a few days later.

Before she left she looked down at Pierre, lying pale and unseeing on his bed, and she vowed to make everything up to him. She wanted to work, to struggle, to find cleansing relief from remorse. And she felt an overwhelming desire to meet Hugo's challenge.

28

AS THE SILVER STAR prepared to cast off, an enormous crowd gathered. The men shook their heads and the women clucked their tongues and they all craned their necks to see what manner of woman would attempt to take a boat up the Missouri.

Oblivious of all the stir she was creating, Cordelia left Marguerite in the stateroom with her nurse and went up to the pilot-house where she could watch the passengers loading. She listened to the sound of rolling barrels, giant hawsers whipping across wooden decks, and frightened horses whinnying. There was to be nothing luxurious about this trip of The Silver Star. Her blackened, scorched decks were packed with humanity and cargo.

Cordelia was so absorbed in watching the lower decks that she was startled when a lanky man with uncombed hair burst into the pilot-house. "I just got to see you, Ma'am," he panted.

Cordelia frowned. "Who are you and what do you want?"

"I'm Joe Ikes," he babbled. "You stopped by my wagon the other day and talked to my wife and baby."

"Yes, I remember," said Cordelia. "You are the man who makes up fiddling songs."

The man's face brightened. "Yes, ma'am. I'm the best fiddler in our part of Kentucky." He dropped his head. "But like Louisa—that's my wife—says, I ain't much good at other things. I lost our passage money."

"Well," said Cordelia firmly, "you don't expect me to haul you free, do you?"

The man looked down at his cracked boots. They would never get him to California, thought Cordelia.

[181]

"Well, ma'am," Joe Ikes gulped, "they were tellin' on the docks how your father Cap'm Riley—the best captain on the Missouri—always gambled on people turning out all right . . . so I thought maybe you was like him. . . ."

There was a silence. Finally Cordelia asked, "And you want me to gamble on you?"

"I know I don't look like much, ma'am," he said, "but I jest *know* I'm going to find gold. I'll give you half, and throw in free fiddling until we get to St. Joe."

Cordelia looked at the gnarled hands and then at his pleading eyes. He was a shiftless drifter with a fiddle under his arm. Then she thought of his wife and the children—especially of the little girl with brown hair—the one with eyes like Marguerite's.

"Very well, Mr. Ikes," she said. "My father once won three thousand dollars on a wood-loading contest. We'll see what I win on you. I'll make arrangements with the purser for your passage and freight. You may load up."

"God bless you!" he said. "You'll never be sorry. Never!" With that he scampered down the stairway, yelling, "Ma, Ma! Load the young'uns! We're going to Californy after all!"

Later that day when *The Silver Star* churned into the Missouri River, Cordelia was still in the pilot-house. She did not trust Fancy Foot Morgan to remain sober, and she had not been able to obtain a second pilot.

Watching the river, she spoke softly, almost silently to herself. "Up the Missouri," she said thoughtfully. "It seems a hundred years ago that I ran away on *The Blue Teal*."

"That's 'cause you're young," said Fancy Foot. "If you was old like me, it'd seem like a minute. Now you watch how I flank this here bend," he said, bringing the boat skillfully around a sharp and dangerous bend.

"See them islands? Sunk steamboats. That one over there," he pointed to a blob of willows, "is full of gold dust and whiskey. A man could raise a lot of hell with that much gold and whiskey."

Fancy Foot talked on, but Cordelia only half-listened. Ahead were the turns, bends and chutes and the rainbows reefs. There were the trees, bent to admire their own reflections, and the dancing, spinning cottonwood logs. But now she knew that trees could fall into the river and become wicked sawyers to rip the bottom from a boat. Islands were silted to ground a steamboat, and the bends were graveyards. As she looked at the wind-whipped river, she saw that the ripples were serrated, edged in white, like the teeth of a shark. Involuntarily, she said, "Pierre always said the river had teeth but I never believed it before."

Fancy Foot looked at her out of his rheumy eyes and said, "The Missouri's always had teeth, gel. But it ain't teeth that worries me; it's that—" He pointed a short distance ahead to where a steamboat laid down a wand of smoke.

"That's *The Hawk*," he explained. "I heered on the docks that your cousin was on it and was out for blood. And back there," he pointed behind them, "is another Knapp boat."

"Then Hugo really does intend to run me off the river!" Cordelia said bitterly.

"Looks that way." Fancy Foot took a big chew of tobacco. "*The Hawk* can pretty well clean up the cargo ahead of you and unless you want to wait around and eat up your profit, and make the passengers mad, the other Knapp boat can loaf along and pick up the next load."

"There must be some way to beat Hugo," Cordelia said thoughtfully.

"There is, gel," said Fancy Foot. "Get ahead of *The Hawk*."

"Then we'll get ahead of him," said Cordelia, staring hard at the smoke of *The Hawk*.

"Cain't hardly do that," said Fancy Foot. "This is a wide river but there's almost no place to pass. The channel's too narrow and you get stuck on sandbars or go to the bottom."

"But there are *some* places," said Cordelia, "some places you can pass."

"A few," said Fancy Foot.

"Then give the engineer the bell!" she ordered.

Sparks flew and the boat shook as Bottle Head Mac pinched the steam and sent *The Silver Star* bucketing against the current. By nightfall she was nipping on the heels of *The Hawk*.

The night was too black to travel, so both boats tied up. When *The Hawk* cast off, *The Silver Star* was no more than a quarter of a mile behind her.

At every landing Cordelia would find that Hugo had taken only the lighter merchandise, leaving the heavy cargo. Rather than leave the shippers desolate, Cordelia took on the heavy cargo. Around noon she picked up a shipment of molasses and lard. "My God, gel!" exclaimed Fancy Foot. "You ought to be takin' on nothin' but wood."

"I know it," she said, "but people have to ship their merchandise.

[183]

They depend on it for a living. Hugo wouldn't take it, and if I guess right, neither will the boat behind us. These people depend on us to take their lard."

"Lard, hell!" said Fancy Foot. "Osage Chute is just ahead and if we don't get there before *The Hawk* we'll have to stay behind, because there won't be no passing anywhere else for miles. That chute's silted in. You can just squeak through now. I'm for dumping the passengers in the muddy and blowing the boilers to Kingdom Come, if necessary, to beat that jackass of a Hugo Knapp."

Word of the boat race had spread up the Missouri, and now every little landing was crowded with men making wagers. Finally it was at a landing that *The Silver Star* came alongside *The Hawk*. Cordelia could not go on; she had to put in for the same reason *The Hawk* had docked: to buy cord wood. This was the last good fueling place for miles.

No sooner had *The Silver Star* docked than Hugo came aboard. The crowd on the docks shouted and craned their necks as Cordelia met Hugo on the wide staircase. Passengers packed themselves on every deck to try and catch the conversation.

"Well, Cordelia," said Hugo, "you should be satisfied now that you've made a spectacle of yourself."

"I notice," she said coldly, "that you are hard put to stay ahead of us."

"You are making yourself the laughing-stock of the river," Hugo said angrily. "A *woman* mastering a *boat!*"

"And you are at last showing what kind of a boat line you run! Charging three times the regular rate and beating me out of honest trade," Cordelia retorted. "Well, I'm on to your scheme of going ahead of me and trailing me with another of your vulture boats. I shall beat you, Hugo. Then we'll see who is the laughing-stock of the river!"

"Bah!" said Hugo. "Within two hours I'll be in Osage Chute where you can't pass, then you're done for."

Cordelia took a deep breath. "Very well, Hugo! I'll make you a wager. I'll be in Osage Chute before you are. And when I do, I want those golden hawk wings from your pilot-house and a promise to leave me alone on the river. If I lose I'll sell you *The Silver Star* at regular prices and leave the river."

"I'll take that wager," Hugo said triumphantly. "You're a fool, Cordelia. You've always thought you could win what you wanted. Well, it didn't get you your soldier, and it won't get you what you want on the Missouri. I came up here to give you a last chance to admit defeat, but since you won't, you'll have to take the consequences." He turned and walked away without another word.

Fancy Foot commented, "Better take care. That jackass brays just before he lays into you with his heels."

Fancy Foot's prophecy was correct. Only minutes later Button came running to the pilot-house to report. "Miss Cordie, there ain't no wood to make de boat go!"

"No wood?" she exclaimed. "Why, the docks are full of it!"

"But Mr. Hugo done bought it all and paid for it," said Button. "Nobody kin sell us any. We can cut some in de woods but that take a long time!"

From the corner of her eye Cordelia saw Fancy Foot uncorking his bottle. "Put that down!" She snatched the bottle from him. "How much wood *do* we have, Button?"

Button shook his head. "Not enuff to make de next landin' wid steam up."

"But do we have enough to make Osage Chute full steam? If we get in the Chute ahead of *The Hawk*, we've won, anyway."

Button rolled his eyes at Fancy Foot. "You'd sure be chancin'," he said.

"Then we're chancin'," said Cordelia. "We're casting off."

At first *The Silver Star* was only feet behind *The Hawk*. But the woodpile dwindled rapidly and the heavier load of *The Silver Star* began to tell, and *The Hawk* began to pull away from her.

"Chute's only two miles ahead," warned Fancy Foot, his breath smelling of the rum which he had managed somehow to swallow despite Cordelia's watchfulness.

"We've got to get up more steam, more speed!" Cordelia stared ahead at *The Hawk*.

"Engineer's got two niggers sitting on the safety hatch now to keep the steam in," said Fancy Foot.

"Oh, you're right," moaned Cordelia. "I shouldn't have taken on that molasses and lard. I ought to throw it in the river. If only it were cord wood!"

Suddenly Fancy Foot let out a string of oaths. "My God, it's better than cord wood! Throw that lard in the furnace! Nothin's hotter than grease!"

"You mean burn the lard?" Cordelia asked incredulously.

"Why, shore," said Fancy Foot. "You can pay the owner for it. He won't care if you burn it or sell it for him." He was treading the wheel in wild excitement. Cordelia was trembling with excitement herself. "Button! Tell the engineer I want to see him at once!"

Burning the kegs of lard, *The Silver Star* leaped forward, belching blinding smoke, and nosed in on *The Hawk*. Less than a quarter of a mile away lay the narrow chute which ran for nearly ten miles. On each side were willows, snags and the dreaded silt.

Every passenger was at the rails—many praying. *The Silver Star* came alongside *The Hawk* and they made neck-and-neck for the chute. Now the narrow mouth of it loomed ahead. Hugo, standing in the pilot-house, shouted and cursed like a madman at *The Silver Star*. Suddenly, as they reached the mouth of the chute, *The Hawk* swung into them.

"He's ramming us!" shouted Fancy Foot. The boat shuddered, passengers tumbled and barrels rolled.

As *The Hawk* slammed into the side of *The Silver Star*, Cordelia screamed to Fancy Foot, "Look out! He's running us down!"

But a wild light had come into Fancy Foot's eyes. Instead of turning or pulling away, he turned full steam ahead into *The Hawk*. When *The Hawk* had struck she had bounded away from the force of the impact. In that split second Fancy Foot by turning into her and giving full steam ahead inched the bow of *The Silver Star* ahead of her. Again the boats crashed together, sprang apart, crashed together again, but the bow of *The Silver Star* was in the chute. Then like a big whale giving a contemptuous lash with its tail, the rear of the boat again struck *The Hawk*. The Knapp boat spun sideways, crosswise and into the silt.

"Let 'em grasshopper out of that," chuckled Fancy Foot as Hugo ran bellowing out of the pilot-house. When Cordelia looked back she saw the spars being lowered and *The Hawk* getting her winches into operation.

A great flood of emotion was released in Cordelia. "I've won!" she cried. "Oh, if only Pierre could have seen this, or my father! All my life Hugo has bullied me. But he'll never do it again. Not Hugo or anyone else. I've won!" She burst into tears and ran from the pilot-house.

"Wimmin!" said Fancy Foot, taking up his bottle.

Back in her cabin Cordelia sent the nurse away and held the sleeping Marguerite close in her arms. "Don't ever be afraid, darling," she whispered. "Please God, you'll always be happy and never be frightened and sad as I have been."

Having won the race, *The Silver Star* tied up to give Fancy Foot a chance to sleep and sober up. By ten o'clock, the entire boat had settled down after the nerve-shattering day. By eleven, the only sounds came from animals aboard the boat and the giant bullfrogs croaking in the tall watergrass along the banks.

29

IT WAS NOT YET MORNING when Cordelia realized that someone was pounding on her stateroom door. Marguerite awakened, screaming with fright, and the nurse sat up in bed, as frightened as the baby.

Opening the door, Cordelia was confronted by a shivering Negress. "Come quick, Missy!" she said breathlessly. "Down on the lower deck. One of them wagon-folks is sick something awful, and there ain't no doctor on this boat."

Wrapping a shawl around her, Cordelia followed the girl to the lower deck. The girl stopped at a distance and pointed to a wagon where a lantern burned. Even at that distance Cordelia could smell the vomit and the fever.

Joe Ikes' worried face peered out at her between the canvases. "Hit's the young'un," he said. "Must have been that catfish she et."

The other children, piled in the wagonbed like so much cord wood, stirred sleepily. Cordelia drew aside the tattered covers and saw that it was the little girl with the brown hair who was ill.

The child was gasping for breath. Her face had a deep bluish cast and her lips were drawn back from her teeth in agony. Again she was convulsed and wracked with terrible vomiting.

"Worst stomick-ache I ever seen," said Joe Ikes.

The child gave a piteous wail; her knees drew up, her head went back. Impulsively Cordelia put her hand under the small back in hopes of easing the child's pain. Her eyes met those of Louisa Ikes, the mother. The two women looked at each other. They had known what it cost to bear a child, and now they knew what it cost to watch a child die.

The little girl's fingers curled, the long lashes fluttered down and she was quiet.

[187]

"There, I told you. She's quietin' down," said Joe. "Now maybe all of us'll get some sleep."

"Sleep!" Louisa Ikes' thin face contorted. "Oh, my God, man! She's dead!" She fell to wailing across the child's body.

Cordelia comforted the Ikes' as much as she could, then set off for the carpenter's cabin.

Although it was scarcely daylight, the carpenter was awake. "No need to make a coffin, ma'am," he told her. "I got one that will fit. Built two since I left St. Louis. Brought eight with me; cholera and steamboats go together these days."

"Cholera!" exclaimed Cordelia. But even as she uttered the terror-striking word, she knew that cholera was what she had just witnessed. Quickly she grasped the carpenter's arm. "You must not tell anyone how the child died. Otherwise, panic will break out."

The carpenter promised. "But, ma'am, it ain't the panic breakin' out that worries me, it's the cholera. I'll caulk the coffin good with pitch."

Cordelia loaned her best petticoat to line the coffin, and the passengers trooped off the boat to form a sympathetic audience when the child was buried in a corner of the Rocheport cemetery. Louisa Ikes did not cry, but as Cordelia watched, it seemed the creases in the tired face grew deeper, as if her inward suffering defied outward expression. But Joe Ikes wept loudly, and because there was no one who could sing proper, he put his fiddle under his chin and made up a song, and the fiddle wept, too.

Back on the boat, the passengers agreed it was a touching scene and an altogether satisfactory funeral, one you could tell about later. But Mrs. Ikes stood apart, silent, looking back until the village where her child was buried was lost to sight.

From that time on, Fancy Foot Morgan slept only in snatches, as did Cordelia. Both of them felt the greatest urgency to discharge passengers at St. Joseph as speedily as possible. Cordelia spoke privately to trusted cooks, and all water was boiled and the food cooked for extra long periods. The Ikes wagon was scrubbed inside and out and sulphur was burned.

But on the day *The Silver Star* rounded a sharp bend where willows grew into the river and Cordelia saw the little village where the Birds lived, she did not hurry the loading and unloading of cargo as she had done previously. For, high on the bluff, she saw at last the house Josiah Callahan had built for Red Maude. Often she had bitterly envisioned a many-gabled house in extremely bad taste, a mansion with red-curtained windows where strumpets sat like spiders, waiting for their prey.

Instead she saw a tranquil house, imposing in size and built of the finest stone with seven stately pillars. Delicate lace curtains hung at the windows. A terrible anger swept over Cordelia. Why should such a woman have such a house?

Finally she turned and looked at the village and saw the steeple of the little church, which must be Reverend Bird's. She thought of taking the baby and going up to the Birds' for a brief visit. She was sure they had not heard of the fire nor of Pierre's terrible accident. But she did not go; she remained aboard *The Silver Star*, staring at Red Maude's beautiful, arrogant, hateful house.

Presently some women dressed in light-colored dresses came out on the porch and walked about as if taking an afternoon stroll. Casually one waved a handkerchief. Then they all disappeared inside a great doorway.

Later, Cordelia watched men passengers walk purposefully toward the village, as if on some errand, but at the top of the hill they set off in the direction of The Petticoat.

That night came on so dark that it was dangerous to cast off, and since St. Joseph was so near, they decided to wait until morning.

After dinner, Cordelia sent the nurse away and played with Marguerite. She wondered, as she constantly did, if Pierre were any better. The doctor had promised that he would live, but little more.

Cordelia bathed Marguerite and curled a soft brown curl around her finger. The baby's big brown eyes were closing and the long lashes swept the perfect little cheeks. Then, putting the child in her crib, she opened the door to her stateroom and looked out into the night. Tomorrow I shall be in St. Joseph, she thought. I have defeated Hugo, and I will be the first woman to take a boat up this river. I know now that I can, and that I will be able to care for those who depend on me.

Then from The Petticoat there sounded a sudden blare of music and raucous laughter. Suddenly her gesture of taking a boat up the river seemed empty. All her tomorrows stretched ahead of her. After this trip, what?

A great bitterness assailed her. She had no laughter, no gaiety. To know gaiety, must not one be like Red Maude? Cordelia hit the railing with her open hand. "I hate her," she said. "I'll always hate her," she said aloud, watching the lights twinkle mockingly in Red Maude's house.

Cordelia heard Marguerite turning restlessly in her crib. As she touched the child she seemed hot and fretful. It was warm and close in the stateroom, so Cordelia bathed the baby with cool water and removed some of her covers.

Suddenly, without warning, Marguerite gave a piteous wail, the tiny knees drew up against her abdomen and she began to vomit. Terrified, Cordelia ran from the stateroom, stopped a steward and asked him to get the nurse quickly.

The nurse came at once, but she, after taking one look at Marguerite, backed away and ran wild-eyed down the passenger deck.

Within minutes, word spread through the boat that the baby Marguerite was stricken with cholera. Terrified passengers and crew huddled in groups, recalling gruesome tales of how whole boatloads of people had been known to die like flies. Some took pills, some burned sulphur and a few prayed. At first, only two people approached Cordelia's ill-fated cabin.

Mrs. Ikes came, but Cordelia sent her away because of the other small children. Button appeared, terrified, and remained outside the door like a faithful dog.

Dazed, hardly knowing what she was doing, Cordelia sat by the side of her child. She knew of no way to ease the agony. Over and over she prayed, "Please God, please God, maybe I loved her too much, but please don't let Marguerite die." She was sure in her own mind that she had carried the dread cholera to Marguerite from the Ikes child. Sobbing and praying intermittently, she looked up to see the bulky form of Reverend Bird standing in her doorway. His craggy face was lined with concern.

"I heard in the village," he said simply. "I have come to help."

"Don't come in," Cordelia told him. "Cholera is sure death."

"That is why I have come," he said. He didn't offer any long prayers. He sat by Marguerite's bed, put his great gnarled hand under the struggling child and lifted her in his arms. "You should raise her head so she won't choke on the vomit," he said. "I have brought some medicine. It is small use with cholera, but we must both pray to God that it will work."

Raising tear-dimmed eyes, Cordelia suddenly knew a great comfort in this man. His broad shoulders were ready to share her burdens —in life, or in death. How could she ever have laughed at him? Here was a man with the courage of his convictions.

Late that evening the ship's carpenter was working on a cherry coffin, carving flowers along one side. It was a nice piece of burl. He could get a good price for it in St. Louis. Then he looked up to see Button, the giant roustabout, standing in the doorway.

"Carpenter man," said Button, his voice deep with grief, "we need a coffin for Miss Cordie's baby. It done died of the cholera."

After Button had gone, the carpenter stood for a moment with his hands hanging loosely by his sides, then he looked at the big cherrywood coffin he had just finished.

The carpenter was an old man and he had been on *The Blue Teal* and other Riley boats before that. He was remembering how, long ago, Captain Riley used to bring his little black-haired daughter Cordelia aboard to visit them when they docked at Hermann. He remembered how she would smile and watch him work. It didn't seem possible that same little girl was a grown woman with a baby dead of cholera. It made him feel terribly old and very sad.

He took up a chisel. He hoped God would let him get that piece of cherry burl out of that big coffin without bustin' it all to pieces.

30

WHEN WORD REACHED WESTON that cholera stalked *The Silver Star*, the villagers formed a posse to keep the passengers from fleeing into the town. Men and women stood in a tight body, grim-faced and determined to keep the deadly menace from their soil.

On board the boat, passengers huddled in their staterooms or their wagons, waiting for the child to be buried as quickly as possible. But when Button appeared on the upper deck carrying a small cherry-wood box on his shoulder, they came out and watched.

A hush fell over the people as Cordelia appeared, tearless, white as death itself, and followed Button slowly down the staircase. Close behind her walked Reverend Bird carrying his big Bible. He had offered a corner of his little church's cemetery for the burial ground. Under a young walnut tree, he had said, and somehow just the sound of "a young walnut tree" was some measure of comfort to Cordelia.

Burial must be made immediately, since Marguerite was a cholera victim.

No one approached the trio and they silently descended the stairway. No one dared, so great was their fear of the dread disease.

But as soon as Button stepped on the dock a murmur arose from the crowd. A large man with a black beard stepped forward, blocking their passage. "I'm the mayor of this town," he said quickly, "and we want you to bury your dead somewhere else."

Cordelia looked at him incredulously. "Surely you would not keep us from burying a small baby. There is no harm in that!"

The man shifted his feet. "This is cholera, lady, and they say that even buryin' the dead can cause it to get a start. You ought to pour pitch on the body and burn it."

"Oh, no!" moaned Cordelia.

"Nonsense!" Reverend Bird advanced, his eyes flashing. "Hiram Graham, I'm surprised at you. One must be charitable. It was only a year ago that I put one of your own children to rest in that cemetery."

Hiram looked down at his feet. "But my child didn't have no cholera," he said stubbornly.

There were murmurs of assent from the crowd.

"Surely you don't mean I can't bury my baby in your cemetery?" Cordelia cried in a high, tight voice.

Hiram shuffled his feet again. "I'm sorry, ma'am, but we got to think of our wives and children. Couldn't you just bury her up by the river somewhere?"

"Out by herself with wild animals!" Cordelia swayed, and Reverend Bird steadied her.

"Stand aside, Hiram," he ordered.

Hiram stepped back before the minister's withering glance, but another man took his place. He held a shotgun. "I ain't a member of your church, preacher, so you got no claim on me. Now take your cholera and git!" He gestured menacingly with his gun.

Button put down the cherry coffin and reached for his knife. Cordelia knew there would be bloodshed in another instant. She put her hand on Button's arm. "Put down your knife, Button," she said. "Please let us come ashore," she beseeched the crowd. But they stood fast.

At last Cordelia turned back to the boat, but a passenger met them at the stage-plank. "We know how you feel, ma'am, but don't bring

[192]

your child back on this boat. Why don't you go upstream and bury her on the bank somewhere?" Cordelia saw the passengers nodding in agreement.

"Better do that, gel. Do like they say," said Fancy Foot, looking at her sympathetically. "I've seen them set fire to a coffin and pitch it in the river many a time."

"Not the river!" Cordelia drew back.

"Effen I was you, I'd do like they did in the old days," said Fancy Foot. "Put your child in a cottonwood log, calk it up with pitch, put iron hoops around it and bury it deep. Then when you ain't got passengers, you can tie a little boat on behind and fetch the log downstream, and bury the child decent-like—out in a Catholic cemetery."

"Pierre would want that, of course," said Cordelia uncertainly, "only I'm afraid that . . ."

"Nothing will bother the log," said Fancy Foot. "Dug up a man been buried that way oncet. Been there two years. He was as good as new."

"I've heard of it," said Reverend Bird. "And I can understand how your husband, especially, would want the child buried in a burial ground of his own faith."

Cordelia looked at the ship's carpenter and he nodded. "I done it oncet," he said, "for a priest that died of cholera. We marked the spot with a high cross, and in the spring, two other priests came and took the log to St. Louis."

"Prepare the log," said Cordelia in a barely audible voice. "At least it will be some comfort to know Marguerite will in time be buried with the rest of the de Vries family."

The crowd on the docks increased when it was learned they were going to walk down the bank in the direction of The Petticoat and bury the child under a large elm on the bluff. It was the most excitement the village had seen since a steamboat had burned on the river the year before.

Women from The Petticoat, hearing the noise and learning the child was to be buried a short distance from their establishment, came out to watch. They stood apart, talking and giggling and flirting with the male bystanders who were not accompanied by their wives.

Finally, a murmur ran over the crowd. "They're coming, they're coming. They've got the log. There she is, there's the child's mother!"

Craning their necks for a glimpse of the woman whose baby had died, they were disappointed to see she was not weeping nor bowed on a supporting arm. She walked straight and tearless, her black hair flowing about her shoulders. Beside her walked Button, the log, with its tiny burden inside, on his shoulder, his eyes rolling in fear.

"She ain't cryin' at all," a woman said loudly.

"Course not!" another replied. "She's cryin' inside and that's worse. A whole lot worse."

Reverend Bird followed them, his head thrown back and his eyes darting lightning at the crowd. Suddenly his wife Martha came running and crying, "Judd, Judd, come back." She hung on to his arm. "You'll die of the cholera! Please, Judd, come away!"

He loosened his wife's frantic grasp, shot her a glance of withering scorn and let it play over the faces of the rest of the villagers. They fell silent, watching the trio on the bank going past the graveyard, walking through the long green grass to where an elm grew high on the bluff.

They were halfway up the bluff when the carpenter ran down the stage-plank crying, "The spade! My God, they forgot the spade! Somebody take them the spade!" He started to run after them, but the crowd shouted a warning. The silence deepened, and people looked everywhere but at each other. No one moved.

Then a voice, deep for a woman's, spoke up. "All right, you yellow-bellied fish. I'll take them the spade." Down from a little rise walked Red Maude, her bosom half-exposed to the gaping men. The women pointed and buzzed. The men shifted and looked uneasy. Quickly Red Maude jerked the spade from the carpenter's hand. The crowd parted as if cut with a scythe as she swept through them and hurried up the bluff after the burial party.

Button had just put down his burden under the giant elm in the soft soil when he remembered. "Oh, Miss Cordie, the spade!"

"Oh, no, Button!" she gasped. Involuntarily she looked back toward the boat. It was then that she saw Red Maude coming with a spade in one hand, and lifting her skirts just short of the mud with the other.

Red Maude came up breathless, her hair tumbling down. For a long moment the two women looked at each other. Then silently Red Maude handed Cordelia the spade.

"Thank you," said Cordelia through numb lips. She realized it was Red Maude, but she was too drained of emotion to think.

Without replying, Red Maude turned to Button. "We'll take turns, the preacher and I, helping you dig the trench. It oughta be good and deep."

Most of the crowd had shamefacedly dispersed before Cordelia and the others returned, but the passengers came from their staterooms and watched as she came back. They saw her walk, straight and frozen to her cabin. The door closed behind her.

All evening they talked about how she had sowed fleur-de-lis on her child's grave, and how Button had erected a high cross. They gossiped about the famous hussy who had taken them the spade and helped bury the log. They said she had seen lots of cholera in the war and being what she was, she wasn't afraid of Old Nick himself.

Joe Ikes, the fiddler man, made up a sad song about Cordelia. He called it the "Song of the River Witch." It was all about a beautiful river woman with raven hair, who buried her baby in a cottonwood log. The passengers wept when he sang it, and even his wife said, with her voice unsteady, it was the best song he had ever made up. But Cordelia never heard the song. She remained in her stateroom with the door closed. She was not seen again until *The Silver Star* tied up at St. Joseph. And then she appeared only at a distance, high in the pilot-house.

At St. Joseph, Cordelia watched with bitter eyes as passengers stampeded in their eagerness to leave the boat. Reverend Bird, who had insisted on making the trip with her, came to tell her goodbye. "I can only say to you, my dear, that in time God will soften your grief," he said.

Cordelia looked directly into his eyes. "Nothing, neither God nor time, will do that," she said in a flat voice.

"Excuse me, ma'am." Joe Ikes shuffled up, interrupting them. "I just want to say how sorry we are about your baby gettin' cholera from ours."

"Let's not speak of it." Cordelia looked away.

Joe Ikes stood, shifting first to one foot, then the other. "I made up a purty song about you and your baby. I called it the 'Song of the River Witch.' I could fiddle and sing it for you. If you was to cry, it might help."

"I don't want to hear any fiddling," said Cordelia, her voice strained to the breaking point. "Be off with that family of yours so you get to California before winter."

Joe Ikes ducked his head. "Is there anything I can do—anybody I can pass the word to about your husband bein' hurt and about the baby?"

Josiah's dark face flashed before Cordelia, but she shook her head. "I have no one," she said. "No one in California."

When Joe Ikes was gone, Reverend Bird asked, "Surely, Mrs. de Vries, you do not feel hard toward that poor man?"

Cordelia's voice was low and hard as she answered, "My father always said I loved everything I loved a little too much. I hauled that worthless man because I was sorry for him. He brought me death— death to the thing I loved most in this world. I used to love the people on the boats and the landings, but I'll never love them again!" she said vehemently.

"It was only that they were so afraid of the cholera," he protested.

"I hate them!" said Cordelia. "I'll never love anything again."

"My poor child," said the minister. "I do not like to leave you like this, without forgiveness in your heart."

"Reverend Bird," she said, "I shall never forget what you've done, and if Pierre could only know, he'd be even more grateful. But don't ask me to forgive those people, because I never will." With that she left the minister gazing sadly and helplessly after her.

When *The Silver Star* docked at St. Louis, a crowd had gathered on the levee. As Cordelia came out on the deck they pointed at her.

"Why are they staring at me?" she demanded of Fancy Foot Morgan. In the back of the crowd she saw the Abbé and prayed that he had good news of Pierre.

"Folks want to see what you look like," explained Fancy Foot. "You're the first woman ever to take a boat up the Missouri. Then, too, they heard about the baby bein' buried in a cottonwood log, and they like to make over things like that."

"Curiosity-seekers." Cordelia's lips curled bitterly.

"Don't be angry with them," Fancy Foot said. "Folks are funny. Now that you're the talk of the levee, everybody will want to get on this boat. First thing you know you'll be the richest woman on the river."

Cordelia looked at Fancy Foot with stony gray eyes. "Rich?" she said. "What good is *rich*, when I am the loneliest one?"

PART THREE

31

Two years later Pierre de Vries had recovered sufficiently from his injuries to pilot *The Silver Star* again. And the boat had become the most popular one on the Missouri. Fancy Foot Morgan's prediction had come true; Cordelia had caught the imagination of the public, and the title bestowed on her by the singing fiddler had become a by-word. Passengers had a notion that both they and their cargo were safe as long as The River Witch was aboard.

River-men told over and over how Cordelia had taken a raft to bring her child's body down the river—only to discover that the entire bluff-side had been gobbled up by the hungry Missouri. They told how for days she had stood on the deck while the crew searched for the cottonwood log, and how, when it could not be found, she had shaken her fist at the river. They whispered that Cordelia, swearing vengeance on the river, had become its master. There was true witchery in her success with the boat.

For the past six months, Pierre had insisted that Cordelia remain at Beaver House, but to his distress she had refused. There was money in their bank account—the success of *The Silver Star* was a fact—but Cordelia herself was emotionally bankrupt. Inwardly she seemed to be burning with restlessness, but outwardly she appeared indifferent to everything she had once loved.

Now on this June morning Pierre was leaning on the railing, watching the crews loading cargo at Westport Landing, one of the fastest-growing towns on the Missouri River. He was scarcely aware of what they were doing because he was deeply perturbed about the rumors he had heard on the levee. Summoning Button, he began to question him. "Button, is it true that Negroes are telling that Miss Cordelia is still looking for the cottonwood log?"

Button would not meet his eyes and evaded a direct answer. "Well, Mistah Pierre, you know how she always make de boat stop so she can look at de place where de baby wuz buried, and how she keep looking where dat fancy-house fall in . . ."

"Yes, I know, Button," Pierre said, "but you haven't told me . . ."

"Mistah Pierre," Button burst out, "will Miss Cordie evah be laughin' and lovin' any more?"

"I wish I knew a way to make her laugh, Button," Pierre said sadly.

"She cain't *laugh* 'cause she cain't *cry*," said Button. "You ought to make her cry, Mistah Pierre. A man got to do dat—onct in a while anyways. It keep a woman happy."

After Button was gone, Pierre took out his pipe and began to smoke thoughtfully. Darkies were direct and elemental. He remembered a nigger roustabout he had had once. He used to slap his woman to the deck, and when she came crawling back, push her away until she cried. Then he'd wait, and finally she'd smile and he'd pick her up and carry her into the bushes if it was anywhere near dark. Pierre smiled wryly to himself. That was a nigger's way. But he was white. And Cordelia . . . Cordelia was a woman who had taken this boat up the Missouri with only the drunken Fancy Foot to help her. Pierre shook his head. Cordelia had strength, dignity and warmth. He sighed. It had been a long time since she had shared her warmth.

Pierre had been so absorbed in his thoughts that he had not realized some sort of commotion was going on below. But now he saw that the whole crew had ceased loading cargo and had gathered around a tremendous fish lying on the docks.

Looking down with interest, Pierre saw Fancy Foot Morgan shoulder his way through the crowd and cover the fish with a canvas. Beside the fish, covered with blood and grinning like a gargoyle, was No Legs Harry.

As the crowd pressed closer, Fancy Foot held out his hat and began to bark, "Step right up, folks, and see the monster catfish—the demon fish of the Missouri! Weighs three hundred pounds and caught by No Legs Harry!"

Three hundred pounds! *Mon Dieu!* What a feat, thought Pierre, awed. Then he smiled to himself. At last No Legs had caught his catfish, and now he'd be what he always said it would make him— the tallest man on the river.

"Step right up, folks," bellowed Fancy Foot. "You can put your head in the fish's mouth for a penny." Pierre laughed, as villagers and even passengers began flocking to the docks to pay their pennies. Then his smile faded and he gripped the railing as he saw Cordelia hurrying down the broad stairway, frowning.

Walking out on the docks she stopped in front of Fancy Foot. "Just what do you think you're doing?" she demanded sharply.

"I've caught the monster catfish!" No Legs broke in jubilantly. "Look!" He drew aside the canvas. "A long time ago I promised your father I'd catch it; and he said it would make me the tallest man on the Missouri. And he was right! See how these people are a-standin' and lookin'!"

"And so does the crew look—at my expense," said Cordelia. Her voice was harsh now. "You, Fancy Foot, why are you defrauding people of money? You, No Legs, why aren't you peeling potatoes?"

"No, Cordelia!" Pierre said to himself. "Mother of God, what has happened to you, Mimi? Let No Legs have his day. Don't take away his dignity!"

"I was going to give you the fish," said No Legs slowly. "Or only the head if you want. See, you really can put your head in this fish's mouth!" He ducked his dirty head into the fish's wide mouth.

Cordelia drew back. "Get rid of that filthy fish and get back to work!" she ordered. "If you don't, I shall find a new cook!"

A sudden hush fell over the crowd and the crew scurried nervously back to rolling barrels. No Legs sat stunned, his arm thrown protectively about his fish. Then slowly he dragged himself across the docks and back to the boat.

Pierre was waiting for Cordelia when she came back to the stateroom. "Pierre!" she exclaimed when she saw his face. "Are you ill? You're as white as death!"

"No, Cordelia." His voice shook. "I am very, very angry. I cannot remember when I have been so shocked."

"At what?" she asked.

"At you," he replied. "I heard you just now on the docks. How could you! How could you have done that to No Legs Harry when you *knew* what that fish meant to him?"

She flushed slightly. "I *was* a little hasty, I guess, but they were wasting time and—we are behind schedule."

"Schedule!" exclaimed Pierre. "Cordelia! Mimi, what has happened to you?" he demanded. "You were not hasty, you were cruel! There is no boat, no shipment on any river, that is worth the price of a human being's dignity. For once, this legless man would have been looked up to. Today he was important—and you took it away from him. I will not have it!"

"Pierre!" gasped Cordelia. "How dare you speak to me like that."

"I am your husband, Mimi," he said.

She drew back. Never had Pierre spoken to her like this. "Dignity!" she cried. "No one left *me* any dignity. People would not even let me bury my child decently. You can talk of loving people, but when I needed help, on whom did I have to depend? A common prostitute."

"And I do not even think you have, in your heart, forgiven Red Maude, even though she did help you," said Pierre. "She, too, could have protested your burying our child so near her house. Have you never wondered where she was or what became of her after the flood washed her house into the river?"

"You told me yourself," said Cordelia, "that girls like Red Maude might get hungry, but they seldom starved. I know her kind. She'll get what she wants out of this world!"

"You see," said Pierre, "you still have a resentment against people —and that is understandable—but not when you take it out on a helpless man like No Legs Harry."

"He should have been peeling potatoes!" Cordelia said fiercely. "If, when you were ill, I had run this boat in a sentimental manner, I should have lost it. I watched every penny! I have never—since the day I hauled that wretched Joe Ikes—allowed anyone to take advantage of me!"

"I would rather have lost a thousand boats," said Pierre, "than for you to have lost your love of humanity." There was a silence, and finally Pierre said, "Mimi, I beg of you, talk to the Abbé about the way you feel. I know he can help you."

"I told you," Cordelia said, "I cannot, will not talk to the Abbé. I am still a Protestant at heart. I do not believe as you do that . . ."

"Mimi! Do you think I am trying to force my faith on you? You know better. You took my faith when you became my wife but I do not demand that you practice it as I do. I only know the Abbé can help you find peace of mind."

"I'm sorry," said Cordelia. "I did not mean to be cruel to No Legs. And I never saw you so angry before." Her tone had softened.

She laid her hand on Pierre's arm, but he did not relent. "Sooner or later, Mimi, you must make your peace with this world or your hate will destroy you—and all of us," he said. "Now I am going up to the pilot-house, and I think you'd better go down and see No Legs Harry."

Cordelia meant to find No Legs Harry. She knew she had been cruel, but she remained face-down on her bed where she had flung herself. She was deeply disturbed by what Pierre had said about Red Maude. More and more she had begun to wonder what had become of Red Maude. Slowly Cordelia had come to realize that now she knew how Josiah Callahan had felt when Red Maude came along and tended his wounds. But she tried not to think about that, or about Josiah. For thinking of Josiah Callahan was like floating down a deep river that had no end. She pressed her hands to her forehead as she heard the Negroes singing a mournful song on the lower decks.

She did not know it was the song that Joe Ikes, the fiddler man, had written about her. For two years now, while Negroes shocked corn in fields, rolled barrels on wooden docks, or just sat full of johnnycake and sorghum in the boiler room, they sang of Cap'm Riley's daughter, "The River Witch."

> "Cap'm Riley's daughter was a River woman
> River woman on the Old Missouri, Oh.
> The Old Missouri, Oh!
>
> "Her little baby died of cholera
> Died of the cholera, Oh.
> Now Cap'm Riley's daughter is a River Witch,
> A River Witch.
> Callin' for her baby . . . Oh.
>
> "Listen early in the mornin',
> Listen late at night,
> River Witch is callin' high, and callin' low.
> Cap'm Riley's daughter,
> Lonesome Missouri woman, Oh . . ."

The sound of the music depressed Cordelia, but she had no idea that the "Song of the River Witch" was being fiddled in every coffee house and barroom across the country, or that like "Joe Bowers" it was sure to bring a tear to the eye and a penny to the hat. Cordelia did not know, because she no longer cared for songs, or for the people who sang them.

Listening high in the pilot-house, Pierre de Vries knew every word of the song. But he knew of no way to break through the wall surrounding the woman about whom it was sung. Cordelia was his wife, but she might as well have been upon another boat, on another river.

32

In August, at Cordelia's insistence, Pierre purchased another steamboat, a trim side-wheeler which Cordelia promptly christened *The Marguerite*.

But when she announced her intention of taking *The Marguerite* upstream while Pierre remained on *The Silver Star*, he protested vigorously. "It was all very well for you to go on the river when necessity demanded it, but now there *is* no necessity. I am well and strong and we have everything we need. Besides, I do not want you on a boat with some new pilot who probably does not know the river well."

"Oh, but I've found one of the best," protested Cordelia. "His name is Sid Howe."

"Sid Howe!" exclaimed Pierre. "Do you mean you've already engaged this man without consulting me?"

"Why, Pierre!" Cordelia tried to tease him. "Is it possible you think no one else can pilot a boat as well as you?"

Pierre flushed. "You have a sharp tongue of late, Mimi. Perhaps it is just as well my mother has gone to live with Janette. I fear you two would not get on so well now as you used to."

"I'll always love your mother," said Cordelia. "It was lonely for her here while we were gone. But you are evading the subject. What is wrong with Sid Howe?"

"He is a good pilot," said Pierre, "but he is new, impatient, and he is a hot-headed Southerner. He has had trouble with the free Negro roustabouts." He shook his head. "He's not the kind of river-man you've known all your life. He is the type of man your father would never have hired."

At the mention of her father, Cordelia sat silent a moment, then she replied stubbornly, "I'm sorry, Pierre, but I have already hired him for this trip. If he does not work out, I shall have another pilot on the next trip."

Cordelia and Pierre had been sitting at the big cherry desk, going over their accounts. Pierre put down his quill and said quietly, "There's not going to be a next time, Cordelia. This is your last trip up the river, except for pleasure."

Cordelia stared at her husband incredulously, her eyes wide with surprise. "Do you mean you're *forbidding* me to go on the river?"

Pierre got up from the desk and attempted to take her in his arms. "Look at me, Mimi," he said, putting his hand under her chin and tipping her head back. "This can't go on any longer—you on the river looking for something, or running away from it, I don't know which. Beaver House is our home. We shall have other children, a new life—perhaps another Marguerite."

"Don't say that!" She whirled on him. "Don't ever say that! You know there will never be another child like Marguerite!" Then, seeing his face, she faltered. "Pierre, you know I'm not the sort of woman to occupy myself with needlework."

Seeing the hurt in Pierre's eyes she added, "Your mother has always been content with Beaver House, just as you are content with being a pilot. But I'm not like that. I can't help it."

Pierre turned and walked away. He stood looking out the window for some time before he answered. Finally, he said, "Yes, Mimi, I know that—and I know now that I should never have urged you to marry me. I know your heart has often taken wing—and that you have always wished you'd married someone like Josiah Callahan—a man who has gone places and done things in the world."

Cordelia made a gesture of denial but Pierre went on. "You do not need to deny it," he said. "It is a relief to speak of it frankly. But you did marry me, Cordelia, and we have had a child and lost her. That makes a bond between us that only God can break. I should believe that, even if I were not a Catholic."

A feeling of remorse swept through Cordelia. Pierre had known about her errant thoughts all this time! "Pierre!" she cried aloud in a strangled voice. "I've tried to be a good wife . . . I know I've tried . . . I didn't mean to fail you. . . ."

"Every trip you make up the river I lose a little more of you,"

[203]

he said. "That is why I cannot—and I will not—let you continue. This must be your last trip."

Cordelia was white to the lips. "You can't mean that! You can't do that to me!"

"I'm sorry, Mimi," he said, "but that is final."

Cordelia could not believe Pierre would not relent, but in the days that followed, he remained firm. She boarded *The Marguerite* with a sense of uneasiness, almost wishing that she were not making the trip since she would have to return forever to Beaver House. But her pride kept her from saying so.

On the new boat, things went badly from the start. They almost grounded the first day out at St. Charles. Sid blamed his co-pilot, and the co-pilot blamed the engineer. As the trip progressed, Cordelia grew more tense. Pierre's attitude and his reference to Josiah Callahan had shaken her. For, though she had determined to bury all thoughts of Josiah, she found herself scanning the faces of men on returning wagon trains, in the hope that he might be among them. It was true that her heart had taken wing at times, and it humiliated her to know that Pierre had been so aware of it.

On the day *The Marguerite* passed the Knapp plantation, Cordelia looked at it bitterly, as she always did. After Cordelia had defeated Hugo in the boat race, Virginia had sent a curt note saying that Cordelia would no longer be welcome either at the plantation or at the Knapp house in St. Louis.

The hurt went deep. All those long months when she had struggled on the river, when Pierre was ill and Marguerite was gone, not a single word of sympathy had come from Virginia. Although Cordelia knew this, too, had probably been on Hugo's orders, still she found it hard to forgive Virginia.

To her considerable surprise Cordelia saw two of Virginia's servants standing on the landing, signaling *The Marguerite*.

Button, who, at Pierre's insistence, had accompanied her, saw them waving. "Please, Miss Cordie, cain't we even see what the darkies want?"

"I'm sorry, Button," she said. "You know why I can't stop!"

"Miss Cordie!" Button burst out. "I 'most never see my Anna any more, only when Mr. Pierre fix it so I can. I ain't seen my woman for more'n six months. I cain't stand it no more!"

"I'm sorry," Cordelia said with finality. She went into her stateroom and closed the door so she could not see the frantically signaling servants, or the look in Button's eyes.

The farther she got from the Knapp landing, the more Cordelia regretted her decision. Had something happened to Virginia? Or to little David? But *The Marguerite* steamed on up the Missouri. They reached St. Joseph ahead of time, but by then Cordelia knew Pierre was right about Sid.

He was not like any river pilot she had ever known. True, some of the old pilots were drunken, egotistical and erratic, but they did not set the crew snarling at each other's throats or shout at the Negro roustabouts until they subsided sullenly. She found herself wishing for Fancy Foot Morgan—rum bottle, Indian cures and all. Yet in the next instant she was glad he was Pierre's relief pilot.

It was with a feeling of depression that she watched the passengers stream from the boat and the new ones come on. My last trip, she thought. From now on I must be at Beaver House. After Beaver House, what? The sound of the rolling barrels made her head ache. Where was the excitement she had once felt at such a scene?

Waiting to come aboard was the battered remnant of some wagon train returning from a fruitless search for gold in California. The horses were so worn their ribs almost cut through the flesh, and the canvas on the wagons was in shreds. As always Cordelia wondered . . . but, no, men like Josiah Callahan never came back. They walked with sure steps into the adventures of the world. Sometimes they asked a woman to walk with them, but if the woman . . . ? She shook her head. What *was* the matter with her?

Looking at them more closely, she noticed that a crowd had gathered about one of the wagons, and as she watched a wild, half-starved-looking man stood up and began to fiddle. Cordelia caught her breath at the sound of his rusty voice and his squeaky fiddle. It was Joe Ikes.

> Come join in the chorus and sing its fame,
> You poor lonely settler that's stuck on a claim.
> Farewell to this country, farewell to the West.
> I'll travel back East to the girl I love best,
> I'll stop in old Missouri and get me a wife
> And live on corn-dodger the rest of my life.

A shout of laughter went up. A few people tossed coppers into the hat he passed. Joe Ikes and his gold! Cordelia thought scornfully. It was a miracle he'd lived to get back to Missouri. The image of his cracked boots flashed before her. To get them off her mind, she turned abruptly and went into the purser's office to check the new passenger list.

She looked up later to see Joe Ikes slouching against the doorway. He coughed two or three times in an apologetic manner before Cordelia would allow herself to recognize him. "Howdy, ma'am," he said. "Well, I got to Californy."

"And back, I see," said Cordelia dryly.

"I found me a real good claim," said Joe defensively, "but this here feller and I got to playin' cards and I put up my . . ."

"You put up your claim and you lost it," Cordelia said scornfully.

"Yes'm—" he ducked his head sheepishly, "that's why I ain't got no passage money. I was wondering," he plunged on despite Cordelia's frown, "if you would give me a ride on *The Silver Star.*"

Deliberately Cordelia put aside her pen. "This is *not The Silver Star.* This boat is called *The Marguerite!*"

Joe Ikes dropped his head. "Named after your little baby that died, I reckon."

"Yes." Cordelia looked away.

"I sure wish you could have heard the song I made up about you, ma'am," said Joe. "Folks in Californy liked it real good."

"I'm sorry, Mr. Ikes," Cordelia picked up a ledger with a shaking hand, "but we have no room for you on this boat."

After Joe Ikes had gone the purser cleared his throat. "Mrs. de Vries, we *could* put that fellow on the lower deck. . . ."

Cordelia shoved back the passenger list. "I charge a fair rate for passage on my boats. If people have the fare, I haul them; if they haven't, I don't. Is that clear?" She pushed back her chair and rose abruptly. "I'm going to the dining room. After that I will check your accounts. On the last trip with *The Silver Star* you were off nearly a hundred dollars."

Cordelia could not eat. She kept seeing Joe Ikes' pleading eyes. And late that night, lying sleepless on her bed, she felt impelled to rise and look down at the docks. A lantern burned in Joe Ikes' shabby wagon. Where was his family? she wondered. She sat on the edge of her bed until morning.

In the morning, just as *The Marguerite* was casting off, Cordelia was again drawn to the railing. Yes, the old wagon was still there.

Now the children had come out and were scratching about like a brood of hungry sparrows.

Suddenly the ragged canvas parted and Louisa Ikes stepped from the wagon and stood waiting for *The Marguerite* to cast off. Cordelia gripped the railing and she felt a terrible wrenching inside of her. For a moment she thought she would faint.

For Louisa Ikes held a small baby in her arms. Born somewhere in the desert, or perhaps in a tent in a gold-rush camp. Louisa Ikes' life had gone on, despite the brown-haired little daughter in a lonely grave. Cordelia realized that Louisa Ikes had known what she had not known—what Pierre had once tried to tell her—that life could not be static. Not grief, not love—no, not even hate. Not even hate, she thought, trembling—not even hate.

Without warning the long-delayed tears came to Cordelia's eyes. It was like ice breaking up in the river in the spring—uncontrollable, and a little terrifying.

Word spread throughout the crew that the "Boss Lady been cryin' all day." "Miss Cordie cryin'!" Button whispered softly to the old roustabouts. "That's good," they said. "Thank you, Lawd, that's good." All that day the Negroes sang softly, and late that night, lying on the wooden decks, they looked up at the stars and talked about living and dying and singing and dancing and loving and about the white woman crying. "Lawd, that's good!"

This gave Button courage to approach Cordelia again when, on the downstream trip, just before they reached Franklin, he saw the same two Negro servants signaling from the Knapp landing.

"Miss Cordie," his brow was wrinkled with worry, "darkies wavin' from de landin' again! Please, Miss Cordie!" he begged. "Put in for to land. They looks scairt to me."

Cordelia tried to summon a refusal, but she could not refuse the pleading in Button's childlike eyes. She knew, too, that Virginia would not dare risk communicating with her unless the matter were urgent.

"This landing is not on our schedule," Sid protested. "This poking-along, visiting kind of steamboating is out of date."

"You can find a boat more to your liking when we get back to St. Louis," said Cordelia. "I am the owner of this boat and I order you to put in at this landing."

As *The Marguerite* swung in for her unscheduled landing, Cordelia could see the servants' faces plainly. They kept looking back at the Knapp house in terror, while continuing to flap a big red calico skirt to signal the steamboat.

"Miz Virginia begs you to come quick—for de love of Gawd!" they shouted. "She say somethin' awful goin' to happen if you don't."

As Cordelia hesitated, one of the old Negresses began to cry. "Please come, Missy! If Mr. Hugo catch us, he kill us for suah."

33

HURRYING ALONG after the servants, Cordelia wondered if Virginia was again indulging in melodramatics. But when Virginia admitted her to her upstairs sitting room, she knew the trouble was real.

"Cordelia! Thank God you came!" She threw herself into Cordelia's arms. "I knew you would come, no matter how I'd treated you. I knew that in your heart you'd understand."

Cordelia scarcely heard her words. She was shocked by Virginia's appearance. The once lustrous hair hung in straggly wisps about her face, the fragile cheeks were sunken, and the great blue eyes ringed in shadows.

"Oh, Virginia!" Cordelia burst out. "What has happened to you?"

"Cordelia, take me away! You've got to get David and me away from here before it's too late!" Virginia's fingers dug into Cordelia's arms. "You don't know what it's like! Hugo has been utterly out of his mind ever since you won that race—and now he's gone completely mad over Anna's baby. . . ."

"Baby! Anna has a child?" Button's face flashed before Cordelia.

"Hugo built Anna a little house. She didn't want to live there. She cried. She begged me. . . ." Virginia sank down on the bed, too exhausted to go on.

"I think I know the rest," Cordelia said grimly.

Virginia raised a haggard face. "Hugo would go down to her cabin and stay for hours, and then he always came to me. To me! It seemed to give him a special delight. Then—" Her voice broke. "I found Anna was going to have a child. I hate him. Yes, I do, I hate him!

[208]

You never thought I'd do that, did you? I'm supposed to be a New Orleans girl—who overlooks things like that in her man. But not what *he* did! I hate him!"

"Virginia, calm yourself!"

Virginia drew a shuddering breath. "A week ago, the baby was born. And it was soon plain as can be that it was going to be black!"

"Black!" echoed Cordelia.

"Black!" said Virginia. "And how I laughed and laughed and laughed! Hugo slapped me, but I still laughed. I was glad—glad— that some nigger had got to her first!"

"Virginia!" cried Cordelia. "Hugo might have killed you! *You* know he can't stand to be made fun of!"

"That's why you've got to get David and me away!" Virginia pleaded. "I saw *The Marguerite* go upstream and I tried to signal you. I waited for the day you'd be coming down again . . ." Virginia began to cry. "There never was a minute, a day, that I have not known when you were on the river. I prayed for you—and when your baby died . . . I tried and tried to write. Hugo tore up my letters. . . ."

"Oh, Virginia!" Cordelia put her arms around her cousin, knowing at last the great release of forgiveness. "I'll take you away, of course. Where is Hugo now?"

"I don't know," Virginia said. "He's like a madman. He went to Anna's cabin and I heard her screaming. He made the darkies take away the baby when it was born, and they said it died. I heard her screaming again this morning. She won't tell Hugo who the father is. Every nigger has hidden out—they're frightened to death."

"Which cabin is Anna's?" Cordelia asked.

"The one without smoke," said Virginia.

"Then I think we'd better go down and see what has happened to her. At once."

The door to Anna's cabin was closed, but as they approached, they heard low, animal-like moans. Fearfully the two women pushed open the door.

Cordelia's hand flew to her mouth to stifle a scream. Button was sitting on the floor, moaning and rocking Yellow Anna in his arms. Anna was unconscious, and a trickle of blood ran from the corner of her mouth.

"It was Button!" cried Virginia, beginning to laugh hysterically. "A common roustabout got the best of Hugo! Black Button!" Then she burst into tears. "Poor Anna! She didn't tell. He couldn't make her tell!"

Button seemed neither to see nor hear them. "Oh, Anna honey, your conjure run out. Why didn't you tell Button? Didn't you know Button would come?" Then dazedly he seemed to realize Cordelia was there. "Miss Cordie!" he burst out in an agonized voice. "Somebody hurt my Anna!"

Before Cordelia could reply, the door was flung open. Virginia screamed and, turning, Cordelia saw Hugo filling the doorway. Behind him stood Jean Austin.

Hugo had grown fat since Cordelia had last seen him. He was disheveled, and his eyes were badly bloodshot.

"So," he said in a cold, sneering voice, "it was *your* black bastard that got to Anna." He advanced on Cordelia. "I suppose this is your idea of having the last word—sending your roustabout up here to the best yellow nigger in Missouri to breed black bastards!"

"Monsieur Knapp!" Jean Austin shouldered his way past Hugo. "Anna is hurt!" Then after a closer look, "My God, she's been beaten nearly to death!" He turned and looked at Hugo with blazing eyes.

Hugo shrugged. "Well, don't look at me, you fools. It's that black brute there that did it!" He pointed to Button. "What can you expect? A nigger off the levee. He's killed two or three men, and you all know it!"

There was a low rumble, a growl from deep in Button's throat. He strode to the bed and laid Anna down on it carefully. Then he stood in front of Hugo, his great hands hanging by his sides and his head rolling. "It's you who hurt my Anna, Mr. Hugo. She afraid of— she always afraid of you!"

"Get away from me, you black beast," said Hugo. "If you lay a hand on me you'll be hanged before morning."

Button's voice rose to a shout. "I'm gonna kill you, white man. I'm gonna kill you for what you done to Anna!" His great hands came swinging down and fastened themselves around Hugo's throat.

"Button!" gasped Cordelia, pulling desperately at his arm. Hugo's eyes bulged and his tongue shot out of his mouth. But Hugo had great strength. He gave a mighty jerk and, breaking away momentarily, drew his pistol. But just as the gun went off, Button sent it spinning. Again there was a growl from Button, and his hands gripped Hugo's throat again. "I gonna make your tongue fly outa your head, Mr. Hugo. Then I gonna cut your heart out with mah cannin' knife and stomp on it."

Austin now roused himself and tried to loosen Button's grip. "You fool nigger, they'll hang you for this!" But Button shook him off as if he were a fly.

In desperation, Cordelia ran from the cabin, screaming for help and beating on the doors of cabins as she ran. She was able to find two white men, who gathered up several Negroes and surrounded Button.

Button was banging Hugo's head against the wall. "I gonna feed your guts to de fish, white man!" he shouted wildly.

"Stop him, stop him!" begged Cordelia. Again the men rushed Button. Two succeeded in getting hold of an arm, another grasped him by the throat and one kneed him in the back. At last they pinned the giant Negro, sobbing and foaming, to the floor.

Hugo held his bruised and swollen throat. "Take that nigger out and hang him!" he ordered. "He attacked me."

The white men looked at each other. The Negroes remained silent.

"Send for the sheriff," Hugo gasped. "Lock him up in the house so they can burn him for a torch."

"You can't take Button," said Cordelia, stepping forward. "I forbid it."

"He tried to kill me." Hugo's eyes glittered. "I warn you, Cordelia; if you try to keep that nigger from getting his just deserts, it will be the sorriest day of your life!"

One of the white men looked curiously at Cordelia. "After all, ma'am, he's a nigger, and he did try to kill a white man."

"Let me take him to New Orleans," Cordelia begged. "They'll hang him if I leave him here—and he's not to blame."

"You sound like one of them Boston nigger-lovers, ma'am." The man's lip curled. "Come along, we'll lock him up, and let the townspeople hang him if they want to."

The frightened Negroes helped drag the struggling Button away. Hugo staggered after them. "Come along, Virginia," he snarled, "you sniveling bitch!"

Virginia crept from the corner where she had hidden and stumbled after her husband.

Two Negro women appeared and began caring for Anna, casting frightened looks at Cordelia and Jean Austin.

Standing outside the cabin, Cordelia was surprised to see that Jean Austin was on the point of hysteria. "Mrs. de Vries," he said in a strange voice, "what you are thinking of is madness! If you were to take a Negro away—a Negro who assaulted a white man—you would be ruined. Feeling on the slavery question has men at sword's point. You are a woman who is known everywhere because of your activities on the river. You must go. Forget him."

Cordelia knew what Austin said was true. She had seen riots at the slave markets and she had seen steamboats lie idle because they had a Yankee captain. If she helped Button, she might lose everything she had. She knew that to most people Button might be a dangerous badman of the levee, but all she could remember was Button fixing her swing, and carrying her from the river when she had almost drowned. And he had truly loved Anna. Her father would never have deserted Button at a time like this. Neither would Pierre —no, nor her mother. Margaret Riley would have taken Button away, no matter what the cost.

"I've made up my mind," she said. "I'm going to get Button away from here."

"You are determined?" Austin's face had suddenly turned a ghastly color and great beads of sweat stood out on his forehead. He seemed to be burning with some deep intensity. "Whatever the consequences?"

"Whatever the consequences," Cordelia said, taking a deep breath. "I only hope my husband will understand why I have to do it."

"Then," said Austin, forcing the words out, "I must rescue Button. You go back to your boat and wait."

"I'm sorry," Cordelia said, "but I don't trust you, Austin—you've been with Hugo too long."

"Mrs. de Vries, look at me," Austin ordered. "Look closely. What do I look like to you? A Creole? I can see you drawing back. I think you've always suspected. Yes, Mrs. de Vries, I am a Negro. An octoroon. They say an octoroon is free. Free for what? To be a Negro? A white man? Only to *pretend* to be a white man—until Hugo Knapp finds out what he is."

"Then you *are* a Negro," breathed Cordelia. "Once I thought so. . . ."

"Yes." Austin's voice was only a whisper. "I have not the blood to be a white man, nor the courage to be a Negro. But this once I may be something. I will help you."

"But how?" she asked.

"Let us say I have my methods." Austin bowed as if discussing the time of day. "Go to your boat and wait. If I do not appear with Button and Anna within an hour, you had better cast off and forget what you have seen and heard in this place." Then he turned and walked swiftly in the direction of the house.

Frightened and still shaking, Cordelia was confronted with an angry Sid when she came aboard *The Marguerite*.

"Mrs. de Vries," he said coldly, "I don't know what's going on, but I don't like it! The passengers are furious at the delay and it's boiling hot. We aren't picking cargo and it's still daylight. I say we cast off."

"Mr. Howe," said Cordelia icily, "I own this boat and I say we're waiting here for an hour. My reasons are my own!"

"You forget," he drew himself up and regarded her insolently from his narrow eyes, "a pilot is supreme on the river."

"On the river, yes!" said Cordelia. "But a master and owner is in command when we're docked. And we're docked!"

She could feel Sid's eyes boring into her back as she stood at the railing and watched the bluff-side anxiously for what she well realized might be the most fateful hour in her life. Often, in that hour, she told herself she was a soft-hearted fool, but in her heart she knew she had no choice.

34

H u g o K n a p p lay on the wide canopied bed holding a wet towel to his swollen throat. "You and my dear cousin planned this between you," he grated at Virginia, his eyes glittering with malice.

"I've told you we didn't," Virginia said tearfully, bringing another towel.

"You'll play a different tune this evening," Hugo sneered, sitting up painfully. "You'll have the pleasure of watching that nigger hang."

"Hugo! Please!" begged Virginia. "I implore you, let Button go!"

"A fine, loyal wife you turned out to be! Defending a nigger," said Hugo. "I ought to . . ."

There was a sharp rap at the door. "Who is it?" Virginia asked in a high quavering voice.

"Jean Austin," the smooth voice replied. "I wanted to let you know that the sheriff and a posse are on their way."

"Tell Austin to come in," Hugo said. "I have a thing or two to say to him." Then he waved Virginia away. "And you can go."

Hugo lay back down on the bed and closed his eyes. He was dizzier than he thought. When he opened his eyes he found Jean Austin standing by his bed staring down at him.

"Well, is the sheriff coming or isn't he?" Hugo asked irritably.

"He's coming, Hugo, he's coming," said Austin softly. "Any moment now they'll be up from the village with guns and ropes and torches. But, first," he said, "I want the key to the room where you have locked Button."

"Key?" Hugo shook his head to clear it. "What do *you* want with a key?"

"I'm going to free him," said Austin calmly, "before you goad that mob into hanging him—or worse."

Hugo's lips drew back in a sneer. "I always knew you would go nigger on me."

"That is more than I knew," said Austin. "The key—please. Remember, I know you locked your brother in his stateroom when the boat burned. I heard his dying screams."

"You fool!" cried Hugo. "You know he found out we were running fugitive niggers, and he'd have blabbed to my father. It was your neck as much as mine. You were the one who enticed the niggers aboard and helped me sell them back to their owners for a profit!"

"And I have slept no better since than you," said Austin. "The key, please." He held out his long slender hand.

"Why, you dirty yellow nigger!" Hugo lunged to his feet. "You were glad enough to sell your own kind down the river and glad enough to wear fancy clothes and spend my money . . ."

Austin's eyes narrowed and he moved toward Hugo. "Give me the key or I shall take it from you."

"Ha! Try it and see what happens!" Without warning Hugo swung upward with his huge fist and sent Austin reeling against the wall. "You weak-bellied, yellow fish! I can finish you with one hand." He staggered toward Austin.

[214]

Quickly Austin ducked under Hugo's arm and kneed him hard in the back. Hugo had reached for his pistol but it went spinning as he fell to the floor with a loud grunt. Instantly Austin was astride Hugo.

There was a flash and Hugo saw a long slender knife gleaming in Austin's hand. "You fool! Put down that knife. Have you gone crazy over a roustabout?"

"Not a roustabout, Hugo!" Austin's eyes were mere slits and the whites had turned yellow. The knife made a shining arc through the air and came down hard. "Anna was my half-sister! My sister!" he hissed each time as the knife came down. "My sister! My sister!"

Too late Hugo made a superhuman effort to thrust Austin away, but his arms were like lead and there was a great numbness in his chest and a roaring in his ears. He struggled up, tried to pull the knife out, but it would not come. Dimly he saw Austin moving away, and heard the door closing. He was alone.

He lay quietly, trying to think, letting the warm, hot feeling spread through him. He could not believe that this had happened to him. I am going to die, he thought. And there is no one here. Charlie . . . he loved you best, Charlie, and nobody ever loved me. I'm not afraid to die, it's just that I've been alone all my life, and a man ought not to die that way too.

"It's dark. Virginia . . . you know I hate the dark." But the dark was there, rolling over him, pounding in his ears. And he knew there was no way to hold it back.

Aboard *The Marguerite,* Sid had become openly rebellious. "There's something mighty funny going on here, Mrs. de Vries," he said. "Listen to those pistol shots and the shouting in the village."

"I hear them," said Cordelia tensely, looking into the waning light. Suddenly she saw Virginia running down the bank carrying David in her arms.

"You must prepare to cast off in a hurry," she ordered Sid. "There's going to be trouble."

"If you ask me, you've already had it," he snorted, and stalked away.

Cordelia caught Virginia in her arms as she stumbled onto the lower deck and fainted.

Passengers came out of their staterooms and watched as Cordelia ordered Virginia and David carried up to a cabin. What was going on? they wanted to know. Why the delay, and what was this boat mixed up in anyhow?

Their curiosity was further whetted when they heard shots, the sound of running feet and when a man with a gun appeared on the upper bluff. "Halt! We've got you, nigger!" he shouted. Just then Austin and Button, carrying Anna, burst from the bushes. The deck was pelted with bullets that skipped across the water.

Passengers screamed and ran for the safety of their staterooms.

Now, at Cordelia's order, *The Marguerite* had cast off as Button and Austin waded into the water with the posse close on their heels.

The armed men shook their fists at the boat and cursed as Button, Anna and Austin were helped aboard the boat.

"Mrs. de Vries," said Sid, his eyes flashing. "I'll report you in St. Louis because it's all too obvious that you are aiding fugitive slaves to escape. I won't have them on this boat."

"You are forgetting that this is my boat," said Cordelia sharply. "We'll cross the river and land along the bank farther on so it will be easy for them to find their way into free territory."

Anger among the passengers had swollen to a sullen murmur by the time *The Marguerite* discharged the Negroes on a swampy bank, thick with watergrass and rotting logs.

"Oh, Miss Cordie," said Button, his face worried in the eerie light from the jacks. "I'se scairt for you. I can tell folks is mad." Yellow Anna stirred in Button's arms and he covered her with his shirt as one would a sleepy child.

"Where will you go?" asked Cordelia, realizing that once the fugitives melted into the darkness she would never see them again.

"I kin work anywhere," said Button. "Course it won't be the same," he said sadly.

"New Orleans is never curious," said Austin. "Mrs. de Vries, I think I should tell you . . ." Then he stopped. "Mrs. de Vries, why have you done this?"

"I don't know myself," said Cordelia, "except that when I saw them dragging Button away tonight, I knew that I cared what happened to him—and to other people. I had to do it."

"Oh, Miss Cordie . . ." Button's eyes shone in the dark. Without a word, he took the silver chain from around his neck and pressed it into her hand. Then the three were gone, melting into the woods, the darkness, the unknown.

The Marguerite moved on and Cordelia turned thoughtfully toward Virginia's stateroom. But as she approached the door a shadow detached itself from the side of the boat. "*That* for The River Witch and her niggers!" A sharp object struck Cordelia on the temple, and she heard the sound of running feet.

As she raised her hand to wipe away the blood that had begun to trickle down her cheek, she had a feeling that this might be only the beginning.

35

VIRGINIA HUDDLED in the corner of the carriage as she and Cordelia rode to the Knapp house. "What will Uncle Otto say?" she asked.

"He has a right to see his grandchild, and you have a right to his protection," said Cordelia.

"But what will I do if Hugo follows me? You know he will," faltered Virginia.

"Then you must come to Beaver House. Pierre and I will protect you."

"I can't let you do it," said Virginia. "I've already caused you enough trouble. I'll go to New Orleans . . . someplace. What will Pierre say about your risking your business and your reputation? Your life, even."

Cordelia touched her bandaged temple gingerly. "I don't know what Pierre will say. *The Silver Star* is docked, so he'll be at home. I'll go there as soon as I leave you with Uncle Otto."

"Do you think Uncle Otto will let me stay?" asked Virginia, clutching David.

Cordelia glanced down at David's tousled head. "You have nothing to fear as long as David is with you."

Cordelia was shocked at the sight of her uncle. His face had grown thin, and one corner of his mouth drooped. Only his eyes were alive. He turned them inquiringly now on Cordelia.

"So you came back, I see." His words were labored. "They told me you took a boat up the Missouri—you, a woman!" He struggled for breath. "Only a Knapp could do that!"

"Or a Riley," Cordelia reminded him gently. "Uncle Otto," she plunged immediately into her subject, "Virginia has left Hugo. I've brought her to you. She has David with her. I think you should offer her a home, despite what Hugo may say."

"Left Hugo?" The weak old hands fluttered on the bedspread. Then his eyes brightened. "Where is the child? Where is my grandson?"

Cordelia and Virginia watched from the doorway as little David walked into his grandfather's bedroom and stood by the bed, looking with wondering four-year-old eyes at the vast mountain of man propped against the pillows.

"Why are you so big?" asked David.

Otto Knapp's eyes looked hungrily at the little boy, at his buckled shoes, the sweet round face and at the curly red hair.

"'Cause I'm your grandpa, boy," the old man said in a hoarse whisper.

David wiggled with excitement. "Papa said you had a steamboat."

"Lots of steamboats . . ." Otto spoke with difficulty. "When you grow up, you'll have a steamboat of your own . . . Charlie. . . ."

"I'm not Charlie, I'm David Knapp," the child said in a firm voice, "and I don't want a boat. I want a steam car."

Otto raised up in bed, appeared to be choking and fell back on his pillows. "A steam car . . ." he gasped.

"Where did he hear that!" cried Virginia, rushing into the room and snatching David up. "You're bothering your grandfather. Come away."

"No!" Otto struggled to breathe. "Let the child stay . . ." Then, seeing Virginia, he said, "You have left my son—as I said you would someday."

"I had to, Uncle Otto . . ." Virginia said in a broken voice. "There were things . . . things . . ."

Blue eyes met blue eyes in a long look of understanding. "Yes, yes," the old man nodded sadly. "Put your things in the vacant room next to my wife's. You'll be comfortable there."

"Oh, Uncle Otto!" Virginia cried. "If you only knew . . ."

"Hush, you'll frighten the child," Otto cautioned. "Come here, boy," he ordered the child. "Come sit on my bed. So you want a new-fangled steam car, eh?"

Obediently David clambered up on the mammoth bed. "Why is Mamma crying, Grandpa?"

"Because," said Otto, his chin sinking on his chest, "men always make women cry . . . Charlie . . . That's a good boy," he added as David curled up like a small puppy. Otto's strength was spent and he fell back on his pillow and closed his eyes.

David took up his grandfather's nightcap and began playing with the tassel. Then, peering with bright eyes at the old man, he asked, "Grandpa, why are you shaking the bed? Why are you crying?"

"Come," said Cordelia, drawing Virginia away. "Let's leave them alone. You need to lie down and rest." She helped the worn-out girl to disrobe, then drew the curtains. "Try not to think," she said softly. "I'll see you in the morning. I must hurry to Beaver House. Pierre will be worried."

She wanted to be sure to tell him what had happened before he heard it on the levee. Gossip and scandal always rolled down the Missouri faster than a flood.

But when she reached Beaver House she found a white-faced Pierre, with the Abbé Choate attempting to quiet him.

Upon seeing Cordelia, Pierre rushed to her and took her by the shoulders. He shook her slightly. "Mimi! Where have you been? I missed your docking only by minutes. I've heard wild rumors about you on the levee, that you were involved in aiding fugitive slaves!"

"Oh, Pierre! Not slaves. Just Button and Anna!" She began to cry brokenly and the whole story poured out. "I had to do it, Pierre! I couldn't let them hang him!"

"No, no, of course not," he said worriedly, "but you are involved in something far deeper than you know, I'm afraid."

"But I did know what I was doing, Pierre," she said. "I only hope you'll forgive me . . ."

"Look into my eyes," said Pierre gently.

Like a tired child Cordelia raised her eyes.

"The hate is gone!" he said. "It is gone from your eyes."

"I thought I could hate," whispered Cordelia. "I wanted to—when our baby . . ."

"Mimi!" Pierre took her in his arms. "Don't tremble so, Mimi. It's all right."

Hardly knowing what she said, Cordelia went on. "I looked and I looked for Marguerite and I shall never find her. It was as if the river had taken my life's blood. She was the only thing I really loved . . . really loved."

"Yes, Mimi, yes, I know." Pierre smoothed her hair and his eyes met the priest's sadly.

That evening, Cordelia, Pierre and the Abbé were finishing a quiet supper when a rock crashed through the ancient paned windows.

For a moment the three stared at each other, startled, then looked unbelievingly at the shattered glass. "Go to the kitchen, Cordelia!" Pierre ordered, leaping to his feet at the sound of shouts in the street.

Peering out the window, Cordelia saw a mob with torches standing in front of Beaver House. "Bring out The River Witch!" they shouted. "Bring out The River Witch!"

Quietly Pierre opened the door and appeared on the steps. "I am Pierre de Vries," he said. "What do you want from my wife?"

"How come you let your wife haul runaway niggers?" a voice shouted.

Looking into the mob Pierre saw that it was Sid Howe who was urging the motley crowd on.

"So it's you, Sid," he said scornfully. "You always were a trouble-maker. You got a man hanged at New Orleans once for a crime he didn't commit!"

In reply a stone came flying and struck Pierre on the shoulder. As he staggered back, the Abbé appeared beside him.

At the sight of the priest, a hush fell over the crowd; many of the people there were from the Abbé's parish. "None of you is violent and sinful by yourself," he said evenly, "but together you make a bad thing. Go to your homes—all of you!—and consider what you have done."

A murmur ran through the crowd and it began to break up as the men slipped away. But Sid and a small band remained in the yard, shouting insults and threats for hours.

"Oh, Pierre, what have I done?" cried Cordelia. "I don't see why so many people are concerned with what I did."

"My child," said the Abbé, "you do not seem to realize that you are famous on the river and that what you do influences a great many people. Unfortunately, the slavery question right now is white-hot and really explosive in St. Louis, yes, in all the country. What you did, through compassion, may well cause the prejudices and discontents of our people to reach a climax."

He shook his head. "I must go now. Let us hope this is only a temporary thing, started by that trouble-maker, Sid Howe. Perhaps in a few days the levee will have something new to talk about."

But before the sun went down the following day, two men appeared at Beaver House bringing news of Hugo's death. And the next day, it was commonly known that Cordelia Riley de Vries, known as The River Witch, was to be brought before the magistrate in St. Louis, to give just cause as to why she had aided and abetted the escape of a Negro roustabout known as Button, the same presumed to be the murderer of Hugo Knapp.

Cordelia, stunned and bewildered by Hugo's death and by the sudden turn of events, and unable to deny that she had willfully taken Button, Anna and Austin away from the scene of the murder, posted $5,000 bond. She was released, but ordered to appear with counsel on the eighteenth day of March, 1852, when the spring term of court convened.

In the days that followed, neither Pierre nor the Abbé could find a man in all of St. Louis with courage enough to defend The River Witch. Rapidly the storm of prejudice rolled over Beaver House. Threatening letters arrived from rabid states' righters, slave owners and radicals. Money and poems came from Boston. Some called her a blight upon the name of womanhood; some called her noble.

In the controversy over The River Witch, Mexican War veterans, embittered because California had come in free, found an outlet. Men on their way into Kansas, carrying guns, took time to pen notes at the Planter House and states' righters broke out in a froth of oratory on the floor of the Senate.

All that long winter Cordelia dared not appear on the streets. On her one visit to the Knapp mansion to console Virginia, who despite her protestations of hate was desolate after Hugo's death, Cordelia was followed by hoodlums who pelted her with dried manure from the street. Later they carted off the lions that had sat on the Knapp steps since the day the mansion was built.

When the thaw came and the ice broke in the river, neither *The Silver Star* nor *The Marguerite* had cargo or passengers. The boats sat silent and idle, their shining glass a target for little boys with stones.

36

ONE FEBRUARY MORNING Cordelia stood by the window watching the river mist enfold the city.

Turning from the window, she saw that Pierre had entered the room and realized that he must have been watching her for some time. Of late he had spent his days in a little warehouse on the levee, trying to dispose of the goods they had stored there. But this morning he was wearing his best waistcoat and carrying his new beaver hat, so she knew he had more important business than the warehouse.

"I've been meaning to tell you, Mimi," he said casually, bending to throw another log onto the fire. "I have located a lawyer who will take your case. His name is Beaman."

"Beaman!" Cordelia exclaimed. "Not the man in the office over the hemp warehouse! Not that little man who chews on his mustache?"

"Beaman is clever in court, regardless of his address or appearance," Pierre said, "and he is noted for winning controversial cases. In fact, he approached me . . ."

"Oh, Pierre," Cordelia touched his arm, "if only you would reproach or scold me!"

Pierre did not take her in his arms to reassure her, as he would once have done. He had been quiet and withdrawn ever since telling her he knew she was not content in her marriage. Now she missed the old tenderness, but felt she had no right to ask for its return.

"I know how it hurts you not to be on the river," she said, trying to break the constraint between them. "You are a good pilot; other owners would be glad to have you. I beg you not to remain at home because of me."

"Don't make me sound noble," Pierre said, the irritation in his voice betraying for the first time his nervousness over their situation. "I have an appointment with this lawyer within the hour—I want to be on time."

"Are you *sure* he will take the case?" Cordelia asked dubiously.

Pierre looked down at the hat he was holding. "He has already accepted an advance fee, and I have offered him so much more that he cannot refuse."

"But, Pierre, where shall we get so much money?" Cordelia demanded.

"You may as well know now, Mimi," Pierre spoke reluctantly, "I have sold *The Marguerite* and *The Silver Star*. Their new owner will take them over next week."

"Pierre! Not our boats! You *can't* have sold them!" Cordelia cried.

"There was no other way." Pierre straightened his shoulders. "I did it only as a last resort. Surely you know that."

Cordelia drew back as from a blow, but seeing the misery in Pierre's face, she held back her tears. Her voice trembled as she asked, "But what shall we do? How will we live?"

"I have been thinking." Pierre's brown eyes sought hers with concern. "After this is over and you are cleared, we could go away—start over again—go to California if you are willing."

"You, a river-man, on the prairie, going across the country? Oh, Pierre! You *know* you could never go to California! You would never leave this river and you know it!" she exclaimed vehemently.

Pierre gave her a strange, searching look. "I shouldn't think the trail to California would hold more terrors than the Missouri when she is in a bad mood," he said slowly. "But it is for you to decide, Mimi." He turned, preparing to leave, then faced her again.

"Remember, you must remain inside while I am gone. And admit *no one*. I found another of those fanatic letters under the door this morning."

Cordelia shuddered, thinking of the threatening, vitriolic notes that had appeared from time to time. After Pierre had gone Cordelia turned instinctively toward the kitchen where she had busied herself the past few months, under Emil's watchful eye, learning to prepare French dishes.

Opening the kitchen door she knew a brief reassurance at the sight of the familiar copper pots and the strings of herbs hanging by the fireplace. Emil, however, was dressed for the street and was in the act of carrying a basket out the back door.

"Emil! Are you leaving?" Cordelia asked in surprise.

"Yes, Miss Cordelia. I'm taking some food to a sick friend," Emil explained. "To an old man, a friend of my father's, who is nearing his end in an old house on the levee."

"The levee!" Cordelia exclaimed, a sudden idea occurring to her. "If you are going to the levee, I think I shall go with you."

"Oh, no, madame!" Emil protested. "Master Pierre would boil me in my own pot if I took you to the waterfront! You know you must be careful not to be seen on the streets, especially not on the levee!"

"I shall wear a veil," Cordelia said determinedly. "No one will recognize me. *The Marguerite* and *The Silver Star* have been sold, and I must see them once more."

"Please, madame," begged Emil. "The boats are not as you remember them. Vandals who roam the waterfront have thrown stones at them."

"Nevertheless," Cordelia set her jaw, "I must—and I will see what has happened to them. Boats were my father's life, and my own livelihood. I cannot let them go without a last look."

"But Master Pierre has forbidden you to go near the levee!" Emil argued desperately.

"I took *The Silver Star* up the river as its master," said Cordelia. "Surely the St. Louis waterfront can hold nothing worse than the Missouri did." She looked directly into Emil's eyes. As the two gazed at each other, the memory of the laughing baby whom both had loved so dearly rose between them. Finally Emil dropped his eyes and shrugged in hopeless acquiescence to her entreaty.

The fog was lifting and the sun warmed the streets. As their carriage passed the Planter House, Cordelia saw a gay young woman in a flowered bonnet look up laughingly at an equally happy young man. Was it possible she had once laughed like that on the arm of Josiah Callahan, coming out of the Planter House? So long ago, and yet she had only to close her eyes to hear the waltz as the orchestra had played it from their high balcony over the doors.

But when they passed the courthouse, Cordelia shivered at the black iron railing that encircled it, and the dome seemed as high as the sky. A crowd, gathered on the east steps of the courthouse, had overflowed into the street, so the pace of their carriage was slowed. Clearly she heard the auctioneer's voice ringing out. "A sound wench, sixteen years old, good to cook, bake and bear. Warranted a fine slave for life."

Staring out at the crowd, Cordelia saw that few were there for the business of buying a good sound wench. Almost everyone was

[224]

there from idle curiosity. Suddenly she realized that on the eighteenth of March, just such a crowd would stare at her.

"Don't think about it," said Emil, observing her gesture of withdrawal. "Everything will turn out all right, you will see. I have been to the Cathedral every Wednesday to ask it of the Blessed Damozel."

"The Cathedral! Oh, Emil!"

Tears sprang to Cordelia's eyes, for Emil was a French peasant and a timid man at heart. Never before had he knelt in any but the little parish church, with its simple whitewashed walls and its rudely constructed seats. The thought of his venturing into the vast Cathedral, with its high spire and shining gilt ball, to pray for her safety touched her so deeply she could not speak.

On reaching the wharf she was shocked to see that the condition of her once-proud steamboats was even worse than she had feared. Their glass was broken and someone had pelted the decks with debris. Water-birds nested in the railings, and the choppy Mississippi slapped disconsolately against their sides. They were muzzled, but old steeds of the river that they were, they strained at their moorings with a great sawing of hawsers and clanking of chains. A beady-eyed old crow stared impudently at Cordelia from the pilot-house of *The Marguerite*.

Determinedly, she went aboard to inspect the boats for the last time. In the ladies' cabins, velvet hangings gave off an unaired moldy odor. The cloths that had been put up to protect the great chandeliers were covered with dust and cobwebs. Vandals had torn the Bibles from the tables and the great chains hung empty. Sick at heart, Cordelia turned away and went back to the carriage. Yet as they drove away, she was glad that she had seen the boats this one last time.

En route home, Emil stopped before a dingy boarding house to deliver his basket of food. "I shall only be a minute," he said. "Only long enough to give my friend the food and to give some money to the winey old slattern who has agreed to care for him. Stay well back in the carriage," he added anxiously. "I dare not take you into such a place."

Emil bustled away and Cordelia sat studying the dilapidated frame buildings that showed tired gray faces to the street. Glancing up, she observed that every window was hung with the remnants of old lace curtains, cobwebby reminders of the street's better days. Two skulking, half-starved tomcats met on the street and set up a fierce caterwauling, and suddenly all the windows were peopled with faces, their expressions as dun-colored as the buildings in which they festered their lives away.

Here were the brothels, the boarding houses and the waterfront dives. Here a maggoty mass of humanity crept into the houses like scum from the river, to hide their sores, sleep off rum, end animal desires beneath some dirty lace petticoat, or starve—and so, in the end, be thrown back on the levee. If, like Emil's friend, they had a little money, they could die undisturbed in some dank back room. This was the waterfront life that passengers traveling on high white steamboat decks never saw or thought about. Nor did I, thought Cordelia, repelled and yet fascinated by this dirty shift-side of the city.

Suddenly a weather-beaten door swung open and a sailor stumbled out with a woman on his arm. Once in the street, the sailor thrust the woman from him. "G'wan with you!" he said roughly. "You've rolled me for my pay. What more do you want?"

"In a pig's eye," said the woman contemptuously. "You swilled your pay away into that fat belly of yours."

Without warning the sailor slapped the woman so hard she stumbled and fell against the building. Then he strode away, leaving her alone.

This had happened immediately in front of the carriage and Cordelia was sickened at the sight of the woman's slumped body. But as she watched, the woman straightened, rose to her feet, and as if the incident had never occurred, gave her bonnet a jaunty tug and began looking up and down the street.

Cordelia looked directly into a thin white face, wide tawny eyes —ringed with fatigue—and at glistening red curls that neither time nor the rough and tumble of levee brothels could dim. The woman was Red Maude.

As Red Maude arranged her dress and began to saunter off, Cordelia, without stopping to think, alighted from the carriage, picked up her skirts and ran after her.

"Maude! Wait! Please wait!" she called.

Red Maude stopped, then turned, her eyes sweeping suspiciously over Cordelia. "What do you want?" she asked haughtily.

Cordelia raised the veil from her face. "It's Cordelia Riley," she said, the old uncertainty and childishness she always felt in Red

Maude's presence sweeping over her. "Surely you haven't forgotten me?"

Red Maude's chin went up a notch and the plumes on her faded bonnet quivered. "I never saw you before in my life," she said.

"Maude . . . Miss Renfrew . . . please," said Cordelia. "I never had a chance to thank you for helping me when my baby died. After your house fell into the river and was washed away, I wondered about you—where you had gone. I know it was a terrible blow, losing it."

"I died laughing." Red Maude's tone was mocking.

"I know things must have been hard for you when you lost your house," Cordelia plunged determinedly on. "Let me give you some money—a loan," she added hastily, at the flash of anger in Red Maude's dark eyes.

Red Maude tilted her bonnet and looked out of the corner of her eye at two river-men coming down the street. "You are very amusing," she said contemptuously.

"Please," said Cordelia in a low voice. "I beg of you." She realized it had been a very long time now since she had hated Red Maude, but she knew she dared not let pity show in her voice.

"Why, dearie." Red Maude caught the eye of one of the river-men and signaled to him. He returned her signal. "As it happens," she told Cordelia, "my rich uncle died and left me a fortune. Let's hope yours does the same for you." With that Red Maude flounced away, hips undulating and her tarnished finery trailing.

"Maude! You can't go like this!" Cordelia ran after her and caught her arm.

"Sorry, dearie," said Red Maude, drawing away. "If you're still lost, I'm all out of directions."

"Here!" Cordelia thrust some bank notes into Red Maude's hand. "Don't take them for me, take them because of . . . because of my father—Michael Riley."

Red Maude drew back; her eyes sharpened, then deepened like those of an animal at bay. Fiercely she crumpled the money in her hand, then bending quickly, she raised her dress and stuffed the bank notes into a pocket sewed in her petticoat.

Without so much as another word, she turned and ran toward the doorway where the river-man was waiting. As Cordelia watched, they opened a door with a cracked glass and disappeared into the gray limbo of a brothel.

[227]

Finally Cordelia realized that an agitated Emil was shaking her. "Oh, Miss Cordelia," he cried. "Out here in the street! And giving money to the likes of her! A kind heart is a good thing, but you can't give money to every worn-out old prostitute you see on Battle Row!"

"Don't say that, Emil!" Cordelia cried fiercely. Then she burst into wild crying. "Oh, Emil, say anything about her— But don't say that!"

Emil hustled his mistress back into the carriage and drove home as fast as the crowds and the horses would allow. From time to time he cast an anxious eye at Cordelia and shook his head, as if the evangelical teachings of her childhood, which he considered nothing short of heathen, had put a black stamp on her soul for sure.

Cordelia knew a weary relief when they approached Beaver House. She was dismayed at seeing a strange carriage standing in front, and a Negro she had never seen before holding the horses. Could Pierre have brought the lawyer home with him—so soon?

As she approached the front door it flew open and an excited maid greeted her. "Oh, madame, there is a man inside to see you. I know I had orders not to let anyone in, but he insisted it was of the utmost importance. I couldn't keep him out. He said his name was Josiah Callahan."

37

AFTERWARD, Cordelia wondered whether, if she had waited to remove her cloak and bonnet, her reaction at seeing Josiah would have been otherwise.

The instant she appeared in the doorway Josiah rose from the chair by the fireplace and walked toward her. She saw that his eyes were as blue and piercing as she remembered them, and that he was lean as a whip in his light gray breeches. He has not changed, she thought wonderingly. He is the same.

Josiah spoke but one word, "Cordelia!" and took her hands in his.

The patter of convention rose to her lips but was never uttered. Wordlessly she lifted her eyes to Josiah and time spun backwards as he drew her to him. Instinctively they came together in a hard embrace and his mouth was on hers. This was the wind in the trees, the river around the bend, the other side of the mountain and the wine she had desired since girlhood, but never tasted.

Finally the room came back into focus and Cordelia drew back, glanced dazedly around and removed her bonnet. "Josiah!" she breathed. "I always wondered how it would be if I saw you again." She was still trying to catch her breath. "You haven't changed at all." She let her bonnet dangle limply by its velvet streamers. "Not at all. . . ."

Josiah too glanced about the room as if just realizing where he was. "Forgive me," he said finally. "When I saw you walking toward me, I forgot where I was, or the circumstances. I started for St. Louis as soon as I heard of your trouble. Surely you knew I would come."

"I still can't believe you're here—though I've often wished it. But I thought I should never see you again after that time on the river."

"I knew," said Josiah. "I knew that day when you turned and looked back at me that somehow it could not be the end. I have been wanting to come ever since I heard the song they were singing in the gold camps—about Captain Riley's daughter. I wanted to comfort you when I learned you had lost your baby."

"You knew that? You heard that song in California?" Cordelia asked incredulously.

"I heard the song over and over," Josiah said. "They said a fiddler brought it out to the Coast. I made inquiries and learned that the woman about whom they sang was you." They were sitting opposite each other now, quite some distance apart, yet it was almost as if they were touching, for Josiah kept his eyes on hers. "But I had no right to come then."

"Oh, Josiah!" Cordelia said in a low voice.

There was a silence. A shaft of sunlight, breaking through the mist outside, pierced the mullioned windows, picked up the muted colors in the old chintz furnishings and lay warmly across the room. "But now I have that right," Josiah went on. "I am a lawyer and I have come back to defend you."

Still agitated by his reappearance and her own reaction to it, she stared at him doubtfully. "Surely you can't mean to defend *me*—not feeling the way you do on the slavery question. It would ruin you." She knew Josiah was a slave-owner, ingrained in the Southern way of thinking, and that he was bidding for recognition in politics.

Even now she could remember how he had looked, leaning against the rail of *The Blue Teal,* arguing with her father over Button's position as a freeman. When she spoke, her voice was choked with grateful emotion. "You know how much I need and want your help, Josiah, but I can't let you do it. It would be the end of your career."

"Nonsense," Josiah said reassuringly. "People are fools and are easily swayed. They can just as easily turn for us as against us. I have never forgotten what your father once said: that you were 'a girl who loved everything you loved a little too much.' If the case is properly handled, everyone will be in sympathy with a tender-hearted woman who saved an old servant who had served her well. Judges are never inclined to condemn a beautiful woman for a soft heart. I promise you, Cordelia, I have your defense completely in hand—and if my plan works out, your case will be dismissed the day it comes to trial."

"You have done all this—without my knowledge? How could you, when you have just come back?"

Josiah smiled. "I've been back two months, and I've been working continuously. If your case had not been badly bungled, those Negroes would have been uncovered long ago."

"But Pierre has the authorities searching everywhere for them," Cordelia said defensively. "And just this morning we secured the services of a lawyer named Beaman. Pierre is with him now."

"Beaman is a grasping waterfront lawyer," said Josiah. "And he thinks of nothing but money."

"But Pierre has worked so long and so hard to find someone," faltered Cordelia, "and no one else would take the case. I couldn't hurt Pierre by questioning his judgment. I owe him so much . . ."

"Owe him!" Josiah leaned toward her. "Surely it was not meant that you should think only of duty all your life, Cordelia! Duty is fine, but when carried to the extreme, against one's natural wishes, it . . ."

"I am told it will kill the soul," said a deep, weary voice.

Startled, they both turned and saw Pierre leaning against the door jamb. His waistcoat was rumpled, and there were deep lines at each side of his mouth. His usually neat brown hair was tousled and he looked exhausted.

"Pierre!" Leaping to her feet, Cordelia ran to him and took his arm. "I didn't hear you come in. Josiah Callahan has come all the way from California to offer his services as my lawyer!" she explained breathlessly. "Isn't it wonderful of him?"

The two men shook hands somewhat stiffly. "You came all the way from California?" asked Pierre.

"I came to St. Louis as soon as I heard of Cordelia's troubles," Josiah replied. "I am here to offer you my services as a lawyer. I am confident that, with proper handling, the case will be dismissed before it ever comes to trial."

"We appreciate your offer," Pierre said slowly, "and certainly your reputation as a lawyer is of the best, but I have just made arrangements with a man named Beaman. He is perhaps not the lawyer that you are, Monsieur Callahan, but he is clever and interested. He expects to win our case." There was a slight edge to Pierre's voice as he added, "I am sorry you did not come forward before, if you wished to help."

Cordelia realized then that Pierre was not himself, that he was tired to the breaking point. But before she could speak, Josiah answered. "I did not come before," he said, "because I have been in New Orleans, searching for the culprits myself. I expect to find one of them and have a confession from him in a short time."

"You yourself went to New Orleans to search?" asked Pierre. "Surely you know the authorities have left no stone unturned in trying to locate both Button and Austin. Even if they are found, our lawyer, Mr. Beaman, feels we must use caution in their return. Our priest, the Abbé Choate, says that the emotions of the people now are like dry powder. Any spark . . ."

"Priests always predict the worst," Josiah said calmly, "and after all, it is for Cordelia that we are concerned—not about what happens to some guilty nigger."

"Of course I am concerned for my wife," Pierre said sharply. He passed his hand wearily over his forehead. "I'm sorry if I seem abrupt. We will be happy to have any assistance you wish to give, but I think you will understand that I cannot dismiss the lawyer I have just engaged."

Josiah's eyes gleamed with suppressed anger and annoyance. "Am I to understand that you will not accept me as your wife's legal defense? That you will not allow me to conduct her case?"

"Pierre! Don't be childish!" Cordelia broke in. "Don't you realize Josiah has come all the way from California and risked his political

[231]

reputation to defend me? Even against his own beliefs and principles? Surely you will not let your stiff de Vries pride . . ."

"I think you know, Monsieur Callahan, that I am not ungrateful for your offer," Pierre replied in a strange voice. As he was speaking Cordelia realized suddenly how much her husband had changed. He was much younger than Josiah, but there were lines in his face, and his voice, usually so soft, had grown harsh. She caught her breath as he added, "However, I will not fetter my wife in any way. A woman who can take a boat up the Missouri is capable of making her own decisions. I ask only that she think this matter over until morning. If, in the morning, she still feels she would like you to defend her, then I will withdraw my objections and dismiss Beaman. We have sold our boats, so we will be able to meet whatever fee you ask."

"I want no fee." The color was high in Josiah's face, but upon seeing Pierre's expression, he added, "Very well, if that is the way you want it."

"I think we understand each other," Pierre said. "And let me say again that we do appreciate your offer. My wife will inform you of her decision in the morning."

There was a long, awkward silence, and finally Josiah rose. "In the morning, then," he said.

"Yes, Monsieur Callahan, in the morning," Pierre replied.

"Josiah, you must forgive Pierre," Cordelia said in a low voice. "This affair has hurt and worried him more than it has me. Thank you," she added, "thank you for everything."

As soon as Josiah had gone she whirled on Pierre. "How could you be so churlish? Why will you not allow him to help us? After he has come clear across the country?"

Pierre did not answer her outburst. He took out his pipe, tapped it slowly with a lean brown finger, lit it and began to smoke thoughtfully. Finally he spoke. "You helped Button," he said slowly, "because you thought he was a human being who had been wronged. Josiah Callahan wishes to defend you only on the grounds that you are a beautiful woman with a soft heart. He wishes to defend you, yes, but not your cause. He does not defend your cause because he does not believe in it. He defends you only because he is in love with you."

Color flamed in Cordelia's face. "I do not understand you any more, Pierre. You have changed. Once you would have been glad that he had come forward to help me, regardless of his reasons. Now you are not thinking of me. You are not like the man I married at all any more."

Pierre managed a wry smile. "And you," he said, "do you not think that perhaps you, too, have changed? Have you not yet learned, Mimi, that everything in life changes? The river . . . people . . . people most of all."

"But I want things the way they were," Cordelia protested. "Why must life beat us so that we are changed? I want people the way they were, too."

Pierre rose suddenly and, putting down his pipe, said angrily, "No, Mimi, that is not what you want! It is only what you *say* you want. Ever since I have known you, you have been wishing for the exciting, romantic life you thought you would have with Josiah Callahan. As I told you, I have always known it and it is a bitter burden. A burden of which—suddenly—I have tired. Now your Josiah is back—and he is not changed. When this trial is over, he will go away and you will wish you were going with him. Perhaps he has already asked you."

"He hasn't!" she cried. "You know he hasn't!"

"But he will," said Pierre. "And you know that I cannot offer you your freedom. You know that. But neither will I play the injured husband and follow you to the ends of the earth."

"Do you think I would leave—after all your kindness to me?"

"Kindness!" Without warning Pierre took her by the shoulders and shook her. "I never want to hear that word again in regard to our relationship! Never! Do you understand? Button once told me I should make you cry. He was right. Perhaps I should have."

As Cordelia gasped, he went on, "Yes, I should have." Then his hands dropped to his sides. "But I cannot. For two long years you held it against the world because our child died of cholera, and for five years you have held it against our marriage because you did not have the courage to marry Josiah Callahan when you were free. You married me instead, remember?"

"You're jealous!" Cordelia flared. "Angry, jealous and unfair!"

"Very well, I am." Pierre's voice resumed its normal tone. "I believe Beaman can clear you of these charges as well as Josiah Callahan can, but I will not have you hold it against me because I did not approve of his handling your case. You are free to do as you wish."

Anger had turned Cordelia's eyes a deep green. Her hair had tumbled down on her shoulders when he had shaken her. "Then

Josiah shall defend me," she declared with more stubbornness than conviction, for she was badly unnerved by Pierre's unprecedented outburst. "He shall! I will tell him so in the morning!"

"Very well," Pierre said in his old soft, even voice. "You have made your choice, Mimi." He took up his coat. "I am going out. I may be gone for some time." He left without saying anything more.

For hours Cordelia sat by the fireplace. The fire burned down and she replenished it with a log; now it had burned down again. Emil entered silently, carrying a tray with a pot of black coffee and a cup and saucer which he placed on the table by her side. Then he lighted a lamp and went out without speaking. She looked about, bemused. She had been here all afternoon, and now it was evening, and she was alone with Beaver House.

A lassitude, an aftermath of her emotional storm, crept over her. Exhausted, she put her head back and through half-closed eyes she saw Madam de Vries' little rocking chair, motionless in a corner. High on a shelf sat the gold music box she herself had wound too tightly. Once the box had played a faint but sweet, "Ah, vous diras—je, maman," to a delighted baby. Cordelia turned her head away.

It seemed as if the gray cat should be tormenting yarn with wild battings of his cushioned paws, while Janette and Cecily—both gone now to homes and babies of their own—danced about, taking her hand and chanting delightedly, "Oh, Pierre! Cordelia's hair is like woodsmoke, Pierre, it really is!" Cordelia glanced overhead at the great timbers, hewn more than a generation ago to shelter those who would be born through the years. Now there was no one to shelter. All were gone, fled with the laughter that once had enlivened the house, vanished like the thin cry of the baby Marguerite, who once had kicked in a crib only a few feet away.

A dish rattled in the kitchen and Cordelia started. Emil, she thought, Emil, the silent one. Emil! Why only yesterday he was dropping *croquignoles* in sizzling fat, and singing until his round belly shook with the joy of living. But not now. And who spoke any more of the spirit of Jacques de Vries, the gay beaver trader who once had conquered forests and Indians, and who had come riding down the Missouri on his pelts like a king—home to Beaver House!

Like the young men of "La Guenille" who, on a New Year's Eve, had danced in this very room, so the ghosts of things gone capered in their own rag-dance through Cordelia's mind. Beaver House was only a house now; its gaiety was lost as surely as her boats were lost

[234]

to her forever. Perhaps the house was lifeless because Pierre was not home. But then, she realized suddenly, the house was not mute just today, nor yesterday; it had been hushed for a long time. Cordelia buried her face in her hands, unaware that it was she who had silenced it.

38

O N   T H E eighteenth of March the air was redolent of spring as the sun warmed the muddy streets and winter-wet ground. The bare limbs of the locust trees dripped from the fog that had lifted earlier that morning. The levee was clear, with steamboats white and gleaming on the chocolate-colored Mississippi.

This was the day The River Witch was to appear before the judge to give just cause as to why she had knowingly assisted her cousin's alleged murderer, a Negro, to escape justice.

On the surface the city was placid, apparently giving no more attention to the trial of The River Witch than to any other sensational case; underneath, however, emotions were as discordant as competitive hurdy-gurdys. All week long the Abolitionists had made antislavery speeches. At Planter House more than one soft-spoken Southerner had fingered his gun, and brawls were frequent on the levee.

To the casual, inexperienced eye, the levee appeared its usual clamorous self this morning. There was the familiar clatter of dray wagons, carriages milling about, fowls screeching in crates and hucksters bellowing their wares. But those who knew the levee sensed a difference in tempo. There was a high tension and there were sounds missing. The Negroes were silent.

There were few Negroes to be seen, and those in evidence rolled their barrels or toted their bales with heads down. When approached, they gave sidelong glances from watchful eyes and made themselves as unobtrusive as possible. There was no singing anywhere on the docks; they were afraid. Theirs was an intuitive fear, born of living in an insecure world. Some were hiding in the lower decks of steamboats, and others in the backs of warehouses. Those forced to work in the open gave off the acrid odor of fear.

A levee Negro had a way of knowing things long before they were common knowledge elsewhere. A chain of whispers ran from New Orleans to St. Louis and as far north as Council Bluffs. It followed the river from field to landing, from landing to steamboat —and sometimes it came faster than the boats. But no one knew how it came nor from where. Such a whisper had come up the river last night and was spreading from roustabout to mess-boy to steward and on to the warehouses and docks. The levee buzzed with a secret that made St. Louis an uneasy place for a man with a black skin. All Negroes who had a way out of the city were already gone.

Talk of another kind had gone on over teacups and at the dressmakers'. The women said, "What do you think of Josiah Callahan—coming all the way back from California to defend that river woman?" Thoughtfully curling a feather over a finger, one would add, "If you ask me, my dear, there is more there than meets the eye." This would be followed by nods and general sighings.

Husbands at the breakfast-table that morning informed their wives that, according to the papers, it was plain that the woman they called The River Witch wouldn't have gotten into trouble if she'd stayed home like a woman should have and minded her own business. Furthermore, they went on to say, partaking freely of their fried potatoes and pie, a rumor was going around that some *women* were actually going down to the courthouse to sympathize with that woman. Well, they certainly did not want any wife of *theirs* at that trial—or at any trial for that matter!

According to what people were saying, no one would be caught dead near the courthouse that morning. Feeling on the Negro question was running high and you never could tell what might happen. But hours before the trial began—and long before Cordelia left Beaver House—the streets at Fourth and Pine were jammed with people.

Women suddenly announced to their households that they had marketing to do and ribbons to buy. They might just drive by the courthouse and catch a glimpse of that river woman—and especially of that dashing Josiah Callahan. Men strolled away from their businesses. They'd like to see that Callahan now—Assemblyman, wasn't he? Well, *now* what would happen to his political career? But then perhaps he was after something more interesting than a seat in the

[236]

Assembly! The latter was said with sly winks and laughs, as wharf men, planters, shopkeepers and loafers alike crowded inside and out of the iron railing surrounding the courthouse. But there were men who had come early who did not smile. These men were armed with prejudices and with weapons, because they, too, knew the secret of the levee.

Cordelia, inconspicuously dressed in dark gray silk, her hair drawn back under a matching bonnet, rode in a carriage between Pierre and Josiah. It all seemed like a bad dream, as if this were something that was happening to someone else. But she had only to glance at the faces of her companions to know it was real.

Pierre regarded her gravely and then looked away. He had been silent and withdrawn ever since the stormy scene when she had announced she wanted Josiah to defend her. He had given Josiah his support and answered every question to the best of his ability, but when he and Cordelia were alone, he was aloof. The old tenderness had vanished long ago.

Glancing up at Josiah, she found his eyes fixed on her, reserved but tender. Color swept over her pale face as she remembered the scene in her living room only the afternoon before.

He had been instructing her in the way she should conduct herself today, and she had suddenly been afraid—and had told him so. He had gripped her hands hard. "I won't let you be afraid, my darling," he had said. "Trust me, and everything will be all right. It's all arranged." Then he'd added, "I haven't any right to ask you—but this pretense is foolish. When this is all over, don't send me away again. Come with me!"

"Josiah! I can't," she cried. "You know I can't. I'm bound by the church—and by my obligations . . ."

His hands had almost crushed hers. "But, Cordelia, when a man and a woman belong together—and you know that you and I do—and love each other, is that not better than an empty marriage?"

"My marriage has not been empty," she said defensively. "There have been many things . . ."

"I swear to you," he vowed in a low, solemn voice, "just as I did when you were no more than a child with a yellow ribbon in your hair, that I shall love you as long as I live. If you come with me, you'll never be sorry. I know I have no right to ask, but when I see your eyes I can't help but feel that I do."

"Oh, Josiah," she'd sighed, the tears running down her face, "I'm

[237]

so confused. When you're gone, I wonder where you are. I think of you in faraway places and I fear I shall never see you again. Yet such thoughts are wrong. I am Pierre's wife. We had a child . . . Oh, I can't hurt Pierre any more!"

"He knows?" asked Josiah. "I thought so. He is a fine man, Cordelia, but you know he is not your kind. And you are mine. You always were. You are a Catholic in name only. There are ways of getting around the church."

"But not for Pierre," she had said.

"Oh, my darling!" Josiah had drawn her toward him but she would not yield. "Josiah!" she had begged. "Not now . . . we must wait . . ."

He had dropped his hands. "I won't touch you again," he'd promised, "not unless you come to me. If, when this trial is over, you will put your hand in mine, I shall never let you go . . . never . . ."

Remembering this, Cordelia pressed her hands to her forehead. Then she leaned forward to look out of the carriage.

"No! Keep well back," Josiah remonstrated quickly. "Do not look at the crowd as we pass."

"Yes, Cordelia, he is right," Pierre said in a voice that might have been a stranger's. "You had best not be seen."

The crowds were so dense the carriage was forced to stop until a way could be cleared. Cordelia tried not to peer out, but an old lady, seeing her, hissed, "Look at her! Bold as brass! The nigger-lover!" Cordelia shrank back, but an old man ran forward and peered in. "By God, lass, yer Cap'm Riley's daughter—and I'm all fer ye!"

"I can't face all those people," Cordelia cried as they moved forward at a snail's pace. "I'm afraid!"

"The Abbé wanted to come with us," Pierre reminded her, "but you wouldn't let him."

Cordelia bit her lip. "I couldn't . . . I couldn't . . ."

Finally the carriage reached the entrance and Pierre took Cordelia's arm. "Courage, Mimi," he whispered, holding her back inside the carriage.

"I shall walk in front and clear the way," Josiah said, getting out ahead of them. Cordelia noted how the mob moved back before Josiah.

A murmur swept over the crowd as Cordelia alighted from the carriage. "That's her! That's The River Witch!" Old levee men began cheering Cordelia, while others objected. A planter Cordelia recognized turned suddenly and hit a man to whom he had sold cotton for ten years. By the time they had reached the courthouse steps the murmur had risen to a roar.

"The Abbé was right," said Pierre grimly. "Their feelings are at white heat and this is only an outlet for their pent-up emotions."

Inside the courthouse the rotunda let in a glare of light. "This way, quickly!" ordered Josiah, taking her other arm. "The hearing is to be upstairs in one of the small chambers. There will not be so many to stare up there."

The upstairs chamber, however, was packed to the rafters with the curious, and the room was odorous and stifling hot. A hush fell as Cordelia, walking between Pierre and Josiah, made her way to the defendant's box. Cordelia seated herself as quickly as possible and sat with her head down.

"Hold up your head," whispered Pierre. "You have done nothing wrong."

"No, no, it will be more effective if she keeps it down," Josiah advised hurriedly.

"Monsieur Callahan," Pierre protested in a low, determined voice. But he was interrupted by a sudden commotion in the doorway. The crowd had turned to gape and point, and now they were standing up to look. Cordelia, too, turned—and gasped at what she saw. Three men were entering the doorway, staggering under a strange burden. They carried a great carved chair. And in the chair sat Otto Knapp, calm and haughty as a king upon his throne.

"It's Uncle Otto!" Cordelia cried, rising involuntarily. "He shouldn't be out." She turned to the bailiff standing beside her chair. "He's ill. See how pale he is!" Yet as the men carried her uncle toward her, Cordelia felt a sudden warmth around her heart, and some of the loneliness eased.

"Look!" a woman screeched, pointing. "It's Otto Knapp, the big shipping king!" People stood on their seats to have a better look at this almost legendary figure of the steamboat world. The effect was electric. No one could miss the impact it would have on the judge—that the murdered man's father had come to the aid of his niece.

Cordelia was near tears by the time her uncle's chair was placed beside her. "Oh, Uncle Otto!" She touched his arm. "You shouldn't have come here. But I'm so glad to see you!"

"That's more than I can say, Cordelia," her uncle said testily, breathing hard. His blue eyes looked coldly out over the people.

"But surely you did not think I would leave you alone to be stared at by these peasants!"

Cordelia was grateful and touched because she knew how distasteful were the stares of the curious to her proud uncle. "I love you for it," she said in a low voice.

"Don't be a fool, girl. I had to come." Her uncle folded his hands over his stomach. "This ridiculous thing you have become involved in—and it is ridiculous and unbecoming a woman of good sense—is now a concern of the family. You are a *Knapp,* and I can't forget that. See to it that *you* don't forget it either!"

Her uncle's curt advice was still ringing in her ears when the bailiff pounded for order. The judge entered. He was a fat little man with a pouty face, and the spectators muttered and grumbled and showed him little respect. A few did not even bother to stand, although the bailiff shouted at them to do so.

From that point on Cordelia scarcely saw or heard any of the proceedings. There was a roaring in her ears. She did not realize she had been ordered to stand and hear the charges read against her until she felt Pierre's hand on hers, and Josiah touched her elbow.

Somehow she got to her feet. The clerk cleared his throat and began to read in a monotonous voice. It was then that her eyes met her uncle's. She lifted her chin, straightened her back and turned to face the court.

39

A RIPPLE OF CONVERSATION flowed over the courtroom as Cordelia sat down again. She saw that a strange man had come down the aisle and was holding a terse, whispered conversation with Josiah. Josiah nodded to the man and arose. "Your Honor," he said, "I wish to address the court on a most urgent matter."

The judge pursed his lips and frowned. "Such procedure is most irregular, Mr. Callahan."

Josiah's eyes gleamed with excitement. "But, Your Honor, I have just received evidence that will make this hearing unnecessary, and will save my client much suffering and embarrassment."

"Is this not a matter that can be brought out during the testimony, Mr. Callahan?" asked the judge severely.

"No, sir, it is not." Josiah's voice rang out forcefully. "I can produce a culprit who has confessed to the crime of murdering Hugo Knapp, and who will absolve my client of all knowledge of the same."

Everyone began talking and shouting at once. "Order in the court, or this room will be cleared!" The judge banged his gavel and half rose from the bench. "Mr. Callahan, are you trying to tell this court that you have such a person in custody? If so, why have you not come forward before, instead of employing this irregular procedure?"

"Because, Your Honor," said Josiah, "this man was brought to St. Louis only last night."

"In whose custody is he?" asked the judge. "Can you produce him?"

"He is in the custody of the men I have had searching for him," Josiah answered. "I can produce him at once. He is being held immediately outside the courtroom."

Cordelia saw Pierre lean forward and clutch his chair.

The disorder in the courtroom increased. "Order!" shouted the judge, banging his gavel again. "I will not have this court turned into a circus. Do you wish to produce this man now—or are you asking for a recess?"

"If the court pleases," Josiah replied firmly, "I should like to produce him now and spare my client further anguish."

"Bring him in," ordered the judge.

To a man the spectators rose, peering to see who was being brought in. At first Cordelia could not bear to look, although her heart was beating so fast it felt as if it would burst. She was afraid it was Button, and she felt she could not stand it. But it was Jean Austin whom the men brought down the aisle.

It was a thin, hollow-eyed man, with sweat dripping from his face, who passed Cordelia. For a brief second she caught a glazed, anguished look in his brown eyes and saw a cut over his forehead. At first she had known a sweeping relief that it was not Button who had murdered Hugo, but when she saw Austin's eyes, she suddenly felt a great pity for him.

Again the spectators had to be quieted. "Mr. Callahan," asked the judge, "do you bring this man before me as the professed murderer of Hugo Knapp?"

"I do," said Josiah, his voice carrying to every part of the room. "He has confessed to this crime, and has cleared my client of any implication in it whatever."

"Is this true?" the judge asked Austin.

Austin nodded weakly.

"Stand up, man, and speak out," ordered the judge. "And give the court your name."

"Jean Austin," came the scarcely audible reply.

"Mr. Callahan," said the judge in an exasperated voice, "are you sure this is not a trick to confuse the court? Your client is accused of helping two Negroes to escape, one of whom presumably murdered Hugo Knapp. Yet this man appears to be white!"

"Your honor," Austin's voice was clearer now, "I am a Negro."

"Of course he's a nigger!" a man shouted from the rear of the room. "I'd know him anywhere! He's the one I hauled across the river." It was Sid Howe who was shouting. "I told you they had him here, boys. Let's take him to the docks and burn him!"

"Young man, that's heathen talk!" An old lady struck him over the head with her umbrella, and pandemonium broke loose.

"Clear this courtroom!" bellowed the judge, who no longer looked petulant. "Clear this courtroom!"

Bailiff, guards and clerks started pushing the spectators toward the door, but Sid Howe and a small knot of followers advanced toward the bench, shoving anyone who was in their way ahead of them. Women screamed, chairs were swung and fists began to fly.

"Order! Let's have order!" the judge shouted hoarsely, banging his gavel heavily. "This man has confessed, but he shall have a fair trial."

"*Mein Gott!*" Cordelia heard her uncle mutter. "At least give the man a sword."

Cordelia cringed as she saw Sid, a wild light in his eyes, and followed by his cohorts, form a flying wedge to break the jam. "We're agoin' to burn that yaller nigger!" he shouted.

"No! No!" Austin's voice rose in a thin, high scream.

In vain the judge pounded and the guards shoved, but Sid's group advanced relentlessly through the melee. Bonnets fell off as women tried to escape, heads were beaten with bottles and gun butts. Here and there a would-be peacemaker stood on a chair, only to be pulled down and mauled by both factions.

Crowds in the street, hearing the noise, tried to force their way in, so that those who were trying to flee fell down and were trampled underfoot. Outside, Negroes who had been holding horses and tending carriages left their charges and scampered away. The whinnying of frightened animals and the smashing of vehicles furthered the confusion. The judge, leaping down, stood stoutly in front of Josiah and Jean Austin. Facing Sid, he ordered him to stand back in the name of the court and the law. Finally someone managed to lock the outside doors, but the din was deafening and the sound of the loud breathing was terrifying.

Sid, a fanatical light still in his eyes, took out a long knife and advanced on the judge. Cordelia, crouching under her uncle's chair where Pierre had shoved her, hid her face in her hands.

Suddenly a voice rang out. "Stop, you fools! I demand that you stop!" It was such a strong, arresting voice and carried so much command that momentarily the crowd subsided.

Josiah, she thought, creeping out to see. He would have no qualms about facing such a mob. Then she gasped and clung to her uncle's chair for support, for it was Pierre who had mounted a chair and now stood defying Sid and his followers. Pierre was speaking in a voice she had never heard before, and as he spoke he brandished an old pistol threateningly.

"I should not like to be forced to use this, Sid." Pierre's face was pale but determined. "I have never believed in violence, and I have never killed a man. But if you come one step closer, I shall shoot you down like the dog that you are. I well remember the man whose burning you incited in New Orleans. You will not do that here."

Then, half-turning his head, he spoke to Josiah. "Callahan, take your man away and put him in a safe place."

Stunned, Cordelia stared unbelievingly at Pierre and at the revolver he held in his hand. Quickly she glanced at Josiah. Josiah Callahan's famous silver-handled pistols were still in their holsters!

Surely he was not afraid! Not the Josiah who had fought battles in distant lands, and who had come back to defend her! No, there was no fear in his face, but with a sick feeling Cordelia saw something else—*Josiah did not care what happened to Austin, now that he had confessed.*

Suddenly she realized that Josiah would have gone to any war—

whether to avenge his brother or not—because he loved adventuring. He went to California because it was exciting. He had come back to defend her because he knew she had him in her thoughts. She did not doubt that he loved her, but in her heart she knew he would never have loved her enough to have stayed at home, if need be. And she—if she had loved him enough, would have followed him to the ends of the earth—Red Maude or no Red Maude.

Josiah stood fast with folded arms, but his pistols were not drawn to help Pierre; this was no glorious charge on a battlefield, no high adventure on the plains, no duel for a lovely woman. This was only a demand to preserve the basic rights of another human being.

Sid was panting like a dog after a fox. "*Vide Poche! Vide Poche!*" he hurled derisively at Pierre. His followers took up the cry. "*Vide Poche!*"

Pierre leveled his pistol at Sid's breast. "*Vide Poche*, yes, and proud of it!" he retorted. "All my ancestors had empty pockets when they came here. When my grandfather came, this was a place of savages and mud flats and forests. It was a wilderness with no civilization. With his hands my grandfather cut logs from that forest and built the first church—and homes—so that we might rise above our beginnings."

"Who cares about your grandfather!" sneered Sid, making a threatening movement. "Give us that nigger!"

Again Pierre shoved the pistol toward Sid. "And my father, Jacques de Vries, went up the Missouri River and conquered the forest and Indians. He endured many hardships and dangers, but it was to this place that he was proud to return with his beaver pelts. It was *here* that Beaver House was built, and it was in it that he died. Our buildings are tall now, and our people are many and the name of de Vries is only a name. I am only Pierre de Vries—a river pilot —but I cannot, and I will not, let you sink back to the savagery and the mud flats of my grandfather's time—by burning this man without a trial."

"You fool! He's only a nigger!" a planter shouted.

"I am not questioning his color or his crime," retorted Pierre. "He says he is a Negro, and he has confessed his crime, for which he may very well hang. I am thinking of what you do to yourselves—and to this city—if you burn him on the docks. God created us all, and we are entitled to be treated with dignity and a fair hearing. If you expect a just hearing from your God, so should you give one to your fellow man."

For a moment the crowd was silenced. "*Himmel!*" breathed Otto Knapp. "What that Frenchman could do if only he were a German!"

"Pierre!" Cordelia cried, trying to make her way to him. "They'll kill you!"

The spell broke, and Sid and his followers surged forward. But Pierre had held them long enough for Josiah, the guards and the judge to be able to rush Austin away. Turning in a wild fury, Sid lifted a chair and let it fly. It struck Pierre on the side of the head and he fell, never hearing Cordelia's cry of warning.

Immediately the mob was tamed. Blood had been drawn, their savagery appeased, and now they rushed for the exits.

"Pierre! Pierre! They have killed you!" Cordelia knelt beside him, mopping the blood from his head. "Oh, my God! The blood has opened his old wound!"

"Here, lady." A planter handed her a big linen handkerchief. "Use this." He looked down at Pierre. "I do not agree with him, but your husband is a brave man. To say what you believe when the world is against you, requires more courage than I have."

"Someone get a doctor," begged Cordelia. The crowd standing around, parted, and let the Abbé Choate through. He knelt by Pierre and put his fingers on his wrist. "I do not think he is badly injured," said the priest. "His pulse is still fairly strong."

Pierre stirred, opened his eyes and recognized the Abbé. "I am a fool, Father," he said. "Always getting hit on the head when I am trying to do something."

"Pierre!" cried Cordelia, but his eyes had closed again.

"We had best take him home," said the Abbé, "the doctor can attend him better there."

"Nonsense," said Otto Knapp, trying to command the situation from his chair. "Bring him to Knapp House where there are more servants to care for him. The fool! If this had been in the old days, he would either have been killed or knighted. As it is, he will only furnish St. Louis table talk for the evening, and nurse a cracked head for a week."

"Thank you, Uncle Otto," Cordelia said gratefully. "But I want to take my husband home."

40

AT BEAVER HOUSE the doctor had come and gone and Pierre was sleeping comfortably. The Abbé and Cordelia remained by his bed, grateful that his wound was not serious. Cordelia felt the Abbé's eyes upon her and she wanted to pour out her mixed emotions to him, but she could not. Instead she busied herself bathing Pierre's forehead. From time to time she would rise and walk about the room, then come back to sit by Pierre.

In the kitchen there was the soft clink of pans as Emil made soup he hoped Pierre would be able to eat. The only other sound was the old china clock that marked the hours with a musical chime. The silence between the Abbé and Cordelia lengthened, and presently the priest began to doze and nod.

The great brass knocker on the front door shattered the silence and both Cordelia and the Abbé started. In a moment the little maid appeared and motioned silently to Cordelia. Cordelia rose and, glancing at the sleeping Pierre, went softly out, closing the bedroom door. On the doorstep stood Josiah Callahan, holding his hat in his hand.

"Is Pierre all right?" he asked. "I heard he was injured after I left." "Yes, he was hit by a chair." Cordelia stood in the doorway. "But the doctor says it is not serious. It opened the wound he suffered in the levee fire."

"I'm relieved," said Josiah. "But what made him do such a foolish thing?" he asked, puzzled. "He knows they'll hang Austin anyway. I don't understand it." Then he added, "I have been talking to the judge all afternoon. You will be cleared. In fact, you are free now."

"Free! And you have done this so soon?" Cordelia put her hand against the door jamb to steady herself. "It was wonderful of you to come back and defend me," she said. "I shall remember it as long as I live. I don't know how Pierre and I can ever repay you. . . ."

Josiah looked at her sharply. "Don't thank me, Cordelia! Not in that tone of voice! Oh, my dear, what is it? You've just told me Pierre is all right. . . . But I see by your face that something has happened. What is it?" he demanded.

"Please, Josiah!" she begged. "Not here—wait until I get a shawl. Then we can talk in the garden."

Quickly she threw a pale yellow shawl over her shoulders and led the way into the garden. "Cordelia . . ." Josiah began worriedly, as he followed her down the curving brick walks where the lilies Madam de Vries had planted were showing pale green tips.

When they reached the old stone sundial, Cordelia stopped and put her hands firmly on the edge of it. She kept her eyes downcast as she said, "But I do want to thank you, Josiah, because it is all I can ever do." Her voice broke. "It seems so little. But please accept it—because gratitude is all that I can give. . . . Oh, Josiah, don't you see . . . ?"

"No, I don't see!" he exclaimed angrily. "Cordelia!" he commanded, "look at me. Why won't you look at me? What has happened?" When she remained silent, he asked, "Can you look into my eyes and swear that you don't love me?"

Cordelia would not look up; she looked instead to the spot where the late afternoon sun made branch patterns across the garden. "I only know that I cannot go," she said. "I can never leave Pierre."

"Then you're in love with him!" Josiah exclaimed. "If you cared enough for me, neither church nor convention would stand in your way!" Then he added bitterly, "If I had been content to stay in one small spot on this river that led nowhere, you would have been my wife long ago—would have borne my children."

Cordelia closed her hand around the slender twig of a lilac bush. "I only know that I must stay." She snapped the twig in her hand. "Someday there will be someone else for you, Josiah."

Josiah caught her roughly by the shoulders. "Something has come between us, and I do not understand it. Surely it was not your husband's brave but foolish exhibition of courage that changed your mind. What is it? Is it that you are afraid that someday I will go adventuring and leave you alone?"

Cordelia shook her head.

"I swear to you," he said, "I swear to you that I never really wanted any other woman for my own—and I never will. Wherever I go, you will be with me. What can I do to make you believe me?" he asked desperately.

"I believe you," she said. "I believe you, Josiah." And now she had the courage to raise her eyes to his. With a shock she found that the old magic in them was gone for her. "My life is here," she said quietly.

"I can't believe this is really the way you feel," he said unbelievingly. "Tomorrow you'll see it differently."

"No, Josiah. This must be goodbye." She placed a hand on his arm. "If only . . ." Without warning Josiah took her in his arms and kissed her deeply, then drew away and searched her face. "It is a bitter thing," he said finally, "when you lose the love of the woman you love—but it's worst of all when you wonder if she really loved you." He turned abruptly and strode away from her. "Josiah . . . !" She stifled the cry.

She heard his boots hard upon the bricks, heard the gate opening but not closing, and she knew he was waiting there at the outer edge of the garden. Picking up her skirts, she ran toward the house, and finally she heard the old iron gate clank shut. As she mounted the steps she heard the wheels of Josiah's carriage moving slowly away, but this time she did not turn and look back.

When Cordelia was able to compose herself, she entered Pierre's room and found him still asleep. The Abbé was awake.

As Cordelia seated herself on the other side of the bed she saw that the priest was looking across at her questioningly.

"That was Josiah Callahan," she said finally.

The priest nodded but said nothing.

"He came to tell me that I have been cleared of the charges. Josiah is going away," she added in a low voice. "I have just told him goodbye."

The priest raised his head and looked at her for a moment, his wise old eyes understanding and alert beneath his drooping eyelids. He is as old as time, she thought, and he knows everything even before you tell him.

"You are cleared of the charges," he said, "but your boats are gone. What will you do now?"

"Pierre was talking of going to California," she said thoughtfully. "I saw him studying advertisements of wagon trains, but he was only talking of it because he thought I wanted to see California."

The priest smiled. "Why, child, he always wanted to go."

"Oh, no, Father!" she said. "Pierre loves the river. It is his life. He would never want to leave it!"

"Did he ever tell you he loved the river?" asked the priest.

"No . . . not exactly. . . ." Suddenly she realized that Pierre understood the river—he had conquered it—but never once had he told her he loved it.

"Cordelia, Cordelia." The Abbé Choate shook his head. "It is you who have loved the river. You only *thought* you wanted far places. It was the river that was your life. Did you not know that Pierre felt in chains, going up and down a river all his life, when he longed to see the world? Always he wanted to be an explorer and a trailblazer like his father and his grandfather before him. How it chafed him to carry wagons to departure points when he wanted to ride across prairies and climb mountains, himself! And how he fumed when he could not go away to war himself."

"But why? Why did I not know of all this?" Cordelia cried so sharply that Pierre stirred, in spite of the heavy sleeping potion. "Why did he never tell me of his dreams and ambitions?" she demanded agitatedly.

"Because," said the priest gently, "he had a mother and two sisters and a wife and a baby to protect—and he could best look after his family by staying home. He was on the point of going adventuring when you fled from your uncle's house to him—a frightened little girl with no one to look after you. He hid his ambitions. That took courage. Pierre's courage, like his gun, was never displayed until it was needed. But it was always there if one looked. Ah, yes, I believe that in his heart Pierre de Vries is the most venturesome man I have ever known." Then, seeing Cordelia's face, he added, "I am afraid, my dear, the truth is you do not know your husband very well."

"But I want to." She hid her face in her hands. "I want to, and now I never will. He has grown away from me and I can never get him back."

"It won't be easy," the priest agreed. "He is proud."

"Father," Cordelia turned to the priest, "you once promised me that if I needed your help I could come to you. I need it now!" She dropped her head onto her arms. "Oh, I need it now!"

The priest's face broke into a thousand wrinkles. "You have been a long time in coming, child," he said as he reached across the sleeping Pierre and gently placed his hand upon her shining hair.

41

Two weeks later Cordelia stood at the railing of a steamboat, looking into the silted waters of the Missouri. All afternoon she had been alone, first watching the loading of railroad ties for a track for steam engines, and now watching the banks and the little houses they passed by. She loved this land with its fertile soil and its trees. She loved this angry, captious river that cut through it like a vengeful scythe. Now she was leaving it—perhaps never to see it again. The Abbé was right—it was *she* who had loved it.

It had come as a shock to her to learn that Pierre had been planning to go to California alone. Only by the intervention of the Abbé had Pierre been persuaded to take her with him. They were to join a wagon train going westward from St. Joseph in about two weeks. Looking at the river now and at the little farms, she knew Pierre was the only man for whom she would have left this land. She must find a way to tell him so. They were young, with a new life and a new land before them, perhaps there would be other children. . . .

In time their old comradeship could be restored, but she wished for it now—to talk to him and tell him things.

Earlier, their steamboat had passed the Hermann landing and she had seen her old home high on the bluff. A young girl had come out and stood waving at the steamboats, just as she had waved so long ago. She wanted to tell Pierre how it felt to see the old orange brick house—with the young girl in the sunlight—to recall again how she had run away from that house in her new green velvet dress, and hidden on *The Blue Teal.* And maybe to laugh a little about that dear old terror of a Fancy Foot Morgan! And the uproar when he and her father and Pierre had found her. But it had been a long time since she and Pierre had laughed together and ever since they had left St. Louis he had busied himself with other wagon-men.

She was tired, and it would soon be dark. She knew she ought to go inside, but the thought of opening the door to an empty cabin and lighting the lamp alone repelled her. Pierre had chosen to stay on the lower deck with the wagons.

The sun was slipping behind the bluffs now, turning the river crimson. Along the banks, evening mists were already beginning to drift down, like smoke from snuffed-out candles. Cordelia was so absorbed in her thoughts that she started when, looking up, she saw that Pierre had joined her. He, too, was standing motionless, watching the last bit of sun on the river. His face, under his new wide-brimmed hat, was dark and remote. She felt shy, almost as if he were a stranger. She was trying to think of some way to tell him of how their new life together could be, to bring him close again, when she saw a cottonwood log come whirling downstream, traveling alone on its way to the sea.

For a moment it was caught in the wash from their boat and hung suspended in a little whirlpool of its own. Round and round it went, in the gyratory dance peculiar to old logs and the river. Ripples spreading out from it caught the sunset and sent a thousand rainbows spinning in concentric circles. A strangled cry rose in Cordelia's throat and she felt as if her heart would burst. The log was covered with pitch and bound with iron bands.

She felt Pierre's hand close over hers and felt his arm around her. Together they watched silently until, in a sudden whimsy, the river released the log and sent it floating on downstream.

"Pierre," she cried, "did you see that log?"

"I saw it, Mimi," he said in a trembling voice.

"Could it be . . . oh, could it be . . . ?" she implored him.

"The river is full of logs with iron bands, Mimi," he said.

"But tell me it could have been!" she cried. "Tell me that everything I love is not lost!"

"Of course it could have been," he said, drawing her to him at last. "Of course it could have been, Mimi. Nothing one really loves is ever lost."

The log was gone and the sun was gone and it was dark upon the river. But overhead there were stars aplenty, and a long, deep night for understanding.

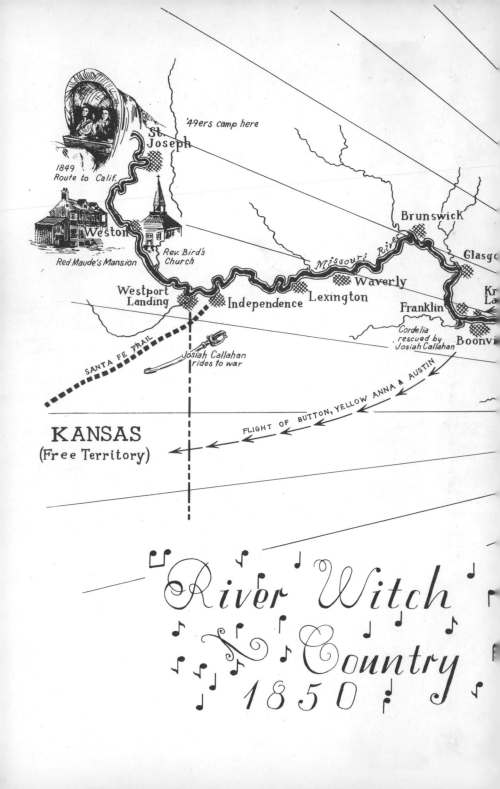

'49ers camp here

St. Joseph

1849 Route to Calif.

Weston

Red Maude's Mansion

Rev. Bird's Church

Brunswick

Glasgo

Missouri River

Waverly

Westport Landing

Independence

Lexington

Franklin

Kr
La

SANTA FE TRAIL

Josiah Callahan rides to war

Cordelia rescued by Josiah Callahan

Boonvi

KANSAS (Free Territory)

FLIGHT OF BUTTON, YELLOW ANNA & AUSTIN

River Witch Country 1850